# Deadly Justice

PATTI STARR

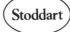

Published in 1995 by
Stoddart Publishing Co. Limited
34 Lesmill Road
Toronto, Canada  M3B 2T6
Tel (416) 445-3333
Fax (416) 445-5967

**Stoddart Books** are available for bulk purchase for sales promotions, premiums,
fundraising, and seminars. For details, contact the **Special Sales Department**
at the above address.

CANADIAN CATALOGUING IN PUBLICATION DATA

Starr, Patti

Deadly Justice

ISBN 0 - 7737 - 2903 - 8

I. Title.

PS8587.T37D4 1995 C813'.54 C95-931149-1

PR9199.3.S73D4 1995

Cover Design: James Ireland Design Inc.
Printed and bound in the United States of America

*Stoddart Publishing gratefully acknowledges the support of the Canada Council,
the Ontario Ministry of Culture, Tourism, and Recreation, Ontario Arts Council,
and Ontario Publishing Centre in the development of writing
and publishing in Canada.*

*To my husband Jerry,*
*and our children, David, Evan, Brooke, Stuart, and Randy,*
*who ride the roller coaster with me*

# Prologue

## November 21, 1994

*A* thin layer of white frost covered the front lawn and clung to the petals of the orange mums, the last flowers to survive the cold nights of late fall. Most of the leaves had been torn from the trees by wind and rain earlier in the month. Winter was close at hand.

Inside the house the heaters had turned on automatically with the dropping of the temperature outside, but Rebecca still huddled beneath the blankets with only the top of her head visible. The phone was ringing somewhere off in the distance, and at first she incorporated its sound into her dream. She didn't want to let go of the dream, at least not until she knew the identity of the man with whom she was making love.

"Get the phone! Dammit! Are you deaf?" her husband Brad shouted from the bathroom that separated their bedrooms.

Rebecca bolted upright. Now wide awake, she picked up the phone.

"This is the AT&T operator in Boston calling for Mrs. Rebecca Sherman."

"This is Mrs. Sherman." Boston? Her heart began beating wildly as she slipped back down into the bed.

"Go ahead," the operator said. "And thank you for using AT&T."

"Rebecca, this is Elizabeth DeLuca."

Rebecca's throat tightened and went dry.

After a few seconds of silence Elizabeth spoke again: "Rebecca, are you there? I know this is a surprise, but Santino asked me to call you."

"I'm sorry, Elizabeth," Rebecca managed as she fought for calm. "I'm still half-asleep."

"I'm sorry to call so early."

"It's all right. I'm just surprised to hear from you after so long." A thousand mundane questions ran through Rebecca's head. How are the twins? How do you like Boston? How's your sculpting? She didn't ask any of them.

"Rebecca, Santino is dying," Elizabeth said softly. "He wants to see you. Please come as soon as you can. We'll make all the arrangements from here as soon as you let me know when you can leave your family."

Elizabeth sounded so composed that it was hard to comprehend what she was saying. Rebecca bit her lip and fought her turmoil. She wanted to cry out in anguish when she heard Elizabeth's words. Memories of Santino came rushing back, but she knew she had to react in a composed and detached manner, so she struggled for control.

Rebecca envisaged Elizabeth as she had last seen her — a willowy five-foot-ten-inch-tall woman with streaked blond hair and green eyes that drew you to her like a magnet. When Elizabeth looked at you, it was as if she were looking into your soul. Elizabeth gave the impression of being the person-ification of propriety. She never had a hair out of place, nor did unkind or foul words pass her lips. She always seemed to be in charge of her emotions, at least in front of outsiders. Her concerns were always with family and tradition.

"Rebecca, Santino wants to see you before he dies," Elizabeth said. "We must honor his wishes. Both of us."

"Elizabeth, I'm so sorry. Please forgive my hesitation. It's just such a shock. It's been so long and . . . " Her voice trailed off as she suppressed the fear that threatened to overwhelm her.

"Will you come?" Elizabeth asked.

Rebecca answered, knowing she had no choice, "Yes, of course I will."

"There's a midnight red eye out of Pearson Airport to Boston tonight,"

Elizabeth told her. "Someone will pick you up and bring you here."

"At four o'clock in the morning?"

"There isn't any such thing as normal time here now," Elizabeth replied. "Our lives revolve around Santino's medication schedule."

"If you're sure." Then more positively: "Yes, the red eye will be fine."

"I'll tell him you're coming; it will help him to rest easier." With that, Elizabeth hung up.

Rebecca sank down under the covers and stared at the ceiling. Santino. She conjured up his image; she thought about their last meeting. She remembered his smile, his wonderful smile, and his strong arms holding her.

"What was that all about?"

Brad was standing next to the bed.

"Santino DeLuca is dying," she told him. "Elizabeth wants me to come to Boston to see him." She turned, and looked at the bedside lamp, avoiding his eyes. "I don't want to go."

"Well, you have to go," he said, his tone somewhat hostile. "You can't refuse his request. Besides, he might remember you in his will. That would be a nice reward for all those years you kept your mouth shut."

She turned to look at him and, seeing the look in her eyes, Brad's tone softened. "Sorry. I never pretended to understand your loyalty. But I do know that, if you don't go, it'll eat away at you. You really have no choice."

He was right, of course. Brad was like a rock. He had appeared at the worst of times and seen her through them. She could forgive him for his dislike of Santino and for his sarcasm. As usual, he had her best interests at heart.

"Don't worry about things here," he said. "I'll take care of everything. How long will you have to be there . . . two days, three?"

"About that, I imagine."

"If there are any emergencies with the preparations for the wedding, Jean can handle them."

Jean was Rebecca's sister, the other rock in her stormy life.

"I'm lucky to have both of you," she said, still distracted, still lost in disturbing thoughts.

Brad leaned over as if hoping to kiss her good-bye. Rebecca reached up to pull him toward her. They held each other and said nothing more. She reminded herself how fortunate she and Lisa were to have him in their lives. What would she have done without him during those awful days?

"I'd better go," he said, standing up. He looked down at her as if waiting for permission to leave, then he forced a smile and turned away.

As soon as Brad had left to go to the office, Rebecca called her sister.

"Elizabeth DeLuca just phoned. Santino's dying. I'm leaving for Boston tonight."

She heard Jean's sharp intake of breath; then there was silence for what seemed a long time. Finally she spoke, revealing both fear and bitterness.

"Becky, Becky, is it happening again?" she asked. "Don't try to kid me. Spit it out. I can't go through that hell again. Neither can Lisa. Santino can't be dying. Only the good die young."

"Very funny, Jeannie," Rebecca answered sharply. "I'm leaving tonight and I expect to be home within two or three days. I'll try to reach Lisa at work, but I think she told me she had an out-of-town shoot. I'll leave a message for her to call you. And, Jean, please watch your mouth. It's all past history. I'll speak to you in a few days."

When she hung up, Rebecca wondered if her phone might be tapped again.

After she started running her bath, she made a list of things to do before leaving. She left a message on Lisa's machine, telling her to call Aunt Jean.

Next, Rebecca made an appointment at the beauty salon. In spite of everything, she wanted to make sure Santino saw her the way he always had liked her to look. "Smooth, soft, and delicious," he used to whisper as his hands and mouth traveled over her body.

Finally, after checking off all the items on her list, Rebecca slipped into the bubble bath, surrounded by mirrors and marble. She turned on the Jacuzzi for fifteen minutes to give herself a chance to relax and think about what she might have to face in the coming days. You've changed, I've changed, she thought, wondering how she and Santino would look to one another.

Her once-long hair was now gone — she'd had it cut very short before she went to prison, and had never bothered to let it grow back. With tiny lines now appearing on her face, she sometimes wondered if longer hair might be a better idea, although the effort of taking care of it would be a pain.

As she looked at her naked body, her eyes avoided the tiny scars on her breasts. Not bad for a fifty-year-old broad, she thought, despite the fact there was a droop to her breasts she hadn't noticed before. She was surprised that the reality of middle age didn't bother her. Once she had been so proud of her firm body, so concerned about keeping it in shape, that she had spent a lot of money on her weekly rituals of personal care.

But life had slipped into a comfort zone now, and her fixation with appearances had gone the way of carnal affairs. There was no point trying to compete with twenty-five-year-old bodies anyway. Just sit back and enjoy good food and good books. It was time to make the most of having no pressures. It was time for peace of mind.

Oh shit, Rebecca, she almost said out loud. Has your brain started to sag, too? Admit it, you miss the excitement, the passion, and, yes, the danger. At least some of the time.

Rebecca looked down. Her hand was resting between her legs, and she remembered how Santino had been turned on by that. He used to love having her lie on the bed, legs spread, stroking herself while he watched. Then when he was overcome with passion, he'd leap on her and bring them both to an orgasm. God, what an incredible man and lover he had been.

The ring of the telephone brought her back to reality. She'd forgotten to bring the portable with her into the bathroom, so she had to get out of the tub, dripping water all over her bedroom rugs, to answer it. She could have just let it ring, but she thought it might be Elizabeth calling again. It wasn't; it was her daughter Lisa.

"Hi, Mom, what's up?" Lisa asked, her voice bright and cheerful. "Auntie Jean said you might still be home."

A smile came over Rebecca's face. "Hi, sweetheart," she answered, water still dripping from her naked body. "I have to go down to Boston for a couple of days. Business. Is everything okay with you?"

Rebecca envisaged her daughter's sparkling eyes and loving concern. Just over five feet tall, Lisa looked more like an adorable teenager than the twenty-six-year-old professional photographer she was. Her outgoing personality and biting sense of humor belied the depth of her sensitivity.

Although Rebecca and Lisa's father Steven Sherman had divorced in 1976, she had kept the name "Sherman" even after her marriage to Brad Ross in order to keep life simpler for Lisa.

She reminds me so much of my father, at least the way he once was, Rebecca thought.

"Everything's okay. But as the wedding gets closer, I get more excited," Lisa bubbled on. "I can't believe it! I'm finally getting married. Even Jeff is getting into it, despite the sour look on his mother's face. Ma, why can't you be nicer to her? She's feeling left out and I have to bend over backward to keep her happy."

"Forget it, Lisa," Rebecca said. "Jeff's mother is a throwback to the dinosaur age. Just put on your beautiful smile, Lisa darling, and tell her if she isn't careful I'll bring my home movies from prison to the rehearsal dinner next week."

"Oh Mom!" Lisa shrieked, laughing. "You are so incredible. But the thought is tantalizing! Gloria would probably have a cardiac arrest and her brother the senator might fall down on his gold-plated canes in a dead faint."

You're closer to the truth than you realize, my darling daughter, Rebecca thought. Senator Jack Jacobs. Otherwise known as Judas Iscariot. I should have had him killed years ago, when I had the chance. How ironic that my daughter should have fallen in love with Jacobs's nephew. I wonder how he feels about Rebecca Sherman's daughter joining his family. I can just imagine it. Oh, well, forget it. Pray that Lisa and Jeff will be happy together.

"Mom," Lisa continued in a more serious tone, "Auntie Jean told me how sick Mr. DeLuca is. Will everything be okay? Will you be all right?"

Why couldn't Jean zipper her mouth? "Don't worry. It was very thoughtful of Mrs. DeLuca to call and give me an opportunity to go to Boston to see Santino, and to say good-bye. He was once such a good friend to all of us."

Lisa didn't comment. "I'll miss you," she said.

"I have to go. Speak to you soon, sweetheart."

Two hours later Rebecca was spread out on the flat table of torture, having hot wax pulled off her legs. Her face was covered in a mask of astringent mud; her hands and feet were flapping in the air to speed up the drying of the nail polish. Despite the discomfort, Rebecca had always found her time at "Marina's" therapeutic because, while there, she could forget about the pressures of her life and indulge in self-pampering.

But today forgetting was harder than usual. Emotions — some long held in check, others kept hidden — were threatening to break out. Memories of Santino and their time together filled her mind. She wondered how she would cope with seeing the man she had once loved dying and helpless. Santino had been powerful, protective, much like a knight in shining armor.

Santino, my darling, she thought, so much of what I am, or ever was, is because of you. Whatever you need, I'll be there.

Her eyes started to fill up, and she knew she'd have to get hold of herself in order to face whatever was coming. Nothing could be allowed to disrupt the life she had built for her family in the past ten years, nothing and nobody.

*I*t was noon and the Florida sun was still burning away the mist from last night's rain. Grant Teasdale was standing by his houseboat, holding the portable phone in one hand and his fishing rod in the other. He was six feet tall, with wide shoulders and a very thick neck. He looked as if he could have been a linebacker for the Dolphins. His once-flaming-red hair was speckled with white, but his robin's-egg-blue eyes were still incredible, even as they narrowed while Elizabeth spoke.

"Inspector Teasdale, my name is Elizabeth DeLuca, Santino's wife. He's asked me to call you and request that you come up to Boston to see him. He's terminally ill and needs to speak with you."

Grant frowned. Tomorrow was supposed to be the start of a five-day fishing trip with some of his business associates. They were driving down to Islamorata, just south of Key Largo, to hire a charter to take them deep-sea fishing in the Gulf of Mexico. He had been looking forward to it as his reward for last year's hard work developing security for Banco National de Argentina's new branch in north Florida.

Grant Teasdale was a retired Mountie. Once the head of a special FBI–RCMP task force on the Mafia, he had become a legend in the law-enforcement field. His record of convictions in relation to the number of arrests was over 80 percent. He was a highly principled man who wouldn't tolerate incompetence or corruption in any of his colleagues. His contempt for political expediency was well known, and he had never tailored an investigation or arrest to suit "the powers that be."

Teasdale was also a very sensitive man, often referred to as "Inspector Teddy Bear" by associates who knew him well. There was some talk about a troubled early life, but since no one really knew anything about him outside his professional career, it was only speculation.

Ten years earlier, in 1984, it had been rumored that he was one of three inspectors in line for the top RCMP job. But suddenly, six months later, he had taken early retirement and moved to Florida with his wife and son. There, he'd opened a security agency known for its efficient and discreet service as well as its FBI contacts. This had made Grant very popular with certain secretive Latin Americans who wanted to travel back and forth between Florida and Argentina without any hassles.

Before Elizabeth DeLuca's phone call came, Grant Teasdale thought he had found a measure of peace in his life; now he wondered.

"Of course, we'll make all the necessary arrangements for you," Elizabeth said.

What the hell is this all about? Teasdale asked himself. It's been ten years since I last saw DeLuca. I don't have anything more to say to him. Is this going to be some kind of deathbed cleansing? Who cares anyway? Let him suffer. Maybe he's going to Mafia heaven. If he is, Massimo Brattini will be there waiting for him.

As if reading his mind, Elizabeth went on. "I know this call is unexpected, Inspector Teasdale. But Santino wouldn't be making this request if it wasn't important, not only for you, but for others who mean something to you — and who once meant something to you."

What the hell is that supposed to mean? Could it have anything to do with Rebecca? Was she in any danger? With Brattini's death two weeks earlier, what risks were left?

He wondered if Rebecca was also going to be in Boston and, if so, how he'd cope with seeing her again.

"Inspector, are you still there?" Elizabeth's voice jarred his thoughts.

"Yes, Mrs. DeLuca, I'm here. Of course I'll come. And, please call me Grant. I haven't been an inspector for ten years."

"Thank you. When should I expect you?"

Canceled, one deep-sea fishing trip. "I have to stop in Miami on some business first, so I'll fly up to Boston from there. I should arrive around noon tomorrow."

"Let me know what time to expect you. Have a good flight."

The line went dead and Grant hung up. At least this would give him an opportunity to visit with his twenty-four-year-old son Kevin. Brain-damaged at birth, Kevin had never matured emotionally beyond the level of a ten-year-old. According to the doctors, the umbilical cord had been twisted around his neck during the delivery, cutting off his oxygen supply. "God's will," the priest had said. But Grant wasn't so sure. He feared that somehow he had passed along a curse to his son.

Kevin was living in the Christopher Robin Home, one of the best group homes in the country for the developmentally handicapped. It was located in Hallandale, a few miles north of Miami Beach, Florida. It was costing the Teasdales $4,500 a month to keep Kevin there, an expensive burden that would last as long as Kevin lived — and that could be longer than his parents lived.

That was why the Teasdales lived on their houseboat. It allowed them to save a considerable amount of money. But the truth was Grant really loved it. The gentle sounds of the water lapping against the boat's hull, the squawking of the sea gulls early in the morning, the cool breezes even during the hot spells — it all made life pleasurable.

After Elizabeth DeLuca hung up, Grant walked into the cabin.

"Who was that?" his wife, Doris, asked. She was toweling her hair as she stepped out of the head.

"Elizabeth DeLuca," he answered.

Doris's head snapped up and her intake of breath was sharp.

"Santino DeLuca is dying and he wants to see me. I'm postponing the fishing trip so I can fly up to Boston. I'm also going to visit Kevin and leave from Miami. I should be back in a couple of days."

"You promised me it was over," Doris finally said, her voice like ice. "No more cops and robbers. A quiet retirement, you promised."

"I have no choice, Doris." His voice was just as cold. "This is the last chapter of an old story, and I want to be there when the book is closed."

He turned and went back on deck. He called the Home and arranged to pick up Kevin later that afternoon for an overnight stay with him in Miami Beach. The two of them would go out for a lobster dinner, which they both loved; afterward perhaps they could catch a movie.

It would also give him a chance to slow down for twenty-four hours and enjoy his son while he sorted out what had just dropped into his life when Elizabeth DeLuca phoned.

*E*lizabeth slipped into Santino's darkened room. Despite the flowers and the air fresheners, the stench of death was in the air. The nurse left quickly when Elizabeth motioned her out.

She looked down at Santino, the love of her life, the father of her sons Peter and Matthew, the man who had brought her from Italy to freedom in America almost thirty-two years earlier. Santino, once so strong and powerful, so sure of himself, was now reduced to skin and bones.

She wondered what was so important, after all this time, that he wanted to bring together the two people who had once been such a danger to his existence. Perhaps the answer was on the audiocassette she hadn't yet listened to, and which was still hidden in her lingerie drawer.

All those years Santino had struggled with his demons. His commitment to the Church and its teachings had clashed with business dealings and his attraction to Rebecca Sherman. Elizabeth knew, as only a woman who loves a man can know, that her husband had once loved Rebecca. But even though he had called out Rebecca's name during his pain-racked bouts of delirium, Elizabeth also knew she had won that battle a long time ago. She had stayed close to him, never wavering, always smiling and gracious, just the way Santino wanted. She had never given him an excuse to leave her, had never made it easy for him to forget his promise of a lifelong commitment to her. Yes, she had watched him. She knew him.

Certainly for the last ten years Santino had seemed to be enjoying their life together again. He had rarely mentioned Rebecca's name, and soon even she had begun to forget.

When diagnosed with inoperable cancer of the pancreas seven months ago, Santino had tried to keep it from her. But she became suspicious of his clammy skin and sudden weight loss, and finally, after much prodding, he had told her of his condition. Elizabeth had vowed to give him loving comfort and care for as long as God let him live.

There had seemed to be a peace within him, and the two of them had spent many hours talking and just enjoying each other and their shared memories. Then, three weeks ago, Santino had a visit from Massimo Brattini. He had flown in from Toronto by private jet and Santino had invited him to stay overnight. Elizabeth knew that Santino and Brattini were old enemies and couldn't understand her husband's motives.

"Always keep your enemies close," was Santino's attitude in these matters, but having Brattini in their home did seem a bit closer than necessary.

When Brattini arrived at the DeLuca home, he had looked at Elizabeth strangely. When he met Peter and Matthew, she had become even more uneasy by the intensity of his stares. He'd hovered around the boys, questioning them about their activities, even trying to join them in one of their video-game battles. He'd kept everyone up talking until almost one o'clock in the morning, and had gone to his room only after Matthew fell asleep on the couch.

But Santino had reassured her that she had nothing to worry about, and he had insisted that Brattini be treated as a welcome guest in their home. Elizabeth knew that, despite his weakened condition, Santino was still in control, and she suspected he would be until the day he drew his last breath.

But when Brattini was murdered less than a week after his visit, Santino had instructed her to call that woman, and that policeman as well.

Why do you want to see them both? she asked silently now.

Santino tossed slightly in his pained sleep. Elizabeth shook her head. It was unfair. He was sixty-eight years old and until four months ago still strong, even virile. She smiled to herself, remembering last summer's "adventure in the pool," as Santino had jokingly called it.

"Come on, Elizabeth," he had murmured in her ear. "The boys won't be back till Monday. Remember how we made love that first time in Michigan?"

It had taken a long time for a convent-school girl like Elizabeth to shed her inhibitions and enjoy sex. But as their bodies and minds reached a spiritual union, she had known the kind of happiness she never dreamed possible.

And now, after everything, this.

I've waited so long to have him for myself. And now he's dying. And still he asked for that woman, that bitch!

Elizabeth crossed herself in penance for her momentary lapse. Evil thoughts about others brought nothing but grief. She had learned that as a child, long before Santino had come to rescue her.

Just then a moan escaped from the emaciated body on the bed.

"Elizabeth?" he asked in a hoarse whisper. "Did you reach them?"

"Yes, my darling. They're on their way."

A smile came over Santino's face just before the pain hit again, and his back arched in a spasm.

Elizabeth took out a syringe and prepared to inject the morphine into his vein as the doctor had shown her.

"Rest, my dear husband," she whispered as she leaned over to stroke his forehead and hold his hand. "Everything's taken care of. There's nothing to worry about. I'm right here with you."

# 1

JUNE
1944

It was quiet today. Only birds flew in the blue sky above the valley. It was a sweet spring day, a day to forget the bombers that so often filled the sky, a day to forget that Italy had surrendered and her soldiers now fought alongside the Allies, that the Germans had killed so many in retaliation. A day to forget the war that still raged on so many fronts. And yet it was because of the war that school had been let out early.

The Allies had taken Sicily in August of 1943 — almost a year earlier. By September they had landed in Salerno, and soon Italy south of a line that stretched from Naples to Foggia was in Allied hands. Then for a very long time fighting had stalled on the road to Rome. The Germans held out at Monte Cassino and it was only months later that the famous shrine fell after suffering extremely heavy damage.

"Utterly, absolutely destroyed!" the Fascists shouted to the world. "No respect for history!"

And so as the Allies moved toward Rome, Italians held their collective breath. But today, June 6, the news had come. Rome had fallen on the fourth, but the great city had been spared the devastation of combat. It was to celebrate this that the nuns had dismissed their students early.

Giovanna Volpe was fifteen years old. She had blond hair, green eyes, an olive complexion, and was barely five feet tall. As she was growing up, she'd often fantasized about a prince on a white horse coming to carry her off to live happily ever after, just like her grandmother. This fantasy was her escape from the unhappy reality of her life at home. Two years earlier, her father had been taken away by the Fascists and sent to a work camp. Giovanna missed him and wanted solace from her mother, but Maria Volpe did nothing but cry and complain all the time. They still worked on the landowner's farm, and her mother took in laundry to earn some extra money.

On this joyous afternoon Giovanna and her best friend, Theresa Vincenzo, walked toward home. Theresa was also petite and much slimmer than Giovanna. She had long dark hair and snapping brown eyes.

She and her baby brother Benito had originally lived with their parents in Brindisi. Three years earlier, their father and mother had been killed by a car that ran them over on the sidewalk. Six months after the tragedy, the driver's mutilated body was found in the center of the village, his kneecaps smashed, his right hand missing, and his throat slit.

Immediately afterward Don Paolo Vincenzo brought his two little orphaned grandchildren, Theresa and Benito, to live with him and his young wife Rosa. They had a farm near Altamura in Puglia, where he raised cattle, grew various grains, and had almond groves and vineyards. It was on his land that the Volpe family worked.

Like many Italians, Vincenzo did not like Benito Mussolini. In fact, he disliked him so much that he changed little Benito's name to Roberto.

"My grandfather says he was never a Fascist," Theresa told Giovanna. "He says the Americans were able to take Sicily because they got Lucky Luciano to help them."

"Lucky Luciano?" Giovanna asked.

Theresa shrugged. "*A capo di tutti capi*, the boss of all bosses who lives in America."

Giovanna said nothing. Theresa's grandfather Vincenzo commanded much respect as head of his family, and he was known to follow the old ways, about which those who were wise neither spoke much nor bothered to learn more.

"Hurry right home," the nuns had instructed them as they left. It was not the usual thing, of course. Normally they would have lived at the convent school, but it had been partially destroyed during a bombing raid and now the students came only during the day.

"Hurry home. Talk to no strangers. Avoid men. Do not take up with boys" . . . and on and on. Don't do this, don't do that.

Since her mother paid little attention to her, most of what Giovanna knew about life — babies and sex — had come from Don Vincenzo's wife. Rosa allowed her to sit with Theresa when the topic of "where babies come from" was discussed.

Theresa told Giovanna that Don Vincenzo encouraged these discussions because, "In spite of his way of life, he intends to send us to America to be educated."

The two friends turned off the main road and walked along the dirt road arm in arm. The air was clear and dry: it had an earthy smell from the dust kicked up by their shuffling feet.

"I heard that Antonia is going out with that boy who just came home."

Giovanna looked up. In front of them were three soldiers, their uniforms dirty and wrinkled, stumbling along in the opposite direction. They didn't appear to be carrying any guns.

"We had better walk faster," Giovanna suggested.

Theresa scowled. The soldiers were making lewd comments as they drew closer.

Giovanna noticed that one of them was tall and thin, with jet-black hair and very fair skin. He looked different from the other two, both of whom were fat. She could not help thinking that he was quite good-looking. Eventually the soldiers' raucous laughter faded as the girls hurried past them toward their homes.

Theresa went on talking, but Giovanna felt a shiver travel the length of her spine. She whirled about to see that the soldiers had turned around to follow them and were all but on their heels.

Two of the men grabbed the girls from behind and dragged them into the scrub woodland that surrounded a great lime quarry. Giovanna and

Theresa screamed and struggled as dirty neckerchiefs were tied over their mouths. They were dragged over a hill toward the deep turquoise-blue quarry where the local children often used to swim when it was hot. The third man, obviously very drunk, staggered along behind them, mumbling to his friends, "Take it easy, don't be so rough."

Even in her panic, Giovanna tried to keep her wits, although Sister Lucia's dire warnings kept ringing in her ears.

Why hadn't they paid more attention to what Sister had said and been more careful? Giovanna's heart was pounding wildly and she began whispering, "Hail Mary, full of grace," through her gag. She knew that Theresa must be feeling some relief because she had her period. No self-respecting man would touch a "dirty" girl, as those menstruating were often called. Yes, the blood was a curse inflicted on evil girls. Men should avoid them at all costs when "that time of the month" came.

I'm sure once they see the bloody rags they'll leave us both alone, Giovanna hoped. She prayed to the spirit of her dead grandmother and tried to distract herself by thinking of a princess being abducted by wicked soldiers, only to be saved at the last minute by a prince on a white horse.

Through the neckerchief she tried to hum a song, the one her father used to sing as he rocked her to sleep. Maybe they'll think I'm crazy, she thought, or maybe someone will come by and hear us.

When one of the soldiers slapped her face, she decided to keep quiet and not struggle as much as Theresa was doing. The man holding Theresa around the neck kept pummeling her head and face, shouting at her to shut up or she'd be even sorrier than she was going to be. But Theresa kept fighting and trying to scream despite the gag.

Finally they reached a clearing where a camp had been set up. Giovanna could see a tent, a fire still smoldering, and some empty tins on the ground. There were also several bottles of whiskey, some of which were empty. The men had obviously been staying there for at least a couple of days.

Giovanna was tied to a tree by several loops of twine, wound around her body from her neck down to her ankles, her arms straight down her sides. The gag in her mouth was more tightly secured. I must keep thinking of the princess waiting for her prince, she thought. Don't watch what's happening to Theresa. Turn your head away.

Just then the thin soldier tried to stop the other two from hitting Theresa.

"No, *no violenza!*" he shouted, grabbing at them. "We were just going to have some fun — maybe a fuck or two. Nobody said anything about any rough stuff. *Cessare!*"

"Come on, cousin," answered the short, fat one. "Don't be a jerk. These two babes are just dying for it. Don't be an asshole."

"No, cut it out!" the thin one shouted. He started pushing his two friends and, in the drunken shoving that followed, slipped and cracked his head on one of the rocks close to the tree where Giovanna was tied. He was knocked unconscious and a trickle of blood soon ran down the side of his face. The other two soldiers looked at him and shrugged.

Then one of them held Theresa's arms behind her back while his friend tore off her clothes. When he saw her firm and full breasts, he gave a jubilant shout and proceeded to nibble on her nipples while he squeezed and pinched the flesh around them.

Theresa screamed and Giovanna felt herself straining against her own bonds. The blue sky, the new spring buds on the trees, the sweet smells of the earth, were all obliterated; she was aware only of the sight and sound of her friend.

Then the brutish drunk started sucking on Theresa's breasts, very hard and loud. "Where's the milk?" he cried. "I want some milk." His sucking grew even stronger and Theresa tried to twist out of his mouth. With that, he slapped her across the face, bringing blood to her lips, and proceeded to bite her nipples.

"If she doesn't have any milk, she must still have her cherry," said the soldier who was holding Theresa's arms. By now he had an erection himself, anticipating his turn at her. "Who goes first?" he asked. "How about me, Giorgio?"

"Wait your turn, Domenic," the first soldier answered. "I'm older than you, so it's my right. Remember when Papa fucked that maid before her wedding? The one who worked on our property? As the *padrone,* it was his right. He let me watch. Like I'm letting you watch!"

Brothers, thought Giovanna. And they're Italian, even though their dialect is strange. Obviously from another region. She cursed herself for even thinking that the one now lying unconscious at her feet was cute when she first saw him.

Theresa's tormentor started to remove the rest of her clothes, running his hands along her waist and licking his lips as if in anticipation of sticking his fingers and then his cock inside this juicy young virgin. He pulled down his pants and his underwear, exposing his erect penis. Then he saw the bloody rags between Theresa's thighs.

"Ugh!" he shouted. "She's got the curse! Who wants to put his cock into a pool of poisoned blood!"

Giovanna couldn't help staring at the large penis. She had never seen one before. It was slightly bent, and the two testicles at the bottom looked like rubber balls she had once played with. Despite her terror she had a morbid fascination about what it did and where it went.

Giovanna's relief over the soldiers' initial reaction to Theresa's menstruation was short-lived when Giorgio said, "Well, I guess we'll have to do it Greek style. Domenic, drag her over to that tree."

The realization of what he was saying hit Theresa like a bolt, and she began to struggle even harder. Giovanna immediately closed her eyes, mumbling the Hail Mary into her gag even as she began to cry.

Domenic started dragging Theresa by the hair toward another tree, punching her in the kidneys as she struggled. He also tried to slip his fingers between her buttocks and insert one into her. He couldn't get it in at all.

"We're going to have a problem with her," he told his older brother. "I think she's too tight."

With that, Giorgio forced Theresa over on her knees and tried to push his penis into her behind. It wouldn't go in.

"Wait, I've got an idea," he said. He stopped what he was doing and went inside the tent. He brought out a bottle of hair grease and poured some over his hand and proceeded to shove his fingers inside Theresa's anus, first one, then eventually four fingers. Theresa screamed out in pain and Domenic

18

punched her in the mouth again. Giorgio then pulled out his greasy fingers, poured more oil over his penis, and thrust it as hard as he could into her.

Theresa's almost inhuman screams of agony sent shock waves of terror through Giovanna as she looked over at her friend's crumpled body, curled up in a ball. Giovanna was shaking, and in her fear and horror wet her pants. She began praying for death because she realized that no one was coming to save them.

Giorgio finally stood up and the brothers walked over to the quarry to rinse their hands in the cold water. They then proceeded to finish off the half-empty bottle of whiskey sitting near the fire.

"I don't care if she's got the curse," Domenic whined. "I want to break her cherry. Come on, hold her for me."

With that, Theresa, still bleeding from her mouth and rectum, was dragged closer to the quarry and turned onto her back. Domenic knelt over her and tried to insert his penis into her vagina, but it wouldn't go in. He kept pushing, but the hymen wouldn't break. He stood up angrily, reached for an empty whiskey bottle, and shoved it violently inside her.

The pain that rushed over and through Theresa was excruciating. In that split second she must have realized that her life was over. She would be forever tainted; she would never be married, never be a mother. Death was preferable. As she writhed in agony, she wanted to exact some punishment on her tormentors before she died. She reached down, grabbed Domenic's testicles, and dug her nails into him as hard as she could. His screams of pain and his attempts to twist himself away from her turned the scene even uglier. Cursing, Domenic picked up a nearby rock and started smashing it against Theresa's face, all the while trying to pry her fingers loose.

Finally it was over. Theresa's lifeless eyes stared up to the sky. The brothers looked at her for a moment and kicked her once or twice. When she did not move, they pushed her body into the quarry.

Domenic, still clutching his testicles, managed to stand up straight, and after a few minutes both brothers looked over at Giovanna. "You're next," they said, almost in unison. "But first we need another drink."

Giovanna was catatonic with terror.

Next to her, the soldier who had been unconscious was struggling to his feet, cursing his companions for their brutality.

"They're just two peasant girls," Giorgio slurred. "Even if anyone misses them, what does it matter? We'll be long gone by then."

Giovanna now began whimpering and trembling as the two brothers, stark naked, tossed aside another empty whiskey bottle and came staggering over to her. As they ripped off her clothes, still leaving her tied to the tree, Giovanna tried to blot out the torture that she anticipated by summoning her pride.

Then, suddenly, the man who had objected shouted, "I've changed my mind. I want a piece of this action. It's my turn to go first."

"You're right," said Giorgio. "It's about time you smartened up. Go ahead and we'll watch. Then we'll have some more fun. At least this one doesn't have the curse."

The third soldier took off his clothes and walked in front of Giovanna, blocking the brothers' full view of her. Tears were streaming down her face and her body was shaking uncontrollably.

"Don't be afraid, little one," he whispered gently as he started kissing her mouth. "I'll try not to hurt you. I'm going to help you."

His words gave Giovanna little comfort after what she had just witnessed.

Keep thinking about being a royal princess, she told herself. Think about ball gowns and jewels. Pretend this isn't happening and maybe it will go away.

The soldier's hands were playing with her breasts, fondling, gently squeezing; then he began to knead her nipples between his fingers. His tongue kept darting into her mouth, but he also kissed her face and her closed eyes. His hands were gentle and he said nothing more.

As his mouth moved down her breasts and his lips covered her nipples, Giovanna got goose bumps despite her determination to shut out what was happening. And the more he sucked on her and licked her, the more difficult it was to ignore him.

When his hands started stroking her buttocks Giovanna froze, remembering Theresa. But his touch was gentle, as his fingers just toyed with the opening between her cheeks. Then they moved around to her navel, and he began softly rubbing the pubic hair covering her secret place. All the time he was kissing her face and neck, occasionally bending down to run his tongue over her now erect nipples. Then he let his fingers play around the outer lips of her vagina, occasionally sliding one along the opening. When he found what he was looking for, he started to stroke her clitoris, lightly at first, then putting it between his fingers and rubbing it.

Despite herself, Giovanna started to respond. She felt moisture down there and, not knowing what it meant, hoped that the shock of what was happening had made her period come. When the soldier felt the moisture on his fingers, he lifted his head and looked quizzically into Giovanna's eyes.

He then lowered himself, all the while running his lips down her body. When he reached her pubic hair, he began nibbling at the outer lips of her vagina, holding her to his face by placing his hands on her buttocks. When his tongue began flicking back and forth on her clitoris, Giovanna felt weak. And when he thrust his tongue inside her, passion overcame her. Why, you're nothing but a slut, she thought to herself. Behaving like a whore. Writhing around with some drunken stranger, after they've just killed your best friend. You deserve to be cursed forever.

In the meantime Giorgio and Domenic were getting excited watching what little they could see. When their comrade told them, "I'm going to untie her so I can really fuck her," they answered, "Hurry up, we can't wait to get at her, too."

The stranger untied her, whispering for her to keep still, and then he lowered her onto the ground behind the trunk of the tree. There was high grass all around and the two brothers couldn't see much.

The soldier put first one finger, then two, inside her as gently as he could. Giovanna was fully lubricated and her clitoris was swollen. He thrust his penis into her quite hard, and the pain of her hymen breaking threatened to overwhelm her. Then he started caressing her clitoris again while his thrusts increased in their urgency. Feelings, unknown to her before and not understood even now, pulsed through Giovanna's body along with his semen, making the pain fade into the background. Giovanna's eyes were now closed, and for a fleeting moment she forgot the horrors she had seen. Her arms were around the stranger's back, and her legs as well.

The hooting and laughing of his comrades jarred her back to reality. As the soldier lifted himself off her body, Giovanna saw the ugly red scar of a cross just below his navel. What did it mean? The image burned into her brain.

Just then the sound of planes filled the air. As her tormentors looked up, several low-flying planes passed overhead in what looked like a formation. All three men started crossing themselves.

"Shit! They're looking for Germans," yelled Giorgio. "Let's get out of here. But first let's kill her. We don't want any witnesses."

Giovanna's lover whispered in her ear, "Listen to me, and do as I say. Pretend you can't swim."

"No! Please save me!" Giovanna screamed as she was dragged toward the quarry. "I can't swim!"

The two brothers just laughed as they let their companion tie her hands and feet. Then they helped him throw her into the water. "Join your friend in heaven!" Domenic yelled as they ran off, pulling on their pants as they went.

Giovanna bent over under the water to pull the loosely tied rope off her hands and legs; then she started swimming under water as long as she could hold her breath. Her lover had made sure the knots would untie easily. Now she could only hope he would lead the other two men away quickly.

She emerged long enough to take a deep breath and look around. They were gone, but still she waited. Finally she crawled naked out of the quarry and hid in the tall grass, panting.

"Oh, Holy Jesus, please forgive me for my sins. Please, please forgive me. I promise I will give myself to God, to the Holy Church. Oh, Holy Mother of God, I shall do penance all the rest of my life. I promise." Tears ran down her face. Tears of fear, tears of gratitude, tears for the terrible things she had seen done to her friend. For a long while she held herself and rocked back and forth, crying and praying, praying and crying.

*T*he hospital was not in reality a hospital at all. The church hall had been converted into two large wards separated only by curtains. Because there were not enough beds, most of the patients lay on pallets on the floor. There was only one doctor, and the sisters who looked after the ill were not really nurses, just ordinary nuns who had been pressed into action by circumstances.

The sounds that filled the wards were largely the muted groans of those who had lost arms or legs, and the whole place smelled of blood, formaldehyde, and vinegar. Wounded soldiers who had trickled back from the front, wounded civilians, and those who had become ill because of unsafe water or putrid food crowded the makeshift hospital.

Don Paolo Vincenzo came to the hospital the day after Theresa's body had floated to the top of the quarry. He didn't suspect that Giovanna hadn't been tortured as badly as his dead granddaughter. He looked at her lying on a pallet, and was filled with sympathy.

"Dear little Giovanna," he said very quietly, "you can't stay here, so I will take you to my house. I will look after you and your family, and I will do what I can."

Giovanna looked up at him. "I want to go to a convent," she whispered.

"After you get better. Giovanna, you must tell me who did this. You must tell me who violated you and Theresa, who killed my granddaughter."

"I never saw them before. They were wearing some kind of uniforms and they spoke Italian, but they were not from Puglia."

"How many were there?"

Giovanna looked into his eyes. She wanted to cross herself. She wanted to run away. She could not betray the man who had saved her, the man who had taken her so . . .

"How many, my child?" Vincenzo asked again.

"Two," Giovanna answered. "Giorgio and — and Domenic. Yes, that's what they called each other."

"Tell me what they looked like." Don Vincenzo leaned over her. "As painful as it is for you to remember, we must know who did this. There must be retribution for my granddaughter's murder. The souls of her parents are calling out to me. Tell me everything you remember, please."

"They were brothers — yes, they said they were brothers."

"Were they tall?"

She shook her head. "No, both were short and fat. One had a scar" — she touched her own arm — "here."

"Thank you, my little one," he said. "Now I can find them so that justice can be done. I'll have the sisters help you to my car. You'll stay in our home till you are well enough to enter a convent. If you are certain that is what you want."

Giovanna was certain. Now she would also have to atone for not telling Don Vincenzo the entire truth.

*N*ine months later, in March of 1945, two months before the surrender of Germany, Giovanna Volpe gave birth to a daughter in the infirmary of the convent where she had gone to live after that terrible day in June. The baby weighed eight pounds and had green eyes and blond hair. It was a difficult labor, made all the harder by the sobs and wails of Giovanna's mother, Maria, who sat outside the delivery room.

"God's curse," she cried. "My husband is still missing somewhere and my daughter is forever tainted! Why is this happening to me?"

No, Giovanna thought, not to you, but to me. This is God's punishment for my sin of passion.

And as a reminder of her own lost dreams and lost life, and her love of royalty and fairy tales, she decided to name her baby Elizabeth, after the English princess, whose picture she had once seen in a magazine. She had never forgotten the little royal daughter of the King of England. And it seemed doubly suitable since British troops now occupied the village.

Giovanna looked down on her tiny baby. "Yes, I shall raise you to be a princess, and then I shall give you to the Church as my penance."

*D*on Vincenzo swirled his glass of red wine and studied its clarity. It was September of 1946. "Patience in all things," he muttered. Tonight he was expecting a phone call. Tonight it would be over.

He leaned back and looked around the sitting room of his villa. His books were undisturbed, his wine cellar intact, his fields still fertile. Both he and his wealth had survived the most terrible war Europe had ever known. Others had not been so lucky. So many homes had been bombed, so many fields torched. So much destruction, and now this terrible new weapon. It defied the imagination, but it also bore a message. North America truly was the future. And he would send young Roberto into that future. His grandson would be groomed for greatness; he would study and he would succeed. He would be where he could be of the most use to his family.

Don Vincenzo lifted the glass and swirled the wine again to inhale its bouquet. Then he sipped it, putting it down only when the phone began to ring.

"We have them, Don Vincenzo," the voice whispered in his ear. "You were right when you said only the Calabrese could inflict that kind of brutality on two innocent young girls. What do you want us to do with them?"

Don Vincenzo had put all his considerable resources to work to find out who had committed the atrocities on his granddaughter and her friend. After two years and many favors called in and given, his "connections" had finally delivered.

"Hold them safe till I get there. I'll be in Rome on business the day after tomorrow and I should get there by Wednesday night." He silently cursed the war. It had utterly destroyed Italy's transportation system. Trains were almost nonexistent, roads were unrepaired, and gasoline was still in short supply. It seemed as if virtually every plane in the country had been shot down. He sighed. Patience, he reminded himself. He had waited two years. He could wait four more days.

When Paolo Vincenzo was shown into the abandoned warehouse basement by his contact, Adolfo Leoni, the two brothers, Giorgio and Domenic

Luchese, were naked and spread-eagled by steel handcuffs attached to the wall. The windowless room was made out of concrete blocks, and the floor had several large drain holes with rubber covers. A terrible stench emanated from them.

Adolfo said nothing, but he quietly handed Vincenzo the truncheon in case he wanted to ask questions.

The terror in the brothers' eyes was a comfort to Don Vincenzo, especially since they didn't yet know who he was, or even why they were being held. He walked closer to the shackled men and spat on the floor. "You two are a curse to the parents who bore you."

"You have the wrong brothers. We've done nothing!" Giorgio wailed.

Don Vincenzo swung the heavy bat and struck Giorgio across the middle, hitting his balls and causing him to scream out in pain.

"You'll soon wish you had never been conceived," he said. "You raped and tortured two young girls a couple of years ago." He glared at the figures suspended before him. "It's taken me quite some time to find you."

"Peasant girls!" Domenic cried. "We didn't really hurt them, it must have been someone else. Someone who came after we left them."

Vincenzo turned to Adolfo, a bear of a man with narrow eyes and strangely white teeth, and nodded.

It was Adolfo who struck the next blow. "Show respect! This is Don Vincenzo!"

"One of those girls was my granddaughter, and she died from the torture you inflicted on her."

"No!" Domenic cried.

Don Vincenzo turned to Adolfo. "I want them to die slowly, in a way worthy of the scum they are."

Both Giorgio and Domenic began to beg for mercy as they realized what was about to happen to them.

"First cut their tongues out," Don Vincenzo whispered, but loudly enough for them to hear. His eyes narrowed. "I don't want to hear their words. Just their screams."

One week later the mutilated bodies of Domenic and Giorgio Luchese were dumped outside their parents' house. They had been castrated, their eyes gouged out, their tongues cut out. Metal rods, which had once been red-hot, were hanging out of their rectums. An autopsy showed that the two men had died only an hour before their bodies were discovered. They had lived some thirty-six hours after the last torture was inflicted, their vocal cords no longer capable of emitting anything other than the muted sounds of creatures who bore little resemblance to human beings.

Don Vincenzo read the reports. "Justice has been done," he said.

*T*he news of his cousins' horrible death traveled like wildfire. He knew he had to run immediately. He would not even try to say good-bye to his parents.

Rumors swirled around every town in Calabria that the Luchese family would retaliate for this butchery, but he knew it wasn't likely. Even with bloody feuds generations old, the Lucheses' brutal attack on the innocent young girls was unforgivable. He knew that he was guilty as well. After all, what had he done to stop them? Nothing. Being drunk and unconscious during most of the attack would be no excuse if the Don ever found out that he had been there.

He knew his cousins would never betray a member of the family, but why hadn't the girl told on him? He kept remembering her warm and supple body and her responses to his lovemaking. Still, he wasn't taking any chances. Any romantic notions he had of going back to the hills of Puglia to look for the girl with the green eyes were dashed forever.

He used all his savings to buy a one-way steerage ticket to South America because it was still not possible for him to travel directly to the United States. Things were still tight after the war. But he could make his way there from South America. At twenty-one, he still had his life ahead of him. Maybe in a few years, when things cooled off, he'd be able to contact his parents, but for now there was no future for him in Italy. It was time to take off and start a new life in America.

# 2

*I*t was late afternoon when the group of students and nuns finally gained admission to the Sistine Chapel. Sister Mary Margaret watched her wards disperse, each to look at what interested her most.

Elizabeth Volpe was clearly entranced as she looked at the ceiling of the Sistine Chapel. She tilted her head to get a better look at the image of Moses' fingertips reaching out to the hand of God.

"What are you thinking?" Sister Mary Margaret asked her favorite student.

"I was thinking that it seems as if the hand of God directed Michaelangelo's brush strokes. It's as if the colors are blended in such a way that they give a sense of the spiritual. I think everyone who comes here must have a clearer vision of His presence."

Sister Mary Margaret smiled. Elizabeth seemed to be overwhelmed by the magnificence of the Chapel. And that, thought Sister Mary Margaret, was as it should be. Elizabeth had a strong spiritual nature, but the sister knew that the young woman also had a strong sensual nature and a sense of adventure. If those sides of her nature were stronger than her spiritual side, she would not make a good nun.

"It makes me feel humble to be here," Elizabeth added.

Sister Mary Margaret nodded. The hushed voices and rapt expressions on the faces of those around her reinforced her own sense of wonder at the grandeur of the murals. Still, there was lots to see and the crowds slowed them down. "Some of us are moving on," Sister Mary Margaret whispered, "but you can catch up with us if you want to stay here for a bit."

"Thank you." Elizabeth watched as Sister Mary Margaret moved on, then she returned her eyes to the ceiling and her thoughts to the past.

She and her classmates from the International Convent School in Gravina were on a ten-day tour of Rome under the guidance of Sister Mary Margaret and Sister Angelina. The trip was a reward for those in their senior year whose scholastic achievements warranted special acknowledgment. For those girls who intended taking preliminary vows, a trip to the Vatican was a very special religious experience. The families of all the girls had made substantial contributions to the Mother House to cover the costs of transportation by train to Rome, food and lodging in the convent of the Sisters of St. Joseph, and the tour of the Eternal City.

It was, in addition to every other aspect of the trip, a very special time in Rome, in the Vatican, and for the Church. On October 11, a short month away, the Pope, His Holiness John XXIII, would open Vatican II, and the Holy City was already swarming with dignitaries, members of the world press, and theologians from around the globe.

Sister Mary Margaret, who had organized the trip, was in fact a symbol of the new wave that was sweeping the Church. She had been born in Boston of Irish Catholic parents, and for several years she had taught at a Catholic high school in that city's heavily Italian downtown neighborhood. Sister Mary Margaret quickly learned Italian and subsequently fell in love with Italy and its culture. She applied for and received a five-year teaching position in Italy at the International Convent School, where young women from all over the world came to receive a superior academic education within the confines of a religious community.

Sister Angelina, her co-tour leader, had been born in Venice. She was the daughter of a carpenter and his wife, the eldest of ten children. Sister Angelina was as interested in Boston and Irish culture as Sister Mary Margaret was in Italy. They became fast friends, and both were respected as academics and admired for their piety.

Sister Angelina was a rather portly woman, barely five feet tall, with a cherubic face, dimples, and a smile that could melt ice. Sister Mary Margaret was slim, and had blue eyes and freckles. She smiled readily and delighted her listeners with folk tales galore and songs, which she sang while strumming an autoharp.

Elizabeth knew that both nuns had taken a particular interest in her because, unlike most of the students, she was Italian and because both knew her mother, who resided in the old convent in Gravina a few miles from the school.

"You are a special young woman with special needs," Sister Angelina had once told her, "because you have no family and because your mother is unwell."

"Unwell" was probably something of an understatement. Elizabeth knew that after her birth, more than one nun had hovered over Giovanna, trying to coax her back to reality, trying to make her believe that God hadn't abandoned her. But it was no use. Elizabeth's mother flipped back and forth between fantasy and reality, with fantasy winning out most of the time.

Elizabeth grew up surrounded by women, loved and nurtured by the nuns, and too often just tolerated by her mother. Her grandfather had never returned after the war. Her grandmother, whom she did not remember, wore widow's weeds until the end of her life. Maria Volpe had died two years after her granddaughter's birth, still weeping and wailing over the cross she had to bear in life.

Elizabeth thought a lot about her father, a soldier who had been killed in the war, and she wondered what he must have been like. She'd never seen a picture of him and her mother would never talk about him.

Elizabeth only knew that there was an "Uncle Paolo" Vincenzo, whom she had never met and who showed no interest in meeting her, but who had unlimited financial resources. She knew that her mother was given whatever she needed. As a result Elizabeth was dressed in the finest of clothing available, had private tutors, and was given many books.

When Giovanna was lucid and in a balanced frame of mind, she seemed to have only one goal: to teach her daughter how to be a princess so that when she entered the arms of the Church, she would be a special gift. Elizabeth did not pretend to understand her mother's attitude, and now that she was maturing, she was not at all certain that she wanted to become a nun. As for the future — she daydreamed about handsome men; she wanted to have adventures; she wanted her prince to come. But in the meantime she accepted her mother's tutoring.

Giovanna read her stories about nobility from the earliest times of recorded history, highlighting the royal families of Europe, especially Britain. She acquired books on literature and art, and these had opened the door to Elizabeth's creative curiosity.

She particularly recalled Giovanna having afternoon tea parties with her, teaching her proper manners and ladylike behavior that she herself had learned from the books on etiquette that Don Vincenzo's money provided.

And there were books that depicted the upper-class, finer way of life. Giovanna wanted her to acquire the finishing touches that would allow her to "walk with kings," as she said. To that end, the Don's money paid for tutors who taught her English, French, and Spanish.

But who was this mysterious benefactor? And more to the point, why did her mother want these things for her?

Elizabeth sighed deeply, took one long last look at the face of God on the ceiling, and left to catch up with the others.

Out in the sunlight, she blinked and looked around. Across the courtyard she saw her group. They were gathered around Sister Angelina, who was giving a lecture of some sort.

It was then that Elizabeth saw the tall stranger. He had long curly hair and burning black eyes. She felt those eyes on her before she actually glanced at the bench and saw him. He was staring at her. Elizabeth quickly turned away, fantasizing about who he was and if he would speak to her.

Looking over at Sister Angelina, Elizabeth wondered if she, too, had noticed the stranger hovering close by. He was so handsome he'd be hard to miss. But then Elizabeth reminded herself that nuns never noticed men. It would have been a sin.

She remembered the time she'd asked Sister Angelina about her decision to become a nun and if she ever thought about men.

"Of course, during my novice years in the Order I often thought about boys and wondered what it would be like to have a husband and children," the nun replied. "But God's call to me was stronger than anything else, and I've never regretted my decision. And neither will you."

Elizabeth had wondered then if Sister Angelina suspected that her commitment to the Church was not very deep. She thought of escaping from her restricted life, but was afraid to share her thoughts with anyone. After all, she had been told her whole life that she was committed to the Church, thanks to her mother.

"*L*et's stay together!" Sister Mary Margaret called out as they all walked along Via Pancrazio. "Stay together. I don't want anyone to get lost."

The students had filled picnic baskets with sandwiches and fruit in the kitchen of the Mother House before once again setting out for the Vatican and their scheduled tour of St. Peter's. They planned to have lunch in a park nearby and fully expected that the day would be as beautiful as the whole week had been. It was fall, but that only meant cooler mornings and evenings. The days were warm and sunny and the parks still smelled of flowers even if the grass was sometimes wet with dew.

It's a wonderful city, Elizabeth thought as they walked along. It was, she admitted, a sensual city filled with colors, aromas, and sounds. Red-tiled roofs and white stucco walls abounded under a blue sky. Sparkling mosaics, beautiful terrazzi, gleaming marble balconies were everywhere. Business and residential areas surrounded historic ruins, monuments, and buildings so that a turned corner could easily bring an unexpected encounter with Rome's glorious past.

At every corner it seemed that the olfactory senses were assaulted: the wonderful mouth-watering smell of fresh bread and the perfume of flowers mingled with exhaust fumes and the odors of many fish markets. And certainly Rome was filled with discordant sounds as wailing dogs sang over church bells and honking cars drowned out street musicians and the sound of what seemed like endless and constant construction. Even now, seventeen years after the end of the war, there was still much rebuilding left to do, especially on the roads and bridges.

When the group reached Gianicolo Park there were a few other people there. Elizabeth noticed a sailor who was sleeping under the huge weeping willow tree with a big dog curled up beside him. Close by, a pregnant woman was pushing a toddler on one of the swings. The little boy was shrieking with delight as he kicked his legs trying to go higher, begging his mother to push harder.

Elizabeth also noticed someone else right away. A shiver ran through her. It was the man she had seen on the bench in the Vatican the day before. Dressed in beige slacks, a beige sweater, and a tweed sport jacket, he looked as if he'd just stepped out of a men's fashion magazine. Somehow she wasn't shocked that he'd found her again or that he was again staring at her.

"C'mon, we're ready for some exercise," Sister Mary Margaret called out. She sent Sister Angelina off to be goalie and she put down the ball and kicked it to start play.

What the man saw as he started to approach Elizabeth was a group of girls who had just begun to play some form of soccer, with a portly nun acting as the goalie. They were giggling and squealing as they kicked the ball around and around, trying to get past her into the line of picnic baskets being used in place of the goalie's net.

The willowy blonde with the incredible eyes was laughing and her hair was blowing around her face. To him, she was a vision — tall, flaxen-haired, and so elegant in spite of her youth.

As he continued walking toward her, she stopped running and stood still, looking directly at him. Her green eyes took on a soft glow as she returned his tentative smile. He couldn't take his eyes from hers. He felt as if he'd been hit by a bolt of lightning. Never in his thirty-six years had he ever reacted in such a way to a woman, and this was no woman — she was just a girl. As he continued to look at her, their eyes locked. It was as if there was no one in the park but the two of them.

From somewhere across the park voices called out to him in English: "Hey, Santino, stop drooling over that jail bait. You're old enough to be her father. Come on, we have to go. We'll find a couple of young broads for the party later."

He was hoping she didn't understand their words, but from the look in her eyes, it appeared she did.

He turned to look at his friends. He waved. Smiled. He was in no hurry. The day was sunny, the park was peaceful, full of happy sights and sounds.

And then the car exploded.

It seemed as if everything happened in slow motion. The green-eyed girl stood frozen in front of him as he took a few swift strides toward her. When he reached her, he put his arms around her and tried to use his body to protect her from the flying debris. They both fell down under a huge tree.

The world around them was filled with screams. The stench of burning rubber, flesh, and cordite filled the air. There was total confusion.

Several days earlier he'd heard a rumor about a hit. If this is it, he wondered, who's the target?

Elizabeth started to struggle, trying to look over to where she had last seen her classmates, but Santino kept her head buried against his chest.

"Don't look, my little one," he whispered, stroking her back and shoulders. "Keep your eyes closed. I'm here, don't be afraid."

But she was afraid. Oh God, she prayed, crossing herself, let everything be all right. But she knew that everything was all wrong. The screams of agony from those who were dying, the smoke and flames and flying debris terrified her. She continued to struggle in the man's arms, sobbing and pounding on his chest, yelling at him in English to let her go. But he held her tight, stroking her hair, whispering words of comfort in her ear, telling her to trust him; he would help her.

Finally her trembling stopped as an inner calm passed from him to her. She looked into his black eyes and at that moment she closed the door on any more fantasies about a life on her own. She put her arms around his neck and rested her head against his chest. She knew then that this man would be her future, her salvation, and her life. Her prince had come.

*S*ister Angelina, Sister Mary Margaret, and three of Elizabeth's classmates had been killed instantly, blown to bits, along with the expectant mother and her child, the sailor and his dog.

Elizabeth was still sobbing when Santino lifted her into a car driven by his friends. They circled around for what seemed like an hour as police cars with sirens blaring and ambulances with lights flashing raced past them. The streets were full of people, some running toward the park, others just milling around. The scene was chaotic.

Finally Santino ordered the driver to pull into the underground garage of a house located in a cul-de-sac near the park. The house itself was gray fieldstone; a high hedge surrounded the property; a large apple tree laden with late fruit towered over the front door, which was painted red.

When the garage doors closed, plunging everything into momentary darkness, Elizabeth started to cry again. As Santino helped her into the house, she clung desperately to him, and by the time they reached an upstairs bedroom, she was almost hysterical. Within the hour a doctor arrived to give her a sedative.

After the doctor had gone, she refused to let go of Santino's hand, begging him to stay with her.

When Elizabeth woke up hours later she found herself in the middle of a double bed. It was dark outside and the only light came from the hall so that she could not really take in her surroundings. When she heard the phone ring in another room, she perked up her ears.

Santino answered it and spoke rapidly in English, his voice rising to an icy pitch. "I don't give a fuck what you think!" he yelled. "I want to know who the target was!"

There was a pause and then: "No, of course it couldn't have been me. I was supposed to be across the city at a meeting with one of Brattini's mules. But I decided to take a pass when I spotted a couple of guys hanging around watching the building.

"I want to know about each of those girls. I also want to know if the convent's itinerary included that picnic. No, it's not crazy. That bomb was powerful enough to knock off several people, turn them into mush."

There was another silence and then he said, "So that's what the papers think — well, I'm not sure I agree. Run the background check anyway."

When he came back into Elizabeth's room, he sat down beside her on the bed and took her face between his hands.

"My name is Santino DeLuca," he said very softly. "I live in the United States, in Michigan, to be exact. But I have business interests in Rome, so I'm here two or three times a year. This is my house and all the people you see around here work for me."

Elizabeth just nodded.

"It's best if you stay here, where I can take care of you, until I can find out what's going on. Now tell me who you are so that I can figure out what needs to be done."

Elizabeth didn't know why she trusted him so absolutely, but she did. She began to tell him all about her life. As she talked, he stroked her face, then her neck and shoulders, keeping his eyes fixed on hers. She felt as if she had known him forever, and so she opened up her soul as she had never done with anyone before, going beyond the simple facts of her background. She poured out her feelings and her hostilities, telling him how trapped she felt and how desperately she wanted to escape from the life her mother had planned for her.

"But then I feel so guilty," she added. "As though I'm betraying some sacred trust. Is it so wrong to want to test my wings and live my own life?"

"No, it isn't wrong," he answered gently. "But you're only a young girl. You don't know the dangers that are out there. You need to be protected.

"Listen, *bella mia*," he continued, "you're going to have to trust me. Since nobody besides my men saw me bring you here, you'll be included on the list of people presumed dead. Most of the bodies were disintegrated by the intensity of the explosion anyhow, and I doubt that the rest will ever be recognizable. Whoever planted that bomb must have been trying to kill one of you girls."

Elizabeth's eyes widened with disbelief and fear. "I heard you say something about the papers," she said.

"Not surprisingly, they think it was terrorists. One of your dead classmates, a Katerina Gruen, was the daughter of a big German industrialist — a man with many enemies."

"You don't think so?"

Santino shrugged. "I'm going to try to find out who's behind this. Can you trust your mother not to tell anyone that you're still alive if you call her?"

"I don't know," Elizabeth said honestly. "Sometimes she's not too clear-headed."

"Then I don't want you to call her — at least not yet. It might mean your life if you do. Once I have the answers and decide what to do, you'll be able to contact her."

Elizabeth nodded her agreement. She silently vowed that over the next few days she would try to sort out where she was, and who exactly this stranger was.

People came in and out of the house very quietly. There was a cook and a man who answered the door, besides the men who had been with Santino in the car.

Elizabeth remained in the second-floor bedroom, so prettily decorated in yellow chintz. Like bedrooms in most European houses, it had its own sink, but the water closet was down the hall. Her windows looked out over the main street, but they didn't open when she tried them. And in spite of the fact that the room was clean and dusted, it had a kind of musty odor, as if it had been closed for a long while.

On the ground below, Elizabeth could see two men with rifles walking back and forth and occasionally looking up. Across the road, the homes were all similar in appearance, each one with manicured lawns and thick shrubbery. Sirens wailed off in the distance. Perhaps this house, she thought, was located near a hospital.

Elizabeth wondered if her mother would notice her absence, or if she would really care that she had "died." At the moment it didn't matter. But of one thing she was absolutely certain: she was never going back to the convent. She decided she was going to stay with Santino forever. God had answered her prayers, of that she was sure.

Three days later Santino still had no answers. His contacts could only tell him that the picnic in the park had been on the convent's tour schedule and that one of the dead girls had indeed been the daughter of a prominent industrialist. The International Convent School as well as the Mother House in Rome had had the itinerary. So had all the parents of the girls. The only fact known was that the car that held the bomb had been bought for cash from a used-car lot a few blocks away. No one there could remember anything about who had made the purchase — even when DeLuca questioned the car-lot owner personally.

As he watched his men bloody the dealer's face and knock out a couple of his teeth, Santino wondered if the man really didn't know who'd purchased the car or was more afraid of what would happen if he talked.

"He's out cold, boss. Should we take him for a ride?"

"Nah, let him go," Santino answered. "But put a tail on him. Maybe he'll lead us to where we want to go."

Maybe some terrorist gang *was* responsible, but DeLuca could not shake the rumors he had heard beforehand — rumors that a family would be hit.

*T*he day had been long and Don Vincenzo, who was feeling each one of his seventy years, had wondered if it would ever end. Rosa, who was fifteen years younger than her husband, had been beside herself with grief, but finally after their long talk she had taken sleeping pills and gone to bed. He himself was tired, but he knew he could not sleep. The house was quiet now as he retreated to his study, poured himself a glass of red wine, and sat down in his favorite chair with his feet up. He picked up the morning paper from the table beside him. He had read the story three times already, but it still fascinated him.

He closed his eyes and the past came rolling back like a film on his closed eyelids. True to his promise, he had provided financial support for the

Volpe family, even though he had been horrified when he learned that Giovanna was pregnant with the child of one of the two bastards who had killed his beloved Theresa. A child would be a constant reminder of the tragedy that had struck his family and would be a heavy cross for him to bear. Tradition required that he eliminate the seed of any who had wronged the blood of his blood. This meant the child would have to die.

But Rosa, knowing full well what was in his head, had absolutely forbidden it. "It's the old way," she had said over and over. "It's barbaric. It's wrong." She had begged him to show mercy, had fallen on her knees reminding him of God's commandment of forgiveness for those who had sinned.

"Besides, the child is innocent," she implored him, "and its murder will forever taint your immortal soul."

Yes, he had thought, but the sins of the fathers . . .

He had been reared to keep his own counsel, to keep traditions. So in order to placate his wife and still live with his own code of honor, he had promised her that she would never live to see "the child die by my hand, or by my orders." For her part, Rosa had had to promise her husband that no member of their family would lay eyes on Giovanna's daughter for as long as he lived. And so he had directed his *consigliere* to make all the payments necessary to provide for Giovanna and the child in any way she wanted.

Rosa had been forbidden to say anything to her grandson Roberto about the death of his sister Theresa, other than that she had been killed by soldiers. In war-torn Italy that was a reasonable explanation for a child.

"When the time is right," he had told his wife, "Roberto will be told. And I will be the one who does the telling."

I remember that day, too, Don Vincenzo thought now. As he conjured up Roberto's image, he felt a pang of regret. His grandson had been away a long time now, and the old man admitted he missed the boy even if he didn't always approve of Roberto's behavior.

By the time he was fourteen, Roberto had grown to be a tall boy with an olive complexion much like his late father. A bright boy, he'd been tutored in several languages, and was fluent in English, French, and Greek.

Don Vincenzo shook his head. You were the apple of my eye and I spoiled you, he thought. But then he recalled why: he had been terrified of losing his only remaining grandchild. So he had assigned his best lieutenants to watch over Roberto as he was growing up, and they had put very few restrictions on him. Not their fault either, he conceded. After all, he was a powerful and important don, and Roberto was his heir.

He also admitted that his grandson had been quite an arrogant fourteen-year-old when he learned for the first time what had really happened to Theresa ten years earlier.

"Your sister was raped and murdered by two Calabrese," Don Vincenzo had told him. "She died an agonizing death. Her friend Giovanna Volpe, who was with her at the time, was also defiled, but she lived."

Roberto's face had contorted. He was old enough to know what all this meant, old enough to feel hatred surge through his veins.

"It took almost two years, but I tracked down the two butchers," the Don had continued. "And I sent them to hell where they deserved to go."

He then had gone on to describe what had been done to the Luchese brothers. As he spoke, his gravelly voice conveyed his own undying rage.

Don Vincenzo saw now that it had been easy for his words to inflame Roberto, enough to burn hatred for the two murderers and their families into his heart and mind forever. Roberto had never forgotten his sister, even though he had been barely four years old when she was murdered. After all, she had taken the place of their mother; but somehow he never reached out to Rosa. It was only his sister Theresa that he wanted. She had comforted him at night when he cried out for Mama — just as he had cried out night after night for Theresa when she was killed.

Then, when Don Vincenzo had told Roberto about Giovanna's pregnancy, the boy's face had turned red with rage.

"I didn't kill the baby," the Don had continued. "Rosa made me swear to the Holy Virgin that, despite the need for retribution, I would never take the child's life."

He remembered Roberto had spat out a flood of oaths.

"But my promise to her was that it would never happen as long as she lived. Now that we're both getting older, it's time you knew the facts."

Don Vincenzo remembered now that Roberto had been seething inside, that he had become obsessed with exacting retribution for his sister's death. "Then, and only then, can she rest in peace," he had said.

Roberto never had spoken to him again about Theresa or retribution. He had left the next year for Canada, but Don Vincenzo knew he had not forgotten. He knew he would never forget.

When he had read about the bomb blast and the death of Elizabeth Volpe that morning, Don Vincenzo had experienced a sudden sense of completion, even though he had feigned shock and sorrow.

He had been able to swear to his wife, on the Holy Bible, that he "knew nothing, did nothing, and paid for nothing." I kept my pledge to her, he said to himself. Keeping his pledge protected his immortal soul. But in the recesses of his mind, he wondered about his grandson.

Roberto Vincenzo was now the keeper of traditions. And if he was responsible, then who could blame him? No matter. It was done. It was really over now.

*S*antino came into the bedroom and put a large box down on the end of the bed. "I'd like to take you out," he said, "if you think you're up to it."

Elizabeth looked up at him and smiled. "Oh, I am. I've read all the magazines and papers you brought — I really need to get out." She seemed to have forgotten the horrible bombing and deaths in the park.

Santino smiled. "I thought as much. There are some clothes in the box. Please wear the sunglasses and the hat for me. Just a little precaution. I wouldn't want anyone to recognize you."

He left her to change and a little while later he returned. The dark dress he had picked out was very stylish; it made her look older and more sophisticated. The hat had a large brim and a scarf that covered the hair. It wasn't what he normally would have chosen, but in this case it was a perfect way to conceal her features. The sunglasses were the final touch.

Santino smiled. "You look like a movie star hiding from her public."

"It's what you wanted."

"Well, it's what I feel is necessary."

He escorted her to the car and drove her to a tiny bistro that specialized in cappuccino and homemade desserts. Elizabeth became animated and chattered away lightheartedly, obviously delighted to be out of her confinement. When they returned to the house, Santino led her into the library. He took her hands in his and looked into her green eyes.

"I've given your situation a great deal of thought," he began, "and I'm afraid your life may be in grave danger. So I've decided what needs to be done."

He went on to explain that he wanted to obtain false papers for her and take her back to the States with him. If she agreed, she could never tell anyone about her background, at least not until he found out who planted that car bomb and why. "I don't know for how long, but you'll have to live a lie," he finished.

"Why are you willing to do so much for me?"

He looked at her tenderly. "I think I've loved you from the first moment I saw you in Vatican Square. And I want you to become my wife. But only if you feel the same way about me."

Elizabeth started to speak, but he put his fingers over her lips.

"Don't answer me yet. You need to get to know me better and understand the kind of world in which I live. Tell me after your life has settled down and you've had a chance to grow up a little more."

Later that night Elizabeth lay in bed looking out the window at Rome's twinkling lights. She thought about what Santino had said — and what he hadn't said. She wasn't as naïve as he thought she was. It hadn't taken her long to figure out what his line of work was. The Mafia was an integral part of life in southern Italy, and even those cloistered in a convent knew what was going on. In fact, given the corruption of the government, many ordinary people were very supportive of the mob, including the townspeople back home in Puglia.

Elizabeth could tell by the deferential way everyone spoke to Santino and the way he barked orders on the phone that he must be an important man. Whatever he wanted, happened, and whatever he asked for, arrived. And, of course, there were the guards downstairs. She'd also noticed the guns inside the jackets of his friends, and the rifles near the front door.

Elizabeth knew instinctively that Santino wouldn't want her to be too knowledgeable about such things, so she'd feigned ignorance about his activities, and the conversations she often overheard.

She also knew that if she went with him now, there would be no turning back. Ever. Even though beatings, vendettas, murders, and the rest of it horrified her, she would have to accept them as part of his life, and keep quiet about them, as so many other Italian women had done before her.

In her young heart she knew that this was the man she wanted, so she would just have to learn to play her part well and never let him know just how much she really understood.

Forty-eight hours later Elizabeth Volpe had a new birth certificate and a passport. She and Santino were booked on a flight leaving Rome for New York the following night, exactly one week after the bomb had exploded.

In spite of Santino's warning, Elizabeth felt she had to find the right moment to call her mother. The opportunity came when one of Santino's men took her to shop at a nearby department store to buy a few clothes and some personal toiletries.

Once there, Elizabeth told the bodyguard she needed to go to the washroom. As he hovered around the door, looking embarrassed, she went into the ladies' lounge and proceeded to call her mother.

When Giovanna Volpe answered her phone in a broken voice, Elizabeth was momentarily stunned. Does this mean she misses me? she asked herself. Could she really love me?

"Mama, please don't faint or scream," Elizabeth whispered. "It's me, I'm alive. If you make any noise, I'll hang up the phone."

Elizabeth couldn't see her mother crossing herself, but she did hear the whispering of the Hail Mary and the thanks being given to God.

"Mama, I'm going away," she went on. "I promise you, I'm all right. And I know I'll be very happy. I can't tell you where or with whom, at least not yet. But soon."

After a few moments of silence, she went on. "Mama, are you there?"

"Didn't you tell me not to speak? Well, I guess I should be happy that you were off with some boy instead of with the others, where you were supposed to be."

Somehow her mother didn't sound happy, and Elizabeth felt sad again, but only for a moment.

"Good-bye, Mama," she said. "Please don't tell anyone that I'm still alive. I'll contact you again as soon as it's safe."

*G*iovanna clung to the phone long after the line went dead. She hadn't said the words she wanted to — words about love and loneliness. Too many years of escaping into fantasy had blurred her senses, although not enough to keep her from realizing that in some way her daughter was at risk. That bombing was no accident — everyone knew it. And somehow she knew that it had something to do with her daughter.

She thought again of Elizabeth's father, that tall boy with the sensitive hands and gentle voice. Where did he go? she wondered. Was he really unconscious when Theresa was being brutalized? Was he really trying to save me or just satisfying his lust? Why didn't he ever come back for me?

Giovanna sighed and walked over to the crucifix. She prayed that the child of their union would be kept safe.

# 3

LATE SEPTEMBER
1962

*R*oberto sipped his coffee and looked out at the Canadian Falls. He spent most of his weekends in Buffalo, and on his way home on Sunday afternoon, he liked to stop for lunch at the rooftop restaurant at the hotel. From his usual table by the window, you could see for miles. Both Canada and the United States were beneath you, and although it was only a small portion of both countries, it gave him a feeling of power, as if he were a king overlooking his domain.

On this occasion, however, he was not returning from a weekend in Buffalo. He was returning from Italy and he had chosen to travel from La Guardia via Buffalo rather than leave directly from Toronto International, which was, in any case, under construction. Still, he had arrived at lunchtime, and so he had stopped here, at his favorite restaurant.

He unfolded his worn copy of the Rome newspaper and once again read the story on the bomb blast that had killed two nuns, four students, and several others who had been nearby. He smiled to himself. It could not have gone more smoothly. In fact, he thought with some pride, his whole life had gone rather smoothly.

When Roberto Vincenzo arrived in 1954, shortly after his fourteenth birthday, he was immediately placed under the protection of the Salerno family of Buffalo, some eighty-three miles to the south of Toronto. The

Salernos were his second cousins. Roberto knew he was the chosen one. His marks in school had been exceptional and he had had the benefit of private tutors. When he left Italy he had been given a new name and when he arrived in Buffalo the Salernos enrolled him in Upper Canada College in Toronto. He had been given two orders, and two orders only. The first was to study hard. The second was: "You want fun, you come to Buffalo. In Canada you keep your nose clean. You make the right friends."

His grandfather, Don Paolo, had provided the money for his upkeep and tuition, and when Roberto had graduated from Grade Thirteen, he had entered the University of Toronto. He was now studying law at Osgoode Hall.

The Don had plans for Roberto to move into Canada when the time came. He would be the Salerno family's guide as well as mouthpiece. Given his elegant appearance and charming manners, he was certain to help dispel the image of violence and criminality usually associated with the Mafia.

Roberto put down the paper. Yes, even his mistakes had been turned into pluses. He recalled his nineteenth birthday. He'd almost screwed it up . . .

He had gone to Sassie's, a Buffalo brothel that specialized in S&M. A long time ago he had discovered that rough sex was what really turned him on, and Sassie's was one of the best places to get it. He pushed his way through the smoky main room. It smelled of whiskey and cigarette smoke, and was filled with leather freaks.

The available broads were all lined up against the wall in the back, like so many cabbages on a vegetable stand. He chose a shapely black girl with a butt that looked like two round firm melons.

They were given a clean room upstairs because he was who he was, and he got special treatment. He slapped her around a little and then tied her to the bed, butt side up. He gagged her, grabbed a razor strop, and proceeded to beat her, knowing that it would be a while before he was ready to stick it in her and ejaculate.

Suddenly she started to cough and then choke on the gag he had stuffed in her mouth. But he was about to come! He threw himself on top of her in spite of her writhing. He was really turned on when she struggled harder. He took her from the rear and was still pumping into her when he realized she had stopped moving.

Roberto recalled now how he tore the gag out of her mouth — but it was too late. She was dead. Luckily for him, the brothel was owned by the family, and run by a madam who had once been the favorite of Gino Salerno himself.

When he went to Sassie she gave him the prostitute's address and told him she had lived with her brother. Two hours later he was climbing the rickety stairs to 4 C, the apartment of the late Iris Judson. Her body could be got rid of, and it could all be kept quiet, if no one stirred the pot.

The five-story apartment building was old and grungy. From behind spray-painted doors came the cries of babies, voices raised in argument, and curses.

"Who the fuck is it?" snarled the voice behind the door when he knocked.

Roberto remembered speaking in his best English accent. "May I speak with you, sir? It's a matter of extreme urgency."

The door was flung open by a man not much older than Roberto himself. He was unshaven and dressed in stained jeans and thin T-shirt.

"May I please come in, sir?" Roberto asked as he walked in. His eyes surveyed the room which was furnished with old overstuffed chairs and a sofa. On a table were some empty beer bottles. The place smelled of cheap perfume and burned coffee.

"I'm afraid I have some terrible news for you, sir. Early this morning your sister Iris died of a heart attack."

"What?" the man shrieked. His hands pulled at his hair; his bloodshot eyes filled with tears. "My big sister, my Iris? No, it can't be true. How could she be dead? She's a nurse at the hospital. Wasn't any doctor around to save her? Where is she?"

Something stirred deep inside Roberto, a mixture of sadness and, strangely, sympathy. Even though the man standing in front of him was dirty, the apartment like a pigsty, he related to his anguish. He thought of his own beloved sister Theresa, and how much her death had affected him. As he fingered the gun in his jacket pocket, he made a split-second decision: I won't kill this scum, at least not right away. Maybe I can use him.

"Your sister wished to be cremated, and arrangements are being made. I'm one of the hospital's visiting lawyers, here on an exchange program. Your sister cared for you very much, and took out an insurance policy on her life, with you as the beneficiary. But it's only payable if she died from natural causes."

"Insurance policy?" The young man's eyes narrowed. "She didn't tell me about no insurance policy. How much?"

"Well, if you sign a release right away, it's $25,000. Otherwise, delays and legal fees could reduce it quite a bit."

It wasn't a release, of course. It was an identification document and an order for cremation. A "doctor" had already signed the death certificate, which put all the paperwork in order. There would be no questions.

"By the way, I don't know your first name or what you do for a living." In his mind, Roberto had already worked it all out. The man's accent was heavily Southern. Iris had probably come north first and lied about her profession. Her brother had probably come recently. It was all too typical.

"Ev, Everly Judson. I been up here only six months. We was from North Carolina. My sister sent me a ticket to come up here after I finished school. One of her patients — did private home nursing to make extra money, you know — got me an interview for a job with the immigration department. I just got a letter yesterday telling me that I be hired as a temporary out at the airport. Iris was so happy when I told her . . . and now she's gone. I just can't believe it."

Ev Judson started sobbing and Roberto thought, I'm in luck. So what if Buffalo airport is penny-ante — it's a start.

"Okay, Ev, I'll tell you what," he said. "I thought the world of your sister. She was so warm and so cooperative, and we became such good friends. Out of respect for her memory, I'm going to help you. It's what she'd want me to do.

"First you need a proper place to live. Then you have to learn to speak better English. It wouldn't do for a future immigration officer representing the United States of America to speak like someone just out of a cotton field."

"I used to pick cotton," Ev said, "in the summer."

"Okay, then, what's it to be?"

There was a moment's hesitation, then: "Well, I can't bring Iris back. I'd be very thankful for your help. What about the money?"

"Oh, don't worry about that," Roberto answered. "Why don't I lend you some money to get a new place, some new clothes? And I'll also invest your sister's insurance bequest for you, no charge, and you can use the interest to supplement your wages. I'll also be happy to help you with your new job, so you can have a shot at becoming permanent and maybe even get promoted."

"Say, why are you doing all this?" Judson questioned.

"In memory of Iris. As I told you, she was a good friend of mine. Well, what do you say?"

"Okay, yes, thank you," Ev said, gratitude replacing his initial feelings of suspicion and grief. "Maybe one day I'll be able to pay you back for your help."

"Oh, I'm sure you will."

The documents Roberto had taken out of his briefcase earlier lay on the table. Judson signed them without so much as a second glance. Roberto withdrew $1,500 in small bills from his wallet and put it down. Everly could hardly believe his eyes as he fingered the money.

"Someone will be here tomorrow morning to get you. They'll bring you some clothes. Leave everything else behind."

"Hey, you forgot to tell me your name!" Judson shouted as Roberto turned to leave, pleased that he had killed two birds with one stone. He'd covered up Iris' death and he'd placed a man in Immigration for the Salerno family.

"Bob, Bob DeSalle," he answered without turning back. Over the next three years, he and Ev Judson became close associates. With his benefactor's help, Judson rose quickly through the ranks of the Immigration Department. To show his appreciation, he passed on information about any new government policies, special waivers given to wealthy immigrants with questionable backgrounds and which politicians had lobbied for them, and loopholes for circumventing the regulations. Most important of all, Judson personally handled any "special favors" for Roberto and his friends.

He also alerted them to the possibility that Canada would become a circuitous route of entry into the United States. He had heard the beginnings of scuttlebutt concerning Canada's loosening immigration policies, and in anticipation of its happening, Judson personally began to develop a network of contacts within Canadian Immigration.

The only problem he foresaw was the close involvement of the RCMP, who couldn't be bought off. So Judson decided to proceed slowly and recommend Canada as a port of entry only when he was sure there'd be no problem. Once in the country, a person could easily be slipped into the United States via Buffalo or Niagara Falls.

Judson's growing network enabled the Salerno family to add immigration, specifically Italian immigration, to its power base. They could open or close the door into the United States via Buffalo and the Eastern states for anyone they chose. It soon became known that those with problems might be able to enter or exit the country if the Salernos helped them. And in a typical quid pro quo, for those who cooperated with the Salernos in connection with their growing drug business in Asia, the promise of a haven in the States was a large carrot.

The Salernos also had ammunition, powerful ammunition, to use for or against certain politicians. This was very helpful in their other operations, especially when they needed liquor licenses for their hotels, restaurants, and clubs.

Everly Judson was deemed to be a "special friend" and, as such, was given special treatment.

His initial $25,000 inheritance had increased to the point that the interest on the money covered his living expenses. He took classes to upgrade his working skills, and his friendship with Roberto opened the door to fast cars, high-grade marijuana, and hot women. He had no idea who the Salerno family was or that they were behind everything he had become. And if he had known, he wouldn't have cared. Memories of his past had faded. Only an oil painting he'd had done of his late sister, which hung above the mantel in his living room, reminded him of where he'd come from . . .

Roberto looked out the window as he finished off his coffee; then he leaned back with a satisfied smile and lit a cigar. He told himself he could thank his grandfather's money and connection with the Salerno family for the network of muscle men and henchmen that now linked him to the crime families across the Northeastern states. He would never have a problem finding the right people to do any job he wanted done. Here or in Italy.

A few months ago he had decided that the time had come to take the matter of avenging his sister's murder into his own hands, despite Don Paolo's instructions that he wait until Rosa died. He had felt the moment was right — and he had struck. He again glanced at the paper and smiled. Theresa was avenged. He felt a sense of completion.

*S*antino, Elizabeth, and the two men walked across the Detroit airport lounge toward the doors where cars and buses hugged the curb.

"Elizabeth Rizzo," she repeated over and over in her mind. If someone addressed her, she couldn't look up and say, "Who?" Still, the worst was over. They had cleared U.S. Customs and Immigration and she hadn't flinched despite her nervousness.

The two men took their luggage and soon they were in a long black car speeding away from the airport. Elizabeth looked out the tinted window.

"Not much to see," Santino said. "We're pretty far out of the city, and we won't be going through it to get home."

They turned onto the highway and headed north.

Santino was right. There wasn't much to look at. But she could smell the city and its factories even though the windows were closed and the air conditioner on. She leaned back against the leather seat and put her hand on Santino's.

"Your life has been turned upside down in one week," he said.

"But you're here to help me," she answered.

"Since neither one of us has any family, we'll have to create one of our own."

"I want a family. I want your children."

He smiled and squeezed her hand. "You won't be eighteen till March, so we won't marry till then. I want you to use the coming months to be sure in your heart that I'm the man for you."

"You are," she said, turning to look into his face.

"Hear me out. If, for any reason, you decide you don't want to marry me but you want to stay in the United States, I'll make sure you're looked after financially. My office will find you a place to live. There will be no strings attached, I give you my solemn word."

"I won't change my mind."

He ignored her and continued to lay out the ground rules of their relationship. She listened carefully: when it came to rules, she knew he would always be the one who made them.

"In the meantime, my housekeeper, Mrs. Leone, who's been with me for years, will be our chaperone. She'll teach you everything you need to know about life here in America as well as how to run a home.

"And when the time is right — if you're as sure of your love for me as I am of my love for you — we'll get married. Then I'll teach you every-thing you need to know about being a woman."

His words, his promise, sent a chill of anticipation through her. She wondered vaguely if he realized how much she wanted to learn that lesson right now. But she said nothing. She just leaned against him, letting him know she understood and accepted his rules.

*S*antino's study was a warm, comfortable room lined with leather-bound books and expensively furnished with leather chairs, a huge sofa, several small inlaid tables, and a large mahogany desk. It was cool enough this late September evening for a fire in his fireplace.

DeLuca leaned back in his favorite chair and for a time thought about the beautiful young woman upstairs. Then he began to contemplate his life.

They called him shrewd and, when it came to business, he knew he was just that. He was an unemotional decision maker who could be ruthless when necessary. Under his direction the fortunes of the Detroit-based Villano family, for whom he'd worked since his arrival in America, had grown tremendously along with his own. The only thorn in his side was the constant conflict with Massimo Brattini, once his closest friend and colleague. When their friendship had ended several years earlier, Brattini had gone to work for the Salerno family based in Buffalo. Gino Salerno and Luigi Villano had been rivals ever since their schooldays back in Sicily, so when Brattini left the Villano family to work with the Salernos, open warfare developed between him and Santino.

DeLuca thought of Brattini and of their lives together back in Italy. Who could have imagined that the two of them would ever become enemies? What had happened to turn him into such a cold and ruthless man?

He shrugged. Their paths still continued to cross, directly and indirectly, with the common denominator usually being land development and waste disposal, a mega-million-dollar industry.

Being on top of any land-development opportunities, and controlling the zoning and rezoning process, was the key to power. A good developer had to know real estate trends and land sites that had good potential for rezoning. Buying the right properties from some local farmers at a bargain price could yield a tremendous profit when the land was rezoned and then flipped for resale.

The most important component in all this was waste disposal — and that meant sewer allocations. Getting them was critical. Without the necessary sewer allocations, no parcel of land could be developed for commercial or residential purposes. Finding out in advance which parcels of land would be approved for those allocations meant a tenfold increase in the profit margin.

And this was where the payoffs to the politicians who made the decisions became a part of everyday business. Keeping track of which politicians could be bought off quickly, and for how much, was a fulltime job, one usually assigned to a trusted lieutenant.

But most elected officials went to the highest bidder. So a promise of approval today, along with an agreed-upon "fee," might change tomorrow, if a rival offered more. In the Old Country, a few broken bones and the occasional murder kept that kind of reneging from happening more than once. But this was the New World, and the public wouldn't stand for too much violence. So other forms of persuasion had to be devised.

Cash, of course, was the favorite. But there were others: women, drugs, jobs for friends and relatives, and, on occasion, little boys and girls to satisfy perverted sexual fantasies. Santino drew few lines across which he would not venture, but he had one hard, firm rule. Neither he nor any member of his organization dealt with children.

The avoidance of any violence — at least any that could be traced — was critical. Subtlety was the operative word — otherwise known as blackmail and extortion. Get something on the decision maker and then make him do your bidding. It was a game as old as time. And Santino knew no one was better at it than the Villano family, under his control. His network of contacts who owed him favors reached up to the highest levels of government, and he had no hesitation about calling in those markers.

Still, it was a dangerous business, even if you were good. He had taken out his own insurance policies and he had invested a lot of what he earned in legitimate businesses. One day, he promised himself, he would retire and live off them.

Again he looked up, thinking of Elizabeth, who by now would be asleep. She was the foundation on which he intended building a real family. His own family.

*E*lizabeth put on the white satin robe and looked at herself in the full-length mirror on the bathroom door. Her hair was loose and she shook it out and made a pouty face. She smiled at her reflection. The robe clung to her and she had nothing on underneath. In a few minutes she would go downstairs and join Santino. She sat on the end of the bed and slipped her feet in and out of her satin mules, wondering how he would like her tonight.

Mrs. Leone, who accompanied her everywhere, had enjoyed watching her shop for this robe. "You have a magnificent body," she had said. "Anything you put on looks beautiful."

Santino had opened a bank account for her the day after they arrived in Detroit, and he began depositing $2,500 a month in it. As well, she had the use of his credit cards. She had taken driving lessons, and the day she got her license Santino had given her a red Thunderbird.

Sometimes Elizabeth wondered if she had simply traded one form of constraint for another. But she put such questions aside and reminded herself of how much freedom she really had. She haunted bookstores on her own and often went out to galleries. The list of what she was allowed to do was long. The restraints placed on her largely had to do with safety. For a while she had continued to ask Santino if he had learned anything more about the bombing, but once she settled down in her new life, she stopped asking. It had been months now and she decided not to bring it up again.

Lately Santino had begun taking her out for dinners with some of his associates. She'd often express her opinions on those she found interesting, but she was careful never to indicate that she understood, or even heard, anything that had to do with his business. But she did, and underneath her cool veneer and apparent disinterest, she had to admit to herself that despite her occasional misgivings, she found his world fascinating.

Like so many generations of Italian women before her, she was expected to concentrate on home and family and leave the business to her husband. She wanted desperately to believe that the independence she had longed for during her convent days could be found within the shelter of Santino's world . . . as long as she never forgot who he was and what he did for a living.

Elizabeth crept downstairs. He was in the game room alone watching television. She walked over to the sofa and curled up beside him.

"I love you, Santino," she said. "You're the only man I will ever want or need. I need to be in the cocoon of your world in order to have the security to expand my own."

He looked at her and kissed her gently, stroking her hair. Elizabeth wanted him to kiss her all the time, and every time she anticipated their wedding night, her skin would get flushed and her heart would pound.

"You tempt me," he whispered. He wanted to keep her for their wedding night. But restraint was becoming more and more difficult, and Elizabeth's flirtatious behavior didn't make it any easier.

He looked at her robe, which was half-open. Her well-developed breasts were very firm and she wore no bra. He leaned over and kissed her again. This time he probed her mouth with his tongue and she returned the favor. It was something she had not done at first. At first she had kept her lips closed, not knowing what else to do. But after a while, she parted her lips to let his tongue inside her mouth. Soon her tongue was inside his lips whenever they kissed, and he, who had never had a shortage of women anxious to sleep with him, was struggling to control himself.

He slipped a hand inside her robe and let it cover one of her breasts. Their necking was getting heavier of late, mostly at Elizabeth's instigation. She clearly loved having his hands on her breasts. When his lips passed over her bare skin and he took one of her nipples between them, it drove her nearly to distraction.

"You know, I'm too old to be necking with a gorgeous young girl like you," he mumbled.

Elizabeth was moving under him, around him, and any other way she could press herself closer to him.

"Enough," he said, pulling himself away. "Enough." He stood up.

"Set our wedding date, Santino."

She was looking at him with those wonderful green eyes. He let out his breath, hoping his erection would disappear before she noticed it.

"You set it," he said.

Elizabeth smiled. "May fourteenth," she answered. "Yes, May fourteenth."

"You don't want to be a June bride?"

She laughed and shook her head. "I don't want to wait that long!"

*T*heir wedding was small, with only seventy-five guests invited to the Mass and another fifty to the reception afterward. They were all Santino's business associates and their families.

Elizabeth wore an exquisite wedding gown, with Alençon lace over peau de soie. It had a long train and her veil was held in place by a jeweled tiara Santino had had made for her by Van Cleef & Arpels in New York. He wanted this to be a day for her to remember, and clearly he knew that she, like most young girls, dreamed of looking like a princess on her wedding day.

*I*t was early evening when he drew the horse to a halt in front of a white clapboard house that overlooked the lake.

They had come to spend their honeymoon on Mackinac Island, at the northern end of Michigan. It was a wonderfully quaint locale. No cars were allowed; only horse-drawn buggies or bicycles were. Santino had chosen a buggy. On their way through town they passed Murdick's Fudge Store.

"We'll come back tomorrow," he had promised, "and the next day, too. We'll treat ourselves to a different flavor each visit."

The clapboard house Santino had rented was right on the eastern shore, and the views from their porch were spectacular. They could see several smaller islands in the strait, and despite the rainfall the mist and the cool breeze outside their windows were refreshing.

"Let's walk," Santino suggested.

"Yes, along the shore," she replied.

They left their cases unpacked and set out immediately, hand in hand. They walked for a long way in silence before finally turning back. In front of the house they stopped and he bent down and kissed her. They looked at each other and without speaking knew the moment was right.

Elizabeth didn't bother putting on the peach peignoir she'd bought for her wedding night. As soon as Santino closed the door, they were in each other's arms.

"I've waited so long for you," he whispered as his hands ran up and down her body, removing her clothes as they went. When she was naked, he stood back from her and in the moonlit room looked at her body.

She was beautiful, and he reached out to touch her everywhere. Then his lips found out hers and his tongue caressed the softness inside her mouth. Elizabeth wound her arms around his neck, feeling goose bumps pop up all over her skin.

She began to unbutton Santino's shirt, kissing his chest and running her hands along his back as he slipped it off. She could feel his erection through his trousers, and she put her hand on it, taking him, and herself, somewhat by surprise.

"I've never seen a man before," she whispered as he unbuckled his belt. "But now I'm your woman, your lover, and your wife. You are my protector, my lover, my husband. There will be no other man for me, ever. I want to make you happy. Please help me to do it." She continued moving her hands over him.

Santino struggled to control himself, knowing how innocent Elizabeth was and not wanting to hurt her. When all his clothes were off, Elizabeth couldn't resist looking at his penis. She barely noticed the scar just above his navel.

His penis was throbbing and even though she wanted to touch it, her inhibitions held her back. Santino kept kissing her neck and shoulders as he moved his hands over her buttocks.

Slowly he backed her up to the bed and eased her onto it. He lay down beside her, spreading her legs with his hands as his lips moved over every inch of her body.

Elizabeth felt tremors of pleasure pulse through her body when Santino slipped his fingers inside her. She wanted to give him the same pleasure he was giving her, but she didn't know how.

"Elizabeth," Santino whispered in her ear, "you are magnificent, and I love you."

She felt pressure building inside her. All she knew was that she never wanted him to stop what he was doing and she kept rotating her hips as Santino's fingers moved back and forth inside her.

"Oh, Santino," she practically sobbed, "something's happening to me." Her cries aroused him even more and soon he was unable to control himself. He mounted her and pushed his penis into her, climaxing almost immediately. Elizabeth gave a little cry from the unexpected stab of pain.

After a few murmured words of love to each other, Elizabeth cried out to Santino that something was wrong — her bodily fluids were pouring from her body.

He burst out laughing, delighting in just how naïve she really was. He jumped out of bed toward the bathroom and soon came back with a towel and a damp cloth and put them next to the bed.

"How come, in the movies, the man never jumps up like that?" she asked him. "After the big love scene they just lie around having a smoke."

As Santino started washing her with the cloth, he became aroused again, and they started all over. This time he spent much longer kissing and stroking her body, but when he lowered his head to put his lips where his fingers had been, Elizabeth froze.

"Santino, what are you doing?" she cried. "Is that allowed?"

Santino couldn't stop himself from laughing again. "Oh, my sweet princess," he answered, kissing her face and running his hands through her hair. "We're married now; everything is allowed. It might take some time, but I want you to learn to experience the ecstasy that lovemaking can bring. And oh, am I going to enjoy teaching you."

They made love again, but this time Santino was able to penetrate her completely. Elizabeth loved watching him have a second orgasm even more intense than the first, and felt totally fulfilled and content.

They spent most of the next two weeks in bed, making love three or four times a day and trying many different positions. Santino DeLuca was very experienced with women, and knew how to please them, but nothing had prepared him for the delight he felt in his wife's enthusiasm for his body and her awakening sexuality. It was wonderful. When Elizabeth eventually achieved an orgasm during oral sex, she cried out as her body arched in a spasm of sexual delirium.

I'm a lucky man, he thought. I don't really deserve it.

*S*antino DeLuca had waited a long time to get married. In his home he was a loving and considerate man with a fine sense of humor. He loved to tease Elizabeth until she begged him to stop, and then he'd smother her with kisses and love bites ever so gently.

He began to teach his young wife to enjoy good wines, good food, and the finest of material things. She taught him about ancient literature, the royal houses of Europe, and the joys of giving and sharing with someone you love.

When Elizabeth and Santino celebrated their first wedding anniversary, Elizabeth's concerns about not yet being pregnant were just starting to stir. Considering the frequency with which she and Santino made love, it was impossible to believe that the right moment of ovulation had been missed. When she raised her fears with her husband, he dismissed them.

"In God's good time," he'd say. "After all, you're only nineteen. There's plenty of time."

Despite Santino's reassuring words, Elizabeth wasn't satisfied. She decided to call her mother to see how long it had taken her to become pregnant.

This was not the first time she'd called her mother since she'd left Italy, despite Santino's previous warnings. Fearing his anger, she'd never told him about the calls.

It was four o'clock in the afternoon in Italy when her mother answered the phone, sounding strained.

"Hello, Mama, how are you?"

"Fine, thank you," Giovanna answered, in a very cool voice.

Elizabeth went on to talk about what was happening in her life and how happy she was with her husband, never mentioning his name. When she told her mother about her infertility concerns and then asked some questions, there was a noticeable intake of breath.

"I really don't remember," Giovanna answered. "Please don't talk of such things again." And then she hung up.

Elizabeth was disconsolate. She felt that her mother was totally useless. I'll never treat my children the way she treats me, she vowed. I'll take care of them and protect them. Then she started to cry, but after a few minutes got control of herself.

What Elizabeth didn't know was that her mother wasn't alone when she had phoned. Rosa Vincenzo had just come by for a visit and the two of them had been having coffee. Giovanna had had the presence of mind to say nothing in front of Rosa that might raise her suspicions. Everyone, including the Don's wife, had to continue believing that her daughter Elizabeth was dead, killed in a tragic explosion a year and a half earlier.

# 4

## OCTOBER
## 1971

*I*t was fall and the big maple tree in the front yard was covered with red-gold leaves. A perfect day, Elizabeth thought as she parked the car in front of the triple garage. They called it Indian summer here, and it was wonderful, by far the best time of the year. The days were warm and sunny, the nights cool, the mornings frosty.

She climbed out of the car and paused to pick up a particularly beautiful maple leaf before going into the house. As she turned her key in the lock and the door swung open, she heard Santino yelling at someone in Italian, threatening and cajoling, behind the door of his den.

He wasn't expecting her. Usually she stayed at church after Mass to help the priest serve lunch to those in the congregation who had no family; but today there were enough volunteers, so she'd left early. She walked quietly by the den door and went directly upstairs. Once in their bedroom, she went over to the phone and picked it up.

Santino was on it. From the static, she guessed it was an overseas call, and the static would cover the sound of the extension being picked up. She was about to replace the receiver when she heard her husband say, "Kill him when you find him!"

The phone froze in her hand.

"And Pedro, where's Sal? He's been inside Brattini's operation for six months and should have reported by now. I've had a boat in Marseilles harbor for two weeks, waiting for him. Vinnie's snitch says there's no scuttlebutt, except that Mario Grazie arrived from Buffalo last week."

"Shit, that's Brattini's man," said the other voice.

The name Pedro wasn't familiar to Elizabeth.

"Exactly," answered Santino. "I'm worried. Grazie doesn't surface unless Brattini wants a personal whack. Try and find him first and take care of it."

"The cops made a major raid on Salerno's factory last week," said Pedro, "but I heard the merchandise was already gone. Maybe that has something to do with Lata going missing."

Santino said, "Do what you can. Sal's been with me a long time. And it's all I can do to keep Jimmy from going over to look for him. They've been together since the Old Country."

"Okay, boss, I'll get back to you."

The line went dead, but Elizabeth still held onto the phone. Her insides were mush; her blood felt like ice. It was the first time she had heard Santino order someone killed. Vaguely she wondered if it had anything to do with their conversation that morning.

When Santino had come into the breakfast room she had sensed how tense he was.

"Elizabeth, I want you to be sensitive to the fact that we might be under scrutiny," he had said without bothering with any kind of preamble.

So that's it, she had thought. I've had the feeling I was being followed a couple of weeks ago. But she had said nothing to Santino.

"You know there's always some investigator looking to make a name for himself, trying to get the dirt on anyone with an Italian name," he had continued, trying to downplay his warning. "Just be careful, and let me know if you see anything suspicious."

"What makes you think it's the law and not one of your competitors?" she had asked.

Santino had smiled as he looked at her quizzically. "You always amaze me," he had said finally. "I keep underestimating your instincts and your perceptions. Nevertheless, I don't want you to think about anything more than what I've told you to think about. This is my responsibility, and I'll take care of it. Just be careful."

But that hadn't stopped her from thinking about it anyway. Men are too direct, she had thought. If I was trying to undermine someone, I'd do it indirectly, making sure they'd never suspect I was behind it. And what could be better than leaking just enough to the police to create suspicion, and carelessness. Then I would have an advantage.

Elizabeth had immediately crossed herself, shocked at her own Machiavellian thoughts.

But now this. Someone was to be killed. Push what you've heard away, she told herself firmly, or you won't be able to go on. You knew what he was before you came here. Where would you go? How would you live? Besides, face it, you love him, totally, passionately, and forever. It's a way of life. Is he any worse than the corrupt politicians you've met? Hang up the phone. Forget it, wipe it from your brain.

Elizabeth knelt in front of the crucifix in the bedroom. She pulled out her rosary and began to pray silently. God, forgive me for what I know, and give me the strength to put it away. I will try to serve you in other ways as penance for my husband's deeds.

Elizabeth regained her composure and her resolve. She slipped quietly down the stairs to the front door, opened it quietly, and then slammed it.

"Santino," she called, "I'm home, darling. And guess what? My temperature is up."

Santino smiled as he heard her voice, trying to conjure up romantic images to replace the anger and fear of his telephone conversation. It wasn't always easy to do. He was under constant pressure from various law enforcement agencies interested in his business operations. On top of that, the Salerno family now had a connection in the Immigration Department and Luigi Villano was screaming bloody murder. Things had gotten so bad that it was nearly impossible for the Villano family to deliver their people to a safe haven.

Santino was also under a lot of emotional pressure from his wife, who was frantic about her inability to conceive.

By 1965, when Elizabeth still wasn't pregnant, he had started to be concerned as well. Finally he had agreed that she should see a fertility specialist.

For the last six years he and Elizabeth had spent most of their time having sex according to the calendar and her temperature. Their original spontaneous passion for each other's bodies was replaced by "It's that time of day, or that time of month," and gradually sex became a chore rather than a thrill.

His world outside the office now consisted of having sex on demand, keeping temperature charts, and going to different doctors to suffer the necessary tortures inflicted on those couples having trouble conceiving a baby.

The final straw for him occurred some six months earlier when the most recent in a chain of fertility specialists wanted an early-morning sample of his sperm. Santino was informed that he would have to masturbate into a sterile jar and then have the sample delivered to the doctor's office right away.

Elizabeth could hear him cursing behind the door of their bathroom as he tried to do it. When she knocked on the door and asked if she could help, he yelled at her to go away and leave him alone. Finally, holding his penis in one hand and the bottle in the other, the deed was done. But he found it so repugnant that he refused to repeat the exercise again.

So the doctor had decided to give it one more try. He had put Elizabeth on clomiphene, a strong ovulation-producing drug, and told her she and Santino were to have sex every day for the ten days that the drug was stimulating her ovaries to produce eggs. Her hips had to be elevated on a pillow during intercourse, and she couldn't move for two hours afterward.

Not very conducive to romance.

"I'll be up in a moment," Santino called out. Poor Elizabeth, she wanted to conceive so badly . . .

He put thoughts of business out of his head to concentrate on the task at hand.

*O*utside, the January wind howled as ice rather than snow pelted down on Detroit. This first storm of

1972 had caused traffic to come to a standstill in Motor City.

Elizabeth stood by the window, clasping the curtain as she looked out on a frozen world. This was silly. She'd been waiting for the phone to ring for over an hour. Curse this damn storm! In all likelihood the doctor hadn't even got into the laboratory today. She should put it all aside and forget it. She wouldn't hear until tomorrow, and after so many years what possible difference could twenty-four hours make? Perhaps she should have told Santino she had missed two periods, but she was afraid to believe she might really be pregnant.

Just then the silence was broken by the phone. She fairly leapt across the room and caught it at the end of the first ring.

"Yes, yes, this is Mrs. DeLuca." She could hear her own heart beating.

"Your test was positive."

"Oh thank you! Thank you!" Elizabeth felt like jumping for joy.

"You should book regular examinations with your doctor," the woman on the other end of the phone said.

"I will. Oh thank you." Elizabeth put down the phone and flew down the stairs. "Santino! Santino!"

He opened the door of the den and stood in the doorway as she ran into his arms.

"I'm pregnant, Santino, I'm pregnant! The baby's due in mid-July."

What Elizabeth and her doctors didn't yet know was that Santino's overworked sperm had managed to fertilize two eggs. There would be two babies.

Santino hoisted her in the air and then lowered her, holding her close. "Thank God," he said under his breath as he nuzzled her neck. "*Mia amorosa*," he whispered. "Tonight we'll celebrate."

"Here? Shall I make a special dinner?"

Santino shook his head. "We'll go out. It's a very special night and we've two things to celebrate."

"Two?" she said, lifting her brow.

"Your wonderful news and mine. Elizabeth, we'll be moving to Toronto."

Elizabeth could not contain herself. They had visited that city a number of times. It was so much cleaner than Detroit; it had a kind of electricity; it was growing and changing.

"I take it you like the idea."

"Oh yes," she answered. "Very much."

*T*hey bought a five-acre estate in the Bayview section of Toronto. The property had mature maple and birch trees and a large man-made pond behind the main house. The only access to the estate was along a winding road entered through a guarded gatehouse.

It was June, and it seemed they had barely settled in when she went into labor — a month early. Santino became very agitated, pacing around the house, sweating, yelling for the doctor, phoning Jimmy to tell him to "get everybody on alert," running up and down the winding staircase looking for Phillie, their driver, who was calmly waiting by the front door.

He acted like a character from an *I Love Lucy* TV episode, something Elizabeth had never seen him do before.

She understood that his behavior was simply a cover-up for the love and concern she knew he was feeling, and despite her pains, she kept assuring him that everything was going to be fine. But her labor and delivery were difficult, and after thirty-six hours the doctors decided to perform a caesarian section.

Elizabeth and Santino became the parents of healthy, fraternal twin sons, Peter and Matthew, each weighing just under five pounds.

As Santino hovered over her, Elizabeth felt an exhilaration and inner peace she had never imagined was possible. She was tired, and her insides felt as if a Mack truck had just rolled through her, as she reached up to her husband and pulled his head down to hers.

"See," she said, laughing. "Wasn't all your hard work worth it?"

"Oh Elizabeth," he answered, burying his head in her neck. "I love you. Being a father is unlike anything I've ever felt before. It's like being reborn. I feel as if my life has just begun."

# 5

## MARCH
## 1972

*R*ebecca Sherman reached out the car window and took the parking ticket from the machine. Then she slowly guided her car up the winding ramp until she reached Level 5, where she found a parking space near the elevator.

"President of the Women's Auxiliary, Children's Hospital," she said aloud as she turned off the ignition. She glanced at her watch. She was early. It was never good to be early. She decided to sit in the car for a few minutes and meditate.

She had just been elected president — a position that gave her a seat on the hospital's Board of Directors. It was a feather in her cap, a position that would bring her into constant contact with the powers-that-be. Prominent members of the twenty-member board included Senator Jack Jacobs, Q.C.; Sir John Mecklinger, chairman of the Canadian Overseas Investment Fund; and Santino DeLuca, chairman of DeLuca Industries.

The only person Rebecca had known when she was elected to the board was the senator, who had invited Rebecca to lunch with him a few days before this first meeting.

"I thought I'd take you through the politics of a board such as this," he had said. "You might say this is an orientation."

Rebecca had enjoyed the next half-hour listening to Jacobs talk about the different people she'd meet and how to deal with them.

"Whatever you do, Rebecca," he had advised as they finished their coffee, "don't be too aggressive. With the exception of DeLuca, these people are genteel WASPs. They dislike Jews to begin with, but they dislike pushy ones the most. Just put a pretty smile on your face, never say anything controversial, and let me show you the way."

Rebecca doubted she'd be able to sit like a mouse the way Jacobs suggested, but she did appreciate his advice. They might have been friends, were it not for his wife Charlene, a woman with whom Rebecca was always uncomfortable.

Charlene Jacobs was a viper, or at least that's how Rebecca saw her. She was a thin blond woman with blue eyes that never looked directly at anyone for more than a few seconds before they darted away to see if anything or anybody else was more interesting. She smiled at everyone, never openly disagreeing about anything. But behind your back, watch out. She and Rebecca sat on several charity committees but Rebecca refused to have anything to do with her beyond their polite exchanges at meetings, even though Charlene made constant overtures about having lunch together.

Senators and important boards. In one sense Rebecca had come a long way; in another she was always asking herself, is this all there is?

Seven years earlier, she had met Steven Sherman at her friend Jackie's wedding. He was in business with his father, who ran a steel company. After only three weeks of dating, Steven had asked her to marry him, and she had said yes.

Steven was nice. He was rather stocky, with sandy-colored hair and watery blue eyes. She knew he'd never let her down, as David Winter, her previous love interest, had done. Steven was also very rich and she was tired of counting her pennies. She had decided that it was time to learn more about life, and start pursuing her dreams.

Rebecca was the daughter of Sam and Naomi Singer. Sam had come to Canada from Russia in 1935 to marry her mother, something that had been arranged by the local matchmaker. He was a kind man, but with few skills and very little English. Their first daughter, Jean, was born in 1937,

Rebecca in 1944, and their only son, Baruch (Barry), in 1948. Sam's parents had been killed — victims of Hitler's "final solution." As a result, his children were particularly precious to him.

In 1954 her brother Barry was killed in a car accident. Although they tried to put on a brave front, her parents never fully recovered from their loss.

In April of 1966 Rebecca and Steve were married. On their wedding night, she enjoyed having Steve make love to her and was surprised that it didn't hurt as much as her friend Jackie had said it would. Although she didn't find sex that exciting, she pretended otherwise. For his part, Steve had seemed surprised when he discovered that she was still a virgin and thrilled with his sexy and "horny" wife.

Two years later their daughter Lisa was born. Rebecca soon quit the job she had with an investment firm because Steven wanted her to be a full-time mother. She pushed her own ambitions aside, telling herself that Steven was right about not having Lisa raised by a stranger. But she started taking art courses and interior decorating classes. She became a volunteer with several community organizations, learned to play bridge, and settled into the routine of a wealthy businessman's wife.

Her parents were quite happy to become grandparents, and for a short time they seemed to find a renewed interest in life. Naomi loved to have the baby placed on her lap so she could croon Yiddish lullabies in her ear, as she had once sung to Barry. Sam, too, was exhilarated, and often visited Rebecca's home on his own to play with his "*sheine maidele*," as he called Lisa.

Several times her father asked her if she was happy, as if he sensed that something was wrong; but when she brushed off his questions, he didn't pursue the matter. Sam had never felt comfortable discussing personal matters with anyone, especially his daughters. From Rebecca's perspective, it wasn't that anything specific was wrong; it was just a vague feeling she had that something in her life was missing. But what?

As the wife of a successful businessman who made substantial contributions to various organizations, Rebecca was invited to sit on many community boards. She enjoyed participating because it gave her an opportunity to meet interesting people. She also liked the fact that she was acquiring a reputation as a skilled administrative volunteer with an instinctive feel for the fund-raising techniques that worked.

Her short-lived career in the money market after graduation had taught her financial management, and she was one of the few volunteer board members, male or female, who could understand the financial statements of community-based agencies. She decided to build up her network of contacts so that, when Lisa was in school full time, she could start a company of her own dealing with the funding and management of such organizations.

Rebecca was aware that she had impressed many people over the years, but she also knew that her husband's money didn't hurt. As her volunteer commitments grew, she kept putting off her plans to start her own business. Sometimes she'd look in the mirror and ask herself if she wasn't just copping out. Finally she did open her own office in one of Steve's buildings.

He was happy to provide Rebecca with an outlet for her energy. He'd seen what was going on in the lives of some of their friends — free love, LSD, hippies, drugs galore — and he didn't want it for his family. Clearly, it was all right with him if she was up to her eyeballs in community volunteer work: it kept her busy, amused, and out of trouble.

Recently she had become so busy that she had decided to hire a secretary, a woman named Ruth Feld who had been recommended to her by Senator Jack Jacobs.

And as her reputation grew, the premier opportunists in any city, state, province, or country — the politicians — came out of the woodwork. They lived off the publicity that prominent people could provide, and the best way for them to benefit was to stay near and offer assistance whenever the opportunity arose. It followed that those who had access to the decision makers gave one clout. Steven was a good example: his connections increased his influence with those sitting at the negotiating table.

Money–connections–power–more money. Those were the things that counted, she thought. She glanced at her watch again. She looked in the car mirror: nothing was amiss. She climbed out of the car and locked it. In a few moments she was being ushered into the mahogany-lined boardroom.

Rebecca felt his eyes on her as she entered. She knew she looked

attractive in her navy suede suit with a silk scarf in shades of navy and
fuchsia draped loosely around her neck. Her suede bag and shoes were also
navy with the slightest of gold trim. Her long dark hair was held back with
a navy suede band; her earrings were pearls tastefully set in gold.

She was twenty-eight years old and had never made love with anyone
but her husband. Nor had she ever had an orgasm. That thought crossed
her mind as she took her seat and looked directly across the table into the
eyes of Santino DeLuca.

*S*teve Sherman loved to gamble, something
he kept hidden from his wife. She thought he only went to Pearl's Health
Club, a very popular exercise and spa facility in the north end of Toronto,
to have a regular steam and massage alongside his cronies. She didn't realize that the club was really a front for an elite gambling and call-girl operation. Although the registered owners were the elderly parents of Senator
Jacobs, there were rumors that the mob had a large piece of the action.

Steven was more interested in the horses than in the broads, and he never
indulged in the kinky group sex that often went on in the club's lower lounge
late at night. He saw it as a risk he didn't want to take. He knew that if his
wife ever found out, his marriage would be over. Even though there was a
growing distance between Rebecca and himself, he still loved her. Besides,
she was very responsive to his sexual needs and never refused him — which
was more than most of his friends could say about their wives.

So why should I risk everything I have by cheating on Rebecca with
some two-bit dame? he asked himself as he came down the stairs that led
to the lounge.

That night Senator Jacobs had arranged an eleven o'clock party with
two hookers and some local city and provincial politicians. Jacobs was known
as a "twenty-fiver": he collected "contributions" for various politicians, but
kept 25 percent for himself. "My consulting fee," he would often say laugh-
ingly. He'd been a senator for ten years. He was also a lawyer and the chief
fundraiser for the former Conservative prime minister. Although he and

Charlene had three children, there were rumors that he was bisexual.

Steve had arrived at the club after having dinner at home with Rebecca and Lisa. He'd heard about the party from Jacobs a few days earlier but had declined the invitation to attend. He had only intended to have a steam before settling down to his regular poker game, and he had planned to leave as soon as it was over.

It was now past midnight. Steven looked down the stairs into the private lounge as he was going for his coat. He whistled softly through his teeth when he saw the mayor, the senator, and some other well-known politicos. Must have been some blast, he thought. He poked his head through the door to get a better view.

Two of the men sniffing cocaine and popping pills were known to him, and he was shocked. One was a well-known politician, Richard Dudley; the other was Bob DeSalle, lawyer to the influential. DeSalle was big-time: although only thirty-two years old, he was one of the most powerful men in the country, having become a special aide to the prime minister right after he graduated from law school. Now he was the senior vice-president of A&B Industries, one of the largest conglomerates in North America. The company had made its money in silver mining back in the early '50s, but was now into mergers and acquisitions, buying up smaller companies at a dizzying pace. The company seemed to have an unlimited amount of cash, which made them tough to beat at the bargaining table. But there were some questions about the company's owner, who, it was rumored, had been convicted of fraud in Texas many years earlier.

DeSalle, in addition to his corporate duties, was the chief bagman for many politicians, the person you had to see before any big deal could be made. Most political problems could be fixed by a call to DeSalle, provided that you were on his favored list.

There were many rumors around town about him, but nothing concrete. His bio said he'd been born in an Italian canton of Switzerland and that he had been sent to Upper Canada College when he was fourteen. It was also rumored that his parents were dead and that he had been left to fend for himself. It was assumed that he'd inherited a lot of money from them because when he was younger, and before he had made it in the business world, he had traveled extensively. He was seen everywhere that mattered, and his home, in a posh neighborhood of Toronto where he lived with an elderly gentleman said to be his guardian, was a showplace.

Steve Sherman supposed Bob DeSalle was handsome, with his dark brown hair and olive complexion. He had a mustache that he combed whenever he walked by a mirror, and his vanity was fodder for many jokes.

As Steve continued to watch the scene below, one of the hookers went over to speak to Billy, the club security guard. He then went out the back exit, only to return a few minutes later with a big German shepherd. The men at the party formed a circle with the two girls and the dog in the middle. Even though Steve felt like throwing up, he couldn't stop watching. Soon the men were in a frenzy, with no one caring who was doing what to whom.

Pills were popping; liquor was being consumed right from the bottle.

The dog was soon curled up in a corner sleeping.

Finally Steve went into the men's room and threw up. When he came out, he saw several naked men still entwined with each other and with the girls. As he watched two naked bodies bobbing up and down on each other, Steve was shocked to realize that one of them was David Winter, Rebecca's first boyfriend and now a lawyer in the attorney general's office.

Too bad I don't have a camera with me, Steven thought. Pictures of this would be good security for my old age.

As he turned to leave, he didn't notice the tiny red light in the air vent at the top corner of the lounge, almost parallel to his line of vision. Inside the vent was an automatic camera and it was taking some very clear and interesting pictures. The ripple effect they would cause would be felt long after Steven Sherman was gone.

*F*rom that first moment in the boardroom Rebecca was fascinated by Santino DeLuca. Tall and well built, with thick curly hair that was more gray than black, he reminded her of a TV commercial she'd seen about E. F. Hutton. The one that went "when E. F. Hutton speaks, people listen." Santino was the one who spoke.

Yes, she admitted, she couldn't stop thinking about him. She'd heard he was one of the Mafia, but then most southern Italians were tainted with that brush. She knew he was powerful in the construction industry and that he had a young and beautiful wife.

She'd also read his résumé with great interest, which had been included in the Board of Directors' kit. According to it, he'd been born in Italy in 1926; this made him forty-eight now. His hobbies were listed as billiards and bocce, the Italian version of lawn bowling. He was a past president of the Italian National Congress and was now an executive officer of the Canadian Council of Christians and Jews. He had recently moved to Toronto and had a home here as well as two homes in Michigan and a condo in Bermuda. She still wondered why there was no mention of children. It was hard to imagine an Italian family without them.

She tried to maintain a cool detachment whenever she saw him, which was frequently. Government cutbacks had forced all health-care facilities to tighten their belts, and the finance committee of Children's Hospital was meeting biweekly to try to come up with a workable budget.

One April afternoon, when a meeting had to be extended in order to complete the hospital's budget proposal on time, everyone had agreed to break for a light supper and return at seven o'clock to put the finishing touches on their submission. She was trying to figure out how she could get Santino to join her for a snack when he came up behind her and asked her to join him. They went to the Roof Garden of the Park Plaza where they found a corner table amid the giant vases of geraniums and mums that graced the dining room. The sounds of traffic and blaring horns coming from the busy Yorkville shopping district eighteen stories below had competed with the violinist strolling among the diners.

They made small talk until their drinks arrived. Vodka and soda for him, white wine for her.

She was disconcerted every time she looked at Santino because she couldn't help envisioning the two of them in bed together. It was almost a fixation, although a laughable one, given the fact he wasn't Jewish. She had remained insulated within the Jewish community her whole life and had never even dated a non-Jew.

So why am I fantasizing about an Italian who is only one step away from being a common laborer? she asked herself over and over.

"Rebecca," Santino said, "you are a very clever woman, but you're much too abrasive. Have you ever thought about softening your approach a little? You get more with honey than with vinegar. And you'll never move up in this world if you have too many enemies."

She couldn't speak. Her face felt as if it was on fire. All the time she had been fantasizing about sleeping with this man, the only thing on his mind was humiliating her and putting her down. She tried to maintain her cool by taking a sip of her wine, but to her horror, her hand was shaking and she had to put the goblet down.

Santino, seemingly unaware of her reaction, went on. "If you're really as smart as you want everyone to think you are, show them by suggestion, by consultation, by consensus. Your strategy for overhauling the hospital's grant submissions is brilliant. But most of the board's members don't understand the long-term benefits or see the global perspective. Beating them over the head with it makes them feel intimidated, resentful, and stupid. Do you understand what I mean?"

He had such a pleasant smile on his face that she almost missed what he had just said. Then she thought, no one has ever talked to me this way. What the hell is the matter with me? And then she wondered, how could I have ever had lewd fantasies about this schmuck?

"I'm sure you believe everything you've just said to me," she answered in her most controlled voice. "But I see it a little differently. Life is short. I can't be bothered dancing around the egos of some mental midgets who get paid more than they should. Or somebody's wife with no brains and big boobs. The name of the game is delivery, and I always deliver."

He didn't answer for a few moments; he just kept looking at her. "Something is driving you, Rebecca, and I'm not sure what it is. You've got too much talent to be wasting it on petty squabbles that result from your impulsiveness. If you're as hungry for success as I think you are, you'll try harder to curb your impatience. Unlike you, I am patient. I'll wait."

"For what?" she asked him, trying not to lose her cool.

"Why, you, of course," he answered, his expression softening. "But you knew that from the first moment we met. To quote that famous board member, what's-her-name, 'Life's too short to waste it dancing around somebody's ego,' etcetera, etcetera."

Rebecca made no response but just returned his steady gaze over the rim of her wine glass.

For the next few weeks she made a concerted effort, at least for her, to soften her approach. She waited for Santino to ask her out for dinner or drinks or to do something to follow up on their last conversation, but he did nothing. So she decided to bury herself in other projects.

For some time Senator Jacobs had been suggesting that she get involved in politics. "That's where the real action is," he'd said. He'd made it sound so fascinating that she'd agreed.

"I have just the right project for you to start on," the senator had said. "Do a good job, and you'll be right up there."

So Rebecca agreed to coordinate a fundraising dinner in June for Richard Dudley, the province's youngest cabinet minister and deputy premier. At thirty-five, he wielded a lot of power in the government. He was so pleased with the results of the event that Rebecca had organized that he asked her to be a permanent member of his party's team.

"One day I intend to be the Prime Minister of Canada," he told her. "And I'm starting to build a team now. I want to get away from the old-time bagmen and hangers-on. There are changes in the political winds and I don't want to get blown away."

Soon afterward she was asked to serve on a community task force being established by the mayor, Howard Brennan, to improve cooperation between the business community and the city government in order to facilitate increased investment from Hong Kong. Rebecca spent the next few months immersed in learning about city politics, trying to put thoughts of Santino out of her mind, without too much success. She was totally puzzled by his come-on, which had had no follow-up. Then the reason became obvious. In September a note was attached to the hospital's board minutes. It extended congratulations to Mr. and Mrs. Santino DeLuca on the recent birth of their twin sons. Rebecca froze when she read it.

Why, you two-bit bastard, she thought. You were just fishing while your wife was pregnant.

Even though they continued to see each other regularly at the Children's Hospital board meetings, she avoided any more flirtations with him.

When Rebecca was asked to cochair a newly created nonprofit housing agency, her husband Steven raised some objections.

"Isn't this volunteer work of yours getting to be a bit much?" he asked. "If you're not out at a meeting, you're on the phone. What about Lisa and me? We need some attention."

She felt guilty, knowing he was right. She'd try to spend more time with them and concentrate less on Santino and more on Steven, for whom she wanted desperately to feel some real passion. But every time he put his lips on her body or touched her, it was all she could do not to push him away. Still, she had to continue with the charade to keep her marriage intact.

In May her mother had died in her sleep. It was a blessing, since her mental health had deteriorated a lot during the past two years. But her father was inconsolable; he'd always loved Naomi despite her nagging and her nasty disposition. Rebecca's sister Jean hadn't come home for the funeral even though Rebecca offered to pay her fare. Jean had been living in England for over ten years, having moved there just after her fiancé left her a month before the wedding. She had never got over the pain and vowed never to get emotionally involved with any man again. She was still hiding in her cocoon in England, and was afraid that if she left it, she might never get back in it.

Rebecca and Steven asked her father to come and live with them. They had a large home and she knew Lisa would love to have her *zaidy* around more often. Sam thought about it for a few days, but declined the offer. He was set in his ways and wanted to remain in his own house. He promised to visit them as often as possible.

From time to time Sam still asked Rebecca if she was happy, expressing concern that her community involvements had taken over her whole life.

"What about Lisa?" he would ask. "A mother should be home for her children, not running around all the time, especially with all those *goyim.*"

"Don't worry, Dad," she would answer with a smile. "Lisa is just fine. It's a different world today. Women don't have to stay home doing nothing any more. Besides, aren't you proud when you read all the stories about what I'm doing?"

"I'd be proud of you even if you did nothing," he told her. "But, *meine sheine kind,* it's important that you don't forget who you are and where you come from. To 'them,' you'll always be a dirty Jew, no matter how nice they are to your face."

She didn't agree with him and she kept on working.

# 6

*R*ebecca turned the pages of the financial report slowly, aware that she wasn't fully concentrating. Spring fever, she thought as she looked out her office window. It was a beautiful day; yes, spring was very much in the air.

Her phone rang.

"Rebecca?" Santino asked.

"Hi," Rebecca responded, aware of a sudden increase in her heart rate.

"What's doing?" he asked.

"Nothing out of the ordinary."

"Want to have lunch?"

Say no, you jerk, she thought. Tell him to fuck off and get home to his wife and babies. But she didn't, couldn't. "What a lovely idea," she answered, pulling out her mirror and hairbrush.

"Park Plaza, twelve thirty okay?" he asked.

"I'll be there," she said as she hung up.

She stared at the phone for a long moment and then she fixed her face and combed her hair. "Damn," she muttered.

She picked up her jacket as she headed for the outer office. "Ruth, cancel my lunch meeting," she called out to her secretary. "I have to take my father to the doctor."

She told herself she was behaving like a stupid schoolgirl as she walked toward the Park Plaza, but there it was: after two years Santino DeLuca still held a fascination for her. But she had buried herself in her job, working tirelessly on behalf of Children's Hospital. Ruth Feld was looking after her other projects, keeping everything running in smooth order.

As Rebecca walked toward the hotel she finally acknowledged the real reason for the intensity of her efforts on the hospital's behalf: Santino DeLuca. A few minutes later she reached the revolving door that led into the lobby of the Park Plaza. She took a deep breath and went through it.

*A*s soon as Rebecca left, Ruth Feld switched off the tape recorder she'd hidden behind a painting in Rebecca's office. Although the equipment was rather amateurish, it still worked. Usually Feld took each tape home at night, listened to it, and then stored it away. Today she played this one back while eating her sandwich at her desk.

Why is Rebecca lying about having lunch with that mobster? Feld asked herself as she listened to the tape a second time. But then she smiled and called Charlene Jacobs.

Maybe things are starting to look up, she thought.

Ruth Feld was Charlene Jacobs's cousin, and the two of them had come up with the idea of secretly taping Rebecca's conversations in the hope of coming up with some juicy dirt on her and others.

Until now Feld had heard only some colorful and unprintable comments — nothing of any significance.

"Santino DeLuca," she said aloud. "My, my."

*A*s Rebecca walked into the elegant dining room with thick carpets, the only sound she was aware of was the tinkle of crystal and silver.

She was glad she was wearing her peach silk blouse when she entered the dining room and saw how Santino's eyes softened as he caught sight of her. The V neckline showed just enough of her cleavage to interest a man who appreciated a woman's body. The pearls around her neck added a demure touch.

After a few minutes of chitchat Santino told her the reason for their lunch. It wasn't what she had hoped.

"I've noticed how much your attitude has improved in the past two years," he said. "Even though I know you don't really mean it, some of your critics believe it's a sign of maturity. They think you're ready for bigger things."

She said nothing, just kept looking at him, trying to appear sensual and businesslike at the same time. She was not sure where the conversation was leading, but she decided to play along. She wondered how Santino would react if he knew what she was really thinking.

"And what do you think?" she asked, her eyes sparkling.

"I'm not sure what you mean."

"Well, I know how extensive your interests are. And whatever I've learned on my own these past few years can't compare with what you could teach me."

Forget about the rule of never mixing business with pleasure, she decided.

Santino's black eyes seemed to be looking into her soul, but his face was expressionless. After what seemed a long time, he spoke:

"DeLuca Industries is planning to set up a nonprofit trust, a foundation, to handle our charitable contributions. Our subsidiaries are constantly inundated with requests for donations and our accountants are spending too much time making sure we don't exceed our tax-deductible limits. I've decided to put it all under one umbrella. I've been thinking of putting someone like you in charge."

Rebecca willed herself not to let her own facial expression change. Is he serious? What does "someone like you" mean? If I appear too eager, he might back off. Should I play hard to get?

Santino continued. "DeLuca Industries plans to deposit $5,000,000 in the trust fund to purchase dividend-bearing bonds yielding about $500,000 annually." He paused. "The capital can be reinvested as the trust sees fit. I think the money market is going to fluctuate over the next ten years, so there will be great challenges for anyone not afraid to consider alternative investment opportunities."

"Why would you want a volunteer like me?" she asked. "You could hire the best administrator money can buy. As good as I am, I don't have the education or the credentials of a professional."

"That's exactly why I do want you," he answered forcefully, dropping the "someone like" phrase. He leaned over the table. "The business of charity requires an added dimension — an understanding of and a sensitivity to need. Only someone with a great deal of volunteer experience like yourself can provide that."

As he spoke, Rebecca could see down the road. As the head of the trust fund, she'd be in control of a tremendous sum of money, a position that would give her considerable power and influence. And ultimately all the doors to even more power, influence, money would open to her — doors through which she desperately wanted to walk.

She fought not to appear too anxious. "After listening to you I must say it certainly does sound most interesting. It offers the kind of challenge I feel confident I can meet — as long as you stay close by while I learn everything I need to know."

There was silence for a few moments as Santino looked steadily at her. Rebecca panicked inside, wondering if she'd answered too quickly, too confidently, and put him off.

Finally he spoke. "Well, I think you can handle it. Now, let's talk about your expectations in terms of remuneration."

"I think it's important that I continue my community involvements so that I don't undermine my credibility," she suggested. "Therefore I'd rather not take any salary or benefits from the fund, or from you, for the first year. Then, if I do the kind of job I expect to, and if you're pleased, we'll discuss the subject again."

Rebecca wasn't exactly sure what the slightly twisted smile on his face meant, but she thought it could be a combination of the cat-about-to-swallow-the-canary look, and admiration.

"You're on," he said, lifting his drink to his lips.

*I*t was raining. One of those awful thunderstorms that Toronto so often has in the summer. Not that the rain was a surprise. The humidity had got worse with every passing day. Then this afternoon all the dark clouds had gathered and when the wind changed, the heavens opened up.

Rebecca had been looking forward to the break in the weather, but when it came she cursed it.

She looked at the clock in the car. It was one-fifteen. Lisa had called thirty minutes earlier to say her grandfather was complaining of chest pains. Rebecca had left her office immediately; but then the rain started, and lightning must have struck some generator somewhere because all the traffic lights went out. The traffic was a nightmare and she cursed the storm, the rain, and the cars that seemed to surround her. Finally she saw an opening and she pushed into it, even though the man behind her swore and gave her the finger.

"Fuck you, too!" she shouted back.

She turned the corner and took three side streets, then she pulled into her driveway and hurried to the house. Lisa opened the door even as she was fumbling with her key.

"I've called an ambulance," her daughter said with surprising authority. "*Zaidy* asked me to. He thought it was indigestion, but then he said it hurt too much." Sam Singer had come to spend the day with his granddaughter.

"Oh God," Rebecca said under her breath. Lisa wasn't even seven, but sounded very grown up.

Rebecca hurried to the living room where her father was lying on the couch. His breathing was abnormal and he was ashen. She put her hand on his face. It felt very cold. Lisa knelt next to him.

"*Sheine poo'nims,*" he said to them, his voice barely audible.

In the distance Rebecca could hear the ambulance siren.

Her father reached up to stroke Lisa's cheek and then hers. "Don't cry, my *sheine maideles*," he said. "I'm going to be with my dear Naomi of blessed memory and my beloved Baruch, my baby boy. I'll miss you both, but I belong with them. We'll be watching over both of you, and Auntie Jean, too, waiting till we all meet again in 120 years. I love you."

He gasped the last part of the sentence, then he closed his eyes and his head fell to one side.

Rebecca was holding her father's hand when Lisa opened the door to the ambulance crew. They took his pulse and then tried to resuscitate him, to no avail. They turned to Rebecca and shook their heads.

Rebecca started sobbing uncontrollably, and Lisa, who had never seen her mother cry before, put her arms around her and patted her back.

"Oh Lisa," Rebecca cried to her daughter. "Now I'm an orphan."

# 7

## JANUARY
## 1975

*O*utside, a cold winter wind blew. It was the week after New Year's Day, 1975. Elizabeth DeLuca lay in her tub luxuriating in the hot, perfumed water while the steam filled the room. Her thoughts, not unusually, had turned to her mother.

When she had called her just after the New Year, she had found Giovanna very lucid, wanting to know everything about her life and asking her detailed questions about the babies' care. Their conversation had been warm and intimate — as if they had been in close touch — belying the fact that they hadn't seen each other in almost thirteen years.

Elizabeth thought about the call she'd made to her mother three days after the twins were born. She'd used a pay phone in the maternity ward waiting room.

"Mama, I'm a mama!" she had cried in delight when Giovanna picked up the phone. "You're a *nonna*!"

She hadn't seen the smile that lit up her mother's face, nor had she seen her cross herself and kneel down in her room in front of the crucifix on the wall. But she had heard her mother's voice clearly when she said, "May you and your sons be blessed, my daughter. You have given meaning to my life."

Why couldn't she be like this all the time? Elizabeth asked herself now.

But she knew her mother's state of mind was unpredictable from month to month.

She turned her thoughts to Santino. Once again she'd overheard some late-night conversations he'd had with his associates in Europe, and Massimo Brattini's name had kept cropping up. Obviously, Brattini was creating problems for Santino that were hard for him to deal with from home. But he'd refused to leave the country because he wanted to be with his young sons, who were nearly three.

In order to keep the vow she had made to God three years ago, she had become a tireless volunteer for the Church and a generous sponsor of its projects. She hoped it would offset her husband's activities in some small way.

Elizabeth realized that Santino was trying to reconcile his old-time, traditional Italian background with modern times. *I must try to be more understanding, too,* she reminded herself. *This is all he knows, and he's doing the best he can.*

But she could not forget the way he had behaved after the children were born. Her life had consisted only of feeding the babies and trying to catch some sleep. At first Santino had loved to watch her nurse the boys. He told her that she reminded him of a Renaissance painting.

However, by the time the boys were three months old, and both sleeping through the night, Santino still had not made love to her. Several times she'd cuddled up to him in bed, trying the usual seductive signals a wife sends to her husband when she's in the mood for love, but he had not responded.

One night, after Santino returned late from a meeting, she had crawled into their bed naked. She had kissed him passionately, running her hands over his buttocks. Then, when she'd started stroking his penis, which was only semi-erect, he had pulled away from her.

"Elizabeth, what are you doing?" he had asked. "You're a mother now. Conduct yourself properly."

She hadn't known whether to laugh or cry. "Santino, I'm still a woman," she had answered, continuing to stroke his body and kiss his back. "And I miss having you make love to me. Surely being a mother doesn't mean staying celibate for the rest of my life."

He had been silent for a while, then he'd turned toward her and made love to her. Not as he had once made love to her, but she deemed it a start.

Now, she sighed deeply and turned on the tap to run more hot water in the tub. Santino was more controlled in his lovemaking, as if he was fulfilling a duty. Now that she was the mother of his sons, he had put her on a pedestal, one that was too high, and she wanted to get off.

She had begun to wish she had someone she could talk to about her insecurities, but she had no close friends, at least none she felt she could trust enough.

She remembered how, in desperation, she had finally raised the matter with her mother during one of their monthly phone calls.

"Silly girl," Giovanna had said to her. "That's the benefit of being an Italian wife. Once you become a mother, your husband starts to give you real respect by satisfying his disgusting lusts with others, leaving you alone."

Elizabeth had been struck dumb. But her mother had continued.

"Sex between a husband and his wife is for the creation of children only. Italian men are raised from birth to think of women only as mothers, sisters, wives . . . and the rest."

"Well, I intend to be a wife as well as one of the rest," she had said. "I have no intention of letting some other woman get close to my husband."

But the truth was she had found her mother's remarks particularly troublesome. Lately she had the feeling that Santino was thinking of something or someone else whenever he made love to her.

He'd been talking a lot about the woman he'd put in charge of the trust and with whom he'd been working on his community committees — a Rebecca Sherman.

"I'm really enjoying working with Rebecca. She's shrewd, smart; sometimes I think she must be a man disguised as a woman."

Elizabeth wiggled her toes worriedly, no longer enjoying the bath. She began to wash herself distractedly. Santino talked about the Sherman woman often, recounting every one of her successes, laughing and beaming over "how I've taught Rebecca everything she knows."

Elizabeth smelled trouble, but she knew she'd have to keep cool and pretend to be interested in, and impressed with, her husband's protégée. She didn't want him to think that she was suspicious or resentful.

"As long as he keeps talking to me about her so openly, I have nothing to worry about. I hope." She was talking to the bar of soap, turning it over and over in her hand.

"Soon," she said. She was finally going to meet this Rebecca Sherman at an upcoming ballet fundraising gala. "Then I'll have a better sense of what my strategy will have to be." Yes, she had to work out how to deal with a woman she sensed had become — or might become — a threat to her security and that of her family.

*I*t was one of those deceiving February days. The sun was shining and the sky was a deep blue. From inside it looked warm outside, but in reality the outside temperature was below zero.

Rebecca had just hung up her winter coat and taken off her hat and gloves. She hadn't worn boots because she went from inside her garage, which was connected to the house, to her underground parking space beneath the building in which her office was located. Naturally she kept boots in the car in case of an accident or a breakdown. Driving in winter, even in the city, could be unpredictable.

No sooner had she edged behind her desk than the phone rang. She picked it up and a crisp voice said, "Hello, Mrs. Sherman. This is Senator Jack Jacobs's office calling. Hold, please."

"Rebecca?"

"Yes, Jack. What can I do for you?" She hoped she sounded as crisp as his secretary.

"I'd like you to join me for lunch. I have a few friends I'd like you to meet." His voice was nasal and whiny, reminding her of one of Lily Tomlin's parodies.

"As it happens, I am free," she said, trying to sound as cool as she felt.

"Il Posto at, say, one?"

"Fine," she answered. "See you then." She replaced the receiver and for a long moment looked at the phone.

By now she knew she was a very well-connected woman, influential with politicians from all parties as well as with the movers and shakers within society. Her position at DeLuca Industries gave her the power to designate large sums of money to various charities, and put her name on everyone's "A" list. According to some, she had become as powerful as the senator.

She shook her head. Her initial admiration for Jacobs had turned to contempt. He was always looking for a payoff — cash, free tickets, free dinners, recognition for community work actually done by others — anything would do. She and Steven always referred to him as "Senator Schnorrer," a Yiddish expression of disdain for a person who is a chiseler and a cheapskate, a moocher.

She'd had an argument with Jacobs only last week when he'd refused to pay for his tickets to an upcoming gala that Rebecca was chairing to benefit children with disabilities. He wanted "freebies," tickets designated for politicians and special guests.

"What's the matter, Jack?" she'd snapped at him. "Can't you afford a few hundred dollars for charity?"

"My presence is worth something," he'd answered with no embarrassment. "Didn't I make phone calls for you? Didn't I use my connections to get your committee door prizes? Why should I have to pay, too?"

Santino was irritated when she recounted the conversation. "It's a mistake to start up with someone like Jacobs," he said. "I've told you before. Don't make any enemies."

It was easier to be nice to some people than it was to others, she told herself. With that thought in mind, she went to the coffee maker and poured herself a cup. There was work to do before lunch.

When she arrived at Il Posto, one of Toronto's most fashionable restaurants, the senator was already there, working the tables, shaking hands, and making jokes with the staff.

When the weather was nice enough, tables were set in the courtyard that also served as a walkway from Hazelton Lanes to Yorkville Avenue. The shops there were on a par with those on Fifth Avenue, Rodeo Drive, or Palm Beach's Worth Avenue. Those who wanted to see or be seen managed to find their way into that courtyard during the hours of noon to two o'clock. In the winter everyone was forced inside, but the shops and restaurants of the area were still very much the place to be seen.

When Jacobs saw Rebecca, he came over very quickly, almost bowing as he kissed her hand. What a bunch of hypocritical garbage, she thought. At first she had imagined Jacobs to be better than his wife. Now she realized they were very much alike.

"Dear Rebecca, I want to introduce you to Bob DeSalle."

She'd heard about this man. He's a young Gilbert Roland, she thought, recalling the old movie she'd been watching on late-night TV last week. But unlike the movie idol, Bob DeSalle had eyes that were cold, calculating. She'd heard rumors that he was working to reinstate the political career of Richard Dudley, who had been caught *in flagrante delicto* with some bimbo in his office last year.

Current gossip, which had not escaped Rebecca's ears, had it that the lady in question had been bent over the antique mahogany desk in the Cabinet Room while the "Right Honorable" man of distinction was *shtupping* her in the rear.

Someone had opened the door at a critical moment and snapped a picture. The price of silence, so the story went, had been in the six figures. In spite of the payoff, some of the media got copies of the color prints in brown envelopes, and Dudley quickly resigned from office, citing his wife's illness as the reason. But what exactly she was ill with, the public never learned. Six months after his party lost the next election, she was miraculously cured following a visit to Lourdes, a fact mentioned prominently in the press releases.

"Perhaps," suggested some cynics, "in the hope that this revelation would attract Roman Catholic sympathy, along with their votes, should the dear man decide to re-enter public life."

The juicy tale circulated in various forms for a long time and, despite the efforts of the best spin doctors and public-relations experts, Richard

Dudley was always the butt of jokes. In fact, the name he was called forever more, behind his back of course, was Big Dick Studley.

Bob DeSalle smiled even though his eyes remained cold. "Call me Bingo — it's what all my friends call me."

"That's an interesting nickname." Vaguely she wondered if he had any real friends.

"When I finally pushed my way into the world, after a lengthy labor, the doctor cried out, '*Tombola!*' That's Italian for 'Bingo.' As a kid I was called Tombola, but when I moved to Canada it got Anglicized. Anyway, that's the story."

Given his background — or at least what was known about him — she thought it was probably just that, a story.

As he talked, Rebecca noted his custom-made shirt, his cashmere sport jacket, his large, heavy gold cufflinks. Every woman in the restaurant was looking over at him, and she was amused to observe some of the older "ladies who lunch" making repeated trips to the ladies' room, presumably to catch his attention. You really are one gorgeous hunk, she mused. Gorgeous but ... Her instincts warned her against him. She sensed that beneath his suave exterior he was one of those men with a violent streak.

At that moment Sir John Mecklinger, Rebecca's colleague on the hospital board, along with Alex Goldstein, a well-known developer, ambled up to their table.

"You know Sir John, of course, and Alex Goldstein," the senator said as the two men sat down.

Rebecca looked up and smiled.

Goldstein stood barely five feet four inches tall and weighed about 150 pounds. He was a meticulous dresser, famous for his flamboyant silk ties. Although he was nearly bald, he made no attempt to hide the fact with a toupée, and even made jokes about it. He was soft-spoken, fluent in German, Yiddish, and Polish, and most charming.

He was also the volunteer president of the Jewish Community Council, of which Rebecca was a board member. They'd worked together raising money for Jewish dissidents in the Soviet Union, trying to buy their freedom from the communist bureaucrats with cash bribes. This was the explanation given to the community's more prominent members, very discreetly, as to why they would have to forgo tax-deductible receipts for these donations.

Both she and Goldstein were familiar with the nuances of cash transactions — for charity as well as "other business."

Unobtrusive waiters began to serve lunch. She had ordered risotto and rapini salad, grilled monkfish, and finally the restaurant's famous tiramisu. But as soon as the meal was under way, Jacobs began talking.

"Rebecca, my friend here, Alex Goldstein, has a problem, and he's asked me for help. Naturally I couldn't turn him down — though I did suggest that any problems he might have in this province could more easily be solved with your involvement as well."

How kind of you. And how much are you charging him for your kindness, I wonder? But her sarcastic question remained unasked.

"Goldstein's Development Consortium owns five thousand acres of agricultural land ten miles north of the city. They want to build a community center, a library, and several office towers, which will attract new businesses to the community and kick-start its sluggish economy. They also want to build some affordable housing, which will include several acres of parks." He stuffed a large forkful of salad into his mouth, then continued.

"As I'm sure you already know, from your dealings with the Mafia — oh excuse me, just a joke — your friendship with DeLuca, before any redevelopment can take place, sewer allocations are needed. This requires the rezoning of the site from agricultural to residential–commercial land use." He ate more salad and took a breath.

"Rezoning agricultural land is a very sensitive political issue right now. There are some local politicians who want to make their mark by attacking the establishment and whipping up the public with scare tactics about losing greenbelts and farmland to satisfy the greed of money-hungry developers."

She knew that this was the kind of headline that the left-wing press loved to print, and the publicity-hungry politicians loved to milk. And when he spoke of local politicians, she presumed Jacobs was referring to city councilor Jim Hollis. Hollis was a draft dodger who had slipped into Toronto three years earlier and, as a joke, had run for local municipal office. He'd won, and now the joke was on his constituents.

"Getting this project approved needs more than the usual political strategy," Jacobs went on. "It requires someone who can coordinate all the necessary components to make it work, but whose motives can't be attacked by the likes of Hollis and his friends in the media.

"In short, Rebecca, this project needs you."

Alex Goldstein patted the senator's arm and took over.

"We've just found out that Peartree, a property next to one we own, is one of three sites being considered for a garbage dump by the environmental agency. If Peartree were in fact chosen, it would render our site useless for development, and we'd lose our shirts. After all, who wants to live and work right next door to a garbage dump?

"So we decided to buy the Peartree property ourselves, get it rezoned residential, and include it as part of our overall development plan. But for some reason our usual strategy in dealing with a rezoning issue such as this one hasn't been working. In fact, we're getting nowhere fast."

After a few minutes of discussing the politics of the day and possible tactics to try, Rebecca asked Goldstein when they had acquired the Peartree property and for how much.

"I'll also need to know what the soil tests showed," she added, "and which politicians are already on side, and for how much."

The men all looked at each other, unsure who should answer, or if they should answer.

"Listen, gentlemen," she told them, "you've asked me here for a reason. You said you needed my help. Obviously the esteemed senator can't deliver, or at least not alone. If you don't want to tell me what I need to know in order to help you, that's fine. Let's finish lunch and forget it."

DeSalle's lips curled into a wolfish smile as he watched her. The senator looked furious. Then Sir John spoke up.

"Ah, my dear," he crooned in his very British accent, "how refreshing it is to see that your subtle and gentle approach hasn't been tempered by your increasing public prominence. I'm here to lend my support to this project as a member of the mayor's task force. As you know, we are seeking to build a better relationship between the local municipalities and the business community. We are also hoping to attract some Hong Kong investors to this city. Many are now sending their money to Vancouver. It's common knowledge that rezoning regulations there are much more flexible than ours."

As the conversation continued, it became obvious to Rebecca that the only reason these gentlemen had approached her for help was because they'd run out of options. This seemed strange: getting a dump site changed or removed from a short list was often difficult but almost never impossible. Her association with DeLuca Industries had made her very aware of just how much these decisions were contingent on the sum of money paid out to the politicians who made them.

When Santino had included her in some of his business lunches, it had become even clearer. Although he and his associates spoke Italian most of the time, she had come to understand certain phrases, and their body language often spoke louder than their words. They bought and sold thousands of acres of land among themselves, all by oral agreement. They haggled over their percentages, but once a deal was made, a handshake was all that was required. Then they'd get on to their most important agenda items: an emotional rehashing of old grudges, gossip about old enemies, and tales of greed and corruption practiced by politicians. Rebecca often felt as if she was witnessing a scene from a Damon Runyon novel. Nonetheless it had been instructive.

She had no doubt that Jacobs and Goldstein had the same knowledge and experience as the Italians on how and when to make payments to politicians, and she wondered just why they were acting so dumb.

"Why not allow Rebecca a day or two to consider all this? In the meantime I'll send some info over to her."

DeSalle's sudden conciliatory attitude made it more of a mystery. He was such a wheeler-dealer. Surely he didn't need her at all.

"As a matter of fact," DeSalle continued, turning to her, "why don't the two of us take a walk over to the museum's prehistoric display and sit down under Tyrannosaurus Rex? I think it's a fitting place to discuss the reality of politics."

His eyes were cold but his smile was humorous.

Goldstein picked up the lunch bill, and the group dispersed.

Rebecca and DeSalle took a brisk walk over to the Royal Ontario Museum. It was only three blocks away, but the biting wind made it seem farther. They hurried inside and headed for the lounge. As soon as they sat down a white-jacketed waiter approached.

"I noticed you didn't have a drink at lunch," DeSalle said. "Why not join me for a glass of sherry now?"

"Why not?" Rebecca answered, still trying to size him up. "Tell me, Bingo, why is it so hard to find politicians who stick to their principles? They change their positions with the daily changes of newspaper headlines."

"For a woman with your smarts, that's one hell of a naïve question. The answer is real simple: everybody's got a price. Find the price and you can change anyone's opinion — or, in this case, anyone's vote."

"My, you are a cynic," Rebecca countered. Not that she wasn't. But she wanted him to keep talking so that she could figure him out.

"Truth isn't in their vocabulary," DeSalle went on. "All you have to do to see it for yourself is to ask them questions to which you already have the answers. It's the easiest way to find out who's a liar. And once you do, then you can play with them, throw out carrots, see who'll take them right away and who will keep up appearances until they can come up with a rationalization for their greed."

Now he's getting into it, she thought.

"By seeing how long it takes for them to push their 'principles' aside and take the bait, you'll be able to get a sense of who will be reliable and who will sell out in the flick of an eye."

As DeSalle spoke, she realized just how much she'd hardened. His words not only made sense to her but caused her no discomfort. After all, it was all business, pure and simple, leaving no room to think beyond the task at hand.

She'd suspected, right from the beginning, that Santino's empire was, at the very least, in the gray area of legitimacy. But she had loved the action, had wanted a piece of it, so she'd quickly dismissed any qualms she might have had about where the $5,000,000 to set up the trust had come from. Well, she'd rationalized, at least some of it is going to good causes.

But rationalizations aside, she was also in love with Santino DeLuca. And that was the bottom line.

Rebecca and Bingo finished their drinks and as they walked back to their cars, she asked him if he was involved in the Goldstein project because of Big Dick Studley. He smiled at her use of the disparaging reference to Richard Dudley.

"I presume he's trying to find a project he can latch onto," she said. "Something that might earn him some points with the public before he makes his bid to return to politics."

"Dudley made things a lot easier for some of your friends when he was in power," Bingo replied. "Remember, the wheels of government have to be greased, and since the public has such a short memory, yesterday's loser is today's winner. I try to be of help to everyone and make no value judgments."

He was so sanctimonious she had to control her desire to laugh.

"You should do the same," he went on. "The name of the game is getting the job done. Nothing else matters." Then he took her hand and kissed it, bowing ever so slightly.

As Rebecca drove home, she thought about what she was going to do. This was a stroke of luck for her — and she was going to seize the moment. It was a golden opportunity to break into the big-money world on her own. She'd understood exactly what Bingo DeSalle had been talking about in terms of the politics. In fact, she probably understood it better than most. She'd observed the way DeLuca Industries moved their projects, both here and in the United States, through the political minefields. She was anxious to stickhandle a project herself just to prove that she could.

But most of all, she wanted to be financially independent.

She decided to say nothing to Santino. If he knew, he might try to stop her, or at the very least control what she would do. No, it was time to test her wings.

*T*hree days later Rebecca called the senator and asked him to come up to her office. As soon as he walked in, Ruth Feld switched on the hidden tape recorder.

"Here's the deal," Rebecca said to Jacobs as they both sat down on the couch. "A $100,000 retainer, payable immediately to my personal holding company. Another $100,000 payable to a charity of my choice, up front. When the project is put to bed successfully, which I'm sure it will be, I want another $250,000. I'm to have absolute control of the deal until it's done — no interference by you or anyone else in terms of who gets what and how everything gets done."

Jacobs's sour look turned mellow. "Done," was all he said.

He left and she leaned back in her chair. She felt a certain exhilaration. Making things happen, dealing with large sums of money, was something like taking speed — or being in love.

The next day a certified check for $100,000, written on a numbered company, was delivered to her office. Ruth Feld steamed open the envelope and photocopied the check before she put it on Rebecca's desk, resealed.

A week later an announcement was made to all media that Senator Jack Jacobs and his lovely wife Charlene had raised $100,000 for the Combined Jewish Appeal.

*T*he first person Rebecca wanted to see regarding Peartree was Lois Richardson, the mayor of Greenfield.

Richardson was a feisty woman in her late sixties who had passed up the traditional woman's role long before it was fashionable, and had carved herself a power base that reached across the country. She was the daughter of a former provincial cabinet minister, had been in politics her whole life, and was known as the most important politician in rural Ontario. Her name had never been linked seriously with any man, and some people who had known her family over the years said that she was really in love with her father and that no man could ever live up to him in her eyes.

The municipality of Greenfield was located ten miles to the northeast of Metropolitan Toronto. With an increased influx of immigrants expected over the next two years, Greenfield was ripe for redevelopment.

When a return call from the mayor's office indicated that an appointment had become available for the next morning, Rebecca went home early to prepare. Part of that preparation was the selection of clothing. She was always careful about how she dressed, and this time she decided to wear a simple gray suit, a pink cotton blouse, and pearls. In short, she decided to be conservative.

Greenfield's municipal offices were located in a typical small-town setting — a white clapboard building with green painted shutters on the windows. There were large apple and pear trees on the front of the property, but the parking lot, an unwelcome necessity, was hidden behind the building. Rebecca had driven past it at first because there was no sign.

When she was ushered into the inner sanctum, she decided to play this one very gently. She could smell the anti-Semitism all over the room. Small-town Ontarians still viewed Jews as rich moneylenders trying to plunder the land and wipe out all vestiges of British heritage.

"Well, Mrs. Sherman," Mayor Richardson said with a pained smile pasted on her very lined and sallow face. "What brings one of you people out to our little hick town?"

"I'm interested in the Peartree property," she answered, ignoring the mayor's use of the phrase, "you people." "And I'm wondering what your thoughts are concerning its development."

"I never have any thoughts about development," the mayor replied, the same smile still frozen on her face. "I am simply a servant of the people, one who tries to respond to their needs and wishes."

"Well, Madam Mayor," Rebecca said, "I certainly respect that."

"Oh, please, call me Lois," the mayor interjected.

"Well, thank you, and please call me Rebecca. I understand the present owners of the site are thinking of selling. It seems they've just about given up on their dreams of creating a new community that encompasses quality housing, retail opportunities, recreation facilities, and access to the arts."

She paused, a regretful expression on her face. "It would certainly be a shame if the only potential purchasers interested in the site had no community spirit, no interest in enhancing the environment, and no desire to work in close cooperation with your office — especially since Greenfield's present bylaws permit the land to be used as a graveyard for broken-down cars and trucks."

"Over my dead body!" Richardson snapped, her body stiffening and the smile leaving her face. "It doesn't matter what the bylaws say. It's only what I say that counts."

She quickly got herself back under control and regained the smile. "But, of course, I know you won't tell anyone that I said that," she said sweetly, "because if you do, then you and your friends won't be able to jew down the present owners for a better price."

You anti-Semitic bitch, Rebecca thought. You've already sold out. I wonder for how much. "Thank you so much for your time," she said as she got up from her chair. "I'll have to tell Sir John I wasn't successful."

"Wait," the mayor said, her voice going up in pitch. "Sir John who?"

Rebecca smiled. "Oh, I'm sorry. I assumed you had already heard that Sir John Mecklinger has accepted the position of chairman of the board of the Peartree Redevelopment Corporation. He's also the chairman of the Canadian Overseas Investment Fund. Is he the same gentleman to whom you were referring?"

The mayor swallowed hard.

Rebecca didn't wait for further conversation. Her last thought as she left was that the mayor should buy some really good perfume. What she wore was far too floral, far too strong. In fact, it smelled like gardenias and it gave Rebecca a headache.

She got into her car, but as soon as she got a few blocks away from Richardson's office, she pulled her car over to a phone booth to call Goldstein.

"Alex," she said breathlessly, "you've got to appoint Sir John chairman of the board of your new corporation. Don't ask me what new corporation. I'll let you know as soon as I get back to my office. I think the old witch took the bait. Find Sir John, wherever he is. Bermuda? Even better. No one will be able to reach him till everything's set up. Arrange a conference call for an hour from now. And get Walker & Associates to backdate the incorporation documents. No, no, don't worry. Just tell them it's for me."

Rebecca got an anonymous call later that evening at home. The voice sounded muffled, but it was clearly a man on the other end of the line.

"I thought it would be helpful if you knew that the mayor recently received a $35,000 'campaign contribution' from CanMor Corporation. They own all the land west of Greenfield as far as Kitchener. It's known as Millersgrove, and it was removed from the short list of potential dump sites only last month. I also suggest you take a look at the soil tests for both properties." Then he hung up the phone.

Rebecca slumped into a chair. The call was clearly from someone in the know. But who? And she wondered why someone would give her so much inside information, unsolicited. Usually, in circumstances like this, little dances around the mulberry bush were a necessary part of the ritual that preceded the "reward" for such critical assistance. But she decided she'd better check it out.

By the next afternoon Rebecca had obtained the soil tests on both properties. But no one could give her any information on CanMor, other than the name of the legal firm that represented them and the fact that they were based in Bermuda. As a private corporation, it did not have to disclose the names of their directors.

The environmental reports Rebecca had received on the two sites made it clear that the water wells under Peartree were the purest in the entire region. The sources were free-flowing springs, uncontaminated and deep enough to stay that way. While Millersgrove's water wasn't polluted, it wasn't as pure or as plentiful.

So any political decisions that turned the Peartree property into a garbage dump, while exempting Millersgrove, would cause a tragic waste of a natural resource that couldn't be replaced for generations to come.

And the old lady mayor had planned to sell out for $35,000.

Rebecca knew she now had to decide which strategy to employ. She could offer to pay off Richardson with more money and hope that CanMor didn't find out about it before Peartree was exempted — because, if they did find out, a bidding war might ensue between the two vested interests, and who knows where that could lead.

Or she could get really nasty and simply leak the information on the soil testing, along with CanMor's "campaign contribution," to the media, and let their bonfires start burning.

She paced round her office and thought of Santino. He had often warned her about pushing people into a corner — "there's only one way out," he'd say, "and then you have an enemy for life."

Rebecca decided to use tried-and-true methods. She'd seen it done often enough: first you wine and dine, then you find out what or how much is wanted — then you have it delivered. She had never made the delivery herself, but if she had to, she would.

Anyone who has ever dealt with public officials knows that real power comes from the ability to deliver votes, and mayors, no matter how powerful they think they are, still need the back-up votes of their council to enact or rescind any legislation. And their council knows it, too.

Since most politicians accept special treatment as part of their just reward for public service, Rebecca invited each of the five members of Greenfield's city council, separately, to have lunch with her, "to get to know you better." Of course, her real agenda was to lobby them independently and to try and get them on side, thus going around the dear mayor, Lois Richardson. All of them were happy to be entertained by someone as prominent as Rebecca Sherman.

But in spite of her charm and personality, the catalyst for success on the Peartree deal would ultimately turn out to be Sir John Mecklinger.

*T*he day after Sir John returned from Bermuda, Rebecca met with him and Alex Goldstein to discuss the situation. Not wanting to run into anyone they knew, they met in the bar at the Royal York far from the Hazelton Lanes crowd. The room was dark, furnished in red-velvet-covered chairs and dark wooden tables, and it smelled of expensive pipe tobacco. Over sherry, she gave them her assessment of her meeting with Lois Richardson. "The only way around the anti-Semitism and short-term vision up in Greenfield is you, Sir John," she said. "Peartree needs a WASP, and a knighted one at that, front and center."

Sir John and Goldstein concurred with her analysis, and Sir John agreed to become the figurehead of the Peartree project — for a fee of $25,000 a year, tax-free, plus expenses, for five years.

"I'm chairing a gala evening for the National Ballet in three weeks," Rebecca then told them. "Let's use it to dazzle the Greenfield town council as well as some of the federal and provincial people we'll need when it's time to get the sewer and housing allocations. In the meantime I'll contact the senator and fill him in. Maybe he knows something more than can be of help to us."

They all agreed, had another round of sherry, and then parted. Rebecca retrieved her car from the parking lot and began the long ride home. It was nearly rush hour, so the roads would be crowded.

She felt tired but excited about the challenges facing her on this project. She thought of what she would do when she got home and hoped Steven would be out at the health club so she could be alone.

Their life together had deteriorated into one of mutual convenience. Neither one of them wanted to confront the emptiness of their relationship, so their conversations consisted mostly of pleasantries. Their lives moved on different levels. She was immersed in her life of high society and politics, and the more she got involved, the more she got hooked on the excitement, the challenges, the game itself. Steve spent most evenings at the health club.

Rebecca believed he was still faithful to her, although she suspected that he knew she wasn't really enjoying sex with him. But, since their seven-year-old daughter was the most important person in both their lives, both of them kept their feelings inside, afraid of causing any disruption to Lisa's young life.

*R*ebecca walked toward Il Posto and a luncheon meeting with Senator Jacobs. She paused to look in the window of a chic boutique, then hurried on. As soon as she entered the restaurant she saw him. This man should never play poker, she thought. He looked as if he was about to burst.

"I've found out who controls CanMor Corporation," he said as soon as she sat down. "But before I tell you who it is, you'd better take a deep breath."

"Tell me," she urged.

"Massimo Brattini!"

Oh God. It was as if a light went on in her head. A setup. I'm dead. Her skin got clammy and she felt nauseous. Somehow she got through the rest of the meal. She didn't know what she was eating; she didn't hear what the senator was saying. She couldn't wait for the lunch to end. She excused herself before the coffee came, saying she had an appointment. But she went directly home.

She spent the rest of the day sitting in her den, thinking over her predicament. That night she couldn't sleep. How could I have been so stupid? she asked herself over and over. Why didn't I tell Santino what I was doing from the beginning?

She had initially put the $100,000 retainer from Goldstein into a thirty-day deposit, waiting for the right moment to tell Santino about it. Now she realized that the right moment had been on day one, before she had agreed to get involved in the Peartree project. And now, thanks to her own stupidity, he was going to learn about it elsewhere, and he would probably lose his trust in her.

Why hadn't she given more thought to how it would look if it became known that the chief administrator of a charitable trust, funded through DeLuca Industries, was acting on behalf of a private corporation against one of their competitors?

If she hadn't been so goddamn arrogant, she might have asked why the Peartree group had come to her in the first place — why they hadn't gone with a tried-and-true power broker. That would have required more money, maybe even a piece of the action, but the old boys' network would have been intact. Her presence was disruptive just by the fact she was a woman.

But maybe they had come to her for that reason — and the fact that her reputation was unblemished. Even though there were rumors about her and DeLuca, including the innuendos that he was a mobster, her excellent administration of the trust had proven how unimportant these rumors were.

She could imagine the newspaper headlines when Brattini's people leaked that information to them. No one would bother reading the small print about the fact that the trust itself wasn't involved.

By three-thirty in the morning Rebecca came to the conclusion that the setup had probably been arranged by Brattini himself. The perceived conflict of interest would reflect not only on her but on Santino as well, and that would make Brattini very happy. It would be a great opportunity for Brattini to stick a knife into Santino while playing the innocent victim.

By four o'clock she decided that her first assumption had been wrong. Someone else, someone with close ties to Brattini, must have set this up before realizing that exposing her involvement would also expose Brattini's. This would then damage his plans for the site even more, especially in light of the rumors concerning a joint FBI–RCMP task force investigation of organized crime.

Brattini's reputation as a mobster and ruthless land developer had always kept him out of certain quarters and he resented it. Adding to his undesirability was the fact that the media, both in Ontario and in New York, were always writing "background pieces" on his empire, reporting, as best they could within the slander and libel laws, all the allegations of brutality credited to him. If any of the media found out that Brattini had a piece of this deal, even from the opposite end, it would be blown sky-high. They'd come crawling all over the place, looking for a story, a scandal, anything they could use to create some headlines. The politicians would then run for cover, and the whole deal would be off. Any media scrutiny was usually the kiss of death in a development deal.

So which of Brattini's friends was it? she wondered. Was there someone in the Peartree group who was in his pocket? Had they realized yet that they'd misjudged the situation?

Alex Goldstein? Surely not, unless the Peartree land was so heavily mort-gaged that they were in trouble and the mortgagor was a dummy compa-ny fronted by lawyers.

Possible, Rebecca thought. She knew how the Italians usually structured their moneylending operations. Offshore numbered companies. She'd bet-ter have it checked out as soon as possible.

What about Bob "Bingo" DeSalle? He was so political, so well con-nected, so powerful, and so rich that it wasn't likely he needed anyone like Brattini.

The senator? No way! He had alerted her in enough time to try and sal-vage the situation before Santino learned about it himself.

What about Sir John Mecklinger? As chairman of a major government-funded investment corporation, he wouldn't dare be in the pocket of some-one like Brattini.

Why not? she then asked herself. The chances of anyone finding out were minuscule. But knowing Sir John, she found it hard to believe. He had been knighted by the Queen herself. Born in London, England, he had been raised to view all "foreigners" as fit only for servitude. And Italians were only one level above Jews as far as he was concerned.

"But, of course," he would then go on to say, "some of my best friends are Jews."

When it came to business, religious biases meant nothing, which is why Sir John's prejudices had been overlooked. It was the price and the profit potential that dictated how deep one's convictions ran. It didn't matter to Goldstein or others like him whether they or their religion were liked or respected. And neither did it matter to her. It was business, pure and sim-ple. Whoever could do the job was the person retained. It was another of the lessons Santino had stressed.

"So what if they call you a dirty Jew or a dumb Wop behind your back?" he'd say. "Closing the deal and visiting the bank is the best revenge. Then you have the last laugh."

Most of the time the intolerance worked both ways. The Jews would cut up the *goyim* as much as they themselves were cut up by their colleagues.

The Italians would refer to WASPs as "whitebreads," or "*mangi-cakes*," ridiculing them for being insipid and gutless.

Sir John had spent most of his adult years as a career diplomat with the Department of External Affairs. His appointment to his present position was a reward for his years of service. Sir John was also a homosexual, although his discretion kept the fact a secret from most people.

But what if Brattini's people had found out and were blackmailing him? He'd be immediately ostracized from the social world in which he now traveled. How important was it to him? Or was it simply a matter of money? Maybe he hadn't invested wisely over the years, or maybe he was just worried about getting older with very little financial security.

Rebecca had always got as much "insider" information on her associates as possible. One of the lessons she'd picked up from Santino's operation. It was better to know in advance what might be a problem down the road and be prepared for it than to be caught unprepared if something unpleasant surfaced.

For this kind of "research" she'd used Vinnie Bratuso, DeLuca's "minister of information." Santino had encouraged her to make use of all his resources before she got too involved with any project or person. In this way she would be aware of the skeletons living in the various closets around town.

But she daren't use Vinnie now unless she "confessed" to Santino first. So she decided to do just that. She'd speak to him at the gala next week and make arrangements for them to get together.

In the meantime she knew she had better get as many facts as she could on the Peartree–Millersgrove–CanMor dynamics before she had to face Santino. She hoped he would forgive her impulsiveness and perhaps then, they could develop a strategy together, as they did so often with his own projects.

Maybe I can salvage something from this fiasco, she told herself as the sun was coming up.

# 8

## MARCH
## 1975

*T*he black-tie gala fundraiser for the bal-
let was spectacular. Over 500 people had paid $250 a piece to attend. The
O'Keefe Centre lobby was decorated with hundreds of yards of cream silk
organza draped with magnificent tassels, and interspersed with rows of
tiny lighted bulbs, giving the place the appearance of a fairy-tale castle.

As Rebecca and Steven were getting dressed for the evening, Lisa had
sat on their king-size bed, watching them and asking to try on some make-
up and jewelry. Both parents delighted in their little girl, and her presence
eliminated any awkward silences between them.

When Rebecca had finished dressing, she was rewarded by Steven's reaction. She was wearing a black silk suit. The skirt came down to her ankles
and had a thigh-high slit up one side. The double-breasted jacket, which
had a deep V neckline that showed off her luscious cleavage, was embroi-
dered with off-white seed pearls. She wore the diamond and black pearl
choker that Steven had given her for their last anniversary.

Her hair was piled on top of her head with wisps of ringlets around
her ears. "You look like a Victorian portrait," he had told her.

Those in attendance that evening included the prime minister of Canada
and his wife; the governor of Michigan, who was in town for an economic
conference, and his wife; several Ontario mayors, including Howard Brennan

of Toronto; several cabinet ministers; and assorted politicians of all stripes.

Very evident by their presence were Mayor Lois Richardson and the town council of Greenfield, along with their guests. Richardson, wearing a black lace dress and silver shoes, must have gone to a new hairdresser. Her once-gray, curly hair was now blue-white. Don't be a bitch, Rebecca reminded herself as she struggled not to burst out laughing when she looked at her.

Sir John hovered around the Greenfield group, and it was obvious from the way Mayor Richardson fawned over him that things were going well.

Rebecca began to drift through the crowd, to see what little groups were forming. She prayed nothing would go wrong. True, she felt good, self-confident, but she also felt tight. She had all the political nuances to think about, she had to tell Santino everything, and, to top it all off, she was going to be meeting Santino's wife Elizabeth for the first time. She wondered if her erotic thoughts about Santino would ease up once she came face to face with the woman who shared his bed. Strangely, that question vied equally with another in her thoughts: Who is my enemy?

Since Massimo Brattini and his wife were also scheduled to attend the gala, she was hoping that when she looked directly into his eyes, the truth would be evident. You've been reading too many bad novels, she told herself. Though she'd met Brattini only two or three times over the years, she knew he was like stone. He never showed any emotion other than suppressed hostility toward everyone. She suspected that something, or someone, must have hurt him very badly to make him so cold and unresponsive.

Finally she went over to join Sir John Mecklinger standing inside the main entrance of the lobby, ready to greet the VIP guests personally.

When Michael Covan, Minister of Housing, arrived with his wife, they both greeted Rebecca with air kisses and phony compliments. Covan, a notorious womanizer, had been caught on more than one occasion entertaining other women. It was hard for Rebecca to visualize because he had a pot belly and wore a hairpiece. He looked like a caricature of W. C. Fields. But he was a powerful member of the cabinet and, as well, had inherited a fortune from his late parents.

Money and power — that did it every time.

Covan's wife Marion was as tall and thin as he was rotund. And she couldn't have cared less about his infidelities. She was a known lesbian, involved in a torrid affair with the wife of the president of the civil service union. Which is why none of this juicy dirt was ever played up publicly. The politicians remembered what had happened to Big Dick Studley, and the union executive couldn't afford to have any scandals stain their holier-than-thou public stance.

Rebecca whispered to Covan that she had some "business" to discuss with him. Another word for "consulting fee."

"Lunch next week," he suggested. Winking, he added, "Let's make it Friday."

That would be after next week's city task force meeting in Mayor Brennan's office, she noted.

Her eye caught Senator and Mrs. Jack Jacobs approaching her. "Why, Rebecca, you look so gorgeous," Charlene Jacobs purred, her eyes never leaving Rebecca's throat. "I have a necklace at home that looks just like yours. I got it in a flea market down in Florida."

"How nice for you. As for me, I prefer to be in the company of the real thing."

Charlene's nose twitched ever so slightly. She didn't like being outcatted.

Rebecca gave the senator a hug and whispered her thanks to him for the information on CanMor.

At that moment the arrival of Mr. and Mrs. Massimo Brattini, in the company of Bob DeSalle, caused a stir among those members of the press who were not in the bar. He had never attended a charity event such as this before and rarely appeared in public with his wife.

Brattini was fifty years old, well over six feet tall, with black hair and a fair complexion. He wore rimless glasses that exaggerated his gray eyes.

Donna Salerno Brattini was a short, stocky woman. Though she was thirty-nine years old, she looked ten years older, thanks to her hair and the extra pounds she carried. Her complexion was too dark for her yellow-blond hair. Rebecca thought she needed a better hairdresser. Or did Donna do it herself?

Obviously Mrs. Brattini was delighted to be at the gala. She kept smiling and saying hello to everyone, most of whom she had never met. Her smile could light a thousand rooms, and Rebecca liked her immediately. It was obvious from her excitement that she rarely got to attend social events, and didn't want to miss any of it. She kept turning her head to watch people as they walked by.

Rebecca was amused to see "Bingo" leaning over to whisper in Mrs. Brattini's ear the names of the various VIPs while her husband glowered at her and tried to steer her over to a corner where they wouldn't be noticed.

When Rebecca finally walked over to greet them, Brattini gave her an icy stare. Oh nuts, she thought. He must know. If looks could kill . . .

Rebecca took his wife's arm and asked if she'd mind helping her straighten out the guest cards for the post-ballet party. Donna's appreciation and delight at being asked to help made Rebecca feel terrific — even though she sensed Brattini's eyes boring into her back. Too bad Donna's stuck with that creep; she seems like a warm and loving woman, Rebecca thought as she led her over to the volunteer table and introduced her to some of the committee members, who were being organized by Ruth Feld.

"Ruth will take care of you, Mrs. Brattini," Rebecca said. "She's invaluable to me, and the rest of the committee as well."

As she turned around she came face to face with Massimo Brattini.

"There's an old Arab proverb," he said quietly under his breath. "'Choose your enemies carefully, for they are the people you will most resemble.'" Then he turned and walked away.

Rebecca stood still, letting her eyes follow him while she tried to regain her composure. Then she heard Santino's voice.

"Hello, Rebecca."

As she turned to face Mr. and Mrs. Santino DeLuca, she took a deep breath and smiled.

"I'd like you to meet my wife Elizabeth," Santino said.

Whatever she had hoped for, Elizabeth wasn't it. The woman was stunning. There was no other word to describe her.

She must be twenty pounds lighter than I am, Rebecca thought glumly, and vowed to go on a diet the next day. Elizabeth Santino was also a little taller. She had the most compelling green eyes Rebecca had ever seen.

She wore her ash-blond hair in a chignon at the back of her head. She was dressed in a white lace blouse and a full, satin floor-length skirt. Around her neck was a magnificent cameo hanging from a diamond chain.

She had an elegance that no amount of money could buy. It was the kind of innate class with which old-time WASPs like Sir John were born. And Elizabeth DeLuca had it in spades.

Suddenly Rebecca felt awkward and unsure of herself, just as she had when she was a child.

"Santino speaks of you often," Elizabeth said, her smile warm and her voice friendly. "I've been looking forward to meeting you for so long."

The three of them made small talk before the DeLucas moved on to socialize with other guests. The governor of Michigan made a beeline for Santino and stayed next to him most of the evening.

Rebecca felt as if she had a knot in the pit of her stomach. Let's face it, I'm jealous, she lectured herself. Then she straightened her shoulders and forced herself to mingle with other new arrivals. I still have things to see to, she kept telling herself.

With the arrival of the prime minister and his wife the evening festivities got under way. After the ballet performance a sumptuous midnight supper was offered to the major contributors in the downstairs lounge. Rebecca was pleased to see how happy Donna Brattini appeared to be as she moved around the room as part of the volunteer committee. She also noticed how Bob DeSalle seemed to be hovering close to Mrs. Brattini, and wondered why. She certainly wasn't his type, she thought.

Rebecca didn't get an opportunity to speak to Santino alone until the evening was almost over. Every time she looked over at him, he and his wife were talking to other guests, including Steven, who was accustomed to fending for himself at these kinds of functions and actually enjoyed it. "I get to meet lots of interesting people and catch up on the local gossip," he would tell Rebecca. "I don't have to concentrate too hard when I'm listening to those snobs bullshitting each other. It's like sleeping on your feet."

When Rebecca saw Elizabeth go to the ladies' room, she approached DeLuca.

"Santino, I have something important to discuss with you," she said, looking into his eyes and hoping the beating of her heart couldn't be heard.

"You're exquisite tonight," he whispered to her, that wonderful smile of his crinkling his eyes. "What can I do for you?"

"We can't talk here, and I don't want to talk in the office," she said. "Let's have lunch, just the two of us."

His eyes narrowed a little. "I'm leaving for Detroit tomorrow," he said. "I'll be gone for two weeks. Can't it wait till I come back?"

Rebecca's eyes filled with tears. Santino took her arm.

"*Bella*, what is it?" he asked, his voice full of concern. When she couldn't answer, he said, "You know what, I'll call you tomorrow afternoon at the office and we'll arrange something."

Why do I feel like such a shit? she thought as Santino turned, saw Elizabeth return, and walked back to join her. I almost started to cry, right here in the middle of the gala.

But she hung on his words, "We'll arrange something."

*R*ebecca spent the next day in her office, finding out all she could about those involved in Greenfield. She made a call to Bermuda, using her own network to trace the Bank of Nova Scotia branch that CanMor had used. When she got the manager on the phone, she identified herself as an investigator with their head office in Toronto.

"Revenue Canada is on our backs," she'd said in her most officious tone. "They're investigating someone they say has been funnelling profits from a Canadian company into one operating out of your branch in Bermuda. They say that no withholding taxes have been paid and they're threatening to put the screws to us up here if we don't cooperate."

"Which company is it?" he asked.

"CanMor Corporation."

"Oh baby!" he whistled. "That's strictly off limits. I've got a red tag on it from the governor of the Bank of Canada himself. You'll have to clear anything you want on this account through him. Do you want me to alert him that you'll be calling?"

"No thanks," she answered. "I'll take care of it from here."

Then Rebecca called her own bank manager at Western Trust.

"I need to know if there's a mortgage or an outstanding loan on a development company's property outside Toronto. And if there is, who holds the paper? And if it's a numbered company, where was it incorporated and which law firm was used?"

He was about to speak when she continued: "Before you start yelling at me to get an investigator, this is very confidential stuff. And as my favorite bank manager, the one who not only uses my money to earn interest for his shareholders but, to some extent, used the trust that I control, along with my husband's money and all his companies, I know you want to save me time and trouble."

"Ah, Rebecca, you're so subtle. Okay. I'll see what I can find out."

When he called her back, less than two hours later, she was stunned by what he told her. CanMor had been the owners of the property next to Peartree, the one that Alex Goldstein had recently bought. But there was no clue yet as to who was behind the numbered company that owned CanMor. He said he'd keep trying and let her know if he found anything more out.

Oh God, Rebecca thought. CanMor has covered both sides of the town — both sides of the fence — both ends of the deck, and who knows what else.

As Rebecca was mulling over all of this, she got a call from Santino's office. Arrangements had been made for her to fly to Detroit the next morning. Someone would meet her at the airport.

*W*hen Rebecca's plane landed in Detroit, Jimmy Bono was at the airport to pick her up. Even though the DeLucas had moved their residence to Canada, Santino still spent one week a month in Detroit overseeing his business operations there, and Jimmy Bono always accompanied him.

"The boss got tied up in a meeting," he said. "He wants me to drive you around and show you some of our projects. He'll meet you at the apartment around five o'clock. You're having dinner at Franco's — a new steakhouse he's got a piece of."

The tour was impressive. She noticed that every construction site had a different company listed as the owner, presumably for political reasons. The American media, which loved to go after "big, bad developers," had already crucified some of Santino's associates who controlled several mega-projects in New York. So each of DeLuca Industries' U.S. projects was incorporated separately, traceable only to their lawyers, Walker & Associates.

"The less attention we bring on ourselves, the better," Santino always said.

Rebecca asked Jimmy to drop her off at the apartment at four o'clock so she could relax and collect her thoughts before she had to face Santino. She also wanted to check out whether or not Elizabeth was a resident there. She knew enough about "the games people play" to realize that he would never make love to her in the same place his wife stayed.

She snooped over every inch of the one-bedroom apartment. There were no scents or feminine hygiene products or lotions. There were no cleaning utensils, no detergents, no dishwasher soap — nothing. Only a man could live without cleaning in between the visits of the domestic help, she thought. He probably used one of the professional cleaning services, she thought.

The apartment was beautifully furnished, but it looked more like a hotel than a home. The only clothes in the closets and the bureau drawers belonged to Santino.

She was about to take a bath when she heard the key in the door.

"Shall I make us a drink?" he called from the living room.

"I'll have a bloody Caesar," she answered, and turned on the water taps. "Spicy, please."

When she came out of the bathroom wearing his heavy velour bathrobe, his eyes ran up and down her as he smiled and handed her a glass.

"Santino, I have to tell you something, right now!" she said, gulping down half the drink. "And when I'm finished, if you want me to leave, I will. And then I'll turn over everything from the trust to whomever you want, whenever you want."

His expression didn't change. He just indicated the sofa and she sat down. For close to an hour Rebecca told Santino everything about Peartree and her involvement in it.

She admitted that she'd only recently learned that Alex Goldstein was heavily in debt to a numbered Ontario company on which she was trying to get more information. She left out nothing, including her assessments of her associates in the Peartree deal. Finally she outlined everything she had done, and everyone she had spoken to, in an attempt to get more inside information on CanMor.

His face was a mask as she spoke, neither angry nor sad. He just listened.

"Santino," she went on, "I only wanted to test my wings. I'm tired of spending my whole life financially dependent on someone else. The best skill I have is what I've been doing as a volunteer all these years.

"I just wasn't comfortable taking a fee for administering the trust, even though we'd discussed it in the beginning."

She finished her drink and waited in silence as he made her and himself another. He still said nothing.

"I wanted my relationship with you to be different from the kind you've had with others," she told him. "I wanted to achieve success in your world on my own first, and then come and tell you what I'd done and wait for you to be proud, knowing that everything you'd taught me wasn't wasted.

"But, now I see that I wasn't ready." Her voice was starting to break, but she went on. "I was a dupe, a jerk. I couldn't see the forest for the trees. I wanted to succeed so much that I forgot the most important lesson of all: 'Never believe your own press clippings.'

"Santino, please forgive me," she whispered. "And, please, don't ever think that I knowingly betrayed your trust. I've loved you from the first moment I saw you."

And then she did break down and began to cry. When Santino didn't speak, didn't get up and try to comfort her, she knew it was over. In a few minutes her tears and her shaking stopped. Okay, she thought. That's it. Lift your head, get your clothes, and walk out of here like a lady.

She started to get up.

"Sit down," Santino said. "How did you find out that CanMor was owned by Brattini?"

"The senator told me."

"That wasn't my question. I said, how did *you* find out that CanMor was owned by Brattini?"

She looked up at him. His eyes were boring into hers. And then the light went on. She had assumed that Jacobs was telling her the truth, or at least the truth as he knew it. She hadn't considered the possibility that perhaps someone had given him false information and that he had simply accepted it and passed it along, just as she had done.

Or maybe the senator had misled her on purpose. It was certainly possible. But why? For kicks? For revenge? To appease his wife?

But she was supposed to know better. She was supposed to have learned a long time ago that you never take anything at face value. "Make sure for yourself in all things to do with business," she'd been told in the past, not only by Santino, but by her first boss, William Jackson. "If you didn't see it, or hear it, or prove it for yourself, then don't accept it as truth."

There was nothing more she could say to Santino. She stared down at her hands, not wanting to look in his face for fear she'd start crying again. She'd blown it.

"If you hadn't been so anxious, so impatient, and then so full of guilt," he said, his voice very controlled, "I'm sure you would have stopped and asked the right questions before you got into this."

She nodded silently and he went on. "But now that you're into it so deeply, finish the job!"

For a long moment there was silence.

"Now," he continued as he got up out of his chair, "let's discuss the rest of your confession. I liked that part much better."

He walked over to her and pulled her up. He grabbed her shoulders and pulled her close. As his mouth reached down for hers, he whispered, "I've wanted you for so long, I can't wait any longer."

His mouth covered hers, their lips finally pressed together, their tongues mingling.

Santino was very strong. She could tell by the way he held her and moved his hands up and down her back that he would be overpowering if he ever lost control. A long shiver ran through her whole body.

As his lips moved down to her neck, he undid the belt of the robe and pulled it open. His eyes roamed over her body very slowly, his hands caressing her breasts and upper thighs as he stared.

Her nipples were already hard, standing out from the tips of her breasts, and she could feel her insides churning.

"Come into the other room," he said, his voice strained. "I have some things to teach you."

When they were next to the bed, he pulled her robe off. Then his lips returned to hers as his hands reached for her breasts again. She arched her back as he kneaded her nipples between his thumb and forefinger.

She put her arms around his neck, and when she pushed her body hard against his, she could feel his erection. Then Santino lowered her onto the bed, his breathing much heavier and his kisses more passionate.

He started sucking on her skin, his lips traveling all over her body. She sat up and ran her hands through his long hair and then leaned over to run her lips over his chest which was covered with black hair.

When Santino slipped his fingers inside her, it felt like a series of hot shocks, and she began to writhe around on his fingers, chasing a sensation she'd never felt. His kisses increased in intensity, and when he started flicking her clitoris with his thumb, she gave herself up to the sensations that overwhelmed her.

And soon nothing mattered any more. Just being with him — to touch him, to have him in her hands, in her mouth, and inside her body — was all she wanted. She reached over to take him between both her hands, but when she leaned over to take him in her mouth, he stopped her.

"Slow down," he whispered. "I'm the one who leads in this dance. And I want to enjoy you a lot more before I come."

"But everything feels so good that I don't want to stop. Can't you rest afterward and then we'll do it again?"

Santino burst out laughing. "This is the craziest seduction I've ever been party to. If this were a movie, the audience would be booing. Now shut up!"

He gently pushed her back down. His mouth moved slowly down her body, kissing, and nibbling as he went. When his lips and then his tongue reached her most private places, she cried out.

"Santino! I don't want you to ever stop!"

Her body started to shake as spasms ran through her. Her cries soon turned into moans of unparalleled pleasure. When she opened her eyes and looked up at him, she said, "I knew you'd be the one. You were worth waiting for."

He mounted her, his hands clutching her buttocks as he thrust his penis into her deepest crevices, whispering, "*Ti'amo, bella, ti'amo,*" as he reached his climax.

For the next two hours they made passionate love. Santino was over-powering, using her body as though it had been made only for him. She experienced the most delicious sensations as he introduced her to new positions and brought her to ever-more intense orgasms.

When they were finally resting in each others' arms, Rebecca dozed off. When she awoke, Santino was raised on one elbow, looking at her lovingly as he stroked her hair.

"You and I have a chemistry between us," he said, leaning over to kiss her gently on the lips. "We've had it from the first moment we looked at each other in that hospital boardroom. I thought I knew exactly what I wanted in this life. But now I'm not so sure."

His face was serious as he looked into her eyes. "I have no intention of getting into the typical kind of conversations that lovers who are married to others do in order to justify their adultery. And I won't rationalize what I'm doing with you by putting the onus on my wife. I love her, and I love my family. And, until you, there's never been anyone else."

"Santino, I've never really been in love before, and until you, I've never even had an orgasm. My life has followed a pattern that was set generations ago. And now I can see that it isn't enough, at least not for me."

"And?" he asked as he gently touched her cheek.

"I'm going to break the pattern. I've been thinking about this for a long time, even before you and I met. I don't think I was ever meant to be married. Steve is a kind and generous man, but he's getting shortchanged — and so is Lisa.

"As for you and me, well, I only care about the time we can spend together. So, for as long as it lasts, let's enjoy each other."

He began to massage her neck as she spoke. When his hands started slipping between her legs again, she gave him a few playful punches.

"Whose idea was it to rest in between?" she laughed as she jumped out of bed to turn on the Jacuzzi, her insides sore.

"Yours," he answered, following her out of bed, his bathrobe barely covering his erection.

As Rebecca eased herself into the tub, the feel of the warm water streaming over her body from the side jets was wonderful. She lowered her head against the backrest, closed her eyes, and lifted one leg over the side so that the water could rush between her legs.

When she opened her eyes, Santino was standing next to the tub, staring down at her. She was still sore from the intensity of his thrusts into her body, and was hoping that the warm water pulsing inside her would ease the aching.

Slowly she slid a hand up his leg toward the erection that was pushing open his robe. She put one of her hands around the back of his buttocks and pulled his robe off with the other.

When she took him deep into her mouth, he started to moan, and tried to reach down to lift her out of the tub. The feel of the warm water inside her was too soothing, and she pushed his hands away.

She got on her knees, the water foaming around her up to her hips, and, using her tongue on the tip to get around the folds of his foreskin, pushed him deeper into her mouth with the pressure of her hands. He had to hold on to the wall to keep from falling.

Rebecca was amazed at how many times a man Santino's age could come in a two-hour period. She wondered why some women never appreciated the extraordinary joy of giving singular pleasure to someone you loved. And the power it gave you.

# *9*

NOVEMBER
1976

*I*t's time to put my life back together, Rebecca thought as she drove to her office. So much had happened over the last few months that she felt she'd been in the center of a maelstrom.

The confrontation with Steven wasn't as bad as she had anticipated. He'd realized by the determination in her voice that divorce was inevitable. And she thought he had been secretly relieved. No more pretense, no more lies.

They'd agreed on settlement terms, including his unlimited access to Lisa. Rebecca kept the house and her car and Steve would pay their upkeep for five years, along with $3,000 a month in child support payments until Lisa reached eighteen. In addition, he gave Rebecca $100,000 in bonds in exchange for a waiver on any future claims to his assets.

When it was all over she was surprised at how sad she felt — not for Steven but for herself. I'm a driven woman, she admitted. I don't think I'll ever find any peace. Why couldn't I have been happy with the simpler things in life?

But she resolved to put the past behind her, and began concentrating on closing the Peartree deal. She met with the key political figures necessary for its final approval, and as she turned into her parking garage, she decided it was time to meet with Lois Richardson again and find out exactly what the dear lady wanted. Within the hour she had made all the arrangements.

Centro, one of Toronto's best and most popular spots for dinner, was selected. The food was exquisite, the wines even better, and the large, open space would allow for the kind of conversation Rebecca intended to have with Her Worship. No one watching the group, which included Bingo DeSalle and Jack Jacobs, would ever suspect what they were really discussing. After all, who arranged payoffs and kickbacks in the midst of Toronto's rich and famous, those who liked to see as well as be seen?

She turned away from the telephone and smiled to herself. Things were moving along, and she was following Santino's advice to finish what she had started.

Michael Covan, the Minister of Housing, wanted $5,000 in small bills, to recommend to the cabinet that part of the Peartree site be approved for co-op housing, a necessary requirement in order to have the land rezoned residential.

The money had been delivered to his home in a florist's box containing two dozen long-stemmed roses addressed to his wife. The enclosed card read, "Happy Birthday, from your loving husband."

Unfortunately for Covan, Marion was home at the time and had opened the box. Rebecca felt a certain grim satisfaction when Covan complained that he had to split the money with his wife or she would have kept it all.

The Greenfield town council, led by Mayor Richardson, were poised to amend the bylaws and rezone the Peartree land from agriculture to commercial–residential. They were also prepared to remove Peartree from the short list of dump sites.

Rebecca could only guess at what Richardson had been forced to tell the CanMor group to justify her "change of heart." She smiled to herself. Perhaps she would find out at dinner tonight.

Centro boasted snow white tablecloths, candles, and fresh flowers as well as an incredible menu. And, she thought, it smelled as good as it looked.

Dinner was accompanied by wines from northern Italy selected by the restaurant owner, and by the time dessert and coffee were served, along with the grappa, six bottles of wine had been consumed.

"What do I dream of?" Lois Richardson mused. It was her way of letting it be known to those present, not so subtly, what she wanted for her cooperation. "I dream of a new house, complete with an indoor pool." She smiled and lowered her voice, "But I don't want one tiny little piece of documentation tying me to the Goldstein–Peartree group in any way."

"Leave it with me," Rebecca said. At last the woman had spit it out.

They all went on talking, but Lois Richardson's dream confession was the reason for dinner, and so after that most of the conversation was just meaningless.

*I*t was nearly Christmas and outside a gentle snow was falling, the first of the 1976 season. Rebecca ducked into City Hall and proceeded downstairs. Bingo DeSalle was meeting her for coffee before the meeting of the city task force.

He waved to her across the empty room. "Over here!"

"I love it here after hours," she said.

"Not a soul around," he replied, pulling out a chair for her. "Here, I got two pots when I bought mine. Do you want a snack or anything?"

She shook her head.

They weren't friends. No one was really DeSalle's friend, but she enjoyed discussing strategy with him, especially when she was dealing with municipal politicians, usually referred to as the "lowest of the low."

City task force meetings, which both of them attended, were standard fare for the *quid pro quo* deals that were needed to keep the wheels of government greased and running smoothly.

The matter of Lois Richardson had been settled in a matter of months. And within six months the whole Peartree project was now on track.

After her lengthy discussion with Alex Goldstein and the senator, it was agreed that a numbered company would be set up to build a new home for Richardson as soon as she listed her present home for sale.

As "luck" would have it, one of Alex Goldstein's cousins was in the market for a home just like the one Lois was selling, and the sale could be handled privately.

The proceeds, $75,000, along with $50,000 from a mortgage that had been arranged through a friendly trust company, would cover the purchase price of her new home without raising any eyebrows. The documents in the registry office would list the construction costs as $125,000, even though the actual costs were closer to $300,000.

Goldstein had downgraded everything on the building plans. He wanted to make sure that no overzealous reporter who might be looking for a story would find anything. It would have taken an experienced assessor to spot the fact that the quality of the house actually built for Mayor Richardson far exceeded the specs shown in the plans.

"I must say, it's a pleasure to deal with you," the mayor told Rebecca after all the details had been worked out. "You don't leave anything to chance, do you?"

The rest of the town councilors were happy with two-week holidays, all expenses paid, with their families. Three went to Florida and two went to Hawaii. An envelope containing $1,500 in cash was delivered to each of them the night before they left.

All travel and accommodation arrangements were made through the Siena Travel Agency, owned by City of Toronto councilman, Maxwell Gallow. His company earned over $200,000 a year arranging these kinds of discreet trips for politicians and bureaucrats. It was a double benefit for those using his services — they were paying him off at the same time as the others.

But the payoffs were only a part of a successful project like Peartree.

Without quality in design, along with tangible benefits for the community and the people who were to live there, the press would crucify those making the political decisions. Attention might then begin to focus on how and why the politicians, advised by their bureaucrats, came to their conclusions. Those kinds of questions might be followed by investigative reporting and the risk of exposure.

So it was critical that there be substance in projects such as Peartree. And that substance had to include quality construction, affordable housing, access to recreational facilities, easy public transportation, and most of all, jobs.

Rebecca knew she had become an expert in how to balance the

politics with the substance in order to make the mega-projects palatable to the public and salable to the bureaucrats who controlled the politicians.

But not as expert as Bob "Bingo" DeSalle, with whom she now shared a pre-meeting coffee.

Since the first time they'd met at the beginning of the Peartree project, she had really come to enjoy Bingo's company. He was a personable liar who told more funny stories than anyone she knew. Sometimes he kept her laughing as he recounted some of his escapades with the politicians and bureaucrats in his stable of contacts. It was good to laugh with DeSalle and, she suspected, dangerous to laugh at him.

"Rebecca, do you remember old Jake Davos?" he asked her. "You know the city alderman who represented Little Greece?"

"Yes," she answered. "I met him once at a City Hall reception. He looked as if he weighed close to 300 pounds. Didn't he die in his office?"

"Not exactly," Bingo replied, starting to chuckle. "He died in the saddle." And then he laughed so hard he doubled up.

"Come on, Bingo," Rebecca said. "At least tell me what's so funny."

"Well, Davos would never vote for any developer's project unless he got a case of Crown Royal and two hours with a young blond prostitute. The last time we needed his vote, three of us had to lift him up on top of the girl because he'd got so fat, and that's when the dear man met his Maker."

Rebecca wrinkled her nose in disdain as Bingo continued laughing. "Very funny, Bingo," she said sarcastically. "You guys sell out for so little."

"Come on, Rebecca," he answered, still snickering. "Don't be so up tight. Some guys got it, and some guys got to buy it. That's the way it is. Besides, I'll bet there's plenty of women who pay for young lovers, too. You just don't know any . . . yet."

She studied his expression, trying to see behind it. He was an enigma. Cold eyes, warm conversation. Black and white. She enjoyed him, but she didn't trust him.

DeSalle sometimes talked about his personal life, but only superficially. He told her that he'd had a sister, but that both his sister and his parents had passed away many years earlier.

"I've really never had a family life," he had confessed, "so I don't know what I'm missing. But I'm used to being a loner, and, to tell you the truth, I like it. When I see some of my associates' problems with their elderly parents, I'm glad it's not me."

She asked him about his social life, noting how many different women he always had on his arm.

"Now, Bingo," she'd said, "as the consummate Jewish mother, I need to know what your plans are for marriage. Or at least which of the gorgeous young creatures I always see hovering around you have caught your fancy."

"All of them," he'd told her. "I like variety. But I'm not interested in marriage or children. End of discussion."

Rebecca suspected that Bingo might have some sexual hang-up or maybe just kinky taste. But it didn't matter to her because they were only acquaintances, mutually cynical.

In business, if Bingo promised it, it always happened, no matter what "it" was. In the past few months she had often marveled at his access to those people who really had the power to implement the promises that were made, including officials in the United States who could speed up or delay waivers, visitors' permits, and construction materials not always available in Canada. Many corporate executives counted on Bingo, too. Cash earmarked for Brennan, Covan, or any other senior politicians needed for key votes was usually passed through DeSalle.

When Rebecca had asked him if he wasn't in danger of being "an accessory before, during, and after the fact," he'd smiled and answered, "That's my best protection. If they try to renege or shaft me, I've got the goods on them. Believe me, it's worse to receive than to give."

"Still drinking coffee? It's time to go upstairs for the evening's entertainment," Brad Ross said cheerfully as he approached their table in the corner. He was carrying a coffee to go. Brad was a city accountant and he *was* Rebecca's friend.

Both she and Bob DeSalle stood up. "Into the lion's den," she said cheerfully.

They reached the inner sanctum by way of the silent high-speed elevator. Inside the quiet wood-paneled boardroom were Toronto councilors, among whom were Jim Hollis and Louise Cornwall. In addition, Sir John Mecklinger, Senator Jack Jacobs, and former cabinet minister Richard Dudley were present. Dudley had become a political consultant hoping to earn some big bucks and keep his fingers in all the pots until he took another run at public office.

Brad Ross pulled out a chair for Rebecca and then sat down next to her. He was present to monitor any budget considerations for the taxpayers. The two of them often had coffee together and almost always he bought her drinks after meetings. She had even had him over for dinner. Brad was an all-around nice guy, one of those men she judged too good to be true. The complete opposite of DeSalle.

The two politicians on the task force, Hollis and Cornwall, were also members of the "party" in power and, as such, carried on their tradition of selective hypocrisy. They had no problem accepting perks from these "corrupt and evil robber barons" sitting on the committees with them, even though they would regularly castigate them in the media and pretend to have no dealings with them.

Land-rezoning deals, programs that involved enticing international corporations to invest in the province so that hundreds of jobs would be created, and anything else that needed the recommendation of the task force before the government would approve them, were usually held up until the two of them, Hollis and Cornwall, got their "fee for service."

Jim Hollis was trying to get Oliver, his live-in boyfriend, appointed to the Police Commission, and wanted City of Toronto Mayor Brennan to make the recommendation.

"The cops love to beat up on my friends," he complained.

"Gee, I wonder why?" Brennan snapped. "Maybe they don't think it's proper for youngsters to see men getting off on each other in public parks."

Then Brennan turned to Rebecca and Louise and said, "Oh, excuse me, ladies, but I'm getting sick of this faggot and his friends trying to legitimize their perversions."

Cornwall then piped up. "I think Jim has a point, Mr. Mayor. We can

*127*

at least apply some pressure to the commission to reprimand any police officer suspected of beating up on someone because of his sexual orientation."

"Hear, hear," Dudley said. "Sex between consenting adults should be
allowed, no matter what their preference."

"What about sex between adults and consenting dogs?" Sir John mumbled. Until now he had been silent. Although he himself was a homosexual, he believed sex should be enjoyed in the privacy of a bedroom, not public
places.

Dudley shot him a dirty look while the senator continued to stare out
the window.

Then Louise Cornwall insisted that Arnold, her live-in boyfriend, cur-
rently unemployed and on probation for smuggling illegal immigrants
into the country, be appointed vice-chairman of the board of the Housing
Corporation. The per-diem salary for its executive board members was $175
for the days that the board was considered in session. That translated into
$50,000 a year.

The Housing Corporation was the agency responsible for overseeing the
administration of 75,000 subsidized housing units across the city. The residents were low-income families and single mothers on welfare.

The corporation also tendered out some $15,000,000 in contracts every
year for maintenance and repairs on its buildings. It didn't take a rocket
scientist to figure out just how much power and influence the person or per-
sons overseeing the awarding of these contracts could wield.

Rebecca remembered the first time she'd spoken to Jack Jacobs about it.
They'd been out for lunch at his favorite haunt — Abie's Delicatessen, still
in the same downtown location on Spadina Avenue even though it was now
in the heart of Chinatown. Abie's was the last vestige of the once close-knit
Jewish community that had originally settled there forty years earlier but
which had long since moved north. As long as its patriarch and founder,
Abie Rosenbloom, was still active, his sons intended to keep the deli in its
original location.

Jacobs loved it because he could pig out on corned beef on onion
buns, crispy new dills, and french fries with gravy without his wife finding

out. Charlene wouldn't be caught dead in that part of town.

"Charlene would kill me if she ever found out what I'm eating." He'd grasped his bun, trying to keep the corned beef from falling out onto his shirt. Jacobs's bald spot was gleaming with sweat, and his thick glasses were getting steamed up.

When she'd asked him about how rigged tendering worked, he stopped eating to look up at her.

"Perception is everything when dealing with public funds," he'd said. "That's the only thing that matters. And the way it's done is simple. The contractors — electricians, plumbers, landscapers, painters, elevator maintenance people, and the like — get together and divvy up the jobs in advance. For example, electricians A, B, D, and E overbid a job so that C can win it by submitting the lowest bid. Next month one of the others in the group wins out in the same way, and so on. This is the way the game is played for 90 percent of the jobs tendered out.

"But that's not the best part," he'd continued after another bite. "Once the tender price is agreed upon, and the work is under way, a firm can submit a 'request for review.' This means that they can get an increase in their original projected fees by claiming 'unexpected' costs — most of which they knew about before they submitted their original tender. Even if someone in the bureaucracy starts hollering, it is almost impossible to prove 'intent' or 'prior knowledge' in terms of these unexpected costs."

"What happens if a contracting firm doesn't know about the deal, or doesn't want to go along with it?" Rebecca asked, her interest piqued.

"Ah, that's where the staff and key board members come in. Before any firm can even bid on these kinds of jobs, they have to be included on an 'approved' government list of contractors–service-givers. You can bet that any firm that isn't cooperative, appreciative, and discreet will never get on that approved list, which means they could never be considered for a contract."

When Rebecca related her discussion with Jacobs to Santino later that evening, he had added another bit of information.

"Most of those contractors are related to each other, either by blood, marriage, or related companies. There's $15,000,000 a year involved — that's major money. Who but a fool would leave that kind of business to a legitimate public tendering process that had no checks and balances in favor of the insiders?"

Rebecca had wondered out loud to Santino if DeLuca Industries had a piece of any of those "approved" contractors. He had looked at her with a wry smile and said, "Don't worry, we don't do repairs and maintenance. We hire someone from the 'approved' list. It saves me a lot of headaches."

So, when Louise Cornwall suggested that the Housing Corporation's board would be a good place for Arnold, Rebecca's antennae went up.

"If you don't give my Arnold a piece of the pie," Cornwall threatened when Brennan balked, "it'll only be because you're racist. And then I'll have no choice but to give an interview to all the media about some of the discussions that really go on around this table."

Bingo leaned over to Rebecca and whispered, "Blackmail and extortion are what I believe we are witnessing. Where's the Mafia when we need them most?"

The two of them burst out laughing while the rest of the committee appeared ready to acquiesce, white-faced, to Cornwall's blackmail.

Rebecca could stand it no more. "Louise," she said, "don't you think that Arnold is a bit underqualified for this position? And what about conflict of interest? After all, he was convicted of smuggling illegals across the border from Buffalo, and many of those under the aegis of the Housing Corporation could be his former clients."

"You Jews have had it too easy," Louise snapped back angrily. "What do you people know about poverty and abuse and racism?"

"Plenty, as a matter of fact. We also know about working hard and not making a career out of living on the dole," Rebecca retorted, her voice hardening.

"Hey, you bitch," yelled Cornwall, "are you suggesting that my brothers and sisters are lazy welfare bums?"

Before Rebecca could answer "yes," Bingo put his hand on her arm.

"Your comments and threats are beneath a public official," DeSalle said with a certain mock self-righteousness as he turned to Cornwall. "And

I personally find your tone toward Mrs. Sherman offensive. I agree with her that your boyfriend has no place on the housing agency. I suggest he look for a job elsewhere."

Cornwall said nothing more. DeSalle was too powerful a player to confront head on.

Then Bingo looked around at the group. "Come on, let's stop all this bickering. This task force meeting is supposed to discuss ways of attracting new business to the city, so more jobs will be created, along with more housing. When I brief my friends in the government on our progress, I want to be able to encourage their continued support of what we're doing. Besides, if the press ever gets wind of what really goes on at these meetings, it'll be all over but the shouting."

The flare-up was defused.

When they left the meeting later that evening, Rebecca thanked DeSalle for his support.

He responded by playfully jabbing her back.

"You've got more balls than most men I know, Rebecca," he said. "And I'd rather fight next to you than across from you."

# *10*

*JANUARY*
*1980*

*I*t had been eight years since Rebecca Sherman had first met Santino DeLuca, and for the last five she had been his lover. Their desire for each other hadn't abated; in fact, it had grown more intense as time went on.

When Santino was in town they usually spent two evenings a week together having dinner, discussing business, and then making passionate love. On occasion Santino took Rebecca with him when he went out of town, and eventually she became a familiar face among his associates in Bermuda, Detroit, Buffalo, and, on one occasion, Rome and Marseilles.

Rebecca's daughter Lisa was twelve years old. She was aware of her mother's business relationship with Mr. DeLuca and was accustomed to seeing him around the house, sometimes having dinner with them, other times spending hours with her mother on mountains of paperwork. But Santino and Rebecca made certain, on the rare occasions that they did make love in her home, that Lisa was asleep. Most times they went to a suite DeLuca Industries maintained in the Sutton Place hotel.

They were having dinner at Centro; it was January 10, the first time they had been together since before the New Year.

"Happy 1980," she said, looking into his dark eyes. She sensed Santino's disquiet and she reached over and took his hand in hers.

"Considering the excellent financial report I've just given you on the trust," she said, her eyes filled with love and concern, "your enthusiasm is underwhelming."

"I'm really feeling the heat," he said, squeezing her hand. "The FBI keeps trying to infiltrate my U.S. operations and I don't know why."

"Could it have anything to do with the take-down of Brattini's overseas trading?" she asked, her eyes never leaving his.

Santino couldn't camouflage his surprise. He stared at her, saying nothing.

"Oh, come on, darling," she continued softly. "If I'm as sharp as you keep telling me I am, don't you think I'd have picked up a thing or two during the past five years? I'd like to give you my thoughts on some of them. May I?"

Santino still said nothing, but he kept looking at her intently, his face a mask. Rebecca had the sinking feeling that she'd gone too far by dropping her guard and letting him know just how much she'd figured out about his businesses. People had disappeared for less.

Well, he did take me around with him, she thought, fighting her panic. And he had to know that I'd eventually put the pieces together.

After what seemed like an eternity, Santino spoke, his voice cold. "Why don't you tell me your ideas, Rebecca? It will give me a perspective that could prove to be helpful."

"The first thing I think you should do," she answered, relief flooding over her, "is call a truce with Massimo Brattini. As long as the two of you spend so much time trying to undercut each other, you're vulnerable to attack from the outside.

"And I also think you're overextended. Too much, too far-flung, too diverse. Get out of Asia. Let Brattini have it. Expand the offshore holdings and buy into companies that have a vision for the future."

She couldn't tell how he was taking her comments because his expression didn't change and he remained silent. She decided to spit it all out, to finish what she had started.

"The world is changing, Santino. Now is the time for you to build a better base for your sons. The old ways are just that, old. Let Brattini wallow in them. You're too good for that garbage."

"You know what happened to Sal Lata," he answered. "There must be retribution. And there's more than just me involved in these decisions. Luigi Villano started life as a shoemaker's son. He built an empire on the blood and guts of his family and himself. And his father was killed by Gino Salerno's uncle. There can be no forgiveness for that."

"But, Santino, you're not a Villano. And Brattini's not a Salerno, even though he's married to one. And from what I've come to know about Donna Brattini, she isn't one of them either."

"That's where you're mistaken, *bella*," he said, his face finally softening. "We are what we are. Outsiders cannot understand it, which is why, no matter how much pressure is put on us, we ultimately triumph. My fate was sealed thirty-five years ago. And so was Massimo's. There is no leaving. The die is cast."

Rebecca decided to let the matter drop. As they got into the back of Santino's car, she leaned over and put both arms around his neck. "I am as close to being one of you as I would be if I were born to it," she said. "And my loyalty to you, and yours, is as strong as the ties that bind you to your heritage. If you need me, no matter what it is, I'll be there."

Santino didn't answer. He put his hands on her face and pulled her to his lips. As she returned his passionate kiss and pulled him closer, she knew she had crossed over a bridge into a world from which she could never return.

*A*s the plane took off that bright April morning for Boston, Elizabeth DeLuca leaned back in her seat, closed her eyes, and took very deep breaths. She had been in a plane only once before, when she'd left Italy with Santino. Since then they had driven between Buffalo, Detroit, and Toronto. On two occasions they had driven to New York. Santino had traveled to Europe, but she had remained at home, at her own request. The truth was, not only did she not feel comfortable in airplanes, she had a fear of heights, and, on occasion, she suffered from vertigo. But today she was on a plane, and for the first time in her life, she was traveling alone.

This trip had been unplanned. Two days earlier she had lashed out at Santino when he'd announced that he was going on another business trip without her. It seemed that all her fears and insecurities had erupted at the same moment, and she'd said some pretty strong words to him — strong at least for her.

Elizabeth, painful as it was, relived that scene: "I want to be more than just an afterthought to you! Why should I be content with the scraps you throw to me? When was the last time you took me with you to Detroit? Or to New York? You know I love the galleries there, not to mention the theater. And I've never been to Boston."

"I asked if you wanted to go to Europe last year," he countered.

"You know I couldn't leave the twins then. Santino, I'm sick of being the 'little lady' you trot out for show, forced to make small talk with a bunch of glassy-eyed women whose only challenge in life is what to order in for dinner."

"Elizabeth, lower your voice," Santino snapped. "You'll upset the boys if they hear you. Why are you shrieking like this? I've never seen you behave this way. I don't understand why you're so upset. All I suggested were a couple of excursions that you might take with the boys while I'm away. You know I have some business in Boston that has to be taken care of as soon as possible."

And is the ever-present Mrs. Sherman going with you too? she wondered. "Yes, I know," she answered sarcastically. "It's always business. What a convenient rationalization for so many things. And speaking of business, don't you think it's time to reassess some of your questionable involvements, now that we have a family?"

Elizabeth had recently overheard Santino and Jimmy Bono discussing their problems with one of Brattini's top lieutenants and how best to neutralize him. Their conversation had been no different from those she'd been hearing over the last eighteen years.

Santino's face turned gray at her words, and he stared at her, his eyes narrowing.

"Don't look at me like that," Elizabeth said, throwing her head back defiantly. "This isn't Italy. You've got your children's future to worry about. Codes of honor, *omertà*, and the sanctity of women and children are going out the same door the drug trade is coming in. Things aren't the way they once were."

When Santino finally spoke, it was in a whisper.

"Elizabeth, I'm going to ignore what you've just said. You know better than to talk of such things. And what do you mean by implying that I don't worry about you and the children? You're all that matters to me — I'd protect you with my life."

She asked the most important questions silently. And what about your protégée? Would you protect her, too? In spite of her anger, she had been smart enough not to mention Rebecca Sherman. She wasn't ready to open that can of worms yet . . .

Elizabeth looked out of the plane window and thought of how much she loved Santino. But did he still love her? She wasn't so sure. Ever since the boys' birth, the intensity of his passion for her had waned. She sensed that his head was somewhere else. And she feared that the somewhere else was in bed with Rebecca Sherman.

It had been three months since she and Santino had made love. And then it had been more perfunctory than anything else. He had barely touched her, responding to her overtures by simply turning over, running his hands over her breasts and between her legs, and then thrusting himself into her body. The whole exercise was over in five minutes.

Elizabeth didn't know how to handle the situation. She understood that Santino was a man steeped in Italian customs and traditions. Wives had clearly defined roles: mother, housekeeper, cook, and occasional sex partner. Most of the men in Santino's circle kept mistresses — it was almost expected. But she didn't want to be part of a threesome; she wanted her husband to herself.

Elizabeth thought back to the rest of their conversation. "Okay, I'll tell you what," Santino said after a few moments, his voice softening. "I'll make arrangements for the two of us to take a trip to Boston in the fall, or just before Christmas. We'll leave the boys at home with Mrs. Phillips and really do the town."

He's placating me, she thought. A few pats on the head, a few baubles thrown my way, maybe even an obligatory ten minutes of sex, and after that, everything back to normal.

"No! I won't be patronized, Santino. I'm not prepared to continue living in your shadow. I'm thirty-five years old and what have I ever accomplished? Do you realize I've never had a job, never been to university, never belonged to any clubs — why, I've never even had a date with anyone besides you. I went from a convent to marriage."

He just looked at her sadly.

"I'm floundering, full of discontent, except with my children, and I don't know what to do about it. I can't explain it; I'm not sure I even understand it myself. I'm an observer of life, not a participant, and I'm afraid it's passing me by."

She paused for a moment. "You can't change what you are, even if you wanted to," she continued, softening her tone. "Male dominance and its perks have been ingrained in your psyche, and that of your associates, for generations."

He shrugged, but his expression remained the same.

"Maybe I can't change what I am either. But I want to try. I'm afraid of what I see for me in the future. Emptiness, living my life through my children, waiting for them to call or visit. I'm angry and confused and, worst of all, unsure of what I want out of the rest of my life."

Santino turned and walked over to the window, but not before she saw the guilt on his face. She wondered if her words had been too harsh, or too honest. Did her reference to anger alert him to the possibility that she suspected something was going on between him and the Sherman woman? When he didn't ask her what she was angry about, she knew she had her answer.

Good, she thought. Suffer. I'm not going to make it any easier for you.

After a few minutes of silence, Santino took a deep breath and turned to face his wife.

"Elizabeth, why don't you go to Boston this weekend on your own?" he said, strain showing on his face. "It will give you some time to think things through. I can postpone my trip for a few days until you come back. You can browse through the galleries and museums and shop to your heart's content. Mrs. Phillips and I will take care of the boys."

It was her turn to look surprised.

"I'm not as set in my ways as you think," he continued. "Living together should be a matter of choice between two people, not an obligation. I've never had any doubts about wanting you for my wife since the first moment I saw you. And I don't want you to have any doubts either.

"I'm prepared to give you the space you need to see if I'm still the man with whom you want to spend the rest of your life."

Elizabeth could see the clouds, so close now, and she could also see the expression on his face as he had talked to her that day. He had been trying to be sensitive and understanding, and she knew how hard it must have been for him. He was fifty-four, and his feet were still planted in two worlds — the past, with its traditional roles for men and women, and the present, with its militant feminism, drugs, open sex, and contempt for Old World values.

But she'd opened the door with her words, and she was determined to walk through it. So she'd taken Santino's seat on the plane to Boston, and here she was. But without him to hold her hand and comfort her, she felt panic-stricken.

For heaven's sake, control yourself, she thought. Don't be such a baby. You're thirty-five years old.

"Excuse me, may I be of any help?"

She turned to look at the young man sitting next to her, an expression of concern on his face. "Are you feeling sick? Shall I call the stewardess?"

"No, thank you, I'm fine," she answered. The stranger next to her had the biggest brown eyes she'd ever seen. "I'm just nervous on airplanes."

"That's okay, so am I," he told her. "Here, hold on to my arm. Just squeeze it every time you feel nervous."

Just then the plane made a steep bank to the east and Elizabeth let out a whimper as she grabbed the stranger's arm.

"It's okay, honest," he said, taking her other hand in his. "I know it feels as if the plane's about to turn over and fall straight down, but we're just turning east toward Boston. Here, I'll close the window shade so you won't notice the tilt so much."

Elizabeth bit her lip. She felt as if her breathing could be heard all over the plane. She struggled to hold back her tears.

You idiot! she wanted to yell at herself. Coming on this trip alone was your idea. You're making a fool of yourself in front of this stranger. Why did you ever think you could fly on your own?

"Hey, did you feel that?" he asked, a smile crinkling his eyes as he patted her arm. "The plane is leveling off. Soon you'll hear two little beeps, which means everything's just fine. Then the attendants will start serving breakfast."

"I'll never be able to eat. I'm so terrified. There's no use pretending I'm not."

"Oh, you'll be able to eat," he assured her, laughing warmly. "Here, let me pull down the tray. We'll pretend we're sitting on a yacht cruising around Monte Carlo. Think of the plane's movements as a gentle ocean swell."

She couldn't help smiling at him. Yes, he *was* a very good-looking young man, with blond hair and a large birthmark on one cheek. He also had big dimples and very white teeth, she noticed. And was as charming and sweet as he was handsome.

"My name is Larry," he said, introducing himself. "I'm a computer programmer." It was partly true. He didn't mention that he was an FBI agent and that today was his twenty-eighth birthday.

"I'm Elizabeth," she responded. She reminded herself to be cautious. He might be charming, but he was a stranger.

"Are you going to Boston on business?" he asked.

She shook her head. "I'm planning to visit some galleries, do some shopping, as well as visit the Kennedy Library. I've wanted to see Boston ever since President Kennedy was elected in 1960."

He laughed. "I'm sure you were only a child when he was elected."

She felt herself blush ever so slightly. "I was fifteen," she answered. "But my favorite teacher, a nun named Sister Mary Margaret, was from Boston. She used to tell us about Boston by the hour. And she adored the Kennedy family, so she talked about them all the time."

"Well, they're a pretty interesting family. And Boston's a pretty interesting city." He could have mentioned that old Joe Kennedy used to be one of the big "importers" of Scotch whiskey, that during Prohibition he and the Bronfmans had divvied up the cross-border hooch business, and that both of them were thick as thieves with the mob. But he didn't want to spoil her illusions.

"Are you from Boston?"

"No. I'm just on my way there to attend a seminar on some new high-tech computer programming. I'm also hoping to catch tomorrow night's hockey game between the Bruins and the New York Rangers."

"Are you Canadian then?"

"Yes and no. I grew up in Vermont, though I was born in Northern Ontario. Now I'm working out of Rochester, New York, but the way the computer industry is growing, I expect to be transferred again quite soon. That's what it's like when you work for a large company."

"Well, at least you aren't stuck in one place."

"Yeah, I do get to visit the most interesting places and meet the most interesting people during my travels."

He hadn't taken his eyes off her.

He's flirting with me, Elizabeth thought. I'm sure of it. It's nice to feel attractive again. Besides, what harm can come from it? Once the plane lands we'll never see each other again.

"I was born in Detroit," Elizabeth lied. "But now I live in Toronto."

"Married?" he asked, glancing down at her ring.

"Quite. I have twin sons who are almost eight years old. They're a real handful, but such a delight." She gave him a quick glance and looked away. "Are you married?"

"No, but I've been seeing someone for a while. She's a senior O.R. nurse at Toronto General. I've just spent the last two days with her."

Elizabeth's face went red. Grow up! she thought. Everybody does it today without being married. You're a throwback to the Victorian era.

The two of them spent the next two hours chatting about art, of which Larry admitted he knew nothing; hockey, of which Elizabeth admitted she knew nothing; and politics.

"It's hard to believe," Elizabeth said, "that the same people who once elected John F. Kennedy president would even consider electing a flaky, over-the-hill movie star like Reagan to walk in the same halls of power."

"I don't think it's that hard to understand," Larry answered. "First, it's twenty years later. And the pendulum needs to keep swinging politically in order to keep things in balance. Besides, it's time for a little law and order. What could be worse than another four years of Jimmy Carter?"

She didn't answer. She supposed things had to keep changing. After all, that's why she was on this plane in the first place.

"Americans can't continue to rationalize drug use and criminality by looking for cop-outs to justify inappropriate behavior, especially in young-sters. Allowing them to blame everyone and everything but themselves for their actions will only weaken the fabric of our society, opening the door for even more criminal activity as they grow older."

As he spoke, her eyes never left his face. Elizabeth didn't realize that her intense interest in what he was saying might cause Larry to think she was flirt-ing with him. She couldn't know that he had originally intended to use his spare time during this Boston trip to do some serious thinking about his future — to see if it included a long-term commitment to Judy MacQuire.

But sitting next to this lovely woman who looked like an elegant princess, and whose incredible green eyes caused his heart to keep skipping beats, had changed all that. He was instantly smitten, and his only thought was how he could arrange to see her again.

When the plane began its descent, Elizabeth's self-control vanished and she turned and buried her head in his shoulder, squeezing his arms.

"Shh, shh, don't worry." He held her close. "Everything will be okay. Soon you'll hear the sound of the wheels being lowered . . . See, there it is. Now we're lining up our approach, and in just five minutes we'll be on the ground. This has been a very smooth flight."

When the wheels touched down, Elizabeth crossed herself. Her taupe silk suit was soaking with perspiration.

As they walked through the main terminal building, Larry asked where she was staying.

Elizabeth hesitated for only a moment before answering. "At the Four Seasons." He is so attractive and was so sweet to me, it's a shame to lie to him, she thought. But I'd better not play with fire. Especially the way I'm feeling now.

They shook hands and said good-bye. As Elizabeth walked over to the carousel to wait for her luggage, she could feel his eyes on her back. After a few minutes she turned and saw him walking toward the exit door. Soon the crowds blocked her view and she didn't see him stop and go over to the pay phones.

Larry dialed the number and waited for the familiar voice to answer.

"I've been waiting for your call."

"Well, you won't be happy. DeLuca wasn't on the plane."

For a long moment there was silence, then: "Oh, c'mon. He must have been."

"I'm telling you, Bob, DeLuca wasn't on the plane! . . . Of course I know what he looks like . . . No, I couldn't have missed him. I made so many trips up and down the aisle to go to the john that the stewardess asked me if anything was wrong."

"Geez," Bob muttered. "He was booked on it."

"You'd better check with your people again. Maybe it was the wrong day . . . No, it couldn't have been the wrong flight number because there's only one plane out of Toronto to Boston this morning. Call me back at the hotel and let me know. Oh, by the way, I'll be staying at the Four Seasons. Last-minute change of plans."

Not very subtle, Larry thought as he hung up the phone. Bob Lantinos, his boss, wouldn't be happy if he found out he was mixing business with pleasure. Or trying to.

Well, I'm not going to worry about it. Lantinos would be spending the next couple of days trying to find out what happened to Santino DeLuca, and why he hadn't been on the plane to Boston as scheduled. In the meantime he decided he wasn't going to walk away from the delicious woman with whom he had shared the flight.

Elizabeth was looking around for a porter when she heard his voice.

"Here, let me help you with those. We'll just get one of these carts and pile the luggage on it."

He moved so quickly and so confidently that Elizabeth couldn't think of anything to say. When they got outside, Elizabeth waved for a cab. She turned to Larry with a warm smile, intending to thank him again for all his help.

"Oh, you'll never believe this coincidence," he said as the cab pulled up. He put his luggage with Elizabeth's in the trunk. "My office made reservations for me at the Four Seasons, too. Now we can share a cab."

Elizabeth inwardly chastised herself. This is what happens when you tell a lie. God's punishment. Now what am I supposed to do?

It was a thirty-minute ride from the airport to downtown Boston. Larry made small talk and Elizabeth tried to appear interested in what he was saying, although her mind was racing, trying to figure out what to do next.

Then she opened her purse, pulled out some papers, and let out a small cry. "Oh, Larry, I can't believe how stupid I am. I never looked at my new itinerary. I thought I was staying at the Four Seasons, but this says that I'm booked at the Omni Parker House."

"Oh, that's too bad." Larry's disappointment showed in his voice.

By the time they reached her hotel Elizabeth was back in control. She thanked Larry again and waved as the cab pulled away. Out of sight, out of mind, she told herself.

After checking in, she had a quick shower, changed into casual clothes, and took off for Quincy Market in the Faneuil Hall complex. She checked her guidebook and then headed down Court Street, passing the Government Center. It was straight downhill to the Faneuil Hall area.

It was five-thirty when she looked at her watch. She'd been so caught up in the enjoyment of browsing around the market that she'd forgotten about the time. Before going back to the hotel, she decided to walk up to Washington Street and over to the Old Corner Bookstore, which the concierge had told her about. It was, after all, on the way.

When her stomach growled with hunger, she realized she hadn't had lunch. She saw a street vendor just outside The Old State House and bought a hot dog. She almost giggled as she thought, Santino wouldn't be too happy if he saw me standing on the street, eating in such an unladylike fashion.

Once inside the bookstore, she browsed through the shelves looking for nothing in particular. Then she found an interesting book on sculptor Jacob Lipshitz that included sketches of his earliest works together with commentaries. She'd been thinking of taking up sculpting herself, so she bought the book, paying for it in cash.

Just as she came out of the store, she heard someone say, "Hi there! Fancy meeting you here."

It was Larry. He had changed into Levis, navy penny loafers, a red-checked shirt, and a jean jacket. She couldn't help noticing his red-and-white-striped socks. He looked like an All-American college student.

She felt vaguely disquieted that her heart started beating faster. "Larry! What a coincidence. Is your hotel close by?"

"Not too far away. It's such a nice day that I decided to take a hike on the Freedom Trail. Sitting behind a desk as I do most of the time isn't very conducive to physical fitness. Where are you off to?"

"Back to my hotel. I spent this afternoon at Quincey Market and picked up a couple of super new games for my boys. They love to compete against each other."

He smiled. "I used to fight with my brother."

"Fortunately, my two are best buddies, so their battles never get too physical or too intense."

"Did you like the market?"

"Oh, I loved it! There's a whole aisle of oil paintings and watercolors that were done by local artists — and they're right there to talk about their work. I really enjoyed meeting them."

Her face seemed to light up as she talked and it made him feel good.

"And what else have you been doing this afternoon?" she asked.

"I managed to pick up two fantastic tickets for tomorrow night's hockey game — right behind the bench."

"I've never been to a hockey game." The words slipped out of her mouth and immediately she asked herself, Are you crazy? What are you doing?

They stood in silence looking at each other.

"Elizabeth, let's go for a walk and I'll buy you a cappuccino."

An hour later they were sitting in Il Dolce Momento munching on grilled proscuitto and cheese sandwiches and drinking double espressos. They laughed over some of the wilder-looking hippies they'd seen on their walk.

It was after ten o'clock when Elizabeth looked at her watch and realized that she hadn't phoned home — in fact, hadn't even thought about phoning home. She also hadn't mentioned one word about her husband. Would Larry think that she didn't care much for her family? The truth was, in the company of this man she felt giddy and carefree and very young. She pushed any sobering thoughts from her head. I guess this is what it would have been like if I'd led a normal life and had a chance to grow up and go to college like other girls, she thought as she looked into the smiling face across from her.

"Larry," she said, rubbing her feet against the back of an empty chair at the next table, "I'll never be able to walk back to the hotel. I'd better call a cab."

"One doesn't call a cab here," he told her. "One has to go outside and wave one over by screeching, whistling, and jumping up and down. Come on, I'll get one for you."

As she was about to get into the cab, he put both his hands on her shoulders, turned her around to face him, and leaned over to gently brush his lips against hers. She didn't move.

"I can't tell you how much I enjoyed tonight, Elizabeth. Let's spend the day together tomorrow. You can take me browsing and give me some pointers on the 'finer things in life.' Then, we'll go to Harvard, which is quite magnificent, and then on to the Kennedy Library. Later we'll have a terrific dinner at the Legal Seafood before I introduce you to the frenzy that is known as hockey."

Say no, Elizabeth. Walk away. Think of your husband and children. You're a married woman. It's not right.

Her lovely green eyes looked into his, and she didn't answer.

"Come on, Elizabeth," he said, his smile so innocent. "I won't bite you. I promise."

She smiled shyly and nodded, even though she knew it was wrong.

When she got back to the hotel, it was ten-thirty. There were no messages. Well, at least Santino meant it when he talked about giving me space, she acknowledged.

"*J*immy, it's Vinnie. My man in Boston just called. She got there okay. She went out shopping for most of the afternoon. But he says some blond guy was tailing her. Eventually the guy spoke to her and they went to a coffee house for a couple of hours. She took a cab back to the hotel alone."

"Holy shit!" Jimmy exclaimed. Then: "Nah, no fucking way. Maybe it's one of her artsy friends or something."

"Do you want me to put a tail on him?"

After a few moments of silence Jimmy Bono answered Vinnie Bratuso.

"No, forget it. The boss just wants us to make sure she's okay. As long as your guy keeps an eye on her, that'll be enough."

*L*arry and Elizabeth set off the next morning at ten o'clock. Larry was dressed in jeans, a turtleneck sweater, and a tweed sport jacket. Elizabeth wore gray slacks, a gray cashmere sweater, and a black double-breasted leather jacket. She had put a single strand of tiny pearls around her neck.

When she came out of the elevator, Larry's look of admiration was obvious, and in spite of all her misgivings and guilt, Elizabeth was elated.

Their first stop was at one of Boston's oldest and most respected antique shops, George Gravert Antiques. It delighted Elizabeth to see Larry so fascinated by everything she pointed out to him. As she explained how one should go about examining antiques to make sure they're genuine and not reproductions, Larry would peer inside a French armoire or turn over a Queen Anne chair, looking for the telltale signs she had described: a signature, a date, or some tiny etching.

He was so interested and so excited by her mini-lesson that she began to feel important, smart, and special — emotions she hadn't felt for many years.

Their next stop was at London Lace, where Elizabeth shopped for a large tablecloth and antique napkins for her home. These were unusual laces, made in England on the only Victorian lace-making machinery left in the British Isles. Larry was fascinated with the intricate embroidery. He held up one of the cloths very gingerly, and Elizabeth noticed how gentle his hands were as they caressed the delicate fabric.

As they walked along Newbury Street the smells of the street vendors' wares filled the air. They looked at each other at the same time and said, "Let's eat!"

Elizabeth insisted on paying for a cab to take them over to Harvard because Larry had treated her to lunch and had bought the hockey tickets. As the cab started to cross the horrible old bridge to Cambridge, Elizabeth was overwhelmed with feelings of motion sickness. Larry noticed her face turn white.

"Stop the cab!" he shouted at the driver. Then he opened the door and helped Elizabeth out to get some fresh air. She started swaying, and leaned against his shoulder.

"Take a few deep breaths," he urged, patting her and gently guiding her along the sidewalk. "Don't look down. We're almost there."

As they strolled through Harvard Square with its winding paths, stately trees, and handsome brick buildings, Larry talked about Harvard.

"Walking through this campus is like walking through history. You can practically taste the tradition. It's awesome." Elizabeth couldn't help smiling at Larry's last comments. "Awesome" was a word often used by her sons. Looking at her companion's handsome face, she resisted the temptation to reach over and hug him.

She inhaled deeply. It was spring and it felt like spring. Clearly it was the season to be in Boston. Everywhere she looked she saw trees budding, tulips and crocuses blooming.

She was sorry to leave Harvard, but there was still a lot to see and do. They took a cab over to Dorchester Point and the Kennedy Library.

Their visit there was an emotional one for Elizabeth. It brought back memories of Sister Mary Margaret and her tragic death. She watched videos of those fateful three days in November of 1963, and then walked through the life of the man whose vision of the world had inspired young people like Sister Mary Margaret to dream of making a difference. She started to cry, and when she looked over at Larry, she saw that his eyes were filled with tears, too.

"The bond between Jack and Bobby Kennedy was really strong," he said. "I can imagine how devastated Bobby must have felt when he lost his older brother. I know how I'd feel if I lost mine." Larry spoke softly and then unconsciously looked around. He rarely stated his views to anyone and never to his fellow agents. Admiring Jack Kennedy was bad enough, but admiring Bobby had been the fast track to oblivion within the Agency for a number of years. Old J. Edgar, known for his vendetta with Bobby, might have been dead for eight years, but his influence lingered on.

Elizabeth looked at Larry and realized neither of them had spoken very much about their personal lives. Elizabeth was very touched by his remarks about his brother, but it also made her feel ill at ease. Better not to get too personal, she told herself. "We'd better go," she suggested. "It's getting late."

It was after six o'clock by the time they got back to Boston, and there wasn't enough time to return to their respective hotels if they were going to have dinner before the game.

They feasted on grilled lobster and scampi and talked about everything and nothing. By the time they'd finished off a bottle of wonderful dry white wine, Elizabeth was giggling and laughing as she hadn't done in a long time.

They just made it to the arena before the opening face-off. Elizabeth couldn't believe the noise level — cheers, whistles, horns blowing, the roar from the crowd at every score. Larry tried to explain how hockey was played, talking about the difference between a forward and a defenseman.

"But if Raymond Bourque is a defenseman, how come he scores so many goals?"

Before Larry could answer, Bourque came on the ice, greeted by a roar from the crowd, who by now were seeing in him a new Bobby Orr. Suddenly a New York Ranger came speeding along the ice pushing the puck, trying to skate around Bourque. Everybody got to their feet, including Elizabeth.

"My God, did you see that? That man pushed Raymond Bourque. Is that allowed?"

Larry burst out laughing, putting his arm around Elizabeth and giving her a hug. She didn't pull back from him.

"You're so cute," he said. "That's a body check. And the guy who did the pushing was Brad Park, one of New York's finest. That's what he's supposed to do."

By the third period Elizabeth was really into the game. She kept jumping up, clapping her hands and yelling encouragement to the Boston team. Larry kept up his running commentary on the individual players and what was happening. Near the end of the game one of the Bruins elbowed Park as he was on a breakaway, causing him to fall. Park got up and went after him, and pretty soon several gloves and sticks were strewn on the ice as a melee broke out between the two teams. One Bruin in particular was swinging and punching like a madman.

"That's Terry O'Reilly," Larry said. "His job is to keep the Rangers at bay. He's a wild man who's always looking for a fight."

Elizabeth was exhilarated by the time the game was over, even though Boston lost to New York by one goal. "I'm too excited to sleep," she told Larry as they walked along looking for a cab. "Let's have some tea and sweets at my hotel. They usually serve it in the lobby till midnight. Then we can talk some more about hockey. I really loved that game."

The lobby was full of boisterous Shriners in town for a convention, so Larry suggested they have their tea in her suite. Elizabeth was still too preoccupied with the game to veto the idea. Instead, she went to the desk to check for any messages — there were none — and then she and Larry headed to the elevator.

Neither of them spoke during the ride up to her floor. As soon as they were inside her door, Larry took her in his arms and kissed her, gently at first, then more intensely. Elizabeth offered no resistance, but inside she screamed, Are you crazy? What are you doing? This is a mortal sin.

But it felt so good to be desired again, and Larry was so young and so handsome and so eager. She could feel his erection, see the desire in his large brown eyes.

He kept whispering, "You're so beautiful, Elizabeth, I want you so much," as his lips caressed her ear and his gentle hands stroked her back.

When he kissed her again, she responded.

After a few minutes he eased her jacket off and slipped his hands under the back of her sweater. When she didn't stop him, he unhooked her bra as his tongue found its way between her lips.

Elizabeth gave in to the sensations that were pulsing through her body. Her arms wound around his neck as his hands slipped around to cover her breasts. When he began caressing her nipples, Elizabeth trembled, remembering how much she used to enjoy having Santino do that . . . She froze.

"Larry, Larry, stop!"

She tried to push him away, but he didn't release her.

"Stop, please! You have to stop! Forgive me, forgive me," she cried. "I'm married, I have children . . . "

Larry dropped his arms. "Elizabeth, this isn't a lark for me. I know it's only been a short time, but I think I've fallen in love with you."

"No," she cried, "you can't! I had no right to lead you on this way, flirting with you. It was wrong of me — I have a husband and a family." She was shaking now. "I didn't mean to be a tease, but I can't do this!"

He didn't say anything. He looked hurt, a bit dazed, and she felt horrible.

"You don't know anything about me," she said weakly. "And for a while, I forgot who I am. I pray that God will forgive me."

Elizabeth started to cry, slumping into a corner chair. When Larry approached her to offer comfort, she pushed his hands away.

"Please don't, Larry. I had a wonderful day with you. You'll never know how special it was for me, and, for that, I thank you. But I beg you, please go. Please forget me and what's just happened between us."

"Elizabeth, I'll never forget you or what's happened between us. You felt something, too. And I don't want to walk away from you."

She looked up at him, her tear-streaked face full of anguish. "Larry, I'm so very sorry. I can never see you again. Please leave."

Then she got up, walked into the bedroom, and closed the door. After five minutes she heard the door to the suite open and close. She threw herself on the bed and let all her emotions pour out with her tears. She screamed and sobbed into the pillow she clutched over her face.

*J*immy was pacing back and forth in his Toronto apartment when the phone rang.

"He's just left her hotel. He was up there for about half an hour. Whatever went on, it was sure a quickie."

"Vinnie," Jimmy said, "can you trust your guy to keep his mouth shut?"

"Sure," answered Bratuso. "Besides, he doesn't know who he was watching. I never give my men any names. Jimmy, do you have to tell the boss? Maybe it was nothing. My guy says the kid didn't look too happy when he left."

"I don't know yet, Vinnie. I'll have to see."

*E*lizabeth DeLuca walked into St. Paul's Cathedral at nine-fifteen the next morning. It was magnificent with its wonderful carvings and inspiring stained-glass windows. It still smelled of incense from the earlier Mass.

Her swollen red eyes were hidden behind dark sunglasses. She approached the priest and asked if she could speak with him.

"Father, I know it's not usual to hear confessions on a Sunday, but I'm from out of town, and I'm deeply troubled. I've never missed communion before, so I hope you can help me."

He was Irish, like Sister Mary Margaret. "Of course my dear. Mass doesn't start until ten o'clock, so we have plenty of time. Come with me."

She entered the confessional and closed the door, crossing herself. "Bless me, Father, for I have sinned. It's been two weeks since my last confession.

"Last night I kissed a man who wasn't my husband. And I had improper thoughts about him, wanting him to continue what he was doing to me."

"Have you ever been unfaithful to your husband?" the priest asked.

"No, never. He's the only man I've ever known. We met back in Italy when I was seventeen, and we got married less than a year later. I've always loved him — he makes me feel so safe. I never looked at another man until two days ago."

"Did you intend to be unfaithful to your husband when you met this other man?"

"No, of course not. It was just that I was feeling so useless and so unattractive. My husband has so many other interests. And this young man made me feel so desirable that, for a moment, I really did want to . . ."

"I can hear that you are very troubled, but you are innocent of any wrong deed, and haven't committed a mortal sin. Wanting to do something isn't the same as intending to do it. You rejected the man's advances. There is no greater love than the love that resists temptation."

"Thank you, Father."

"Now go in peace. Remain faithful to your beloved husband. For your penance, I want you to think about our conversation today until you forgive yourself. Now make a sincere act of contrition."

" 'Oh my God, I am heartily sorry . . .' "

When Elizabeth left the church after Mass, she felt a peace she hadn't known in years. She knew she could not go back to where she had never been, and she now understood that's what her attraction to Larry had been all about. She belonged with Santino DeLuca, in the world he'd made for them, and that's where she would stay.

I'll weather any storm caused by Rebecca Sherman's presence, she whispered to herself.

Remember, you're his wife. And the mother of his children. That's 90 percent, and if you're really smart, you'll recapture the other 10 percent.

*W*hen the plane landed in Toronto Jimmy Bono was there to meet her outside customs. He stood by the railing looking uncomfortable and out of place. He smiled and waved when he saw her, then he took her suitcase. "Car's up one level," he said flatly.

"Where's Santino?" She had been hoping he'd meet her, although in a way she was glad he hadn't.

"The boss took the kids to the zoo this afternoon," he said. "And he promised them they could pig out at McDonald's before you got home."

They got to the car and he opened the door for her.

"Oh Jimmy," she said as she leaned back in the seat. "I have so much to be grateful for — a husband I love and children who are so precious. For a second, I almost forgot it, but God, in His infinite wisdom and love, helped me to remember before it was too late. I am truly blessed."

As the car sped toward home Elizabeth didn't see Jimmy crossing himself.

# *11*

APRIL
*1981*

$\mathcal{C}$herry blossoms were in full bloom along
the Potomac when Inspector Grant Teasdale walked briskly to the meeting
that morning. Now he sat back in the leather office chair and tapped his
pencil on the white pad in front of him. He, RCMP Deputy Superintendent
George Wilson, and three FBI agents were sitting around a table in one of
the conference rooms in the Washington Bureau. In front of each man was
a pad of paper and a pencil, a glass, a coffee cup, and a spoon. There was a
pot of coffee, cream, and sugar in the center of the table, and a pitcher of water.

The rug was dark blue, the walls off-white, the furniture standard
issue, and the four paintings were landscapes by lesser-known American
painters, provided by the Smithsonian loan program to government buildings. There were no windows, but air-conditioning came through two vents.

Grant Teasdale was in Washington because the FBI's special task force
on the Mafia had targeted Santino DeLuca's operations in Florida. So far
they'd got nowhere and wanted the RCMP to help them by investigating
his Canadian companies. To that end, they were suggesting a joint
FBI–RCMP task force. Grant Teasdale knew that he had been recommended as the task force head primarily because of his track record of
arrests and convictions in the area of fraud and corruption.

"You come highly recommended," Robert Lantinos, the FBI's special agent, said. "We're told you're the kind of law-enforcement officer who commands a great deal of respect. We're also told that, as tough as you are, you've got good people skills, and that you'd never ask any of your team to do anything you wouldn't."

Grant felt embarrassed.

Lantinos laughed. "I've also been told that you're often in the forefront of any raids or undercover operations, leading your men, rather than directing them."

"My men often work under tremendous pressure," Grant interjected.

"A leader who is sensitive to those pressures — some call it an inner eye — can see beneath the surface of any situation. Yes, Teasdale, we think you're the man to head this team."

"He's also got an uncanny ability to spot fear and weakness in others, and that makes him very effective against the criminal minds he faces every day," Teasdale's boss George Wilson added.

"Well, what do you say?" Lantinos asked.

Wilson responded to the FBI's suggestion that Teasdale head the joint force before Grant had a chance to speak for himself. "It's a great idea. There's nobody better than Inspector Teasdale. But it has to be a shared project. We want access to your files as well."

"Okay," Lantinos agreed, "but I'll expect you guys to use every loophole you have to help us nail this bastard. He's been making a fortune on his U.S. gambling operations and then laundering the money in Canada in order to avoid paying taxes.

"And that's where the IRS comes in," Lantinos continued. "Since Al Capone we've brought down a lot of mobsters that way, and maybe DeLuca will get added to that list. We'll be adding an IRS man to the team for that reason. It seems DeLuca has been having hundreds of thousands of dollars in cash delivered by courier to various Canadian banks who have so far refused to cooperate with us. That's why we haven't been able to nail him.

"American banking laws require that any cash deposits over $9,999 be documented with proper identification before being reported to the authorities. Your Canadian laws don't have the same stringent regulations."

"And I can assure you that there's no intention of our changing the laws," Teasdale said. "The banks are making too much money."

"Right," Lantinos said. "Most of DeLuca's profits from gambling and prostitution are being moved out of the country as fast as they're made. One of our informants works for his arch-enemy, Massimo Brattini. We're also trying to nail him, too. DeLuca is using couriers he picks up in Florida — probably illegals from South America. If any are caught at the border, they play ignorant, claiming they can't speak English, and are simply deported. Most often they come back and try again.

"The one time we did have a live one, he wound up with a knife in his gut before we could get him to a safe house. And it happened on our side of the border." Lantinos shook his head.

Grant nodded and Superintendent Wilson just scowled.

The five of them went on to discuss what they knew about the relationship between Santino DeLuca and Massimo Brattini. Grant already knew most of what was said, but not all of it.

None of them knew if the two men had been friends before arriving in the United States, sometime between late 1946 and early 1947, although in Italy they had been part of the Luchese family. They knew that both went to work for the Detroit-based Villano family, doing "enforcement" and other special jobs. Since no relatives of the Luchese and Villano families were known, and since the most powerful positions within a crime family usually went to relatives, the two young men knew they'd have to earn a place in the hierarchy by skill and cunning.

In the early '50s, gangland crime was spreading across North America. Ontario was initially seen as small potatoes, so at first the other crime families were content to let the Villanos stake out that province. Quebec, especially Montreal, had been home to crime families since Prohibition and the territory was already carved up.

By the late '50s the Salerno family, operating out of Buffalo, decided they wanted a piece of the Ontario action, too. They'd begun by trying to infiltrate Villano's loan-sharking business; then they moved in on their prostitution and burgeoning drug trade operating out of Toronto and Hamilton.

At first both DeLuca and Brattini had been responsible for eliminating any unwanted competition from the Salerno family in whatever way was necessary. They worked well together — both were ruthless and ambitious, both had no qualms about the use of violence to get the message across. The word on the street used to describe them was "deadly," something Teasdale heard repeated over and over during his investigations. But, so far, there had been no witnesses to any of their crimes, or at least none willing to break the code of *omertà* — the code of silence.

But as their stature within the Villano family grew, along with their personal fortunes, cracks in their once-united front had started to appear. It soon became no secret among their associates that DeLuca was beginning to bridle at Brattini's increasingly senseless use of violence, always looking for an excuse to inflict beatings, or worse. He rarely smiled, never laughed, and no one that Teasdale had spoken to could ever remember a kind word passing Brattini's lips. He was described as cold and ruthless — as they all were on occasion — but they said that Brattini was like that all the time, never showing any feelings other than hate and bitterness.

Teasdale, during his long investigation of both men, had heard a story from one of his informants about the murder of a young prostitute. Don Luigi Villano's son-in-law had ordered that the hit be carried out by both Brattini and DeLuca. The repercussions from that order were rumored to have been the reason for the split between his two top lieutenants, and Don Villano eventually had to separate them. He sent Brattini to Toronto to set up the family's Canadian operations and kept DeLuca in Detroit as his right hand, consolidating the family's construction and hotel interests.

When the old man had had a stroke in 1956, at the age of fifty, his son-in-law, the one who'd ordered the hit on the prostitute, had no stomach for the "business," and moved to Nassau. A fight for control of the Villano family's operation had ensued between DeLuca and Brattini, with the latter returning to Detroit from Toronto to lead the battle himself.

After two bloody years DeLuca had eventually won out.

During that bitter struggle Brattini must have realized he would never command the loyalty of his men the way DeLuca did his and that he'd better get out. In 1958 Brattini had approached the two families operating out of Buffalo under the control of Gino Salerno and offered his services.

The Salerno family was outside the Detroit–Windsor sphere where the Villano operation was based. They had wanted to get into the lucrative Canadian market themselves and needed someone with inside information on how the Villano family worked, so they had been only too happy to take Brattini up on his offer. He had moved to Buffalo and consolidated his power by marrying Donna Salerno in 1959, and the following year he and his new wife had moved to Toronto.

According to Teasdale's information, the struggle for power between the Villano–DeLuca and Salerno–Brattini families continued for the next twenty-five years. Their latest conflict was over the waste-management industry in Ontario. DeLuca's Detroit-based operation had expected to get all the contracts, since they had been laying the groundwork of political payoffs for five years.

But Brattini's organization had made serious inroads with the politicians responsible for the decisions. He had found an ingenious way to bribe them — and launder some money as well: coffee houses, pubs, bistros, and donut shops. He created a numbered company out of the Turks and Caicos islands that sold franchises to certain people for "a share of after-tax profits." Which meant one could become an owner of a cash business with no up-front money as down payment.

It was a great way to pay off and launder at the same time because it was virtually impossible for the authorities to calculate the legitimate take. By inflating the number of patrons, one could justify the large amounts of money shown as earnings. Revenue Canada was happy and so were the "bosses," who could legitimize millions of dollars of dirty money while handing out cash bribes that were untraceable.

It was also a source of several loan-sharking operations with no records and no accounting — where six dollars was paid back for every five dollars lent — or an enforcer came to visit.

The offshore company at the heart of Brattini's operations was made up of a board of directors who were all residents of the Turks and Caicos. There was nothing illegal — unless of course someone discovered that Massimo Brattini was the sole shareholder of the company and the board consisted simply of local illiterates whose names were used in exchange for an annual stipend of a few hundred dollars.

Corrupt politicians and judges just selected to whom they wanted Brattini to give a franchise. Relative, lover, whatever. There was no risk, since this kind of payoff to politicians and judges was not unusual — simply the way business was conducted in the underworld.

The "legitimate" corporations that wished to delude themselves about their own lofty standards of morality rationalized that providing gifts, free trips, insider tips on real estate and stock deals, and political contributions somehow legitimized their activities.

As Brattini's operations started cutting into DeLuca's profits, DeLuca had fought back. He had set up some of Brattini's key people for blackmail so that they would pass information to him on Brattini's operations, especially his drug business, which in turn would be leaked to the police.

It was an effective strategy. Even Teasdale had been impressed with the 1978 bust that netted the FBI over $10,000,000 worth of pure heroin that Brattini was bringing in from Marseilles. The word on the street was that it was one of DeLuca's people who had infiltrated Brattini's operations and had blown the whistle to the FBI.

Retaliation had followed, and the vendetta was still going on. Neither side had been able to eliminate, or even weaken, the other, for more than a few months at a time.

The two Canadians and the three FBI agents had been exchanging information for hours now, and files of documents had been brought to the table.

Finally Lantinos stood up and stretched. "So, Teasdale, when can you get started?"

"I'll be ready to take over as soon as I get my other cases reassigned, probably within a week."

He tried to push away thoughts about his wife Doris's reaction to his decision.

"We'll be in touch," Lantinos said.

They all stood up and there was a ritual of handshakes.

"Shall I call you a cab, gentlemen?" Lantinos asked.

"Thanks," Superintendent Wilson replied.

"Done," Lantinos said cheerfully. "Have a good trip."

*D*eputy Superintendent George Wilson glanced at his companion as the plane leveled off.

Grant Teasdale of the Royal Canadian Mounted Police was thirty-seven years old. He was tall and well built. His flaming red hair and piercing blue eyes captivated everyone who met him. He was an intensely private man who rarely discussed his personal life and never referred to his childhood. Teasdale was, as far as Wilson was concerned, an enigma, and he often thought that, as much as he liked the man and admired his work record, he knew practically nothing about him.

"Would you gentlemen like some refreshment?" The attractive flight attendant leaned over, close to Grant's face.

"Maybe a little later," Grant replied with a smile.

The stewardess smiled back and actually winked. "I'll be back," she said in a low voice.

"You seem quite oblivious to that young woman's flirtations, Grant."

Teasdale had been reading one of the background documents he had brought with him from the meeting. "Flirtations?"

Wilson laughed. "It's her third attempt to make you notice her since we got on this plane, my boy. Are you wearing blinkers?"

Grant shook his head.

"Hey, buddy," Wilson said, "if I were your age I sure as hell wouldn't pass up this kind of come-on."

"No," Grant replied, "I'm not interested. It's not worth the hassle. I've seen too many of my colleagues ruin their careers, along with their family life, chasing some skirt. I've got everything I need at home."

"Wish I could say that," Wilson muttered.

Grant leaned back in his seat and closed his eyes, listening to the quiet humming of the plane as it cruised above the blanket of clouds.

I wasn't quite honest, he thought as he reflected on his comment to Wilson. But what the hell, who says one can have everything?

His thoughts then turned to Doris. They had been married for some twelve years. During that time, as Grant was transferred from one RCMP outpost to another, the two of them had fallen into a comfortable pattern. Conversation was simple, limited to issues surrounding Kevin's care, their home, their families, and Grant's career. Regrettably, they had little in common beyond their son. Sex between them usually happened once a week, and was without surprises. They'd have a few beers, exchange a few kisses and caresses, and Grant would mount his wife in the traditional missionary position, their once-wild enjoyment of each other's bodies long forgotten.

As a young man Grant had dreamed of changing the world, making it free of crime and brutality. He had wanted to expose the kind of political corruption that had kept the abuses he and the others had endured at the orphanage covered up for so long. He would never accept as a given that politics and corruption had gone hand in hand since the beginning of recorded history, and probably always would.

Doris had never spoken to Grant of having any dreams, but he knew she did. She had eventually obtained her paralegal diploma by attending night school and had no problem finding part-time work with legal firms wherever Grant was posted. She had enjoyed the extra money and the interesting legal cases, but when the day was over she went home, leaving her work behind.

Grant knew he did not leave his work behind. Most nights he would be up late, reading over material, writing reports, or researching information from the volumes he brought home from the RCMP archives.

As the senior Mountie in charge of "major crimes" in western Canada, he had overseen the arrest and conviction of more than one hundred criminals during the five years of his stint. The amount of time and effort he'd spent to rack up that kind of record left little room for anything else.

Meanwhile, the pressure on Doris had increased. Kevin, who was getting almost as tall as his father, and almost as strong, had become more and more difficult to handle alone.

Despite the boy's disabilities, Grant had insisted that he continue to live at home. His distrust of government-run social services had never waned over the years, and he never wanted his son to be institutionalized. But Doris was adamant. They had to start planning for his future.

Kevin was a redhead like his father. He loved to play floor hockey and go to the movies. He attended special-need classes and sang in the school choir, and spent hours listening to operas, especially *Carmen*. An affectionate young boy, he was always smiling, and whenever he met someone new, he'd reach out to shake hands before putting his arms out to give them a hug. Kevin loved to stand between his parents, put an arm around each of them, and pull them close, calling it "Kevin's sandwich — Mommy and Daddy are the bread, and I'm the meat."

Lately his behavior had become erratic, and he had occasional outbursts of violence, pushing and slapping his classmates whenever he didn't get his way. Doris had tried for some time to make Grant accept the fact that it was in Kevin's best interests to be with others like himself, that he now required more specialized schooling, and that such schools were only available back east. She had stressed that Kevin would have to become a live-in resident in a special facility. But Grant had refused to even consider it, citing his own memories of institutional life.

Doris had accused him of deluding himself, saying that without Kevin at home as a tie to bind them, he would have no reason to continue living with her. She had cried and said that he would never have married her if she hadn't been pregnant.

Grant understood her insecurities, and had known from the way she spoke that she was terrified that one day he would leave her, despite his denials and assurances. So he went out of his way not to give her any reason to be suspicious or jealous. Of course he'd noticed other women. But when temptation had seemed irresistible, he'd told himself to look away and take a pass. Otherwise he'd be in trouble.

Finally Doris had won out, and Grant agreed to go along with her wishes about putting Kevin in a special school.

When the Teasdales had arrived in Ottawa in early 1980, Grant had been promoted. As an RCMP inspector with administrative responsibilities, what he really did was push paper around on his desk. Bored and unhappy, he had confided to his friend and colleague, George Wilson, that he was thinking of taking early retirement.

"I'm getting atrophy of the brain," he'd said one day after work and a couple bottles of beer. "Doris wants to move down to Florida. She hates the winters here, and there are a couple of good prospects for Kevin's future down there as well. I'm giving it serious consideration."

Teasdale was too valuable an officer for the Force to lose, so when the FBI approached the RCMP to set up a joint task force on Mafia links to legitimate businesses, the Superintendent had immediately recommended Grant to be its head.

"Grant, let's try to infiltrate DeLuca's operation," Wilson said, jolting Teasdale back to the present as the plane began its descent into Ottawa. "That's the only way we'll have a chance. We'll worry about admissibility of evidence and entrapment down the road. At least we'll have some information, if nothing else."

*T*hey had roast beef for dinner and it was cooked to absolute perfection. Grant looked around and felt a bit guilty. Doris somehow managed a job, all the housework, and meals on time. No man could ask for more in a wife, he reminded himself. He sat down in his big comfortable recliner chair and waited. Doris cleared the table, tidied up the kitchen, and then she, too, collapsed into a chair.

"Before you start watching television, we have to talk," he said.

She immediately looked distressed. "What is it?"

"I've accepted a position as head of a joint Canadian–U.S. task force on Organized Crime. I've signed on for another five years, Doris."

"How could you?" she cried. "Don't my feelings count for anything? I'm the one who has to transport Kevin around, do up his boots and skates, deal with his tantrums, and help him with his schoolwork."

"I've never denied you have the worst of it — "

"That's good of you. But you blithely decide, without even discussing it with me, to take on some useless investigation of the Mafia. Who even cares any more what they do? Have any of the important ones ever been caught? No! Besides, they're almost all legitimate already.

"And what am I supposed to do?" she went on, her voice breaking. "I'm almost forty-five years old. When do I get a chance to make some decisions? When do I get a chance to have a life besides sitting home alone waiting for you to finish some investigation that takes almost all your waking hours?"

Not knowing what else to say, he murmured, "I know how you feel."

"Apparently not," she snapped back. "I don't want to live in Canada any more. The winters are awful. I want to learn to play golf and maybe even tennis. And what about Kevin? We've got to find him a good home while he's still young enough to adjust. In five years it might be too late!"

Grant couldn't look at her. She was right, of course. He had been so anxious to take this posting that he hadn't given any consideration to her feelings. But still, he wouldn't give it up.

"Doris, I'm sorry. I know you're right. But I give you my solemn promise that when this job is finished, I'll take early leave and we can move down to Florida. In the meantime I'll be able to develop even better contacts to find the best place for Kevin."

"Grant," she said, looking at him with tears in her eyes, "do you want to split up? Is that what this is really all about? Are you afraid to tell me straight out? Is this your way of pushing me out?"

He got up, walked over to her, and pulled her out of the chair. With his arms around her, he talked to her as gently as he could. "Doris, you once saved my self-esteem, my sanity, and probably my life. I loved you for it then and I love you now. I don't want you to leave me. But please understand: I hate those scum-bag politicians more than the mobsters who pay them off. I need to do this one last job. And after that I'll be done. I promise. You'll see. Everything will work out."

Doris just stood there. Then she nodded her head without pulling away, and without looking at him.

*G*rant finished piling his boxes of records concerning the DeLuca–Villano, Brattini–Salerno case in one corner of his windowless Toronto office at the RCMP headquarters on Jarvis Street. He had put a couple of panoramic scenic posters of prairie wheatfields and rocky mountains on the walls to make the room feel less claustrophobic. He moved more piles of papers off the only other chair in his office and placed them on one of the unpacked boxes. A wide path from the door to his desk was now clear. When his intercom phone rang, he reached over, took the half-eaten pear off his phone, and answered.

At that moment there was a knock on his door. "Agent Lantinos from the FBI is on his way up, sir," the receptionist announced. Grant turned to the door to see Lantinos walk in.

"Lantinos, come in. I was expecting you a little later." Grant extended his hand to the FBI agent and offered him the empty chair.

"Still moving in, I see," quipped Lantinos as he sat down. "Have you had a chance to go through the material I sent you last week?"

Grant picked up the file sitting in the center of his desk. "Yes, and it makes for pretty interesting reading. It looks as if DeLuca's been laundering money through Bermuda."

"I agree that's a real possibility," Lantinos concurred. He paused. "What about Rebecca Sherman's involvement, if any?"

Grant raised his eyebrows and cocked his head, "We're keeping tabs on her. Maybe she's the key to how he's moving the money. She handles a lot of his business."

"To check that, we'll have to get all his bank records — as well as hers. You know, she travels quite often with him," Lantinos said.

"What do you say we discuss this over dinner in a quiet restaurant. What's your favorite food, Bob?"

"Great idea, let's go. Any good Greek restaurants?"

Grant smiled. "Lots of them on the Danforth."

# *12*

MARCH
1982

*T*hey were in the apartment DeLuca
Industries rented in the Sutton Place Hotel. It was a quiet building with thick
walls and thick carpets that muted sounds. Even so, the cars on Bay Street
below could be heard, and now and again there was the wail of a siren as an
ambulance from one of the nearby hospitals sped by in the misty March night.

The lights were out in the bedroom but the room was filled with a
soft rosy hue from the city's lights.

Rebecca turned to the man beside her. "Santino," she whispered in his
ear, "have you given any thought to my suggestion about moving some of
your personal banking to Switzerland?"

"What kind of *après*-sex conversation is this?" he answered, nuzzling
her neck, his hands stroking her back and buttocks. "Can't it wait till
tomorrow?"

She shook her head. For some time she had been concerned that too
much of DeLuca's personal fortune, and hers, was based in Bermuda,
along with his other "business" interests. She had her doubts about the
confidentiality of the Bermuda banks — as well as their loyalty. After all, she
had been able to get the information on CanMor and some other companies by methods that were devious but not that brilliant. Wouldn't it be
just as easy for someone else to do the same with her own private business

Here it is:

affairs? Or Santino's? And if that someone wasn't a friend, who knows what might happen?

She'd also become suspicious of late that she was being followed. It wasn't anything she could put her finger on. She hadn't said anything to Santino, but she was going to ask Jimmy Bono to check it out, just to make sure.

As Santino began to caress her more seriously, she changed her mind. "Of course it can wait."

"I'm glad — because I can't. I've been away, remember?"

She nodded and gave into the feelings he always aroused in her. It was like losing consciousness, yet having all your nerve endings alive at the same time. He gently bit her nipples and the feel of him sent waves of heat through her whole body.

She moaned as he continued to tease her. He loved it when she writhed in his arms, twisting and turning, trying to get him to let her come. He delighted in making her wait and then watching her when she had her orgasm. Sometimes she wondered why their love-making was always so good. Why didn't they tire of one another? Then she decided it was because there were so many imposed separations — and an element of danger. They both sensed that because they both knew just how much each had to lose.

When their passion was spent, Santino got up, put on his robe, and went to the bar to fix them drinks.

"I'm having a fourteenth birthday party for Lisa next month," Rebecca said casually. "I sent you and Elizabeth an invitation, but if you can't come, of course I'll understand."

He turned and smiled. "We'll be glad to come."

His acceptance surprised her since Santino knew that she was uncomfortable being at social events that Elizabeth also attended. And for the usual reasons: guilt, jealousy, guilt, and more guilt.

"Are you sure?"

Santino looked at her. "It's for Lisa. Of course I'm sure."

"Thank you," she answered. And by that she hoped he knew she meant: thank you for caring about my daughter.

Lisa didn't know about them, of course. Her sister Jean was the only person who knew about her relationship with Santino. A year after her and Steven's divorce became final, Rebecca had been able to persuade her sister that it was time to come home. "How long can you keep on living like an old English hermit?" she asked. "You've told me often enough how you have no friends, how lonely you are and how much you'd like to be with Lisa and me. Come home, Jean. The three of us will be all the family we'll ever need." Lisa loved having her aunt around and Rebecca felt less guilty about being out so much. Her late hours and many community involvements kept her from spending more time with her daughter. Although Jean never openly criticized the relationship between Santino and herself, she reminded her more and more of late that she would be forty in a couple of years, and "on the way down."

"Jeannie, you know better than most how driven I am, how focused I can get," she had replied. "I don't want a husband around demanding attention that I'm not prepared to give. I'm happy with my life. It can't get any better than this. I love Santino, there's no other man who can hold a candle to him. I've found my place in the sun. I'm independent. I answer to no one. I come home to a family that I love — you and Lisa. What more is there?"

Jean hadn't bothered to answer.

"You're thoughtful tonight," Santino said now as he refilled their glasses.

"It's almost spring. I always get thoughtful at this time of year."

"A seasonal woman," he said with a smile. Then, à propos of nothing: "What's become of Bob DeSalle?"

"He's in Italy. He said he was going on a sentimental journey."

Santino scowled. "He hasn't got a sentimental bone in his body."

"I know, you're right," she answered. "I've always enjoyed Bob, but I don't trust him."

"Wise," Santino told her. "He's a snake."

She didn't reply, but she suspected that he disliked DeSalle because Bob had given up his Italian roots, trading them for the old boy's network he'd developed at Upper Canada College. God only knew if somebody said,

"Look at that Wop," Bob DeSalle would probably say, "Where?"

"Did he tell you when he was coming back?"

"No, I haven't a clue but I got the impression he was going to be gone for some months."

Santino shook his head and sipped his drink.

*A* cool breeze blew over the Adriatic and caressed the coastal towns of Puglia, that region of Italy which formed the heel of the boot and was composed of the provinces of Foggia, Bari, Taranto, and the great Adriatic port city, Brindisi.

Roberto DeSalle, whose friends in Canada — though few there were — called him "Bingo," drove along the winding road that led inland away from the turquoise sea and toward the agricultural tablelands in the interior.

He did not bother to take the road to Gravina, the quaint walled town that was home to the Cathedral and Castle of Orsini as well as the International Convent School, a Catholic institution that rivaled Neuchâtel in Switzerland as *the* place for young women to study languages and the arts. Instead, he took the road to Altamura, the town near which his grandfather Don Paolo Vincenzo had lived.

Altamura was also a walled city with the famous Romanesque Cathedral of the Assumption. People came from all over the world to see its carved portals and rose window. Nearby there was a huge limestone quarry, but on the fertile plateau, farmers like his uncle kept cattle herds, grew grains, and had vast almond groves and vineyards.

Don Vincenzo was now dead, but Rosa, who was fifteen years younger than the Don, still survived.

But it was not Rosa he had come to see. He pulled his sporty black Porsche to a halt in front of the convent where Giovanna Volpe lived, and where her daughter Elizabeth had been born and lived till she was sent to Gravina.

But Elizabeth was dead. She'd had to die, he thought to himself as he climbed the stone steps. Even though Giovanna was a victim, Elizabeth had been the seed of his sister's murderers. Not that women understood these things, he thought with disgust. Nonetheless he bore no ill feelings toward Giovanna. After all, she had suffered, too, and she had been Theresa's best friend.

He reached the top of the stairs and knocked loudly. A small door within the door opened and a brown eye peered at him suspiciously. "What is the purpose of your visit?" a nun's voice asked.

Such formality! She croaked as he imagined the trolls who lived under the bridge would croak.

"I've come to see Giovanna Volpe. I am Roberto, grandson of Don Paolo Vincenzo."

His grandfather had not been dead that long, and indeed he was something of a legend in the community. Of course when Rosa died he would inherit the land, and then he would have to place a tenant manager in charge.

The great wooden door creaked open. "Come in, please."

Roberto entered the foyer. It was dark and musty-smelling inside. The furniture was dark and massive, the oil paintings on the stone walls dark and religious, the rugs dark and threadbare. The only light came from a low-wattage incandescent bulb dangling from the ceiling some fifteen feet above.

"Wait here. You may visit with Giovanna in the garden."

He almost said "thank God." He certainly did not want to stay in here. Everything about the place gave him the creeps.

The nun disappeared and he waited impatiently, moving around the foyer. He studied each of the paintings, all of which were undistinguished. He read the names in the visitors' book, all of which were unknown to him — except one. Rosa Vincenzo. He frowned ever so slightly. He had not thought Rosa and Giovanna were close, but it appeared that his grandmother visited here regularly. He shrugged. What did it matter?

"You may follow me now," the nun said, reappearing in the shadows.

Roberto followed her down a long corridor and then outside into blessed sunlight. It was a lovely garden with a huge old fountain in its center. Its ledge was caked with the excrement of birds, and its water burbled without the energy of a modern fountain with electrically pumped water.

# DEADLY JUSTICE

Underneath a tree that resembled an acacia — though he wasn't certain it was — a woman sat on a deteriorating garden bench. He knew her to be only fifty-three years old, but the absence of hair coloring and make-up made her appear older than her years.

He walked over to her and she looked up. He felt paralyzed by her eyes. They were green and he had two immediate impressions. The first was that he had seen those eyes before, and the second was that she could see right through him.

"I know you don't remember me," he said after a second. "I'm Roberto, Theresa's little brother."

Giovanna's mouth opened in surprise.

"You know, Roberto Vincenzo."

"Yes, I know," Giovanna said slowly. "I could never forget you. I certainly could never forget Theresa. I pray for her every day. Every day."

"I live in America now . . . " He didn't say Canada because he didn't feel like explaining the relationship of the two countries or the fact that not all Canadians lived in igloos. A lot of Italians knew the name Toronto or Montreal, but they somehow did not connect those cities with Canada. They just shrugged and said, "America."

"Do you like it?" she asked.

"Yes. Very much. I'm a lawyer."

"I see," Giovanna answered without sounding or looking interested. "What city do you live in?"

"Toronto."

Giovanna's eyes narrowed and she seemed to grow even paler than she was already. "Toronto?" she repeated in a somewhat shaky voice.

"Do you know someone there?"

Giovanna quickly shook her head. Then she tilted her head and smiled. "They say I'm a little crazy."

He forced his expression to remain the same. Personally he thought she was a lot crazy. "I wanted you to tell me about Theresa," he said. "You were her friend. I just want to know more about what she was like."

"I can't discuss that day," Giovanna replied.

*171*

"No, not that day. Just what she was like. I was so young."

Giovanna nodded. She supposed she could manage to tell him about Theresa. But she really wanted him to leave. She wanted him to leave and Elizabeth to phone. She had to tell her daughter she was in danger. My God, she thought with a shudder. Roberto and Elizabeth lived in the same city! She reminded herself that she had no proof that Roberto had had anything at all to do with the bomb blast. But if Elizabeth had been the target, who had planned it? She knew it had not been Don Vincenzo.

"Did she do well in school?" Roberto asked.

Giovanna nodded. "She was a very good student. She had lots of friends and she used to tell wonderful stories."

For nearly an hour Giovanna told Roberto about his sister, at least all she could remember. It was a great relief to her when he finally left to go visit Rosa.

# *13*

*I*t was a wet spring. Even though it was May, Toronto was still being subjected to cold, drizzling rain.

Rebecca finished going over her bank statements. The P&M Charitable Trust now had assets valued at $7,500,000 and continued to contribute 80 percent of its annual income to various charities and worthwhile projects around the country. When the interest rates started to hit the ceiling, the trust's disposable annual income reached close to $1,000,000.

Ruth Feld, her secretary, continued to receive a bonus from the trust that covered the hours she spent on Rebecca's other charitable projects. Life hadn't improved much for Ruth, Rebecca thought. She frequently complained to Rebecca that her husband made her life miserable, demanding more and more money so that he could play the horses. She lamented that her son's drug habits had turned him into a male prostitute. Recently, she said, he'd shown up at home wearing two earrings, leather pants, and a studded dog collar.

Someone knocked on Rebecca's office door.

"Come in," she called out.

It was Ruth and she look distressed.

"What's the matter? Can I help you?"

"I'd like to talk with you," Ruth announced.

173

"Well, I have some time. C'mon in and sit down, Ruth."

The secretary came in and sat down on the edge of a chair that faced Rebecca's desk. Distress was not the only emotion evident in her expression — there was something else. Nervousness? At the very least she seemed tense, like a spring about to recoil.

"I'd like a raise, Rebecca," Ruth said.

There was no preamble and her request was unexpected.

Ruth went on. "You're making a fortune with the trust, and my salary of $45,000 is ridiculous, considering all the work I do."

Ruth's rigid body language and the hostility in her eyes made Rebecca's antennae go up, especially since she'd kept the numbers on the trust's investments under lock and key.

"How do you know anything about the trust?" Rebecca asked.

"Without me, you'd be nothing," Ruth snarled, ignoring the question. "I've watched you. Cozying up to that mobster. Hobnobbing with the rich and famous. And who are you anyhow? Just the daughter of a greenhorn!"

Rebecca got out of her chair and walked over to Ruth. She stared at her with a mixture of disbelief and anger. Ruth had worked for her a long time. Her attitude was unbelievable. "What have I ever done to you to make you so vicious toward me?" she whispered.

Ruth didn't answer.

"I signed your husband's benefit forms," Rebecca said, "so he could continue to collect unemployment insurance, even though he was working as a furniture salesman for cash."

Ruth looked up at her unblinkingly. "None of that has to do with my worth," she said evenly.

"I arranged for free tickets to the theater, free repairs on your house, free perks for your kids. And I got your druggy son bailed out of jail, how many times? Haven't I always been there to help if I could?"

"I deserved all of it, and more." Ruth's voice was rising and her face was now red as a beet. "Without my help you'd be nothing. And I want more money. If you don't give me an extra $25,000 a year, plus a clothing allowance, I'll let everyone know all your secrets, especially the fancy snobs who are involved with your precious charities!"

Rebecca looked stonily at Ruth. Clearly, something was very much amiss. Ruth was hinting she knew things she shouldn't. She must have been prying. Her own anger rose. How could this woman betray her?

She narrowed her eyes, "You have two minutes to get yourself out of here," Rebecca said, her voice icy. "And if you don't, I'll escort you out myself."

"Bitch," Ruth breathed.

"And if you ever bother me or anyone involved in the charities," Rebecca continued, "then maybe all your suspicions about my Mafia connections will be proven true."

As soon as Ruth left, she called the locksmith and one hour later all the locks were changed in her offices. As she sat at her desk looking out the window, she thought about calling Ruth at home to try to smooth things over, or at least to find out what had provoked her to such nastiness.

But then she decided against it. "Nobody puts a gun to my head," she said aloud. "Especially someone I've been good to."

The next day Rebecca had one year's severance pay couriered to Ruth's home. She assumed that was the end of Ruth Feld's involvement in her life.

*R*uth Feld pressed her narrow lips together and hurried off to see her cousin, Charlene Jacobs.

Change the locks, you bitch! she thought. It doesn't matter. Virtually every word Rebecca had spoken in her office, on the telephone or in person, over the last ten years had been recorded and stored. Her discussions with Senator Jacobs, Bob DeSalle, Sir John Mecklinger, and others about the strategy for getting favorable political decisions had been taped.

All her personal checks, the trust's checks, and the financial statements of other organizations where Rebecca had served as a volunteer executive member had been photocopied and stored as well.

Any special arrangements she ever made for politicians — gifts, perks, contributions — and the code names of the couriers she had used to make the deliveries had also been recorded.

"I'll get even with you, Rebecca Sherman," Ruth vowed.

*A* week later Ruth Feld and her cousin Charlene Jacobs visited the office of *The Tribune*. At first Ruth tried to sell them the information she had accumulated. When they wouldn't buy, she gave them selected copies for nothing — except their promise to print "flattering pictures" of her when the story hit the press.

She then accompanied Charlene to the senator's office.

Jacobs studied the photocopies in her possession. He gritted his teeth, grimly pleased at the thought that Santino DeLuca would probably pay through the nose to keep all this hushed up. But he didn't say anything right away.

"We've already been to the press," Charlene said self-righteously. "We left them copies of some of these documents."

Jacobs couldn't believe his ears. He looked at his wife and then at Ruth, and felt the distinct desire to strangle both of them. "Are you two insane?" he asked, his tone ugly. "What a stupid thing to do! Both of you together have a combined I.Q. of twenty!"

Then he completely lost his temper. "You fucking stupid cunt!" he screamed at his wife. "Don't you know what you've done? You've opened a can of worms that could wind up crawling all over us!"

Both women turned white, neither one of them able to speak.

"Some of these politicians are friends of mine," he continued through gritted teeth, glaring at his wife. "And they're not going to go down quietly if this thing explodes. So when the bomb drops in the bunker, you'd better pray that I'm not still in it!"

*R*ebecca forced herself to go into the office because there was so much work to do. More than usual, she reminded herself. She had been a week without a secretary, and although Jean had helped her by doing some typing at home, things were really stacking up.

This week, she promised herself, she would start looking for someone new.

She felt distracted as well as uneasy. When the phone rang at ten-fifteen, she jumped, startled at the unexpected sound.

"Rebecca? This is Vinnie Bratuso."

She let out her breath. "Good morning," she answered, trying to sound normal.

"I called 'cause I gotta tell you, your secretary and Senator Jacobs have just walked into the building where the Attorney General's office is, together."

She felt the forebodings begin to surface, but it was important to stay calm. "How do you know that?"

"I just happened to be outside the government building, picking up a racing form, when Feld and Jacobs went in."

"Oh. Thanks, Vinnie. I have to call Jimmy."

She replaced the receiver in its cradle. She tried to compose herself; then she dialed Jimmy Bono's number.

"Did you find anything out about a shadow on me?" she asked when he answered the phone.

"So far, nothing," he answered. "Why?"

Rebecca told him about Vinnie's call. "My nose is twitching, Jimmy. That old witch is up to something. Get Vinnie to check out every office in that building to find out exactly who they went to see."

Two long hours later Jimmy called back. She answered the phone on the first ring.

"I'll pick you up in ten minutes. Don't say anything; just be outside waiting for me."

He was there in seven minutes. His fingers gripped the steering wheel, and he had a very worried look on his face as they sped away. "We got trouble," he told Rebecca. "Your office and telephone are bugged."

Rebecca was stunned. "Who? why?"

"We're still working on it, but it looks like your secretary's been taping all your calls and the meetings in your office. I hope you haven't said anything that you shouldn't have. And we've just found out that the boss's home phone has also had a tap on it — don't know for how long it's been on.

We do a sweep periodically, you know. His lawyers are raising shit with the police commissioner right now."

Rebecca's mind was racing, trying to remember what she might have said that could prove to be incriminating. "How the hell can I remember almost ten years' worth of conversations? And besides, isn't it all inadmissible evidence anyway?"

"Yeah, inadmissible, but useful stuff. It's the inside information the cops might get — the amount of paybacks, the names of the politicians on the take, how and when the deals come down, the contracts — that's the most dangerous."

"Oh God," she said, closing her eyes.

"Yeah, once they got the answers, the questions are easy."

"It's hard for me to believe this is happening."

Jimmy was shaking his head. "Once the police know where to look, they're halfway there. Until then, they're like fish flopping around in a pail of dirty water. But if they know who to put the squeeze on, there's a good chance someone will try to cut themselves a deal and start talking. And then the whole house of cards could come tumbling down."

He pulled to a stop in the circular driveway of the Inn on the Park. Silently he handed her a pair of sunglasses and a hotel key. "You're already checked in under the name of Mrs. Cohen. Room five-three-o. I'll stop by your house and talk to your sister. Don't call home, don't call the boss. We gotta make sure the lines are cleared first. Just try to relax and watch some TV."

"But why do I have to stay here?"

"First, so we can clear the lines and, second, because no one can ask you questions if they can't find you."

"I'll have to answer them sometime."

"Sure, but not right this second. Let's try to do a damage assessment first."

Rebecca nodded and got out of the car.

*T*wo days later a newspaper article appeared about politicians, socialites, and their close ties with Italian businessmen rumored to belong to the Mafia, specifically mentioning Santino DeLuca and Massimo Brattini. According to the "unnamed source," an investigation was being conducted secretly by a joint FBI–RCMP task force headed by Inspector Grant Teasdale of the RCMP. Rebecca Sherman was mentioned as one of those having close ties to both the politicians and DeLuca.

*O*n the morning of her third day in the hotel, Rebecca got a call saying she would be picked up at 11:30. It wasn't Jimmy who came for her; it was a stranger. She was driven into the depths of Scarborough, to a fine old restaurant that offered absolute privacy as well as good food.

"I don't like this, Rebecca," Santino told her over lunch. "There's an undercurrent I can't put my finger on. Why is your name being mentioned so much? We've got to find out who's behind it. We know your secretary is providing the information, but she's not operating on her own."

He unfolded the newspaper. It had the inside information on Peartree and its links to CanMor.

"It must be Senator Jacobs," Rebecca said. "He has to be the 'unnamed source.' He's the only one I told that CanMor had been the original owner of the land next to Peartree and that its ownership couldn't be definitively traced to Brattini, as he told me.

"I also told Jacobs that I intended to drop the trace on CanMor because Peartree was a done deal — so who cares anyhow?"

Santino's face hardened. "I'm going to call Jimmy and have him take you to Jacobs's office."

Bono joined them for dessert. "Rebecca is calling the shots on this one, Jimmy," Santino told him, "so you make sure anything she wants done is taken care of."

Once they were in the car, Jimmy told her that Charlene Jacobs and Ruth Feld were cousins. He also informed her that Mayor Lois Richardson had been on the cash payroll of DeLuca Industries for years. Rebecca wasn't surprised. Having insiders on side was part of the price of doing business, but she was angry at herself for not having spotted the setup herself.

Jacobs set me up right from the start, she thought. First, getting Steven to hire Ruth Feld as my secretary, then the political contacts, finally Peartree. He's been planning this for a long time. But why?

When Rebecca walked into the senator's office, unannounced, he didn't seem surprised to see her.

"You two-bit rat!" she shouted at him, not caring if her voice could be heard through the walls. "You're the only one who could have leaked the information on CanMor to the press. Are you working for Brattini?"

When he didn't answer, she continued yelling. "And why didn't you tell me Ruth Feld was your wife's cousin? What the hell are all of you doing? Why are you setting me up? I thought we were on the same team!"

"Not any more we're not," he answered, a look of utter contempt on his face. "You pushed your way into the world of the big boys, where you didn't belong. Your only claim to fame was the fact that DeLuca was hot for you. Well, now you're too hot — everything's too hot. And it's going to get hotter."

Rebecca's mouth was dry and she was shaking with anger. But she didn't say anything; she let him continue.

"You've made too many enemies, lady, and the politicians are getting nervous. DeLuca should have listened to me a long time ago and hired my firm to look after his trust fund, instead of getting involved with an amateur like you. I told him you'd be nothing but trouble."

Rebecca glowered at him but still did not respond. Instead she turned on her heel and left. In minutes she was opening the door of the limo.

"Jimmy, drive me around for a while," she snapped as she slipped into the front seat next to him.

After five minutes of listening to her curse Ruth Feld, the media, and Senator Jacobs, Jimmy asked Rebecca if she wanted a "special" message sent to the senator.

"The boss called while you were in Jacobs's office. He's just got a report on some of Jacobs's activities, and the shit has hit the fan. A call's already been put in to Buffalo, just in case you want the message to be unforgettable."

Rebecca knew what "Buffalo" meant. That's where most of the "hired help" came from. She ran her hands through her long hair and tapped her feet on the car floor, trying to control her rage, frustration, and fear.

How much damage could the tapes really do to her and Santino if they couldn't be used in court? she wondered as she began a long dialogue with herself.

Not too much. I'm sure I covered all the tracks.

But what if Jacobs decided to give evidence against her?

He wouldn't dare! He'd implicate himself. Besides, he knows what the Italians do to snitches.

Yes, but what about some of the others?

A "message" to Jacobs would no doubt get through to all of them, guaranteeing their continued silence.

But could I live with myself if I turned my back on what I know is in store for Jacobs?

Rebecca turned to look at Bono. "Jimmy, does it ever bother you, knowing all that you do about 'Buffalo' and other matters?"

Jimmy kept his eyes on the road and didn't answer her right away. Then he pulled the car over to the curb, turned, and gave her a cold stare.

"I know nothing about nothing, Mrs. Sherman," he answered, "and neither do you."

Rebecca nodded until they were driving again. "I want to go home, Jimmy. I think it's best."

"Sure," he replied.

When the car pulled up to the house, she said to Jimmy, "Don't do anything about Jacobs, at least not yet. I'm sure I can handle anything that comes along on the Peartree deal. And I'll speak to Santino later about hiring a lawyer for myself, just in case."

*A* few weeks later Grant Teasdale paced around his office. His whole investigative team was there, and every one of them looked as upset as he felt.

"Who the hell leaked the info on the DeLuca wiretaps to the press?" he shouted. "The commissioner's been getting heat from DeLuca's lawyers," he continued, "and I'm on the grill myself about the tap on his home phone. And now everyone has clammed up."

"Maybe it was the senator or that Feld woman who leaked the info," Special Agent Ann Mitchell suggested. She had been seconded to the investigation from the FBI's Boston office. "You can bet it wasn't one of us."

"But Jacobs and Feld didn't know about the taps on DeLuca's phone," Grant said. "And the CanMor–Peartree stuff wasn't in the material Feld turned over to us, so she couldn't have known about that either."

"Unless she saw it, and then destroyed it before she came in to see you," Mitchell said. "Don't forget, the senator is married to her cousin. Maybe she wanted to protect him."

"Nah, Feld's not smart enough, or loyal enough," Grant countered.

"Well, I have a feeling the senator's tied to Sherman a lot tighter than he's willing to admit," Ann said. "I didn't buy all that 'I don't remember anything' crap he gave us last week."

"I think you might be right about Jacobs," Grant admitted. He thought back to the day Ruth Feld and Senator Jack Jacobs had first walked into his office.

As Teasdale had listened to the senator and the Feld woman, he knew that Jacobs was simply there to cover his own ass when the mealy-mouthed little bastard said, "I'm coming forward, unsolicited, to cooperate with the law enforcement officers in any way I can."

"Who knows what really went on?" Jacobs had said to him during the interview. "Maybe she misled me. I certainly had no direct knowledge of anything she was doing. I also don't know how she became so successful so rapidly. Is it possible she was nothing more than a front for the mob?"

Feld had then told Teasdale that Rebecca was laundering money. "I know it for sure," she'd said, pointing to the cartons of papers she'd brought along with her. "And these documents will prove it." Now he wondered if she had neglected to mention that Jacobs had "borrowed" them for a few hours two days earlier.

The agents in the room were silent as Teasdale came back to the present and went on talking, as if to himself, while he stared out the window.

"It's starting to look as if Jacobs played both sides of the street on that Peartree deal," he said without turning. "CanMor's real owner is a DeLuca numbered company, based in Bermuda, which was dormant for years. And guess who has a piece of it? Senator Jack Jacobs. DeLuca probably didn't even remember that it was a part of his holdings.

"Jacobs had to have known the real story when he sent Sherman off on her wild-goose chase to trace CanMor's ownership," he continued. "He must have played on her fears that Brattini had set her up to get at DeLuca. I think Jacobs was simply testing the waters to find out just how vulnerable he really was. If the tenacious Mrs. Sherman couldn't find out CanMor's real owner, then he figured no one else could either. And then he'd be safe, especially from DeLuca. I suspect the senator was cashing in on his Italian connections without their 'permission.'"

"I can't believe how right on you are," Ann said, her eyes lighting up with admiration for her boss. "You always figure things out so quickly."

Grant didn't notice the snickers from some of Ann's colleagues, but he did notice her. He wasn't as unaware of Ann's overtures as it seemed. He did find her very attractive, but he simply didn't play around. So he felt he had no choice but to keep his distance and ignore her not-so-subtle suggestions about getting together for a drink "so they could unwind together."

Why play with fire? he'd ask himself over and over after he'd refused her. But she was persistent, and very difficult to resist.

Ann Mitchell had a terrific personality, was always smiling, and was well liked by her colleagues. She showed a genuine sensitivity to, and understanding of, the problems they had to deal with every day. Grant felt she was the brightest of his team, the one who could sniff out a lie or a cover-up like a basset hound, and he preferred working with her on this tough case.

But he could see that she hadn't given up on having a more personal relationship with him, so he continued to keep himself aloof, not wanting to encourage any unrealistic expectations on her part.

Grant had always frowned on the extramarital shenanigans in which some of his colleagues engaged.

"I don't want you people letting your personal feelings affect the kind of job you do here," he'd say to them. "Life-and-death decisions leave no room for mistakes because of your out-of-control hormones."

But lately he'd been wondering about his own hormones. He was noticing other women too much, especially Ann Mitchell. Still, he ignored her supportive comment.

"I think things are going to boomerang on the senator pretty soon," Ann said, breaking into his thoughts. "DeLuca's like a sleeping giant — one way or another he's going to get to the bottom of this. I almost pity Jacobs when he's exposed, but, when he is, maybe we'll get lucky, and he'll come running to us, singing like a canary, to save his own skin."

"You're right on track as usual, Ann. Let's stay real close to him."

"Okay, people," he said, turning to the rest of the team, "it's time we brought Mrs. Sherman in here for a little chat. Who knows what goodies she might have for us."

*A*nn Mitchell left the meeting smiling. Was Teasdale breaking down? She sensed he did notice her. She sensed he was attracted to her.

Mitchell was almost six feet tall, with jet-black hair and matching eyes. She'd been an agent with the FBI since her graduation from Mount Holyoke College ten years earlier. Her parents had been horrified when they'd learned that she wanted to be a G-woman. Despite their entreaties to "think it over just a little bit longer," she'd applied to the FBI the day after her twenty-third birthday. The requirements for a special agent of the Bureau were that candidates be citizens, twenty-three years of age, and a graduate of an accredited law school or the graduate of an accredited college or university with a major in accounting. Graduates of universities with majors in other subjects could qualify with three additional years of full-time experience. Special consideration was given to those with languages, science, and backgrounds in financial analysis.

Ann had majored in accounting. Thus, given her education and physical condition, she had been accepted right away and sent off to Quantico for fifteen months of additional training.

During her years with the Bureau she'd had a couple of short-term affairs with colleagues that had fizzled. She simply wasn't interested in marriage or children. She was devoted to her career in law enforcement and hoped that someday she'd get to the top, perhaps even becoming the first woman Director of the FBI. As she closed the door to her office she wondered which would be harder: that, or seducing Grant Teasdale.

# *14*

AUGUST
*1983*

*W*hen Rebecca received the first official
letter from Inspector Teasdale two months earlier, asking her to set up an
appointment with him in order to "discuss certain matters now under investigation," she called William Fitzpatrick, the senior counsel at Walker &
Associates. He was also one of the country's most prominent criminal
attorneys.

William Fitzpatrick had been born in Halifax, Nova Scotia, but had
moved to Toronto with his mother when he was ten years old. A brilliant
student, he had caught the eye of one of his professors who had helped to
arrange a student loan so that William could attend Osgoode Hall Law
School. Fitzpatrick had done so well there that he'd received an invitation to
take some postgraduate courses at Harvard.

On his return to Toronto he joined Walker & Associates and remained
there to become one of its highest-billing partners. Fitzpatrick was very
tall, very thin, and very skillful. He was also very black.

"Ignore that letter," he told Rebecca over the phone. "I'll handle it from
here. You've got nothing to say to the police, now or ever."

Santino was very unhappy about the turn of events. The media were
having a field day, reporting on allegations and insider leaks by "unnamed
sources" every day.

Many of Rebecca's former associates, including Richard Dudley and Jack Jacobs, had disassociated themselves publicly from her.

Maybe I should have had a "message" sent to Jacobs after all, Rebecca mused. It might have stopped the lynch mob.

But Bob DeSalle and Sir John Mecklinger made public statements of support on her behalf, highlighting her community service and management of the trust. Their words were of some comfort until Big Dick Studley held a press conference. In it he announced his intention of getting back into politics by running for office in the next election.

He also claimed that he'd severed his ties with Rebecca Sherman months earlier when he'd learned of her questionable dealings.

"But not before he pocketed his monthly $5,000 consulting fee!" Santino shouted as he paced around Rebecca's living room. "God, I hate those sleaze bags. How I wish I could flatten his face with my fist, just like in the old days. Then maybe he wouldn't be so quick to 'give interviews.' By the way, I assume you've got him nailed if you ever need it."

"Yes, I do, Santino," Rebecca answered. "But he's not isolated. Bringing him down might involve others, one of whom is our mutual friend, and that could be a problem."

Early in her relationship with Santino, he had taught her how to deal with corrupt politicians and officials. His most important lesson was on "how to cover your ass." He'd explained how necessary it was to always have back-up documentation on certain kinds of transactions — a tape or a deposit slip or even a signature — and to keep it locked safely away. It kept the politicians in line, and also protected the giver from reverse threats of extortion.

By the time Rebecca received the phone call from Mayor Howard Brennan a week later, she was beyond hurt and humiliation. He suggested she step off his task force until things cooled down.

"After all, Rebecca," he said, "we can't let any outside distractions keep us from the task at hand. As long as you're a part of the committee, the media will focus in on you, and not on the accomplishments of the task force."

And not on the graft and corruption either, she stopped herself from saying to him.

*They* had eaten dinner and returned to the Sutton Place apartment. He fixed them drinks and they sat down to stare at the fire. It wasn't a real fireplace, of course, but it was a fine gas fireplace, with ever-burning logs and glowing coals. It made the place more cheerful than they felt.

Santino was becoming increasingly alarmed about the leaks concerning his own business interests. He looked distressed.

"I know you're worried," Rebecca said as she curled up next to him.

"I don't like all the leaks."

"I don't either, but I don't know what to do about it," she said.

"I'm thinking of leaving Ontario, at least for a while. Not back to Detroit. It's no place for children. Maybe to Boston."

At those words, Rebecca bolted upright and stared at him. She couldn't believe her ears. "Santino, this isn't like you! Giving up without a fight? I'm not afraid of the media or the police. Fitzpatrick assures me they can't do anything to me, other than harass me. They're probably hoping that I'll fall to pieces."

"*Bella, bella,* you can't keep fighting all the time." He pulled her close and murmured in her ear. "Sometimes you just have to fold your cards. Why don't you take off for a year or two, and then come back and pick up your life? You know I'll help you find something. The trust can't function properly now, in any case. I'll put everything on hold till the heat's off."

She closed her eyes, mulling over his words.

I'm not slinking off in the dead of night like some scum bag, she thought to herself. I've worked too hard and come too far to let some petty little people destroy my credibility without a fight.

"No," she said flatly. "I can't leave. I can't let them just win."

"It's your decision," he replied sadly.

*Rebecca* sat in William Fitzpatrick's plush Bay Street office. It smelled of leather books and pungent pipe tobacco.

She had just received a second letter from Inspector Teasdale, informing her that she was now under investigation for fraud and corruption.

"I want to take Inspector Teasdale up on his invitation to come in and see him," she said. "I'm not afraid of the police."

"I see a stubborn look in your eyes, Mrs. Sherman. I would, however, like to dissuade you."

"No. My mind is made up."

"Then let me get the good inspector on the phone. I'll make an appointment for both of us. You must not go alone."

Four hours later as they entered the elevator on their way to the meeting, Fitzpatrick repeated his instructions to her.

"You will not speak to the police or offer any information at all. You will answer all their questions with a simple 'yes' or 'no,' and then only when I give you a nod.

"Remember what I'm telling you, Mrs. Sherman. The police are very tricky, and in this case you're not dealing with ordinary foot soldiers. The FBI and the RCMP have been doing this for too long not to know every trick in the book. And don't believe anything they tell you either. They lie and fabricate evidence all the time. It is something we blacks understand and have had more experience with, so you can just take my word for that."

He noticed the skeptical look on Rebecca's face and said, "Well, with Jews they're a little more careful, but still, don't ever trust them."

"You know, Mr. Fitzpatrick," Rebecca said, unconcerned about the contempt in her voice, "considering how prominent an attorney you are purported to be, I'm puzzled as to why you, in your capacity as a senior officer of the Law Society, have never conducted an inquiry into these 'despicable' law-enforcement officers.

"And, I'm wondering about something else," she went on. "Do the esteemed judges, especially the ones who are occasionally sober, know about these breaches of the law committed by those sworn to uphold it? If not, someone should tell them." She hoped her sarcasm wouldn't go unnoticed.

Rebecca's experience in back-room politics had taught her that those in the justice system could bend the rules to take care of their own, thanks to ambitious and "flexible" prosecutors and judges. After all, judges were nothing more than political appointees themselves, lawyers who were elevated to the bench for life by the politicians of the day. In Canada they didn't have to worry about answering to the voters for their decisions, or getting booted out of office, as those in some U.S. states did.

Even though Rebecca had a more skeptical view of the justice system than most, she was still unsure about Fitzpatrick's pontifications, and his strategy in handling her situation. Her instincts kept telling her that she'd do better trusting the police than the courts. But Santino was insistent that she follow Fitzpatrick's advice, so she pushed her misgivings aside.

Listen to him, Rebecca, she said to herself. Santino can't afford any more police investigations. Just sit there and play dumb. And keep your mouth shut!

They were shown into a waiting room. It was plain, with straight-backed chairs. In one corner there was a tall cactus plant — a lone attempt at decoration.

After she and Fitzpatrick had been waiting for almost an hour, Special Agent Ann Mitchell came out to escort them into the main interview room, which reminded Rebecca of Santino's boardroom.

She and Fitzpatrick were given the transcripts of telephone conversations and meetings that had been held in Rebecca's office over a nine-year period.

"It should take you at least an hour to look over this material, Mrs. Sherman," Mitchell said very pleasantly, noticing that Rebecca had barely glanced at her. "And then Inspector Teasdale will want to speak with you. I'm afraid we can't let these documents out of our hands at present, but if your lawyer wishes to examine them further, we can set up an appointment for another time."

When Ann walked into Grant's private office, she whistled. "Well, now I can understand what DeLuca sees in her," she said. "That woman sure has something. I almost knelt down to kiss her ring."

Teasdale burst out laughing and, without thinking, put an arm around her shoulder.

"Ann, I need a woman's perspective on this one," he said, dropping his arm when he felt her warmth against him. "As smart as Sherman is supposed to be, I think she's being set up. How scared do you think she'd have to be to talk to us? She's got a young daughter to take care of and, without a husband, she's pretty much on her own. Let's play on that and try to get her pissed off enough to finger some of her so-called friends."

"Judging from the way she handles herself, I doubt we'll be able to intimidate her," Ann said, shaking her head. "It's worth a try, though. I can't wait to see her face when she reads some of the stuff her so-called friends had to say about her. In the meantime, I'll go back in and amuse her lawyer so she can read the transcripts without him putting in his two cents' worth every few seconds."

"No," Grant said. "I don't want her to get too familiar with you. Send in one of the others. They all said they'd like to have a close-up look at her, so now's their chance."

Rebecca felt like a balloon slowly leaking air as she read transcripts of some of her recent and not-so-recent telephone conversations, and the indiscreet comments she'd made. Despite Fitzpatrick's assurances that nothing that had been taped without her permission could be used as evidence against her, she knew that somehow the words she had spoken years ago had come back to haunt her — and worse, to haunt Santino.

She didn't bother reading every word in the transcript; it didn't really matter. It wouldn't take a rocket scientist to figure out that Dudley, Covan, Brennan, and others had taken payoffs. Dudley, when he was the deputy premier, and Brennan, even now, while still serving his third term as mayor. She wondered if the Premier knew about the bribes to Dudley.

The transcripts included conversations about some of the business deals that Rebecca had been handling for DeLuca Industries. There were also references to Brattini's thugs and how they were to be taken care of.

Thank God Santino's name wasn't mentioned directly, Rebecca thought as she pushed the papers away for just a few minutes to gather her thoughts.

Behind a two-way mirror, Special Agent Mitchell watched Rebecca. She saw her begin to look anxious as she read the material and then quickly get herself under control when Deputy Inspector Mark Chan walked into the room.

"Inspector Teasdale would like you to have a look at some of these other transcripts, Mrs. Sherman." Chan deposited another carton of files on the desk.

"They're the statements of certain individuals in response to our questions. The Inspector thought you should have a sense of them before the two of you meet."

"I'd like an explanation of what's going on here!" Fitzpatrick snapped, getting out of his chair and walking over to Chan. "Mrs. Sherman agreed to come in here for an interview out of courtesy and respect for this task force, and to show that she has nothing to hide.

"Instead of meeting with Inspector Teasdale, as the letter indicated, she has been required to look through documents — dubious in their credibility to say the least, and certainly inadmissible in any court of law.

"Now, if there's nothing else," he went on, trying for all the world to look impressive as he puffed out his chest, "my client and I are leaving."

Just then the door opened and Inspector Teasdale walked into the room. Rebecca, who was still concentrating on one of the documents, didn't lift her head to look at him. Verbal sparring broke out between him and Fitzpatrick, which she ignored as she continued to read statements by her former associates.

Her initial despair quickly turned to anger. I thought these people were, at the least, friendly colleagues, she said to herself. Instead, they've been sticking knives into my back, tripping over themselves to see who can make the deepest cuts.

"Mrs. Sherman, please, I'd like your attention for just a moment," Fitzpatrick said, his voice sounding strained. "Inspector Teasdale would like to talk with you now."

Rebecca stopped reading and looked up into the bluest eyes she'd ever seen. She felt a spark and, for just a second, she forgot who Teasdale was and why she was here. But she quickly came back to reality and looked him over as disdainfully as she could. She gave him a brief nod, noticing the amusement in his eyes.

"How do you do, Mrs. Sherman," he said as they shook hands. "I'm Inspector Grant Teasdale, of the joint FBI–RCMP task force. Thank you for coming in to see us."

For the first time in his career, Grant really understood the concept of eyes throwing off sparks. She was electric. No fear, no embarrassment — just defiance. Everything about her body language seemed to say, "Let the games begin."

"What do you know about DeLuca Industries' Florida operations?"

"Don't answer that!"

"How well do you know Massimo Brattini?"

"Hardly at all."

"Did you have anything to do with rezoning the property known as Peartree?"

"Don't answer that!"

"Did you have anything to do with the sale of Mayor Lois Richardson's home and the purchase of her new one?"

"Don't answer that!"

"Do you have any direct knowledge of the disappearance of Mario Grazie?"

"No, I don't." My God, that's Brattini's personal hit man. What had happened to him? She looked down quickly, hoping her eyes hadn't given away the fact that she had recognized Grazie's name.

"Which bureaucrat did you pay to get the freeze lifted on the importing of quarry tile from Portugal?"

"Don't answer that!"

How the hell did he know about that?

"What involvement did Santino DeLuca have in the fire that destroyed Paisano's Bakery?"

"Don't answer that!"

"How much of the capital from the P&M Trust came from offshore companies?"

"Don't answer that!"

"Who is Pedro Villela?"

"I don't know." Christ, he's found the link to Marseilles.

"What were you and DeLuca doing in Hamilton, Bermuda, four months ago?"

"None of your business!"

"Do you have any direct knowledge of which public officials are on the cash payroll of DeLuca Industries?"

"Don't answer that!"

"Do you have any direct knowledge of cash payments made to James Sergino for sewer allocations on the Peartree site?"

"Don't answer that!"

How did he find that out? Sergino was the senior aide to Murray Hill, MP from Vancouver Central, whose cabinet portfolio included government services. All sewer allocations in Ontario had to have federal approval from the Ministry of Government Services. Jacobs and Bingo were both there when Sergino accepted the $50,000 in cash on Hill's behalf.

Jacobs must have ratted in exchange for immunity, she decided.

"Do you have any direct knowledge as to whether Jim Hollis or any other member of the mayor's task force received money in exchange for cooperating on certain municipal matters?"

"No."

After another hour of questions Rebecca Sherman still hadn't said more than twenty words.

"Mrs. Sherman, I think you're making a mistake," Inspector Teasdale said in a very gentle voice. "As you have already seen, the transcripts in our possession are very incriminating. All roads appear to lead to you. We'd like to save you the humiliation and stress of criminal charges and a lengthy trial. Why don't you go home and think over what I'm about to tell you. And then give me a call."

"Wait a minute, Inspector," Fitzpatrick snapped, putting a hand on Rebecca's shoulder. "My client knows her rights. Any evidence obtained by tape or wiretap without her knowledge and consent is inadmissible. All you've got is a bunch of words that might very well have been spoken in jest. You're trying to intimidate Mrs. Sherman, to frighten her. Today's off-the-wall questions sound like nothing more than a fishing expedition."

Grant looked at Fitzpatrick as if he were a dead fish.

Fitzpatrick continued. "So, any communications you might wish to have with my client in the future must come through me. Until you can show us something more substantial than the airy-fairy crap we've seen so far, Mrs. Sherman has nothing more to say to you."

The lawyer took her arm, propelled her around, and they left. Rebecca was in turmoil. What did Teasdale want to tell her? Should she listen?

# 15

SEPTEMBER
1983

$\mathcal{R}$ebecca had known for a long time that a parting with Santino was inevitable. The allegations and the innuendoes about her had received wide media coverage in both Canada and the United States. As long as her name was associated with the trust, or Santino, the publicity in the media wouldn't let up. And her refusal to bow to pressure and resign from all her positions when the stories had first surfaced had only made matters worse.

The trust was now under investigation, along with the various charities to which it had given contributions.

The fact that Santino was a married man added to the pressure. If the FBI–RCMP task force decided to leak some damaging evidence about their personal relationship to the press, things would only get worse.

Men like DeLuca went out of their way to avoid publicity, never drawing attention to themselves, to their families, and most especially to their businesses.

On September 5, the day after Rebecca was charged with fraud, she and Santino met at Jimmy Bono's apartment in the Colonnade. She was picked up outside the Farmers' Market near the waterfront. The area was full of Saturday morning shoppers, and when she got into the car she immediately lay down on the floor, hoping that if anyone was following her, they'd lose her. They did. When she reached Jimmy's apartment, Santino was waiting for her. They embraced, kissing and clinging almost desperately to each other, neither one acknowledging that it was for the last time.

He took her face between both hands and looked into her eyes. "I wish you'd listened to me in the first place and taken time off," he said gently. "But now it's too late to stop the frenzy."

Rebecca lowered her eyes. *My God, he looks so tired and pale. And I feel so guilty. Why didn't I just walk away when I had the chance?*

"I've made arrangements for you and Lisa to leave the country," he continued. "You'll be well taken care of. Of course, you'll both have to change your names and live very quietly. But at least you'll be safe, away from all this mess and any danger of going to jail."

Rebecca looked up into his loving eyes and smiled at him.

"You know I won't do that, Santino. I'd never be able to come back to Canada. What kind of life would it be for Lisa? I can't rob her of a future. And hiding out in some foreign country, always looking over my shoulder, isn't for me. Besides, I'm going to fight these charges. Running away will only make matters worse."

He said nothing, but held her closer to him.

"I guess it's over for us," she whispered, hoping he'd deny it.

"Yes, it's over for us, *mia bella*," he said softly. He stepped back, taking her face between his hands again. She nodded her head in understanding. When she looked up at him she was shocked to see tears in his eyes.

"We've both made some wrong choices, and now we have to pay for them," he continued. "In another world we might have belonged together, but not in this one. The intensity of our passion for each other could never make up for the hurt we'd cause to those we love."

When she couldn't hold back her own tears, he kissed her wet cheeks, her quivering lips.

"I was perfect for you as a lover, a protector, a friend," he continued. "But my family is the most important thing in my life. My love and passion for you almost transcended it."

She felt paralyzed. She couldn't take her eyes off his.

"What's happened to our world this past year has forced me to remember who we both are, not who we wish we could be. Try to remember all that we've had together, my darling Becky, not what we couldn't continue to share. And think only of what life can still offer you. Hold the love that was between us next to your heart, and know I'll always be close by."

She nodded again, unable to speak. She felt her heart was breaking as she kissed him one last time, tears streaming down her face.

"*Ciao, bella. Ti'amo.*"

# *16*

*R*CMP headquarters on Jarvis Street looked like a prison. It had few windows and every possible security device. It was certainly no place for anyone even remotely claustrophobic, Grant Teasdale thought. He wished he could look out on a park or even open a window. He hated working in this hermetically sealed coffin of a building.

His office was cluttered; he just couldn't seem to keep empty surfaces empty, at least not for long. He had even had to clear two chairs for Rebecca Sherman and her lawyer to sit on.

He looked back at her. For the first time he thought he saw a hint of fear in her eyes.

It had been nearly four weeks since she'd been charged with aiding and abetting the commission of a crime in connection with favors and benefits paid out to secure the approval of the Peartree project.

The media were still having a field day over the fall of the once-powerful woman who had been so closely associated with DeLuca Industries. It was a daily topic of conversation in the halls of power as far away as Italy.

"My door is always open to you, Mrs. Sherman," Grant said, looking into her eyes and ignoring her lawyer, William Fitzpatrick.

"As I told you last month, I want to help you if I can. If you agree to cooperate with our investigation, I promise you protection — from both your 'friends' and the criminal justice system. You'll be given immunity from prosecution in exchange for evidence against certain politicians and others."

Rebecca took a deep breath, lifted her chin, and stared into his eyes. They both knew who the "others" were: Santino DeLuca and his associates.

"I have no information to give you, Inspector. I know nothing about any criminal activity; not yesterday, not today, and not tomorrow."

Grant admired her style but not her decision. He'd known very soon after he'd begun interviewing some of her former associates that Rebecca Sherman was quietly being cut loose.

He thought of the visits he'd had from Councilor Maxwell Gallow and his lawyer. Gallow was concerned about some of the trips Rebecca had arranged through his travel agency for people who often had issues before city committees. He'd never bothered to declare his conflict of interest, assuming no one would ever connect him with the trips. Gallow's lawyer, worried that Rebecca might start pointing fingers, wanted to offer his client's cooperation as a bargaining chip. Teasdale had promised to let them know.

Richard Dudley had been even more pathetic.

"How could I know she was involved with the Mafia?" he whined to Grant.

"Did you take any money from her?" Grant questioned.

"What do you mean, 'take any money'?" Dudley's eyebrows shot up.

"You know what I mean. Did she give you any money for your re-election campaign? Or any money when you had to retire from office?"

"I don't remember. I never kept the records myself. I had staff who did that for me. But I promise you, Inspector, that if I do remember anything I'll call you. And if there's anything I can do to help you put her away where she belongs, let me know."

I'll bet he's afraid we'll find out about the cash he took, Grant thought as Dudley left his office. I'm sure he'll be on his knees in front of Jacobs within the hour. Too bad we can't use the wiretaps of his conversations with Rebecca and the senator as evidence against him. If we could, the only office he'd be eligible to run for is chief toilet cleaner in Kingston Penitentiary.

The wagons were circling around the politicians and the "establishment."

Grant believed they'd all be quite happy to see DeLuca go down, too — as long as they weren't the ones who had to point the finger at him.

Teasdale knew that Rebecca had the instinct to sense the prevailing political winds. She'd been involved in back-room politics long enough to realize that she was being sacrificed. And he hoped that, when she learned the depth of the betrayal, it would push her over the edge and loosen her tongue. Toward that end he'd offered her a deal. But she wouldn't take it. He wasn't surprised: she'd been too well trained.

"Am I free to go?" Rebecca asked.

Grant stood up. "If that's what you want."

"It's what I want."

"I have a meeting downstairs," Fitzpatrick informed them.

"Do you have a car?" Teasdale asked.

"Yes," she answered, although she wasn't sure Brad was still waiting.

Rebecca walked out onto Jarvis Street and she stood for a moment looking around.

"Over here!"

Rebecca's eyes followed the voice. It was Brad Ross. His silver Chrysler was parked across the street and he was standing next to it, ready to jump in should a meter maid materialize to ticket it.

She waited for the light to change and then crossed the wide street. "Too cheap to feed the meter?" she teased.

"No. I ran out of change."

"You really didn't have to wait."

"I wanted to."

Brad Ross wasn't very tall — about five feet nine inches — but he was very muscular. He had discovered the "joy of fitness" after being warned by his doctor that he was a prime candidate for a coronary if he didn't take better care of himself. He would be forty on his next birthday, and his jet-black hair was as thick as it was when he was a kid.

Rebecca had first met him five years earlier, when he'd been one of the bureaucrats working for the city. They had become good friends. Brad was one of the few she could depend on, one of the few to stick by her as the publicity raged on. In fact, when negative stories about her activities started surfacing in the press, he was the first bureaucrat to approach her with reassuring comments of respect and loyalty.

As the pressure mounted and her isolation from others grew, Ross would call to commiserate with her. When things got worse, he stayed close by, calling more often and developing a friendship with her daughter Lisa. Soon he was a regular visitor to her home, and both she and Lisa looked forward to their evenings together playing Scrabble. He even made some feeble attempts at cooking. He never asked her about Santino or any of the rumors and allegations swirling around them. He simply offered his shoulder and his friendship whenever she needed him, making no demands on her.

Rebecca thought now that she had really never appreciated Brad during those years when she was a member of the mayor's task force. His job as city auditor had been to monitor and assess the expenditures of all agencies and commissions and report back to the city council. His constant presence on most city committees made him almost a fixture. She glanced over at him as he pulled the car away from the curb and thought, I'm glad you're here now.

*T*hat night, as he sat in his den nursing a few beers, Grant couldn't get Rebecca Sherman's face out of his mind. It was her eyes that had given her away. They had changed from anger to defiance to fear and then, worst of all, to helplessness. He knew that she had come to see the reality of her situation and to face the fact that she was totally on her own.

He understood why he felt so strongly about this woman's plight. She reminded him of how it had once been for him, so many years ago. And he wanted to help her.

So many years ago — yes, my God, he did know what it was to be helpless, to be alone, to be abandoned to the worst of all possible fates. He closed his eyes and the past came rushing back as it so often did. Suddenly it was 1954 . . .

"Hail, Mary, full of grace! The Lord is with thee; blessed art thou amongst women, and blessed is the Fruit of thy womb, Jesus. Holy Mary, Mother of God, pray for us sinners . . ."

Those were the first words he heard when he came home from school that day. There were police cars and an ambulance in front of what used to be his home. Once it had been red brick, with white shutters on all the windows with a funny-looking weather vane on the roof. It was a rooster with two tails.

But now his house was all black, and the windows were all smashed. The smell of charred wood and something else, Grant wasn't sure what, was overwhelming.

Where were Mom and Dad? And his little brother Kevin? He tried to run inside but a large policeman held him back.

"Stay out of there, son," he said, "you don't want to see them like . . ."

Grant was ten years old. He had flaming red hair, blue eyes, and freckles; his features were like chiseled marble. He was, in a word, beautiful, and his mother used to tell him how handsome and wonderful he was. "You're my gift from God," she used to whisper as she smothered him with kisses.

Grant and his parents, Mary and Sean O'Connor, had come to Canada from Northern Ireland in 1946, when he was two years old. Kevin was born three years later. They were a loving family who were devout Roman Catholics, and every Sunday they went to church.

Grant didn't like the priest, Father Thomas Wood, who was tall and skinny with a long nose and beady eyes. He had a dark complexion and black hair. His face was pockmarked, and his face reminded Grant of his mother's warnings about what would happen if he didn't stop scratching his face when he'd had chicken pox.

Grant used to wonder what the priest was hiding under the long cassock he wore.

Sean O'Connor used to laugh about how the good priest was putting away too much holy water. But Grant knew what he really meant — the priest's breath often reeked of whiskey.

And on that awful day Father Thomas was standing in front of what had once been his house, saying the Hail Mary. Grant was frozen with dread.

"Oh, my poor boy," the priest intoned as he looked down.

Even now Grant could remember his eyes — the look in his eyes haunted him.

"I'm afraid God has called your dear mother and father back to heaven along with little Kevin. The gas stove blew up and the fire burned everything inside. His will be done."

And then he crossed himself.

Grant put his hands to his head and started to scream, crying for God to come and take him, too.

"There, there, be a brave lad," one of the policemen said awkwardly. "Only sissies and girls cry."

The police asked Grant if he had any family to be called.

"I'm afraid not," Father Thomas said. "At least not in Canada. Poor Grant is an orphan now."

"No, no! I don't want to go to an orphanage!"

Grant was shaking and sobbing. Father Thomas picked him up.

"I'll take him home with me tonight," Father Thomas told the police, his voice almost a whisper, "until the Children's Aid and I decide what to do with him."

Later that night, when Grant was settled in the spare bedroom of the rectory, Father Thomas came in and sat down next to him on the bed. He was wearing some kind of perfume that reminded Grant of the lilac bushes that used to grow outside his bedroom window.

"You can stay here with me until we notify the authorities in Ireland," the priest said quietly. "And if you're a good boy, I won't let them come from the orphanage to get you. Would you like that?"

Then the priest took the little boy's hand in his and began praying for the souls of the dear departed O'Connor family. Grant's blue eyes filled with tears and he burst out crying. Father Thomas put his arms around him and pulled him close. For a few seconds Grant felt just like he used to when his Daddy hugged him after bedtime prayers.

But then the priest took Grant's hand and put it under his cassock.

The boy recoiled. Now he knew what was under there, and Father Thomas was trying to get him to hold it. Grant tried to pull his hand away, but the priest kept putting the little fingers around his penis.

"Just hold it a little," he whispered in Grant's ear. "Then I'll play with yours until it gets big. It'll feel good, I promise. Come on, don't you want to be my special boy?"

Grant jumped out of the bed. No wonder I didn't like him, he thought. He must be a fairy. I've got to get out of here.

"I'll tell on you, you fucking queer!" he had shouted, using words he'd never said before. "Wait till the cops find out. You'll be in trouble then!"

A strange smile came over the priest's face. "You'll be sorry you didn't take up my offer, you little sinner." His voice was cold and full of venom. "Who's going to believe anything you say? Now you'll have to go to the orphanage. And eventually I'll have you anyway. But by then I expect you'll be more cooperative."

Grant couldn't move. He could only watch Father Thomas and listen to his threats.

"Remember, Jesus died for our sins. And your parents and brother have died for yours. If you weren't such an evil boy, they'd still be alive."

"That's a lie!" Grant screamed.

But Father Thomas got up and walked out of the room to call the authorities.

The next morning a social worker from Children's Aid came to take him to the orphanage. She told the whimpering little boy that he would have to stay at the orphanage until the authorities got an answer to the letter that Father Thomas was writing to the relatives in Ireland.

When he tried to tell her what had happened with Father Thomas the night before, she slapped him across the face and told him to keep his dirty lies to himself. Then she crossed herself.

After an hour's drive in total silence, they turned off the main highway onto a winding dirt road. When Grant looked up through tear-filled eyes at the iron gates of his new home, he wondered where the kind and loving God he had been taught lived everywhere had gone.

As soon as he got out of the car, the social worker drove off without even a good-bye.

Mommy, Daddy, I'm so scared.

Carrying nothing at all — no clothing, no mementos of his family — ten-year-old Grant O'Connor left his childhood behind him forever as he walked through the orphanage's front doors into hell . . .

"Do you want another beer?"

He looked up, his eyes moist. It was Doris standing in the doorway of the den. "No, no, I don't think so."

"You're thinking about the orphanage, aren't you?"

"Yes."

"This is the first time you've thought about it in a long while."

He shrugged. "No accounting for the return of memories."

She walked over to his chair and kissed him. She didn't need to say, "I understand." He knew she did.

*G*rant hadn't been in his office the next morning for more than five minutes before his secretary buzzed him.

"Inspector, there's a Mr. Steven Sherman on the phone for you. He says he's Rebecca Sherman's ex-husband."

Another fucking Judas, Teasdale thought as he picked up the phone.

"I'd like to come in and talk to you. I have some important information on the case," Sherman said.

Grant agreed to meet with Sherman later that afternoon, more out of curiosity than anything else.

He was sitting at his desk finishing off a ham and cheese sandwich when Sherman was shown in. His visitor wasted no time coming to the point. He tapped his foot as he spoke, yet, as nervous as he seemed, the man also projected an air of calm.

"Inspector, I'm here because I have serious concerns about those who are advising Rebecca. I think they have hidden agendas. I can't turn my back on her as others have."

Grant said nothing.

"I originally took the videotape I'm about to show you to her lawyer, Fitzpatrick," Sherman continued, "but he said it was irrelevant. When you see who, and what, is in it, I think you'll disagree with him."

Grant held up his hand. "Just a minute, Mr. Sherman. I'm in charge of the investigation that found reasonable and probable grounds to charge your ex-wife with fraud. Defending her is not my job, nor do I wish it to be."

"Let's cut out the bullshit," Sherman snapped. "I wouldn't be here if I didn't believe that you're a man of some principle. The word on the street is that you're a straight shooter. Ten miles above those Attila the Hun types on the police force."

"Just so you understand I'm not here to defend her," Grant told him, ignoring the slur against Toronto's finest.

"If Rebecca is going to have to pay a price for her involvements, so should the guys who were on the receiving end, especially the politicians. And I'm sure that's who you really want anyhow. I'm also pissed off that some of those people now acting holier than thou are really the scum of the earth."

"Mr. Sherman, I don't understand why you're doing this," Grant said as he smiled at the distinguished-looking man. "Most ex-husbands are only too happy to see their former spouses suffer."

"I care about what happens to Rebecca. She's the mother of my daughter, Inspector," Sherman answered. "And she's got more balls than all of those wimps who are now running for cover. I think DeLuca is a piece of shit, too, and he'd be out of business if it weren't for the corrupt judges and politicians who take his money. They're all the same, you know."

Grant did know and he was beginning to like Sherman.

"But I can tell you this. Rebecca will never talk, and they know it. Instead of being grateful and keeping their own mouths shut, too, they're trying to dig a deeper hole for her. I intend to stop them."

"Who is 'they,' Mr. Sherman?" Grant asked. "And how do you plan to stop them?"

"When you see this video, you'll have your answers, Inspector. And when you're finished with it, I'm going to release it to the media. Then we'll see how much credibility Big Dick Studley and his friends will have."

"Big Dick Studley," Grant repeated, and the smile he'd been struggling to control crept around the corners of his mouth. "I like that."

"Here," Sherman said. "Watch it and retch."

"We'll talk tomorrow."

*T*hat night Grant watched the video of a wild sex party at some kind of health club. He was sickened by the antics of two prostitutes and a dog. But when the tape ended, he could understand why Sherman thought it would be helpful to his ex-wife. Clearly visible in the orgy were the naked butts of Senator Jack Jacobs, Richard Dudley, Bob DeSalle, and, surprise of surprises, Bruce Todd, the investigative reporter who had broken the original story on the Peartree affair and who had been leading the charge ever since.

Grant also recognized Judge Ronald Osgoode, who was scheduled to preside over Rebecca Sherman's preliminary hearing. Grant hadn't realized, until he saw him writhing around on the floor with Todd, that the esteemed judge was a homosexual. He hoped Mrs. Osgoode already knew it, because if Steven Sherman really did release this video, she'd find out soon enough, along with the rest of the country.

At midnight Grant called Sherman at home.

"How did you get this videotape?" he asked.

"It was delivered to me personally by Billy, the manager of Pearl's Health Club," Steven answered. "He told me that the video was his retirement annuity. And that it might be of some help to Rebecca, too. When I asked him why he wanted to help her, he explained that he had come to Canada on the same boat as Sam Singer, Rebecca's father. The two of them had stuck together during the trip, sharing their food and protecting each other from the bullies who liked to beat up on the Jewish immigrants traveling in steerage.

"When I asked him if anyone else had seen, or knew about the videotape, he hesitated before answering no. I think he was lying. Why do you ask, Inspector?"

"Because this is hot stuff, Mr. Sherman," Grant said. "And since it certainly doesn't help the prosecution, I'm perplexed as to why Fitzpatrick didn't find it useful. After all, some of those who've been subpoenaed to give evidence against Rebecca are easily recognizable in the video."

"Exactly my point, Inspector. I think Fitzpatrick is more concerned with protecting his friends and associates than his own client. And I'll go further than that. I think he's in cahoots with them, keeping Rebecca isolated while he reinforces her decision not to talk to you. And if I'm right, doesn't that mean obstruction of justice, and isn't that a crime?"

"Not exactly," Grant answered. Steven Sherman had some pretty good points, but the Inspector was pretty sure that none of it was relevant from a legal standpoint.

"Well, I think Rebecca's making a major mistake dealing with Walker & Associates, and I've told her so," Steve reiterated. "And I'm getting more worried about my daughter. This is causing Lisa a lot of stress. Her mother means a lot to her."

"I'm not sure what I can do, Mr. Sherman," Grant said honestly, "but I'll ask a few questions and get back to you."

"Thanks for listening to me, Inspector. I'll look forward to hearing from you."

Something about this case stinks to high heaven, Grant thought as he rewound the tape to get another look at the familiar faces. He anticipated the confrontation he would be having with Judge Osgoode in the morning, and he was sure his visit would be followed by the good judge's immediate withdrawal from the case.

Grant knew that he wasn't handling the Sherman case in as detached and professional way as he should. His concern for Rebecca was approaching a danger zone, and his head kept telling him that he'd better back off, and fast.

Despite the sordid activities on the video and the juicy scandal it could create, he wasn't sure there was any legal significance, at least from the prosecution's point of view. He decided to discuss it with a friend who did special investigations for the Law Society as soon as he got the chance — but only as a favor to Steven Sherman, he rationalized to himself.

When Steve hung up the phone, he was glad he had decided to go around Fitzpatrick and follow his instinct about Teasdale. The warmth and concern in the Inspector's voice had been reassuring.

*B*y noon the next day, Judge Ronald Osgoode had removed himself from any involvement in the Rebecca Sherman case.

That night Brad Ross was in Rebecca's kitchen; he'd just turned on the dishwasher. They had spent an at-home evening eating spaghetti, salad, and garlic bread, and playing Scrabble. Lisa had gone to bed.

When the phone rang Brad glanced at his watch. It was nearly eleven. A forewarning shot through him. Eleven o'clock was not the time for good-news calls. It was his strong sense of foreboding that caused him to walk into the living room.

"Oh, no. Oh God!" Rebecca was saying.

She was standing holding the phone and shaking. Her face ashen, she let the phone drop to the floor. And then she covered her face with her hands and began to cry.

"What's the matter?" He was at her side in an instant and his arms were around her.

"I can't stand it! I can't stand it! How much am I supposed to take?" she said, sobbing now and still shaking. It was so completely unlike her that it frightened Brad.

"What is it, Rebecca? Who was that on the phone?"

"That was Jimmy. It's about Steve," she managed. "He's dead. His body was just found on the golf course. Apparently it's been there all day, hidden by the trees off the eighth green."

"Oh God," he whispered as he stroked her hair. "How did Jimmy find out? Was it . . . ?"

"Jimmy got the call from his guy in 45 Division, the precinct nearest the course. They said it was a heart attack. I don't know if I believe it."

"Oh Rebecca, this is god-awful. I don't know what to say. I'm sure there'll be an inquest to find out what really happened."

"What does it matter now?" she mumbled. Her sobs eased up and a distant look came over her face. After a few minutes of silence, she turned to look at Brad.

"I feel so alone and so responsible for Lisa's well-being. I'm also scared. I've got some tough decisions to make, Brad, and I'm not sure I have the strength to make them."

"Rebecca, I want to help however I can. Surely you know that I love you, that I've loved you for a long time. I want to marry you."

"Oh Brad, you are so sweet, and so kind. But I need time. I need to straighten out my life and my emotions. And to be honest, I'm not sure I can ever love again."

"As long as it takes," he answered, and kissed her forehead.

*G*rant Teasdale answered the phone impatiently. It was eight-thirty in the morning and he wasn't even supposed to be in the office yet. But he'd got the call about Steven Sherman late last night and had come in early to start looking through his files. The preliminary report stated that Sherman had died of an apparent heart attack. Grant knew there'd have to be an investigation, given Sherman's ties to Rebecca. He thought of that video Sherman had shown him.

I wonder how Rebecca will handle this? he thought. And her daughter. "Sorry," he said to the senior crown prosecutor. "I wasn't listening. What did you say?"

"Come down to my office right now. It's urgent."

The phone line went dead before he could say a word. It was a royal command. "Shit," Grant muttered as he headed out the door.

The cream-colored walls of the old City Hall needed painting. The whole place had all the charm of a poorly dressed, ancient dowager with halitosis.

The secretary waved him into the office, and he was startled to find William Fitzpatrick sitting uncomfortably in the only chair. Fitzpatrick looked up and without preamble said, "I've come to discuss a deal for Mrs. Sherman."

Grant felt a mixture of relief and anger rush over him, but he kept his face impassive.

"I like having the crown spared expense," the prosecutor said. "Mrs. Sherman is prepared to plead guilty."

My God, she's throwing in the towel, Grant thought. Sherman's death has pushed her over the edge.

"Well, I'll have to talk with her again," he said to Fitzpatrick, even though he knew she still wouldn't give him Santino DeLuca. "Bring her in this afternoon and we'll try to work something out."

As he walked back up the stairs to his office, Teasdale was filled with anger and frustration.

Shit. She was going down, and all the scum bags were going to walk.

# *17*

*I*t was just after eleven o'clock at night. Grant Teasdale was drinking a beer while the television blared in the background of his thoughts. It was the *Tonight Show*, but he wasn't really watching it. He was trying to push thoughts about Rebecca Sherman out of his mind. He had been ignoring Doris, their life was becoming more tense, and if he didn't get a handle on it, their difficulties would reach the point of no return.

How can I think of other women? How, after all she did — does? He downed the Molsons Light and opened another, leaning back in his recliner chair. He remembered when he'd first met Doris and how she had brought him back from the edge of hopelessness. Again, as it had so often lately, his past life returned to fill his thoughts . . .

He met Doris in 1965 almost five years after he had been removed from the Brothers of St. John Home for Orphans in Pembroke, where he had languished for six long, tortured years because none of his parents' relatives in Ireland ever replied to his letters.

When the government began an investigation into the orphanage because of rumors of abuse, RCMP Inspector Brian Teasdale was put in charge. He and his men were horrified at what they'd found there and several of the Brothers had been arrested, including the senior priest, Father Thomas Wood.

213

Inspector Teasdale took the sixteen-year-old redhead, Grant O'Connor, home to meet his wife Janice. It was love at first sight. The anguish the Teasdales saw in his face haunted them, and, since he had no other relatives, they invited him to come and live with them in their cabin in Vermont.

Brian was semi-retired by now and he and Janice were looking forward to spending most of their time in their cabin on the Quechee River, ten minutes from Woodstock, Vermont. They had never had children, and hoped that the love they had to give Grant would help him to recover from the horror of his years at St. John's.

In 1961 Grant O'Connor was formally adopted by Brian and Janice Teasdale, and in 1963 he enrolled at Bennington College.

Grant was an expert skier and received a limited scholarship. The college was reminiscent of a Wyeth painting, with white wooden exteriors, tall spires with weather vanes, and green shutters. The campus was situated among rolling hills with the greenest of green grass and an abundance of maple trees.

In 1965, on a trip to Montreal with his parents to celebrate his twenty-first birthday, Grant met Doris Page, a cocktail waitress in a local bar. The bar was managed by Michael Hogan, one of the boys who had been in St. John's with Grant.

Doris, who was twenty-eight, made no secret of her immediate interest in the six-foot redhead. Michael noticed Grant's awkwardness and blushing face, and guessed his problem.

"Eh, buddy, have you ever made it with a girl?" Michael whispered.

"I thought so," he muttered when Grant's face turned the color of his hair.

"Come on, buddy, you've got to get over what happened back then," Michael urged him. "You're not like me. I can tell. I've been with enough guys to know that you're not one of us."

Grant wasn't so sure. Deep down, he was afraid that he'd been forever scarred by his experiences at the orphanage. Nevertheless he kept glancing over at Doris, who had sensational legs, and breasts that pressed against the thin material of her blouse.

So he went with her when she invited him back to her apartment for a nightcap. She put on some music and asked Grant if he'd like to dance. He told her he didn't know how, and his face turned red again.

"Come on, I'll teach you."

"Move to the sound of the music," she coaxed as she put her arms around his neck and pulled him closer to her. "Just relax and let yourself go. Follow my lead."

In spite of his attraction to her, Grant was terrified. What if it doesn't work? he thought in panic. What if Michael's wrong?

Doris poured them both a Scotch on the rocks. Grant gulped his down and they continued dancing. Doris ran her hands down his back and rested them on his buttocks. It was the wrong thing to do. He stiffened and started to pull away.

"What's wrong? Don't you find me attractive?"

He couldn't answer; he felt cold and clammy, as though his worst nightmare was coming true. But when he looked at her tear-filled eyes, his heart went out to her and he held her close.

When he kissed her, it felt good, and as his mouth pressed down on hers, she used her tongue to pry open his lips. That felt even better. As Grant's hands moved up to her breasts, a moan escaped his lips. Doris stepped back and lifted her blouse over her head and unhooked her bra. Her breasts popped out of their binding and he was fascinated. They were full and white, with dark brown nipples that stood straight out. He started running his hands over and around them.

And then the most wonderful thing happened. He got an erection.

Doris led him to the bedroom. By now he was very excited, kissing her neck and breasts, letting his hands run all over her body, his lips close behind. Doris unzipped his pants, pulled down his underwear, and took his penis in her hand. As she started stroking it, what he had most feared happened.

Memories of Father Wood came flooding back, and his passion waned. He couldn't look at Doris as he got out of the bed, reaching for his clothes.

"I can see that you're hurting," she said to him softly. "I've been hurt, too. Let me help you, and then, maybe, we can help each other."

When Grant looked into her eyes, he saw how desperately lonely she

was, and how frightened. Again his heart went out to her. After a few minutes of silence, he sat on the side of the bed and took her hand in his. He
told her about his life in the orphanage, and as he talked, her eyes filled with
tears and she started to massage his neck.

"Forget what happened back then," she said. "This is now, and now is
what matters. I'm a woman, not some weirdo. Think of how I feel, how I
look, how my lips and hands feel different on your body — different from
anything you've known before. Think of how much you excite me and how
you make my juices start to run." Then she took his hand and put it where
he could feel just how wet he had made her. His erection came back.

"Kiss me again, and touch me like you did before," she whispered. Doris
began to moan and writhe as his fingers kept sliding in and out of her.
Suddenly, she gave a loud sob and arched her back up. "Oh God, I'm
coming!" she cried as her body started to shudder.

When her trembling subsided, she opened her eyes and whispered to
Grant, "You're a fantastic lover. Too bad you don't realize it yet."

She turned him on his back and began kissing him. Before he realized
what was happening, she straddled him, pushing his penis inside of her
and undulating her hips back and forth. He came very quickly.

His fears that his past would ruin his future were finally over, and, for
that, he would be forever grateful to Doris.

"Stay with me tonight," she whispered in his ear. "I'm off work tomorrow, so we can spend the whole day together."

Grant called his father at the hotel. "Dad, I'm with a woman," he told
him, stroking Doris's back. "I want to stay with her till tomorrow. Tell Mom
something, will you?"

The next twenty-four hours were an orgy of sex for Doris and him. They
hardly left the bed.

From then on, he went to Montreal to see her whenever he could take
the time off. He'd drive the three-hour trip from Bennington to spend a
weekend of ecstasy with her. Sex was on his mind all the time; it seemed as
if he'd never get enough of it.

After graduation in 1966 he decided to follow in his adoptive father's footsteps and join the RCMP. He'd wanted to be a Mountie ever since the moment they'd stormed into the orphanage to rescue the boys. After two years on the Force, Grant knew he'd found the right path for his life. He loved everything about the RCMP, especially the loyalty and camaraderie among the men. In late 1968 he was assigned to a post in northeastern Canada, Cape Breton Island. It was a beautiful locale, but its economy wasn't at all good. Unemployment was high and drinking was the main recreational activity. But Grant was undaunted, he had high hopes of improving life there as he protected the residents from crime.

He also knew that he had to tell Doris that he needed to focus his energies on his career and that their relationship would have to be put on hold for a while. Before he could discuss it with her, and after a night of sex, she told him she was pregnant.

They got married the next week in Woodstock, Vermont, in a little Catholic church just off the main street.

During the Mass, Grant whispered a prayer for his late parents, Mary and Sean O'Connor, and his baby brother Kevin. He asked God to bless his unborn child and to keep his wife safe and healthy. Then he thanked Him for the blessing of his other parents, Brian and Janice Teasdale.

Together, he and Doris left Woodstock to start a new life.

Grant's thoughts were shattered by the ringing of the telephone. It was after midnight.

"Inspector, this is Santino DeLuca. I'd like to meet with you personally to discuss a few matters."

Grant agreed to meet him the next night at Ontario Place, the waterfront park bordering Toronto's lakeshore. The location would enable him to see if DeLuca was being followed, in case this was some kind of setup.

*I*t was a clear, crisp night and Grant sat in his car staring into the distance, watching the cold mist waft off Lake Ontario. When he heard the car's engine behind him, he turned and waited for his old nemesis to get out of the limousine. As the tall, elegant man approached him, Grant couldn't help thinking that DeLuca looked more like a Latin movie star than a hood.

The two men shook hands and started walking along the breakwater, two of DeLuca's aides following behind at a distance.

Without any preamble DeLuca began discussing the old grudges between himself and Brattini. When Grant asked about the prostitute's murder, back in the '50s, DeLuca stopped walking and turned to look at him.

"You really do live up to your reputation, Inspector," he said. "They say that if anybody ever cracks the wall, it'll be Inspector Grant Teasdale. You also have some good informants."

When Teasdale didn't answer, DeLuca began talking about the episode.

The prostitute had been pregnant, and DeLuca, who was still Brattini's associate, had wanted her spared because of it.

"Two-timing Villano's asshole son-in-law didn't deserve that kind of punishment," DeLuca told Teasdale very emotionally. "Besides, killing a woman carrying a child is a mortal sin."

Grant wondered about *that* rationalization. Killing anyone was a mortal sin. Was DeLuca saying he was worried about his own immortal soul? If so, it was a little late for someone who had been an "enforcer." But as a Catholic himself, Grant knew how well the Church had ingrained the fear of an "eternity in hell" into its flock. Better late than never for DeLuca, he thought.

As Santino continued speaking, Grant was able to envisage the scene as it must have played out.

The prostitute had been on her knees, crying and begging them for mercy. She'd said her family in Chicago would help her to disappear with the child, and no one would be the wiser.

"I told Brattini to show some pity and let the child have a life," Santino said. "Killing a pregnant woman was unthinkable. But Brattini only looked at me with a sneer. 'I got over that fainthearted stuff a long time ago. I don't let nothing get to me anymore. That's why you'll never rise to the top,' he told me. 'You haven't got the balls. Villano's the Don. He speaks, I do. Who cares about some two-bit cunt anyway? For all you know, the father is some nigger. She's only a hooker and her kid would probably be one, too.'"

"And then he shot her between the eyes," Teasdale said without missing a beat.

When DeLuca didn't answer, Grant knew that his informant had been telling the truth. He made a mental note of it.

"I turned and walked out of the room," DeLuca continued. "The next day I told old man Villano I wouldn't work with Brattini again."

Grant wondered why DeLuca was telling him all this. *Maybe he wants me to think that he has a heart under that steely exterior.*

But he knew that DeLuca must want something from him, and as if he were a mindreader, DeLuca said, "I'm telling you this story, Inspector, because I believe that you're a man of compassion underneath all your cop's armor. You've suffered enough in your own life to understand the weaknesses and pain of others."

*How the hell does he know that?* Teasdale fought to keep his face expressionless.

"I'm worried about Rebecca Sherman's safety in prison. Brattini's people might use the opportunity to try to get at me through her — especially since everyone knows your task force has my political and business associates under close scrutiny. They've been too nervous about exposure themselves to risk getting involved in protecting Rebecca — and Brattini's people know it."

Teasdale knew that DeLuca had no need to explain why he was so concerned about Rebecca — he'd let the Inspector draw his own conclusions. He was hoping Teasdale would use his position to make sure Rebecca was put on the "don't touch" list of inmates.

Santino had rightly assumed that the police were hoping to draw him out by throwing the legal book at her. Since it hadn't worked, perhaps it was time for them to try another tactic.

"Now that you've met Rebecca, talked to her, you must have developed a small soft spot in your heart for her," DeLuca said almost plaintively. "I'm certain you don't want to see her hurt. Her life could be in danger."

Grant felt uncomfortable. It was as if DeLuca really had been reading his mind. He'd been struggling with his fascination for the woman since he'd first met her. But he was still a professional, and, like his colleagues, he was hoping she might be the weak link and provide incriminating information, if enough pressure was put on her. But it hadn't happened. And if she wouldn't talk, no clemency could be offered.

Teasdale believed Rebecca had had more power within the DeLuca operation than most people realized. His own wiretaps and the videos of DeLuca and his business associates had indicated her presence at many of their meetings. She had run that trust with an iron hand, and despite all his investigations, no evidence of money laundering had yet been found. She had either known exactly what she was doing or had been too stupid to know what she was doing. He doubted it was the latter.

And there was something else. Men like DeLuca could get young and gorgeous bodies any time, and rarely mixed business with pleasure. His relationship with Rebecca would have had to involve more than just sex, and Teasdale still wanted to find out what it was.

DeLuca is a shrewd fox looking for a weak spot, he thought. Play it by the book.

"What are you prepared to give in return?" he asked in his most detached voice. "Your concern for Mrs. Sherman is very touching, but she means nothing to me — unless, of course, she can lead me to you."

DeLuca's response was not unexpected. "I know nothing about Brattini's money-laundering business. Nor his Asian connection. But I'll certainly ask around and see if anyone else does."

It was a carrot that Teasdale grabbed at, even though he doubted that DeLuca would ever deliver. But it would allow him to justify to his colleagues — and to himself — his continuing involvement in Rebecca Sherman's fate, at least for a while.

# *18*

OCTOBER 15
1983

*F*all. She hated that it was fall. It was her favorite time of year. The maples were turning outrageous shades of red, gold, and orange, and Ontario was breathtaking. The days were warm, the nights cold.

Rebecca looked out the window, which was covered with wire mesh. She was forcing herself not to think of anything beyond what was coming. She was afraid that if she lost her self-control, she'd never get it back.

An hour ago, along with six other convicted felons, Rebecca had been led out of the federal courthouse into a paddy wagon for the one-hour trip to the Midland Prison for Women. She'd been sentenced to eighteen months — and for a first offence.

The other women in the van smoked and swore, mostly at each other, for the entire trip. She was glad that no one appeared to know who she was, or what her crime had been. She would have sworn she was the most infamous person in North America by this time — but in this group she seemed to be anonymous.

At least Lisa will be okay, she thought. Between Brad and Jean, she'll be surrounded by love. God willing, I'll be paroled and I'll be able to come home after a year — maybe less. She inhaled and forced real time out of her thoughts.

The van pulled into the courtyard of the prison. The guard riding in the front turned and yelled, "Okay, ladies, you're home."

They were marched single file through double doors, down a flight of cement stairs, and into a long room with smallish cells. Each of them was placed in a holding cell; then one by one they were taken away.

Rebecca sat on the edge of the narrow cot and folded her hands. It was cold in both temperature and atmosphere. There was an absence of color, sounds were hollow as they echoed off the walls, and the smell was that of a high school gym or a locker room, sweet sweat floating on stale air.

After two hours of sitting in the holding cell, she was taken out for processing. She was walked down a long hall and pushed into a room that looked as if it was an infirmary. Three female guards were waiting there.

"Okay, Sherman, take off all your clothes." The woman who gave her the order was a large woman whose hair had dark roots but was dyed a bright yellow. Her plastic-encased name tag read "Josey."

Rebecca couldn't move. The way they looked at her, the way they spoke — she didn't want to strip in front of them.

"Listen, you fucking Jewish cunt," another guard sneered, "take off your fucking clothes. We haven't got all day."

Terrified and embarrassed, Rebecca quickly did as she was told. She was cold, and she was aware that her nipples hardened and she had goose bumps on her skin.

Then Josey told her to turn around and bend over.

Again, she just stood there. Her body seemed unwilling to respond even to her own commands. It was as if she were nailed to the floor.

"Okay, you cunt, you asked for it," said a tall black guard with wide shoulders. Her name tag identified her as "Lola."

She walked over to Rebecca, spun her around, took her neck, and pushed it down toward the floor. She then pushed Rebecca's legs apart with her boots until she was quite exposed. One of the other two grabbed her buttocks and spread her cheeks, pulling so hard that Rebecca started to struggle.

"Better check her for drugs," Josey said, laughing. "And make a note for our reports that we suspected her of smuggling contraband into the prison."

Rebecca heard the sounds of rubber gloves being pulled on, and, before she knew it, a foreign object was being forced into her rectum. She tried to stand up, but Lola kept holding her head down by tightening her grip. The object was being pushed so deeply and roughly that Rebecca thought she'd faint from the pain. When she started to cry, the guards began snickering.

"Well, the famous Mrs. Sherman isn't so cocky now, is she?" they said.

"Well, there's nothing up her ass," Lola announced. "Turn her around; we'll check her cunt."

When Rebecca started to struggle, more in fear than in pain, Josey slapped her across the face and pushed her back against the desk, and her pelvic area over the edge of it. Two of the guards took her legs and spread them very wide, while Josey walked between them. She shoved her fingers inside Rebecca's vagina, twisting them around and around.

"Have to make sure there's no drugs hidden up there," she muttered.

Then she laughed. "She looks disgusted now, but after a few months in prison our famous prisoner will find other women more attractive than the dildo we just used on her ass. Unless, of course, she gets to like it."

Then she stared into Rebecca's eyes. "Okay, you shit, this time you're lucky. We didn't find any drugs — maybe next time. We'll be keeping close tabs on you."

Rebecca shivered as they released her.

"C'mon, let me show you your new home," Lola said as Rebecca was putting her clothes back on.

Down more corridors. At last she was put in a cell in the medium-security section of the prison.

"Keep your nose clean, and your mouth shut," Lola said. "Don't be 'snitching' or 'ratting.' If you think that dildo was bad, wait till you feel a burning hot one up your pussy."

Rebecca summoned herself. "Aren't you guards supposed to protect inmates from abuse?"

"Oh, it's not what the other jailbirds will do to you," Lola said, missing the sarcasm in Rebecca's voice. "They'll only beat you, or make you suck them off, or maybe even kill you if they can. No, it's what we'll do to you that you have to worry about."

As soon as the door of her cell was closed and Lola had left, Rebecca collapsed on her cot and burst out crying.

*T*he other girls she met on the range were a mix of ages and races, and conversations were pretty basic. Soon Rebecca was into a routine of eating, cleaning the common areas, working in the prison's laundry, walking one hour a day around the courtyard, and trying to make the clocks turn faster.

The food served was tasteless and full of starch. Lots of white bread and margarine and macaroni-type lunches almost every day, and boiled potatoes and boiled meat for dinner. Usually the meat was the canned variety.

The girls had to line up for meals and there was a lot of pushing and shoving by the tougher ones to get at the front of the line. By the time those at the end of the line got to the food, there wasn't much left. If, on occasion, there was some fresh fruit or a piece of cake being served, the bullies got it all.

The good news is that I'll probably lose some weight, Rebecca thought as she looked at the unappetizing food. She wondered who planned the menus for these institutions. The inmates were being fed cheap food full of sugar and starch, with very little protein; yet she knew the budgets were high.

Each cell had its own toilet, although the guards could look in any time they wanted, and did. There was no real privacy, no time when she felt she could let down her guard.

Each prison range held twenty-four women. There were only two shower stalls and they could only be used between six-thirty and seven-thirty at night. Hot water ran out very quickly, and after the toughest girls who had pushed their way into line first were finished, she and the rest had to make do with cold water. The guards seemed oblivious to what was going on.

Paint was peeling off the walls, the taps leaked incessantly, and the concrete floors and walls made sounds reverberate like an echo chamber.

In the first few weeks Rebecca noticed a few of the girls arm in arm, and occasionally saw them kissing and rubbing against each other's bodies when no guards were around.

She tried to sign up for every program posted on the bulletin board. Anything to pass the time more quickly. But most of the programs were never held, with no explanation given. The other girls smirked when she asked about it.

"It's a joke — they post the programs so when the do-gooders come around checking on how us 'poor, fallen women' are being treated, the brass can point to all the rehab they're offering," they told her.

Where are all those do-gooders? Rebecca wondered. And where's all the money that is supposedly being spent on prison reform? She had enough experience with creative bookkeeping to know that whatever money was earmarked for programing in this woman's prison was certainly not being spent as recorded in the books.

She very quickly noticed a camaraderie among the girls, even those who were bullies. Fights were common, consisting of a few punches or kicks, but were over quickly. It was as if they had only one another, good or bad, to fend off the screws.

For the most part, she was left alone after the first couple of days. On arrival she was their "celebrity" con, but her distinctiveness soon waned. She was called "dirty Jew" regularly, but once the girls saw that she wasn't rattled, they stopped.

*A*fter a week Rebecca was allowed her first visitor. It was Brad.

Sitting across the glass partition separating them now, she tried to keep a smile on her face and not start crying.

"There's still a lot of fallout from your conviction around City Hall," he said.

"Shake-up in the halls of power," she commented. His eyes looked tired, and she hoped he was okay.

"Jean and Lisa are doing great. We've all had dinner together every night since you left. Both of them send their love — I guess I don't have to tell you that."

Neither of them spoke for a moment; then he asked, "Are they treating you okay? Can I send you any books or magazines?"

Rebecca couldn't help smiling as she assured him everything was fine and she had plenty to read, leaving out the fact that the most up-to-date magazines available were over two years old. And how could she begin to tell him the truth about her treatment?

"I can't believe it. Our time's up already," Brad said.

"Call Jimmy Bono and tell him not to worry — tell him I'm okay."

Brad's eyes narrowed, and Rebecca knew that he suspected it was really Santino she wanted to reassure. But, as always, he smiled and said he would look after it.

"Brad, I only want to see you while I'm here," she told him. "I know you can explain it to Jean and Lisa so they'll understand. I never want Lisa to remember coming to visit her mother in a prison. Also, I want a new lawyer — someone who will help me get parole. Please let me know who you think I should use."

She saw how pleased he was that she was leaning on him. The truth was she herself was pleased, knowing he was there for her.

He forced a smile and waved her a kiss. She returned the gesture.

As she left the visitors' block, she was taken into an anteroom and strip-searched. This time she was simply made to squat, jump up and down with her legs spread, and bend over. The guard made no physical contact.

Her first thoughts were thank you, thank you, until she realized how totally absurd the search was in the first place. How could anyone visiting her across a glass partition slip her drugs or contraband with guards sitting by the doors, watching? And, if a visitor somehow did, how could she pull down her jeans, squat, and shove the stuff inside her body without being noticed by all those supervising the visitations?

No, it was just an excuse to justify the degradation of powerless women who were at the mercy of the guards, some of whom were questionable themselves. Many times already she had noticed the dilated pupils and mumbled words on the part of those in charge of the inmates. And she knew that many of the guards worked in the corrections system because they had been rejected by the police forces.

As she was escorted back to her cell, she heard shouts and curses coming from the isolation range. Just passing that place made her shudder.

Everything about the prison was gray. The walls, the furniture, the curtains, even the gym. What would be so terrible if someone painted the walls in some other color? Unless they *want* to keep everyone depressed.

The only color the prisoners ever saw, besides the sparse grass in the courtyard, was during arts and crafts classes — if there were supplies in stock. Most of the time the only art supplies the girls had to create with were some crayons, five or six small bottles of paint, and three brushes. As for "crafts," there was a bag full of beads and some thread for making bracelets and necklaces.

The instructor was a petite Oriental woman who was a recent immigrant and spoke very little English. But she smiled a lot, which was a nice change. She wore her long black hair in a pigtail which she would decorate with the creations made by her "students."

*R*ebecca still felt isolated from the other prisoners, more by their choosing than by hers. But since she was determined to fit in and not create any animosity toward herself by acting "snooty," she continually sat down with the girls and tried to start a conversation.

After two weeks a few started to respond to her overtures. By the end of a month she had made a couple of friends, including one of the new prisoners, a woman named Kathy Okata. She was the same height as Rebecca, about five feet six inches, but weighed no more than 110 pounds. Her breasts sagged like pancakes, and her skin was beginning to wrinkle. Her hair was half-gray and half-auburn, almost two-toned. Since there were no hair-coloring products available to women in prison, nothing could be done about it. Her teeth were gray and so were her eyes. Rebecca was stunned to learn that Kathy was only twenty-five years old. She looked fifty.

Rebecca learned that Kathy, like many other female prisoners, was a

Native Canadian. She came from Manitoulin Island in Northern Ontario and had been convicted of manslaughter for smothering her newborn baby two years earlier. In court she had claimed that she had no recollection of doing it.

Usually women who committed crimes against children were kept on another range, but it was common knowledge that the father of Kathy's dead baby was her own father, so she was left alone.

During meals six girls would sit around each table, and at first Rebecca didn't know that everyone's seat was reserved. Once, she had inadvertently sat down in someone else's spot, and the next thing she knew, she was flat on the floor, having had the chair pulled out from under her. The guards had a good laugh over that.

Dorotea Herrara, which translated from Spanish into Dottie Smith, another one of the new arrivals, had helped Rebecca off the floor and told the other girls to "fuck off and give the Jew broad a chance."

Dottie, as she preferred to be called, was Cuban and had a slight Spanish accent. She said she and her family had come from Cuba when she was in her teens. "Hundreds of us trickle into Canada," she said. "My parents saved enough for a vacation in the Soviet Union. When our Aeroflot flight landed in Gander to refuel before going on to Havana, we defected."

Dottie was tall with bleached blond hair. She wore glasses, and braces on her teeth. When Rebecca first saw her, she thought she had seen her somewhere before; but when she asked, Dottie had burst out laughing, answering, "Me, a Dago from Havana, know a rich Jew like you? Not likely."

Dottie was in prison for armed robbery and said it wasn't her first time around. She had an aura of toughness about her that made some of the other bullies wary, although Rebecca did notice that Dottie would offer a smoke to some of the more timid girls, and rarely pushed them around as the others did.

One morning while the two of them were cleaning the bathrooms, Dottie gave Rebecca a short lesson in prison etiquette.

"Always ask if a chair belongs to anyone before you sit down," she suggested. "Don't stare at the dykes feeling each other up — they'll think you're interested yourself. And, finally, never snitch, ever, for any reason. The screws are all liars and can't be trusted. Period. End of lesson.

"Oh yeah, and stick close to me," she added. "I've been here before."

After a while Rebecca was allowed to leave her cell door open and move freely within the confines of the range. That meant she could walk to the common lounge, go into the kitchen for a glass of water, or visit other cells in her corridor only.

There were a few male guards on the range, and they made Rebecca feel very uncomfortable, especially when the girls lined up for the showers covered only in towels or in thin nightgowns. She'd notice the guards staring, and many times whispered words were passed between one of them and one of the girls. She often thought that her life was becoming increasingly like something from a Grade B film or some X-rated video.

Kathy's cell was next to hers and the walls were paper-thin. One night while she was staring at the ceiling, unable to sleep, she heard the cell next door being unlocked by hand.

A few minutes later she heard the voice of John, one of the night guards: "Okay, I've got the stuff." Rebecca moved over to the other side of her cell to listen. She actually put her ear against the wall.

Then she heard the sound of clothes being unsnapped and John saying, "Hey, be careful with the zipper. You almost caught my prick in it."

Oh shit, Rebecca thought. What if someone comes by? Kathy'll be the one punished, not that screw.

The sounds coming from Kathy's cell were getting louder and louder, until Rebecca heard John say, "That's it, I'm coming! Suck it harder, you two-bit cunt and swallow every drop."

A couple of minutes later Rebecca heard the cell door open and close again. She looked out her cell window and guessed it was almost dawn, because she could see the beginnings of light in the sky.

That afternoon, on their walk, Rebecca asked Kathy what the hell she was doing with that screw. "What if the other girls catch you? Who knows what they'll do to you?"

Kathy, in addition to being a murderer and a victim of incest, was also a former prostitute and drug pusher. She threw her head back and laughed.

"Listen Sherman," she said, "grow up. This is prison. How else can a person get what she needs in order to live? Most of the girls here would do it with him or anyone else, male or female, to get what they need. In fact, most of them do.

"I give him a blow job and he brings me smokes and the occasional pill. No harm done. Now stop listening and stop watching. Mind your own business. I can take care of myself."

Rebecca was aware that some of her fellow prisoners had sex with each other. They usually went into the shower room where they'd lie down in one of the stalls and close the curtains, if there were any. Sometimes one of them would stand against the door while the other sucked her off. Then they'd switch positions and reverse roles. They used their mouths, their hands, and, occasionally, a dildo, which was passed around for whoever wanted it. It was kept hidden under Kathy's cot, taped to the box spring.

After a short time Rebecca got used to the sounds, and if on occasion she walked in when some "action" was happening, she'd just turn and walk out. The thought of having sex with another woman was distasteful to her, but to each her own, she thought. If this is what helped the girls make it through the days and nights, it was okay with her.

But she never could understand how relationships were sustained the way they were. The wrong word or gesture could provoke one inmate to punch another in the face or give her a kick in the stomach, despite the fact the two had just been intimate with each other.

Unless things got out of hand, the guards looked the other way. Their motto was divide and conquer — that's how they prevented any organized uprisings. As long as the girls were going at each other, they wouldn't turn on their guards.

But the close quarters and the lack of privacy within the prison still heightened tensions. The most debilitating factor was the mind-numbing boredom, which was exacerbated by the lack of any constructive activities.

Brad continued to visit Rebecca twice a week. By the end of her third month she was eligible to complete an application for parole, which, if granted, would be effective in another three months.

Brad told her he'd met with a young criminal lawyer who was highly respected in the legal community. His name was Richard Stern, and he had agreed to take her case.

Rebecca was grateful to Brad. She tried to tell him what his support meant to her, but he just waved his hand.

"Don't tell me. I know," he'd say. "Just come home to Lisa, and to me, safe and sound. That'll be enough."

I will grow to love you, she vowed. How could anyone not love you?

*O*ne evening after dinner Rebecca noticed some of the girls staggering. Trouble, she thought. Someone has smuggled drugs onto the range. If they were caught, all the girls would be put into lockup — meaning no privileges, no phone calls, no mail. Lights out at six o'clock, right after dinner.

Josey, the guard Rebecca hadn't seen since that first awful day, showed up with two of her henchmen, both female.

"Okay, you fucking cunts!" she bellowed. "We got the word. Drugs are goin' down here. Line up!"

Someone must have ratted because the girls showing the telltale signs of drug use hadn't been stoned for more than half an hour. Rebecca thought this was probably a setup, which meant that either one of the inmates was trying to get her sentence reduced by trapping some of the others, or one of the guards was hoping to earn brownie points with her superiors by using the more vulnerable prisoners to trap others.

All the girls on the range, twenty-four in all, were rounded up, lined up in a row, and strip-searched.

At least there's a good reason for this degradation, Rebecca rationalized. It wasn't like the other times.

Three of the girls who showed signs of drug use, including Dottie, were taken away to the isolation range. They would be put into cells with dry toilets. They would be given no clothing except a hospital gown, and they would have no blankets and no mattresses. They'd be fed laxatives and diuretics

— by force, if necessary — to speed up the elimination process. Anything that passed from their bodies into the toilets would be analyzed for drugs. Sometimes drug capsules wrapped in cellophane would be expelled.

Once confronted with the evidence, the girls would then have the option of ratting on the others or spending up to three months in isolation. In addition, time would be added to their sentences if they didn't cooperate.

By the third day Rebecca was frantic. Why haven't they found the culprits and lifted the lockup? Why hadn't Dottie been released? She was in for armed robbery, not drugs. She had told Rebecca that she used to take drugs, but had been off them for ten years.

"Don't worry, I won't ever get hooked again," she had said.

At the end of the week lockup was lifted. There were no explanations although the rumor mill said that the bust had been a setup by one of the inmates.

Rebecca was telling Brad the story one Sunday evening when he came for his visit. His face tightened up, and he looked very worried.

"Rebecca, don't forget who you are and where you are," he warned. "Prison doesn't operate the way the normal world does. Stay clear of this Dottie person, and don't get involved."

"Don't worry," she told him. "I'll be all right."

*I*t was quarter to seven. Rebecca looked around the shower room. Oddly, it was empty. Her spirits rose. Perhaps there was hot water left; perhaps for once she would have a good hot shower.

She shed her clothing and stepped into the shower. It happened almost as soon as she turned her back.

"What —" she gasped. But no other words escaped her mouth.

A blanket was thrown over her head, and she was dragged down onto the floor and a gag was stuffed into her mouth. She was so terrified that she wet herself.

"Well, well, we've got the two-bit rat," a familiar voice said.

She couldn't identify the voice yet, but she knew it was one of the girls, not one of the guards.

"So, you didn't like it here with us and you thought you could buy your freedom by setting up our friends," said another voice. "Well, guess what? It won't have been worth it."

Rebecca tried to speak, to tell them they'd made a mistake, that she didn't know anything, would never rat on anyone, that Dottie was her friend, that she'd never hurt her. But she could utter no sounds except gurgled squeals.

She could smell the lighter fluid, even under the blanket, and hear the sound of something being flicked off and on. One person sat on each of her arms and legs as she was spread-eagled.

"Nice tits you've got there," said the same voice.

Kathy, she thought. I'm sure of it.

"Too bad we have to ruin them."

Rebecca remembered the words of the ancient Hebrew prayer, "*Shma Yisroel.*" It was uttered by devout Jews in times of anguish or danger, and she kept repeating it over and over in her head.

She smelled her flesh burning before she felt the pain of a hot knife making cuts in her breasts. She twisted her body as tears ran down her face, but her screams of pain were choked off by the gag in her mouth.

The stabs were inflicted slowly, the person doing it waiting a few agonizing minutes between each one to heighten Rebecca's terror and pain.

Suddenly she heard the door being pushed open and the sounds of guards calling for backup on their walkie-talkies. The blanket was pulled off her head and the gag yanked from her mouth.

She was crying and choking with pain, and something else — rage. As she writhed on the floor, she had caught a glimpse of four women being handcuffed and taken out by the guards. One of them was indeed Kathy.

# 19

"There," Doris said as the front door swung open. She switched on the hall light and, as she did so, Grant checked his watch.

"It's after ten. You better get up to bed, Kevin."

"Can I watch some TV? Just till I go to sleep?"

"He's excited from the play," Doris said. "It'll help to relax him."

Grant smiled at his son. "Sure," he answered as he took off his coat and hung it up. They had been out all evening at one of Kevin's school plays.

The phone rang. "Damn," Grant muttered as he picked it up.

He felt the color draining from his face. Then he saw Doris's eyes fixed on him. His body tensed.

"I'll be out there first thing in the morning," he said into the phone. "Make sure she's kept in the hospital's isolation wing, under twenty-four-hour guard."

"Can you tell me what's wrong?" Doris asked as he hung up. "You look shaken."

"One of my drug informants was assaulted," he said, avoiding her eyes. He wasn't a good liar.

Since their last conversation about Rebecca Sherman, he had gone to great lengths to feign disinterest in her predicament to his wife. Doris had been questioning the amount of time and the intensity of his investigation of Rebecca's case, including how he seemed to be defending her actions.

"It's almost as if you're trying to find evidence of her innocence rather than her guilt," Doris had said.

She was right, of course. He had talked too much about the case, as if he were obsessed by it and by Rebecca herself.

"That's terrible," Doris said. "I guess that's dangerous work — being a drug informant, I mean."

Grant snapped his attention back to what she was saying. "Oh, yes. Yes, it is. Hey, I hate to be a party pooper, but I've got to get up early. Do you mind if I hit the sack?"

Doris smiled. "No, of course not."

*T*he next morning Grant Teasdale was sitting in the office of the prison superintendent, Claire Jameson, a former OPP investigator and a first-rate professional.

As prisons go, Midland was one of the better ones, but Teasdale knew, along with those in the corrections field, that there would always be a secret network inside such institutions. Nothing could stop it; it was a practice as old as time.

Both Teasdale and Jameson also knew that some of the guards were borderline alcoholics and drug addicts themselves, and could be abusive to the inmates when they thought they could get away with it. Unfortunately, union regulations usually protected them from dismissal.

Even though she was the superintendent, Jameson could rarely move against those she suspected of abuse. Such action required the kind of corroborating evidence that was almost impossible to obtain. None of the guards would rat on one of their own, no matter how much they might want to. And the inmates, especially if they were druggies or hookers, knew that they'd most likely be busted again, and so were afraid of the repercussions if they ever pointed a finger at a guard whom they might meet again on their next "visit" inside.

"I want to know how this happened," Teasdale said. The anger in his voice was obvious. "She was supposed to be protected. Where's Smith?"

"We've got her in isolation with the others," Jameson answered. "I couldn't take a chance on blowing her cover. We've only just found out which one of the guards we think was in on it. She leaked the word to the other inmates on the range that Sherman was a snitch.

"Smith reported that she'd seen Kathy Okata talking with a guard called Mason behind the kitchen earlier that morning," Jameson went on. "And she saw a package pass between them. But she never anticipated this. So far, it looks as if it was Mason who set this up, and that Okata was in on it with her. And now what should we do about Dottie? Maybe it's time to lift her out."

"No, that would be too obvious," Grant said. "She's a tough cookie. No one knows she's undercover but us, and if she's suddenly gone, it'll look suspicious."

Only Grant knew that Dottie Smith was really Ann Mitchell. When Rebecca had been sentenced to eighteen months in prison, even her detractors had been shocked. Ann had seen Teasdale's reaction, and knew that it went beyond that of a detached professional.

"That fucking Ronald Osgoode!" Grant had raged, pounding his fist on the desk. "Somehow he had a hand in this, I just know it! He must have cut a deal with Fitzpatrick on future cases. I wish I still had that fucking videotape!"

"Grant, get a hold of yourself," Ann had said, putting a hand on his arm, trying to calm him down. "What are you talking about? What tape? Judge Osgoode wasn't the sentencing judge. It was Madam Justice Brown. And Fitzpatrick was Rebecca Sherman's lawyer."

Grant couldn't tell her about the tape, which had mysteriously disappeared after Steven Sherman had been found dead. Teasdale wanted to kick himself for not making a copy of that video. I should have, he thought, cursing himself for neglecting to preserve potential evidence. Even though the preliminary coroner's report indicated that Sherman had died of a heart attack, Grant had his doubts. But without an official investigation, there was little he could do.

"Grant, I know you're planning to send someone inside Midland to cover her," Ann had said. "What about me?"

When Grant started to object, she'd raised her hand to silence him. "She'll never recognize me. I'll bleach my hair and use a Spanish accent. And, remember, I won my spurs back in Miami, working undercover on the streets as a drug pusher. So let me go in there. I'll make sure nothing happens to her. At least you'll know that you have someone you can rely on."

"It will take a lot of paperwork to set it up — you're FBI, remember."

"I've been seconded to your task force."

"I know but . . . "

"No buts, Grant. Besides, you never know what else I might pick up."

He had given in. Now, sitting across from Jameson, Grant thought back to that conversation with Ann as well as to DeLuca's expression of concern about Rebecca's safety in prison.

What about Brattini? Grant thought. Could one of the guards be on his payroll?

When he slipped into Rebecca's hospital room, she had an intravenous tube in her arm and her eyes were closed.

He suppressed a desire to put his arms around her. Get control of yourself, he thought, this dame can only be trouble for you.

When Rebecca's eyes opened and looked up into Inspector Teasdale's face, they immediately filled with tears. Again he had an urge to hold her and comfort her.

"Hello, Mrs. Sherman," he said in his most professional voice. "Would you care to tell me what happened?"

"Take a look and you'll see what happened," she replied, trying to sound tough as she opened her hospital gown. Her entire chest was covered in bandages, but he didn't have to see her wounds to know what she must have suffered.

"Did you see who did this to you?" he asked in a more gentle tone.

She continued to stare at him for a few moments, her dark eyes angry, yet haunted, before she answered. "You know I didn't."

"Mrs. Sherman, I tried to help you before you were sentenced to this place. You refused to cooperate with me then and now you see what happened here. If you tell us who's responsible for this, I'll see that you're not harmed."

Rebecca struggled to sit up. "Listen, Inspector, I told you then and I'm telling you now: I have nothing to say to you. Why don't you spend some of your energy cleaning up the sickos that pass for guards in this place?"

Why did he want to hold her so much? Why did he keep forgetting who she was and what she was doing here?

"Mrs. Sherman, I know you think I'm your enemy, but I'm not. I want to help you."

"Thanks a lot." She was hardly able to hold herself in check; she was trying not to burst out crying. "But I'll manage."

*B*y the next afternoon Teasdale had confirmed which guard had set up Rebecca, and by the next morning, she was in his office.

"Okay, Mason," he growled, "spill it — or you'll find yourself inside the joint with the same dames you love to diddle."

At first Josey Mason was evasive, trying to pretend she knew nothing, but Teasdale was too sharp for her. Pretty soon she was singing like a canary.

"My brother was approached by one of his drinking buddies on behalf of some Wop who wanted Sherman fingered. He was ready to pay 1,500 dollars, cash, for the job. After my brother and his buddy got the Wop up to 2,500 dollars they came to me to do the job."

"And who is this Wop?" Grant demanded.

Mason shrugged. "I don't know. All I know is what my brother told me."

Grant then called Lieutenant Larry Lyons of the Metro Toronto major crime squad. Grant had first met Lyons when he was part of the FBI team under Robert Lantinos, and they'd hit it off. When Lyons had married Judy MacQuire, the Canadian nurse who worked at Toronto General, he'd moved to the city, and the two men had renewed their friendship.

"I need the heat put on someone," Grant said to him. "There's a very important drug deal going down and I need to know who the man with the bread is."

Two days later George Mason was picked up on suspicion of drug pushing. When a rock of crack was found in his pocket, he started to shake. Holy shit, he thought, I'm being set up. Somebody planted that stash in my coat. It had to be the cops. Well, I ain't goin' down for any fucking Dago prick.

"The name of Mason's money man is Tony Aiella," Lyons told Grant. "But here's the strange part. He's an occasional driver for Bob DeSalle, that lawyer whiz kid who is so involved in politics. I seem to remember him speaking out for Rebecca Sherman before she was sentenced. It doesn't make much sense, does it?"

Not yet, Teasdale thought. But it will, as soon as I figure out how the pieces of this puzzle fit together.

*W*hen Rebecca was released from the prison infirmary and returned to her cell, she said nothing to anyone about what had happened. Some of the girls came up to her and gave her the high five, an acknowledgment of their acceptance of her.

Dottie, who was already back on the range by the time Rebecca returned, had told everyone that it was a frame-up by Kathy. When Kathy was transferred to another prison, it was a confirmation for the inmates that Rebecca Sherman had never ratted on anyone.

A week later Josey Mason and her brother George were killed in a tragic fire at a rented cottage in Haliburton. A gas heater had somehow been knocked over and by the time the fire department had reached them, their bodies were burned beyond recognition.

When Teasdale heard the news, his blood ran cold. This is big-time, he thought; Aiella doesn't have the clout to order an execution, and DeSalle's clean. He knew then that the Sherman case hadn't been closed yet.

*R*ebecca left Claire Jameson's office under guard, but it didn't matter. She felt she was walking on air. Jameson had just told her that notification of her parole application had been approved. "You'll be free within six months."

It wasn't just good news; it was great news. When she got back to the range she immediately went in search of Dottie. Good news had to be shared.

She tried the kitchen and the lounge; then in desperation she went to the laundry room. The washing machines were twice the size of those made for home use, and the dryers were much bigger than that. They were attached to the walls and had glass doors.

She stopped short in front of one of the huge dryers. Her scream choked in her throat as she stared horrified at its glass window. It was Dottie, her lifeless eyes staring back at her from inside the huge dryer, its door taped shut.

"Oh my God," Rebecca whispered. Her whole body started to shake. Then, finding her voice she did scream and scream and scream.

People came, and they were pulling Dottie out.

"Shit, she got smashed on the head real good," one of the guards said. "Must have been stuffed in the dryer half-conscious."

"It was turned to the highest heat cycle," someone else said.

"Shit, it was sure a slow and agonizing death for her, being tossed around inside, the heat rising, with no way out."

Rebecca screamed again, her hands over her face. Then she passed out.

*O*utside, the March winds howled. Grant sat in the run-down tavern and gulped down another beer. The whole place smelled of stale beer, cigarette smoke, and urine. It was a lousy, dark bar and it suited his mood. No one knew him and he didn't know anyone who came here. The hell with it. He hadn't gone out and got drunk in twenty-five years. But he decided this would be the night.

Why did I leave her inside? he kept asking himself. I should never have let her go in there. It's my fault she's dead. Ann Mitchell's horrible murder played in his brain like a record.

"You're going to be nursing one hell of a hangover tomorrow," Larry Lyons said as he leaned over Grant's shoulder.

"What are you doing in a dump like this?" Grant slurred.

"I could ask you the same thing. But the fact is I was looking for you."

"Well, I guess you found me. Was it worth the effort?"

Lyons straddled a chair next to Grant's. "Yeah. I guess. Anyway, it wasn't very hard. I heard about Ann and so I just looked for the worst bar within walking distance of your office."

"Smartass," Grant muttered, draining his glass.

"Look, you may have a break. I just found out that Claire Jameson tried to kill herself with an overdose of sleeping pills."

Grant blinked and wiped his mouth with his hand. "Where is she?"

"They brought her into town. She's at Toronto General."

"I've got to talk to her."

Lyons shook his head. "She's out cold and soon you will be, too. Let me drive you home. You can go first thing in the morning."

Grant pulled himself up. "Yeah, first thing."

He grabbed Lyons's arm and let himself be taken to the car. On the way home he fell asleep.

*G*rant's head felt as if it might fall off. But Claire Jameson soon sobered him up.

"I'm the one who spilled the beans on Dottie being undercover in Midland. For $25,000 in cash." She spoke in a soft, restrained voice. She looked ten years older than when he had last seen her a few days earlier.

"Two men came to see me. One of them had a fancy mustache that he kept combing. They said they only wanted to know who was protecting Sherman in order to ask her a few questions, nothing more. They promised nothing would happen to whoever it was."

She shook her head. "They knew about Fred — that he gambled

away all our savings, even my retirement fund. Fred is my husband," she added almost as an afterthought.

"Did you ask how they knew that?"

She shook her head. "I just assumed they were associates of DeLuca, and that anyone who was connected to Sherman would be safe."

Grant stared at her. Claire Jameson's explanation for her unforgivable betrayal wouldn't wash. She was a professional, and Grant knew — as she herself knew — that it was impossible to rationalize her actions.

FBI Special Agent Ann Mitchell (a.k.a. Dottie Smith) was dead, and Jameson, and Grant, would have to live with the guilt for the rest of their lives.

*O*n the day she finally walked out of Midland Prison for Women, Rebecca Sherman was different from the woman she had been when she went in. She had made four rules for herself: The past is over. No more high living. No more Santino. And no more politics.

The first person she saw when she passed through the gates was Brad Ross. She rushed over to him, put her arms around his neck, and started to cry. He rocked her very gently, stroking her head and murmuring words of love and encouragement.

Two days after her release, Rebecca Sherman and Brad Ross were married at City Hall. Jean Singer and Lisa Sherman were their witnesses. They both agreed that Rebecca would keep the name "Sherman" to make things easier for Lisa.

Brad and Rebecca spent their honeymoon at the Four Seasons Hotel, in the trendy Yorkville area of Toronto.

Brad was a gentle lover, eager to please. Rebecca hoped that one day her feigned passion for him would become genuine.

But what was important was his commitment to family, and his kindness.

# 20

APRIL
1994

*E*lizabeth sat down on the small seat in front of the pay phone. She always used a pay phone to call her mother in Italy because she could pay for it with cash as soon as she finished talking.

"Hello, Mama," she said in response to the weak "hello" at the other end of the line. "I hope the weather is better there than it is here. We're in the midst of a blizzard — can you believe it?"

"Elizabeth, Elizabeth, I'm so glad to hear your voice," Giovanna answered, her own voice cracking.

"Mama, is anything wrong? I can barely hear you."

"No, nothing's wrong, my darling daughter," Giovanna mumbled in reply. "It must be the phone lines."

So Elizabeth spoke louder than usual, telling her mother about the boys' plans for graduate school next fall.

"They're both going to Harvard — can you believe it, Mama?" she said. "Peter is continuing his business studies and Matthew is thinking of switching to law. Santino is so proud, and so am I."

When she got no response, Elizabeth sensed something was terribly wrong. Her mother had always perked up when the conversation was about the boys, and she had never tired of hearing every detail of their lives, even when she was in her fantasy world.

243

Over the years Elizabeth had come to know, in the first few words her mother spoke, whether or not she was in a lucid state of mind. Admittedly, though, she sometimes had behaved oddly. When many years ago she had learned that Elizabeth was moving to Boston, she had sounded overjoyed. Since she knew nothing about the place, her reaction had seemed very strange. But Elizabeth had just chalked it up to good humor.

Today, even though Giovanna sounded strained, almost desolate, Elizabeth sensed that she was clearheaded.

"Mama, something is definitely wrong. I can tell by your voice. I insist that you tell me what it is!"

"Oh Elizabeth," Giovanna said forlornly, "isn't it sad that our relationship has grown deeper over the years only through a telephone line? That we haven't touched, or smiled at each other, or watched each other change? That we remember only what we once were — never sharing what we have become?

"I've had to create my own reality about my grandsons," she went on. "What they must look like, how they must have been as children, their achievements and disappointments. I've never even seen a picture of them. I know you said it was too dangerous, that the pictures could fall into the wrong hands, or that someone would see them in my room. But everything I know is based solely on your descriptions. I've never been able to share in any of your lives, never been able to exchange gifts, never been able to tell the boys about their great-grandfather and the rich heritage of their ancestors. For one sinful act, I've paid penance my whole life. And now our Father wants more."

"What sinful act, Mama?" Elizabeth asked. She was almost afraid to hear the answer. It was the first time her mother had even hinted about her past life, or shared her innermost feelings with her daughter.

"Elizabeth, I know how lonely and isolated you were when you were young," Giovanna said, ignoring the question. "I'm sorry, I really am, but back then I just couldn't speak of it. And then that terrible bombing — I'm sure it's the reason for the secrecy surrounding your life, the reason that has kept us apart for all these years.

"But, my little princess, I need to be with you again, at least one more time. And I need to see Peter and Matthew, to hold them close to me once before I die."

Elizabeth's blood ran cold. "Die? Mama, you're only sixty-five. Mama, are you sick? Tell me what's wrong."

"I have cervical cancer," Giovanna murmured. "The doctors say it has already spread, so I can expect only six more months of life before the beginning of the end. I'm so afraid. I need you. Please come."

And then, despite what must have been her determination not to, Giovanna burst into sobs, something she hadn't done since Elizabeth had left Italy almost thirty-two years earlier.

"Mama, Mama, stop crying, please. I'll come. I promise. I'll find a way to come."

Elizabeth said good-bye and paid for the call. She went outside and walked through the blowing snow to where she had parked her car. She was still shaking.

She turned on the ignition but just sat there, mumbling to herself. "I'm going to make up for the lost years, no matter how difficult." She knew she would have to deceive Santino and make all the arrangements herself. She also knew she'd have to accept the responsibility for any repercussions, but she was determined to see it through.

I hope I'll have the strength to stick with it, and not fall to pieces, she thought as she pulled away from the curb.

*T*hat night after dinner Elizabeth came into the study. "I had a great idea today, Santino," she said, attempting to look cheerful.

"And what might that be?"

"Why don't the two of us take the boys on a bicycle tour through France as soon as classes are over? It'll be a great opportunity for us to have a special vacation with them before they go back to university. You know that for the last ten years I've listened to you talk about taking up bicycling again.

Well, now's your chance. We can eat our way through France and then bicycle the pounds off."

Santino's eyes softened and a smile lit up his face. Oh God, don't change your spots now, Elizabeth thought, starting to panic inside as she watched her husband mulling over her suggestion.

"Sorry, sweetheart," Santino finally answered. "You know how busy we are in the spring and summer, especially now, with a construction boom just beginning. I can't possibly get away."

Elizabeth tried to keep her breathing even and not heave a sigh of relief. "How about early September?" Santino suggested.

"No, that's too late," she told him. "Besides, you know that there could be an unexpected business crisis at the last minute. It's happened more than once before, and then it would be too late. Besides, I've got too much to do getting the boys ready for graduate school to wait that long."

"Come on, Elizabeth," Santino said, half laughing. "The 'boys' will be twenty-two in July, not exactly babies any more."

After a few more minutes of chitchat, Santino said, "Say, why don't the three of you go on your own in July? You can shop in Paris to your heart's content and take the boys through Versailles or the Louvre without me complaining about being bored."

Elizabeth took a deep breath: Thank you, God, for letting Santino stay true to form.

"If I can, I'll join you, but I doubt it," he went on. "So don't plan to be away for more than two weeks. I couldn't stand being without you for longer than that."

Santino didn't mention the severe pains and cramps he'd been having lately. Elizabeth's absence would give him a chance to visit the doctor without alarming her.

*I*'ll make arrangements to get to Italy as soon as we get to our hotel, Elizabeth thought as the plane began its final descent into De Gaulle Airport that July morning. I'll pay for the tickets in cash so no one can trace our footsteps.

Santino thought she and the boys were planning to bicycle around the French countryside for the first two days of their trip. She told him that they would stay at whatever country inn struck their fancy and that she would not be able to call him until they were settled. That would give them enough time to get to Altamura and back before she had to call him.

Of immediate concern to Elizabeth was how she was going to explain to her sons why, despite their questions, she had never really told them much about her early life. She hoped they would understand now. Feelings of love suddenly swept over her — they were good boys, strong and considerate.

The DeLuca twins were over six feet tall. Peter, the older by two minutes, was fair-skinned with green eyes and looked like his mother. Matthew was dark-skinned, had black hair, and looked more like his father, except for his green eyes.

The brothers had some knowledge of their father's international business interests because in the past year he had begun discussing some of it with them. But no mention had yet been made about that part of his business which was written about regularly in the media — his alleged ties to the Villano crime family. In the last few years, however, Peter and Matthew had secretly discussed between themselves the possibility that there might be some truth to the rumors, and that their mother might be aware of it.

Peter was very pragmatic, a realist. He approached all situations head-on, prepared for confrontation. Even as a little boy, he would sit down and think through a problem and come up with the best strategy to obtain the result he desired. But his quick temper made it just as likely that he'd lash out when provoked rather than react calmly. He was also very protective of his brother.

Matthew was an idealist who believed in the principles of social justice and equality. He was a gentle giant who loved to read and to listen to classical music when the ear-shattering din of rock music wasn't blaring throughout the house. He rarely lost his cool, and often interceded when Peter's temper flared up.

Elizabeth anticipated that Peter would analyze the situation she would soon share with them, and immediately make suggestions on how it should be handled, no matter how difficult it might be. Matthew, on the other hand, would probably just hold her and tell her not to worry — he'd say everything would be okay.

But one thing was certain: nothing would ever be the same again, especially for Giovanna Volpe. Elizabeth intended to bring her home to Boston as soon as the necessary arrangements could be made.

The next morning they took a flight to Brindisi, and in that bustling port town she rented a car.

"This sure is proving to be a mystery vacation," Matthew said with a grin.

Elizabeth pulled out onto the highway. Her heart was pounding, but her resolve was firm. "Boys," she said, "I will explain everything now. Please bear with me until I'm finished, and then you can ask questions."

She began haltingly, gaining strength as she progressed. The brothers appeared shocked by their mother's story, and didn't say a word until she had finished speaking.

They had been told that she was an orphan and had been living in a convent when she met their father. Elizabeth explained how fearful Santino had always been that someone from her past would find out that she had survived that terrible explosion, and for that reason the truth had been kept from them.

"I think Dad was right," Peter said, his green eyes flashing. "I'll bet it had something to do with one of those other girls — probably because of something her father did. But since you were there, and saw what happened, you'd be in danger. My guess is that a contract was put out on somebody. Probably whoever did it is dead now, or very old, so you and Grandmother won't have to worry any more. If not, well, Dad and I can handle it."

"Knock it off," Matthew snapped, his green eyes also flashing. "Right away you think the worst and you want to fight. No! I say it was an accident, a fluke. Who'd want to hurt a bunch of nuns and girls? If it was anything, I think it was a political statement. After all, those were the '60s, and people were all revolting back then." He paused, looking sheepish. "Sorry, I like the pun."

Then he went on seriously. "The greatest tragedy of all is that Mom and her mom have been kept apart for so long. So, don't worry, Mom, I'll speak to Dad. I know he'll understand why you had to do this."

Elizabeth prayed that Matthew's assessment was the right one. If not, she'd jeopardized all their lives, and Santino would never forgive her.

*R*oberto Vincenzo was sitting in his den drinking Sambucca when he decided to make a call to his grandmother.

"Roberto, it's good to hear your voice," Rosa Vincenzo said. "When are you planning to come visit me again? It's been over two years since I last saw you."

"You know how much I look forward to visiting you, Nonna Rosa," he answered, "but I've been so busy lately. I'll try to come soon, I promise."

Roberto thought about Don Vincenzo's villa and cringed. It was really strange that he had once thought it the grandest place on earth, but now it just seemed like a tumbled-down old house in the middle of nowhere. But what the hell, he had gone there only four times in all the years since he had left Italy at the age of fourteen. Besides, he'd soon inherit all of it—the villa, the farms, and the vineyards. And when he did, he intended to burn down the old house and build a new one. Rosa was old. She was about to kick the bucket. He considered his phone calls and occasional visits a duty.

"How are you doing, Nonna Rosa? Well, I hope."

He could hear her intake of breath. "My friend Giovanna is dying," she said.

He frowned slightly. "How sad."

"But it's not so sad. She will die happy, ever so happy and contented."

"Oh? Why is that?"

"Her daughter Elizabeth came to see her this morning. She brought her two sons, Giovanna's grandsons. Such wonderful boys. I met them, too. Her husband, Santino DeLuca, must be very handsome, too."

Roberto's mouth went completely dry. Elizabeth was alive! And DeLuca was her husband! Then he thought of Giovanna's eyes. Yes, just like Elizabeth DeLuca's. That's why she had seemed so familiar to him.

"Are you all right, Roberto?" Rosa asked. "Are you still there?"

It was too much to assimilate so quickly. Shit, now he had to kill the boys, too. Well, that would make Brattini happy. DeLuca would die in agony when his wife and sons were knocked off.

"Yes, I'm fine," he answered. "It must be a bad connection."

Roberto could hardly sit still after he'd hung up. He'd have to start making plans. Getting Santino's family wasn't going to be easy.

He took a few gulps of the Sambucca right from the bottle and called Massimo Brattini.

"I've got some good news for you," he said after Brattini snarled at him for calling him so late, and at home. "You'd better be sitting down."

# 21

NOVEMBER 21
1994

*R*ebecca was happy to get a window seat on the flight to Boston. The plane was crowded even though it was close to midnight.

Most of the other passengers looked like college students and she assumed that was because the rates were cheaper on the red eye. In fact, several were wearing jackets emblazoned with University of Toronto logos — they were probably on their way home for American Thanksgiving.

I must be getting older, she thought. They all look so carefree — guys and girls together, it's hard to tell sometimes which is which, given the same hairstyles and unisex jeans, especially from the back. It wasn't the way she had been reared. In the '50s girls were girls and boys were boys.

As the plane took off, she closed her eyes and tried to relax, knowing that in a few hours she would come face to face with her past — and the man she had once loved so much, the man who had offered her the world on a silver platter, and then delivered it.

Having gone through U.S. Customs in Toronto, Rebecca moved through the gates at Logan Airport quickly, looking around for someone who might be there to pick her up.

"It's been a long time, Mrs. Sherman." She whirled around at the sound of the familiar voice behind her. It was Jimmy Bono, Santino's right-hand man. He looked somewhat embarrassed when she threw her arms around his neck and hugged him, but then he should have been used to it. During the years she and Santino had been together, Jimmy was always the recipient of Rebecca's hugs.

"Jimmy," she used to croon to him, "you look just like a beagle puppy. Adorable and cuddly. Who'd ever believe what you really do for a living?"

His face would always turn beet-red and she'd laugh.

Now, as they got into Jimmy's black Porsche for the drive to the DeLuca home, Rebecca asked, "How is Santino?"

Jimmy's face tightened up. "Things aren't looking so good."

"How come you're driving your own car?" she asked him. It was unusual for Jimmy; he'd always used one of the company's limos or had Phillie drive him where he had to go.

"It's too late, or too early, depending on which end of the clock you look at, to make Phillie drive us," he answered. "Besides, the fewer people who know you're here, the better it is for you."

A wave of apprehension rippled through her. Once she had thought someone was trying to kill her. But that was long ago.

They drove the rest of the thirty-five-minute trip in silence. She didn't ask him what he meant by his comment, and he didn't volunteer any further thoughts.

Rebecca couldn't remember the first time she'd met Jimmy. He seemed to have always been there, next to, or very close by, Santino. It must be close to twenty years since we first met, she thought. Where has all the time gone?

She remembered when Santino had told her about his first meeting with Jimmy back in the late '40s. On the day his ship docked in New York Santino had rushed down the gangplank; he'd been seasick during the entire voyage, and wanted to put his feet on solid ground before he threw up again.

After a few minutes' walk, he'd found a parkette, stretched out on the nearest bench, and dozed off immediately. It couldn't have been a minute or two later that a couple of thugs had pushed him off the bench and stolen his knapsack, which contained everything he owned, including his passport and train tickets to Detroit.

Santino had been reluctant to follow them because he didn't know any of the streets, or which way the thieves had gone. He was afraid of getting lost because he spoke very little English. As panic began to overtake him a teenager and a large man had stumbled out from behind a parked truck, the young one holding the other man, who was almost double his own size, in a headlock. The kid's fingers had been pressing into the man's neck, right under his ears.

"I think this man has something of yours," the youngster had said to Santino in very broken English.

"Let me go, you Dago prick!" the thug had kept yelling.

When they came up to him Santino had taken his knapsack from the boy's shoulder and made sure his passport and tickets were still there. Then he had grabbed the thug by the hair and brought his knee up very hard into his groin.

"See what happens when you steal from a Dago?" he'd said in his own broken English. The man had doubled over, yelling in pain.

Santino had turned to the youngster and asked him, in Italian, who he was and what the hell was going on.

His name was Jimmy Bono and he wasn't a teenager— he just looked like one. He was twenty-five. He'd been living on the streets of New York since he was twelve, doing odd jobs, running numbers, driving for different small-time hoods. His parents, now long dead, had originally emigrated from Reggio, on the tip of the Italian boot across from Sicily.

The young man had been hanging around the docks, hoping to run into some of his friends who had been deported back to Italy during the war.

"I'm sick of small-time action," he'd told Santino. "I been hoping to get into something bigger." He grinned. "When I saw that bum rolling you, I felt it was my duty to protect you."

"This is your lucky day, Jimmy," Santino had said. "I'm on my way to a new job — and a new life — in a place called Detroit. I can use a loyal friend in my line of work. Come on, join me. Let's see where the road takes us."

Jimmy had been with him ever since, over forty-seven years. He had often couriered documents or notes between Rebecca and Santino. But she had never really appreciated his loyalty and commitment to the DeLucas until she became embroiled in the Peartree controversy and learned what the word "ruthless" really meant.

As Jimmy's car sped along the deserted streets of Boston, Rebecca thought back to that morning back in 1975 when she'd received a call from Senator Jack Jacobs, and how it changed the course of her life.

I wonder how different my life might have been if I hadn't been so impulsive, so greedy, so driven, and so stupid? If only I'd discussed the situation with Santino before it was too late, she reflected. If only I'd been patient. If only I'd waited.

*T*he DeLuca home on Brimmer Street in the Back Bay section of Boston was a five-story brick row townhouse. It had originally belonged to a wealthy family in the nineteenth century. In the depression years it became a rooming-house, and remained so until the late '60s. Then, under the watchful eye of an experienced historic renovator and an interior designer, it began its metamorphosis. Wiring and plumbing were modernized, rooms once walled off were opened, and all the original wood trim and wainscoting were restored. Old brick was exposed, stained-glass windows were replaced, and the house emerged a modern mansion for townsfolk.

A stone walkway led to the front door, which was illuminated by a porch light fashioned to look like a gaslight. The house was trimmed in white and had window boxes. The front yard was tiny, but there was a hidden garden in the rear, a garden completely enclosed by the walls of other brick homes.

Ten years ago Elizabeth had fallen in love with the house, which was only the fourth one they had viewed, and that afternoon Santino bought it. Elizabeth, after spending a fortune on antiques and fine furnishings, had turned it into a showplace. In fact, the home and several of its rooms had been featured in a recent issue of *Architectural Digest*, the upscale decorating magazine.

Rebecca paused for a second on the doorstep. On each side of the door was a giant urn; they obviously held flowers in warm weather. She took a few deep breaths to settle her nerves. When Jimmy knocked on the front door, she noticed the camera trained to catch the face of anyone on the steps or in front of the door. But it was high enough so that it couldn't be reached by hand. She wondered if there was another entrance at the rear of the house, which was attached on either side to others.

Elizabeth DeLuca opened the door herself. She was, as always, stunning. Something about her always made Rebecca feel awkward. She was wearing a long tartan skirt and a white tailored blouse; a sweater was draped around her shoulders. Her streaked blond hair was hanging loose and her makeup consisted only of a little eyeshadow and lipstick.

The fact that it was just after four o'clock in the morning didn't seem to faze her.

"Thank you for coming," she said to Rebecca with a warm smile. "It means a lot to all of us."

To the left in the foyer was an elevator, and Vinnie Bratuso, another of Santino's longtime retainers, was standing there. He was wearing what looked like the same navy shantung suit he had on when she had last seen him, over ten years earlier. His purple flowered shirt was unbuttoned just enough to show the heavy gold cross around his neck: a black silk handkerchief was tucked into the breast pocket of his jacket. His shoes were shiny snakeskin and he wore flowered socks. She couldn't help smiling — he always dressed like a character from *Guys and Dolls,* and this early morning was no exception.

"How are you, Vinnie?" Rebecca asked as she turned toward him. "It's been a long time."

"I'm fine thanks, Mrs. Sherman," he answered. "It's too bad we have to meet again under these circumstances."

Rebecca looked around the black and white marble foyer. There were vases filled with flowers everywhere, giving the place a festive air. The whole house was lit up as though it were the early evening instead of the middle of the night.

She could see the white kitchen at the end of a side hallway and a woman in uniform moving around there.

Off that same hallway was a large paneled room with a pool table inside. Rebecca knew how much Santino loved to shoot pool, and smiled to herself thinking what fun he must have had teaching his two sons how to play.

"Let me show you to your room, Rebecca," said Elizabeth, taking her arm. "And then I'll let Santino know you're here."

Her tone was one of warmth and graciousness. She gave no inkling that she knew, or even suspected, that the woman standing in front of her had once been her husband's lover.

"You have a lovely home, Elizabeth," Rebecca said as they got into the elevator. "I noticed some stunning pieces of sculpture in the foyer which I assume you created. They are quite beautiful."

Elizabeth described the layout of the house as the elevator started to rise. The second floor consisted of the help's quarters and laundry room facilities. On the third floor were a screening room, a gym and exercise room, and her sons' bedrooms. Then the elevator stopped on the fourth floor. There was a large den, a small kitchenette, and two guest bedrooms, each with its own bathroom. The entire fifth floor consisted of the DeLucas' private quarters. Rebecca still hadn't noticed another entrance, but of course she hadn't investigated all the rooms on the first floor or the basement.

"This is your room," Elizabeth announced, opening the door to an exquisite bedroom, decorated in different shades of peach and furnished with elegant French antiques and a king-size canopied bed.

"Would you like anything to drink or eat? Some fruit? Or would you prefer a few moments just to freshen up?" she asked.

"No, I'd just like to see Santino," Rebecca answered, wondering what Elizabeth was really thinking.

How can she be so gracious and friendly? Rebecca thought. If I were facing a woman I suspected, or knew, was once my husband's mistress, I'd want to kill her.

"He's fairly sedated most of the time," Elizabeth told her as they walked back to the elevator. "But he wanted to make sure he was awake and alert when he saw you, so we've cut down on his painkillers."

Rebecca didn't want to say how much she dreaded seeing Santino this way. She couldn't.

"Don't be too upset if his skin is clammy and he perspires a lot. There's a button attached to the side of the bed. Push it if you need any help."

When the elevator stopped at the fifth floor, Elizabeth stayed in it while Vinnie held the door open to let Rebecca out. As she walked down the hall to where another old lieutenant, Sal Lata, was waiting, she noticed a glass door in an alcove to her right. It had a heavy metal bar across the bottom. She could see the stars outside and assumed the door opened onto some sort of a roof garden.

As she approached, Sal gave her a warm smile and nodded his head. He couldn't speak because many years earlier his tongue had been cut out by Brattini's thugs. Sal refused to tell them how he'd infiltrated their drug operation and who had ratted on them to the FBI.

Finally she was in Santino's room. There was an overpowering scent of pine, probably an air freshener. She could see the hospital bed over by the window. As she walked forward she tried to steel herself.

"Oh, Santino," she whispered, "how I've missed you."

As she came closer to the bed, the figure in it stirred slightly, and when she saw his gaunt frame she had to choke back her tears. She went to him, took his hand in hers, and began to stroke his forehead. His eyes remained closed and she wasn't sure he realized she was there.

She bent over, putting her cheek against his, running a hand through his thick hair, which was now almost all white, trying desperately not to cry. But seeing him so vulnerable overwhelmed her. As tears began to run down her cheeks onto his face, his arms came up around her and he held her as tightly as he could.

"Shh, don't cry, *bella*," he whispered. "Now, now . . . it's okay . . . you're here with me again. Soon the pain of the past will be over."

She kissed his lips very softly and murmured, "*Ti 'amo, ti 'amo*," in his ear.

By the time Rebecca left Santino's room, it was almost six o'clock in the morning. She was shaken by all that he'd told her, but she knew she'd have to settle down quickly and figure out how to deal with this situation before time ran out.

Sal was still sitting outside his door when Vinnie came up in the elevator, and held the door open for her.

When she got back to her room Elizabeth was waiting for her. "I need to talk to you," she said quietly.

When they got inside the room Elizabeth took an audiocassette out of her skirt pocket.

Well, well, what's this? Rebecca thought. Confrontation? After all these years?

"Rebecca, I have a long story to tell you, or rather let you hear. And then I hope you'll help me. Santino's sons' lives depend on it."

She drew Rebecca down beside her on a small settee. "When I was seventeen years old, Santino spirited me away from Italy after a tragic car bombing that killed some of my classmates. It was only by chance that I wasn't killed, too. But everyone believed I was dead.

"Santino was sure that I was in some sort of danger and warned me not to call my mother before we left Italy, but I called her anyway. I continued to call her every month after that — and never told him. Elizabeth paused, as if recalling these phone conversations.

"Last July, without telling Santino what I was doing, I took Matthew and Peter to Italy, to visit my mother . . . I hadn't seen her in over thirty years.

"Oh Rebecca," Elizabeth continued, her voice cracking. "I never realized how much I missed having a mother until I saw her again. She was so forlorn, so thin and drawn, so different from the last time I'd seen her. Then, she'd been domineering, alternating between fantasy and reality. I never thought she really cared about me; I believed she was keeping me restricted only so she could pressure me into becoming a nun. I resented her so much. I even used to call her a weirdo.

"But the look of joy on her face when the three of us walked into her room will give me comfort for the rest of my days."

Rebecca thought of her own mother, and nodded.

"The twins were amazed at how well their *nonna* could speak English and were really impressed by how well read and articulate she was. We stayed with her the entire day and into the early evening. I explained to her that, as soon as we could get her a passport, we'd make arrangements to bring her here, to Boston, in secret. She seemed really content.

"But when we had to leave to catch our train back to Paris, she clung to me, kissing and stroking me as she'd never done before. She smothered my sons with kisses, as if she knew she'd never see us again.

"As Mama walked us out to the car I had rented, an elderly lady was just walking up the path to visit her. In her excitement my mother introduced us to Rosa Vincenzo, proudly explaining how her daughter and grandsons had just arrived from the United States.

"I thought nothing much of it — after all, they were just two old women. Then my mother and I held each other tightly and she blessed me for giving her life meaning. I didn't understand exactly what she had meant, at least not then.

"When we returned home I knew I'd have to tell Santino what I'd done right away, knowing that, if I didn't, the twins would.

"He wasn't as angry as I thought he'd be. Perhaps the medication he was already taking was affecting him — or, maybe, like me, he thought that whatever danger there might have been thirty-odd years ago was over. We both turned out to be wrong."

As she listened to Elizabeth's story, Rebecca resolved never to let her know that she already knew most of it; years ago Santino had shared his concerns with her, always wondering who had caused that explosion, and why.

"A week after we'd returned home, after all the travel arrangements had been made, I called my mother," Elizabeth continued. "But the Mother Superior told me that 'Giovanna Volpe has gone to be with our Lord in heaven.' She had died in her sleep two days earlier.

"And then, just a few weeks ago, Santino told me that Massimo Brattini, his old nemesis, was coming to visit him to say his farewells, and would be staying here overnight. I found that very strange, given the enmity between the two of them all these years.

"When he arrived, Brattini was very warm and friendly to us, especially the boys. He stared at us so much that I became very uncomfortable, really worried, because I knew what kind of man he was.

"So I did something I never imagined I could ever do. I took one of my sons' tape recorders and put it under the skirted table in Santino's bedroom. I started the tape with my foot before I left them alone together. I needed to know what Brattini had to say to my husband, and if he was going to try to take advantage of his weakened condition.

"Rebecca, I want you to listen to the tape — it's not very long — and then . . . then I need your help."

"Wait a minute, Elizabeth," Rebecca said. "Brattini's dead! Whatever threats he might have made to Santino don't matter any more because whoever shot him sure as hell didn't intend to take care of his old vendettas."

"That's what I thought, too," Elizabeth whispered. "And it's why I didn't bother listening to the tape right away. But when Santino told me to call you and Inspector Teasdale, I became very concerned again, and decided I'd better listen to it. All the answers are on it. Rebecca, our lives are in danger. Mine, the boys', maybe yours . . ."

Rebecca wondered if she looked as shaken as she felt.

"Please listen to this," Elizabeth said as she got up to put the cassette in the tape deck. She turned it on and closed her eyes. Rebecca stared across the room, seeing nothing as the two familiar voices filled her ears.

The first few minutes of the tape were full of greetings and words of respect between the two old enemies who had been childhood friends back in Italy. Santino had left five months before Brattini.

Brattini asked Santino if the scar near his navel was still there. As kids they had decided to become blood brothers, but instead of cutting their fingers and letting their blood mix, as did those who were being inducted into the Black Hand, they heated up their rosaries and made matching scars on themselves.

"Yeah," Santino had answered, "I couldn't be bothered having it removed."

Then Massimo Brattini began his story.

"Nearly fifty years ago, when I was in Puglia with my cousins, we left our unit and headed home. It was a year after the surrender, and things were chaotic. We went out drinking, looking for broads. By the time we passed a couple of young ones walking along the road, we were pissed out of our minds.

"I'm ashamed to say that we decided to give them a fuck, and so we dragged them off into our camp. But things got out of hand and my cousins murdered one of them horribly. In my panic I thought the only way to redeem myself with God was to spare the other girl. I decided to protect her from the Luchese brothers' brutality by fucking her myself as gently as I could, and then somehow finding a way to let her escape.

"The truth was I liked her. She was so young, so frightened, and her big green eyes kept looking at me so pitifully, even as I felt her respond to me."

Santino's grunt of disbelief could be heard on the tape as Brattini continued talking.

"Yes, it's true, she did, and I was feeling something, too, something I'd never felt for any broad before — or since. And I knew I had to save her from my cousins and then, maybe, come back for her. But I didn't know how. When we heard planes, we ran away, but I made sure she'd be okay before we took off.

"I didn't know who the dead girl was until we got back home to Calabria. By then her family had put out the word that they wanted the two soldiers who had murdered her. Since there was no mention of me, I was sure the girl was protecting me.

"When the mutilated bodies of my cousins were dumped on their father's driveway, a couple of years later, I decided to take off right away, without even a good-bye for my parents. I used all the money I had to buy a third-class ticket on a boat to South America.

"When I got to America, the only thing still connecting me to Italy and the past was the scar of the cross, so I had it removed.

"But I still needed to know who the girl with the green eyes was. I wanted to bring her to me. But I couldn't find out because she'd disappeared, and if I made too much of it, someone might start asking questions. I was still a poor *capo* with few connections, so I gave up. But I never forgot her.

"Last month I found out her name — Giovanna Volpe."

They could hear Santino moan, "Oh, my God!" Rebecca sat up straight and focused her eyes on Elizabeth, who hadn't moved an inch.

"Yes, Santino, it's true," Brattini continued. "Your wife is my daughter, and your sons are my grandsons. How can I tell you what it felt like to look at Elizabeth and see her mother in her face? She has the same green eyes. And so have the boys."

There was silence on the tape, and then Brattini went on, his voice breaking.

"Oh, Santino, if only I'd known that Giovanna was carrying my child. Somehow I would have found a way to get back to her and bring her and the baby here. Even when I was with other women, even when I was with my own wife, she was always in my thoughts. And my bitterness drove me to unnecessary violence. I was always trying to prove to myself that I didn't care about anything or anyone, that nothing could ever hurt me again."

There was a moment of silence on the tape. "Santino, do you remember the hooker?"

"Remember?" Santino rasped. "How could I ever forget her."

"Well, neither did I. Not one day of my life has passed since that terrible day without her haunting eyes tormenting me. And now, this."

Again, there was silence on the tape.

"Knowing that Giovanna, that sweet young girl, first protected me and then spent the rest of her life in misery because of me, will haunt me forever."

Now Rebecca understood what "pain" had plagued Brattini all those years, and why he was so cold.

Then Massimo warned Santino that Elizabeth and the twins were in danger from Bob DeSalle, who was Don Vincenzo's grandson — and the murdered girl's brother. Bob had always been a mole in the Brattini organization.

"His real name is Roberto Vincenzo," Brattini said.

"When Roberto learned from his grandmother, old Rosa Vincenzo, that Elizabeth hadn't been killed in the bomb explosion he'd arranged in Rome years earlier, that she had in fact been spirited out of Italy by you, Santino DeLuca, he was in a rage. He's sworn to finish the job himself so that his dead sister can rest in peace along with the soul of his grandfather."

There was another silence on the tape — except for DeLuca's rasping breathing.

"Roberto told me the whole story because he thought I'd be happy to learn of the pain he would soon cause you, especially since he'd blown my instructions about getting your girlfriend when she was in jail."

Brattini's voice clearly revealed his anger. "But he blew it, the prick, because that fucking Mountie had already put a plant inside the prison to protect her."

So that's where Santino had got the information that Teasdale was protecting me from Brattini, Rebecca thought. And I told him he was nuts.

"Roberto was hoping I'd forgive him his past failures if he did this job himself," Brattini said. "In fact, he thought I might even reward him when the deed was done.

"Naturally, it never occurred to him that I was the father of Giovanna's baby — why should it? — and there was no point in trying to explain the story to him and get him to back off. He'd never believe it, and even if he did, it's the kind of information that he would use to bring chaos into all our lives — my wife and my other children — and our mutual business associates.

"So I've decided to take care of this matter myself as soon as I get back to Toronto, even though it's been a long time since I took anyone out."

"That's something you never forget," Santino croaked, compassion and respect for his old enemy in his voice.

"I wanted you to be aware of everything, Santino," Brattini said. "If anything should go wrong, I need to know that my daughter and my grandsons will be safe. And next to me, you're the only one I can trust enough to make sure of it."

As the tape deck switched off, Rebecca knew what she had to do. The two women looked at each other for a long time.

"We have plans to make, Elizabeth," Rebecca said.

Elizabeth nodded her head in silence.

# 22

*NOVEMBER 21–22*
*1994*

*G*rant Teasdale was lounging on a cot by the pool. It was almost five o'clock and the sun was starting to disappear behind the tall palm trees. He was trying to figure out what DeLuca wanted with him. Since their meeting eleven years earlier, the two men had never spoken again. Well, he'd have the answer to that question by tomorrow night.

The sounds of Kevin's laughter brought Grant back to the present. He opened his eyes and watched his son slide down the water slide into the water with an expression of happiness all over his face. He was more determined than ever to find a way to make sure Kevin would be looked after properly when he and Doris were gone.

Kevin jumped out of the pool and came running over to Teasdale, looking like a normal and powerful young man. Only his eyes revealed the child that lived within.

"Daddy, Daddy, can I go over to the playroom and try the games?" he asked excitedly.

"As long as you stay where I can see you," Grant told him.

With that, Kevin dashed off to the glassed-in entertainment room adjacent to the hotel's cabaña.

There were several young boys playing the video games and as Grant watched them, their faces so carefree, moisture suddenly filled his eyes.

He thought back to when he had been young and had been anything but carefree.

If Kevin isn't taken care of, history could repeat itself, he thought, remembering his suffering and that of the others with whom he had shared his early years. A cold shiver passed through his body despite the Florida sun. His worst fear in life was that his son might suffer as he once had.

Teasdale closed his eyes and relived the horror that was once the Brothers of St. John Home for Orphans . . .

Grant had been beaten regularly, for even the slightest infraction of the rules, since he'd arrived at the orphanage in 1954. Ice-water enemas were one of the favorite techniques used by the brothers, and Grant's insides would turn to mush whenever he saw the catheter and rubber bag come out of the cupboard. The punishment room was next to Father Thomas's office.

Many times Grant felt like giving up and becoming a zombie like some of the other boys. But then he'd think of his plans for a new life once he was old enough to leave the orphanage and he somehow managed to endure. In what little spare time he had, he jogged and practiced lifting weights in the Home's makeshift gym.

When Father Thomas started making overtures to Grant again, he knew he was in trouble. The priest called him into his office one afternoon, locked the door, and asked Grant to sit down on the couch. The priest sat down next to him and put one arm around his shoulder while his other hand rested on Grant's knee. The heavy scent of lilacs filled Grant's nostrils.

"You know, I've never forgotten you," the priest said in a soothing voice. "Your little hands on my cock, the way your skin felt so soft. You're an obsession with me."

Grant tensed up, his brain screaming. Don't say anything, don't punch him, remember the punishment room.

Father Thomas's beady eyes looked into Grant's big blue ones, and then he leaned over to kiss him on the lips. Grant pushed him away as hard as he could, jumping off the couch and running for the door. It was locked.

"If I can't have you, I'll make you suffer," the priest whispered, his eyes narrowing. "And you know there's nothing you can do. The only way out of here is there." Father Wood was pointing to the cemetery visible through the office window. It was common knowledge that some boys had already died in mysterious circumstances.

That night fourteen-year-old Grant O'Connor got on his knees and prayed for the first time since he'd come to the Home. He asked God for the strength to face what he knew was coming.

Grant knew all about sex between the priests and the other boys. Michael Hogan had often recounted his experiences to the others, as if, in the telling, it became easier for him to bear. He told Grant all about penetration, how it hurt, and how he had learned to try to arouse his tormentors orally and perform oral sex on them, to avoid the tearing pain that he suffered when he was being sodomized. Hogan was sixteen years old.

Two weeks later, after many beatings and abuse, Grant accompanied Father Wood on a visit to one of the parishes in North Bay. That evening Grant ran about ten miles around the track before diving into the pool.

Father Thomas slipped into the pool and soon swam up to Grant carrying a small flask filled with vodka, which the boy had never tasted.

"Go ahead, have a sip. It will relax you. I've put some orange juice in it."

Grant felt the drink's effects almost immediately. The priest swam behind the boy and started to kiss his back. Revulsion overwhelmed Grant, and his body stiffened. When Father Thomas handed him the flask, Grant took three more large gulps.

Then the priest eased down the boy's bathing trunks, slipped one hand on his penis, and stroked it gently. By now, Grant was in a stupor, and while the priest was caressing his genitals, he was fighting nausea, trying not to throw up.

Soon he saw the priest's bathing suit floating around the top of the pool as the older man turned the boy around. Grant felt his hard penis pressing against his buttocks. Then Father Thomas was parting his cheeks by pushing up his leg.

"I want to play with you for a minute," the priest whispered in his ear. "You're so tight. I can't wait to break you in."

Grant's mind froze with fear and revulsion. *I'd better get good and drunk* or I'll never get through this, he told himself. He reached over for the flask and finished it. The priest was still trying to push his penis into Grant, but it wouldn't go.

"We'll have to go to my room where I have something that will help," the priest said in a frustrated voice.

Okay, remember what Michael told you, Grant thought as they went to the bedroom.

"Father, why not let me take care of you?" he asked, his voice full of a bravado he wasn't feeling.

Then he took the priest's penis in his hand and started to stroke it, trying to bring him to a climax. But with no experience, and even less desire, Grant's attempt wasn't very effective.

Then Father Thomas pushed Grant's head down. "Okay, suck it. Just pretend it's a popsicle."

After five minutes the priest ejaculated into Grant's mouth. The boy vomited all over the bedroom floor.

When Grant awoke the next morning his head felt as if someone was pounding it with a mallet. The mess had been cleaned up and as he recalled the night before, he pulled the pillow over his head and went back to sleep.

He was awakened by kisses on his face and lips and the feel of hands running over him. He opened his eyes and remembered where he was as the priest took Grant's penis in his mouth. This time something did happen. It got hard. The priest was beside himself. "You see, I knew you'd get to like it," he said. "Oh my dear boy, you can't imagine the delights I'm going to teach you."

Father Thomas took a jar of Vaseline from the drawer next to the bed and smeared some on his finger, which he then inserted into the boy's rectum. Grant tried to pull away, but the priest held him down. Smearing Vaseline on his own penis, he shoved it all the way in.

A cry of pain tore from Grant's lips as the priest's thrusts got quicker and stronger. It felt as if he were being torn in half, and he broke down and started to cry, not from joy as the priest had promised, but from horror and despair and shame.

Grant eventually fell into a troubled sleep, and had a dream about his mother. She was smiling down at him, just as she had the last time he'd seen her alive.

"Hang onto life, my beautiful little boy," his vision pleaded. "Keep your faith and don't give up. One day we'll all be together again."

For the next two years Grant O'Connor was the special boy of Father Thomas Wood.

Grant followed his friend Michael's advice, and became the dominant sexual partner, thus avoiding penetration most of the time. But when he found himself responding to the priest's oral sex, he was filled with shame.

Dear Lord, forgive me, he prayed. But I want to live . . .

"Come on, Dad, wake up!" Kevin shouted, waking Grant from his nightmare. "You promised to take me out for lobster and then to a movie."

An hour later father and son walked off down the road toward Captain John's Lobster and Steak House. Arm and arm, they looked at the boats moored along the waterway opposite the hotels, laughing at the sight of two novice sailors trying to steer their sailboat into a narrow dockside space and missing by a mile.

After the third attempt, Grant and Kevin walked out onto the dock and offered to help. Grant yelled instructions at the sailors while Kevin stood by ready to catch the rope and tie up the boat. When it was done, the two elderly gentlemen offered to buy father and son a drink in Neptune's Cove just across the road.

Although Kevin looked hopeful, Grant thought better of it. I'm not in the mood for questions and quizzical looks he thought. Sooner rather than later Kevin's immaturity became evident, especially given his size. Grant was too preoccupied with thoughts of the past to deal with the subtleties required to protect his son's feelings — no matter how well intentioned these gentlemen might be.

So father and son went on their way. After a delicious lobster dinner, they went to see *Home Alone II*. Kevin enjoyed the movie more than Grant did, but they laughed over it as they finished off their ice cream sundaes in the hotel coffee shop before turning in for the night.

Kevin telephoned his mother and related all the day's activities. Grant kissed and hugged his son good night, swearing to himself that he'd find a way to protect the boy from the cruelties that life could inflict on those who were weak and vulnerable.

Tomorrow is time enough to worry, he thought. Tonight is for Kevin.

After flicking the TV remote from channel to channel for several minutes, Grant looked over at the clock and saw that it was eleven-thirty. Kevin was fast asleep, but he was still wide awake. He was tempted to slip out of the room and go down to the bar for a nightcap, but decided against it. He had to be alert for tomorrow's meeting with DeLuca.

As he switched the TV channel to CNN, he saw a familiar sight that gave him a chill. It was a camera shot of the outside walls of the Brothers of St. John orphanage.

Grant had been trying to ignore the recent stories in the media about yet another sex abuse scandal involving young boys. This time the tragedy had occurred in Newfoundland at Mount Cashel, and as a background to their story, CNN was referring back to the infamous Pembroke scandal of 1960.

As the reporter droned on about the prison sentences being handed out to those convicted of molesting the boys in their care, the camera panned over to the steel gates of the Brothers of St. John Home for Orphans, the bars on the windows of the old gray building, and the crosses in the cemetery, where too many who shouldn't have died were buried.

Then a picture was flashed on the screen of the late Father Thomas Wood, the highest-ranking church official ever to be convicted in a molestation case. The newsman was telling the viewers that thirty years ago Father Wood had been found hanging in his office in the church rectory, and that the names of the two boys who had testified against him had been sealed by the court in perpetuity.

I wonder what DeLuca would think if he knew I was one of those boys? Grant thought. Or Rebecca.

*T*he phone's ring woke him up. He glanced over at Kevin who was still asleep and noticed that it was after one o'clock.

"Hi, son, how ya doing?" It was his father. "Doris told me you were in Miami visiting with Kevin before your trip to Boston."

"Is everything okay, Dad?" His parents never called him this late at night.

"Mom and I will be in Boston the day after tomorrow," Brian answered, ignoring the question. "We need to get together with you. We'll be at your hotel around noon. See you then."

He hung up before Grant could get in another word. He frowned: something had to be wrong if his parents were going to so much trouble to see him now. After all, they'd all be together in a few weeks for Christmas in Vermont.

Grant shrugged. I suppose if it were something urgent, Dad would have told me on the phone. Anyway, it will be good to see them again.

*A*fter he put down the phone, Brian Teasdale looked over at his wife Janice.

"My God, how will he handle this news?" she asked him. "And how cruel for this to happen now. Are you sure we're doing the right thing, dear? Maybe we should have just destroyed the letters and left the past as it was."

"You know we couldn't," he answered as he looked down at the letters in his hand, postmarked, "Eire." "Perhaps this is God's will. Maybe He has a reason we don't yet understand."

*T*he next morning Grant and Kevin had a wonderful pancake breakfast together before driving back to the Christopher Robin home. They hugged, and Grant smothered Kevin's face with kisses as he always did whenever he said good-bye to him.

"Only four weeks till we pick you up for the trip to Gramma and Grampa's house," he told his grinning son. "Be a good boy and I'll call you in a few days. Love you, pal."

"Love you, too, Dad. See ya, pal."

As Grant Teasdale drove out to Miami Airport to catch the morning flight to Boston, he wondered again about that strange call from his father. But he pushed it from his mind and after a few minutes began to concentrate on what might be in store for him when he saw DeLuca. Whatever it was, he was ready.

*T*he ringing of the telephone jolted him awake.

"It's Rebecca Sherman," she said as he mumbled an expletive. "I'm in a phone booth in Boston. Listen carefully because I don't have time for explanations right now.

"Brattini told Santino everything before he died, including who you really are and what you intend to do. Now Santino suspects you're the one who took out Brattini."

"Oh fuck," said the sleepy voice at the other end. "Well, what else could I do? Brattini was trying to stop me. I had to eliminate him. And how the hell did you find out about all this?"

"It doesn't matter," she answered. "I just want to make sure the job gets done. That rat left me to take the rap, so he deserves whatever happens to him."

"Whatever little thing I can do," he sneered.

"But you've got to do it fast, before anyone here can tighten up the security. Elizabeth hasn't got a clue about anything. All she wants to do is make sure that everyone who needs to makes peace with her husband before he dies. Some crap about his 'immortal soul.'"

"You're so tenderhearted," he said sarcastically.

"There's a red-eye flight leaving Pearson tonight at midnight," she continued. "It gets into Logan at four o'clock. Jimmy will pick you up — I'll say you have some news about Brattini's murder that DeLuca should know. Santino didn't tell Jimmy what Brattini told him. I'll be waiting for you at the front door." She paused, giving him time to absorb this information.

"The sons and their mother are all here, so you'd better come equipped. Everyone is searched when they come into the house, so you'll have to slip me the piece at the front door. They won't touch me. I'll give it back to you when we get off the elevator."

"Boy, you really hate DeLuca, don't you?" he asked.

Rebecca could imagine the smile on his face. "Wouldn't you, if you were me?" she answered.

"You're right, of course," he said. "I kept telling Brattini that he should try to make a deal with you instead of trying to shaft you all the time."

"It would have been better."

"But you know how the old-timers are. Women have their place, and that's it. But I knew you were too smart not to know when the time had come to change sides and join the winning team, so . . . welcome aboard."

"By this time tomorrow it will all be over," Rebecca said.

Then she hung up the phone and switched off the tape recorder.

*G*rant Teasdale relaxed in the back seat of the limo as it maneuvered through Boston traffic. Even though the driver circumvented the core of the city, it took over an hour to get from Logan to Back Bay via the John Fitzgerald Kennedy Expressway and Storrow Drive. The sun was still trying to burn through the blanket of smoke and fog, and finally succeeded by the time the limo reached Storrow Drive, paralleling the Charles River. Grant noticed the shell where the Boston Pops held their outdoor summer concerts before the car exited, heading into residential Back Bay Boston.

As he stood in front of the DeLucas' house, he noticed the video camera over the front door. He wondered if there was a back entrance.

When Mrs. DeLuca opened the door, he couldn't help being impressed by her looks. She was a tall, elegant blonde. When younger, she could have been a fashion model, he thought. Her beautiful green eyes looked directly into his.

"Thank you so much for taking the time to come," she said to him as he walked into the house. "I know it's been a long trip. You won't mind joining Mrs. Sherman and me for a late lunch before you see my husband, will you? I've just given him a sedative, so he won't be able to talk to you for at least four hours."

"Mrs. Sherman is already here?" he asked. His heart had skipped a beat at the mention of Rebecca. Was she the same? He wondered if her looks had faded, or if she had lost the energy that made her so attractive.

"Thank you for your hospitality," he replied, hoping his face had not revealed his reaction. "I'll be glad to have lunch with you and Mrs. Sherman."

A half-hour later, as the two of them were making small talk over orange juice and champagne, Rebecca walked into the den. Grant tried to remain impassive as he stood and turned to face her, but it was difficult. She was wearing a slim black skirt with a slit up the side that revealed one beautifully shaped leg, and just enough buttons were left undone on her blouse to show off her cleavage. He liked her short hair — she looked perky.

Grant extended his right hand. "It's nice to see you again, Mrs. Sherman. It's been a long time. I can see life is treating you well. You don't look a day older than the last time we met."

Oh shit, he thought. What a corny line.

As Rebecca took his hand she lifted her big brown eyes to his and smiled. Her tone was soft as she replied, "Come now, Inspector, after all the years you spent investigating me, don't you think it's time we called each other by our first names?"

She's flirting with me, he thought. She's up to something. He decided to enjoy it while it lasted.

During lunch Grant and Rebecca exchanged several long looks but kept their voices neutral as they talked about everything from politics to fishing to their mutual interest in British history. Occasionally she would reach out and touch his arm.

Elizabeth didn't seem to notice anything, but Grant was aware that Rebecca's eyes lit up every time she laughed and that she seemed interested in every word he said. By the time they started on a second bottle of champagne, he didn't care why she was flirting with him.

God, he thought, how I want to kiss her — and I don't want to stop there . . .

They were sipping coffee in the den when Elizabeth came back in to the room — they hadn't noticed she'd left — and told Grant that Santino was now able to see him.

"Well Grant," Rebecca said, "it's nice to see that being a cop doesn't mean giving up one's charm and intelligence. I can't remember when I've enjoyed a man's company so much."

She leaned over and kissed him very lightly on his lips. She had a mischievous sparkle in her eyes as she added, "If I'd known how fascinating you were, I'd have been much nicer to you years ago."

With a wave of the hand she turned and left before Grant could think of a smart reply.

As he followed Elizabeth to the elevator, his thoughts were still on Rebecca and how she had managed to frazzle his head so quickly. He barely noticed Jimmy and Vinnie standing guard.

*T*he bedroom was dark, and the clock next to the bed showed four-thirty. As he approached, Grant was shocked to see how much DeLuca had aged. His hair was still full and thick but almost completely white. His face was drawn and pale and his breathing was heavy. But when his eyes opened, Grant noticed how clear and direct his gaze still was.

"Thanks for coming, Inspector," DeLuca said in a raspy voice. "A lot of water has gone under the bridge since we last met."

Grant smiled at him, "A whole lake."

"I understand you've left the Force, live on a houseboat, and have opened your own security business," Santino continued. "I get seasick myself, so I'll never understand how humans can travel and live on water, which is only made for the fish I know you love to catch." He paused, and it was obvious that talking was an effort, but he carried on.

"I'm also happy to hear that your son has adjusted so well at the

Christopher Robin home. I'm sure he enjoyed your visit together before you came here."

Grant wasn't surprised that DeLuca knew so much about him; nor was he offended. "Keep your enemies close," was akin to a prayer for men like Santino. As long as there was a breath of life still in him, DeLuca would learn everything he needed to know about any situation in order to control it.

But Grant also knew that DeLuca wasn't going to threaten him or try to raise his hackles. He needed something, and he needed it badly enough to bring Grant into his home with his family close by.

When Santino tried to reach for a glass of water, Grant helped him sit up. My God, he's like a skeleton, he thought.

DeLuca leaned his head back and took some deep breaths before he went on speaking.

"Before he was murdered, Massimo Brattini hired a hit man to kill my wife and sons. That man is now on his way to do the job."

Seeing the look of skepticism on Teasdale's face, Santino said, "I know what you're thinking, Inspector. Old-time Mafiosos don't kill women and children to settle their debts. That's right — most of the time. But this vendetta goes back a long time and runs through three generations."

Santino DeLuca then told Teasdale a story worthy of Aesop, with just enough truth to make it plausible. When DeLuca spoke of his love for Elizabeth and his children, Grant could only wonder why this man would pour out his heart to someone who represented what he despised most of all in this world — a onetime law-enforcement officer.

"The killer's the same person who had your undercover agent, Dottie Smith, wasted, along with those two pigs who tried to frame Rebecca in prison," DeLuca told him finally.

Teasdale stiffened. "Have you got proof of that?"

Santino ignored the question. "He was also the press leak during the Peartree affair. He's been blackmailing former cabinet minister Dudley, among others, for years. It seems they liked kinky sex orgies and dogs. And he's always worked for the Brattini–Salerno family."

Grant's reaction of surprise confirmed Santino's suspicion that — despite all their investigations — the police hadn't yet found the link between the families and some of the politicians, but suspected that Rebecca had known about it.

"The man's an animal," Santino went on. "He'll stop at nothing to get revenge. So I want to hire your firm to take care of this matter — to protect my wife and children."

Santino's voice had grown stronger. "When it's done, I'll put $1,000,000 into an interest-bearing bond, in trust for your son Kevin, with you as the trustee. The yield won't be less than $80,000 annually, more than enough to take care of him properly as long as he lives.

"There'll be no tax implications for you because the trust will be set up in Bermuda so that no one can trace its source."

"Taking care of this matter," said Grant, almost to himself, "means taking out this guy."

"Yeah, that's the idea," Santino answered.

Grant raised on eyebrow quizzically. "Why me? You don't have to pay me — you've got a whole crew of loyal men who have a lot of experience and who would die for you."

"Sure I do, and I thought about that. But, if someone from my organization does it, that won't be the end of it. There will be retaliation — we'll be back where we started from. No, right now he's the only guy who knows anything and if he's taken out, say by accident or by an ex-cop defending himself — well, it won't have anything to do with me or mine."

Grant's head was already in a struggle with his heart. What's the difference? he thought. I'm not a cop any more. So another hood bites the dust, who cares? And Kevin will always be cared for properly. Doris can stop worrying — and so can I.

"Who's the guy?" he asked DeLuca.

Santino's answer jolted Teasdale right down to his toes.

After a few moments of silence Teasdale said, "I'll let you know tomorrow."

"Tomorrow may be too late," Santino replied, putting his hand under the bedcovers. For a second Grant thought he might be going for a gun, but DeLuca only pulled out an envelope, which he handed to Teasdale.

"This is a list of his Swiss bank accounts, his safety-deposit boxes, the name of the Supreme Court judge he owns, and his police informant.

"As soon as I know that my family's safety is assured, you'll get the documents for your son's trust."

Santino was sure, from the look on his face, that Teasdale was going to take him up on his offer.

# 23

NOVEMBER 22
1994

*T*easdale patted the gun inside his jacket pocket when he heard the knock on the door. He glanced at his watch: seven o'clock. He'd been drinking straight Scotch for an hour, thinking over DeLuca's offer, fighting his urge to grab it, thinking of his father's principles and integrity, and trying to remember that both of them had spent their whole lives upholding the law.

He'd also been feeling guilty about Doris. He expected that she'd fall apart if he ever left her. But seeing Rebecca again had thrown him for a loop, and this time he didn't want to walk away. He'd been burying his desires for a long time.

"You only go around once," one of his friends used to say.

"Yes, who is it?" Grant asked as he walked toward the door.

"Room service."

She was smiling when he opened the door.

"I've come to seduce you, although I'm not sure I remember how it's done. And if I've forgotten, I won't know how to save face if you don't want me."

He grabbed Rebecca's arm, pulled her into the room, slammed the door shut with his foot, and latched the lock.

"Want you, you silly woman?" He slurred his words ever so slightly. "I've wanted you since the first time I saw you — but you knew that, didn't you?"

She slipped off her coat and draped it over a chair.

"I'm so glad you're in a hotel and not staying with the DeLucas. If we were both there, this wouldn't be possible."

It was part of the plan. She had insisted he stay in a hotel. "It's important we get Inspector Teasdale out of the house," she had stressed.

Rebecca just stood looking up at Grant, hoping things wouldn't move too fast. I want you, too, she thought, but . . .

He pulled her into his arms and kissed her, their tongues intertwining as his hands caressed her body. When he felt her tears, he lifted his face to look into her eyes, but she pulled his head down again.

"I wanted you, too," she whispered between kisses. "More than I realized. It's been so long since I felt like this." And that part was true.

Finally she pulled away and put her finger on his lips. "I hate rushing into things, Grant. I think I'd like a drink now."

He smiled, his face flushing slightly. "Sure. I guess I'm overanxious." And he was. You don't, after all, open your hotel room door, drag a woman inside, and take her right away. Women needed foreplay. Just because they had been thinking about each other didn't negate the need to go slow.

He smiled at her. "I'll fix us drinks."

He'd been up since early morning. From the airport he had gone directly to the DeLucas' house, then he'd been brought directly here.

"Why don't I take a quick shower," he suggested. "There's plenty of choice in the mini-bar, and I've got an open bottle of Scotch over there."

"I take it that's what you'll be drinking?"

"Yeah, I started on Scotch, I better stay with it."

With that he disappeared into the bathroom.

Rebecca waited until she heard the shower go on. Then she went to the mini-bar and got out some rum and a Coke. She mixed herself a drink and then poured him a Scotch, adding plenty of ice to both glasses. Then she opened her purse and took out the envelope of white powder. She emptied it into the Scotch and watched it dissolve instantly. Let this work the way it does in the movies, she thought.

A minute later Grant flung open the bathroom door and emerged in a fog of steam. He was wrapped in a bath sheet which was knotted round his hips. He looked very masculine, and very appealing.

"Stop looking at me like that, you beast." She laughed and handed him his drink. "*Lechaim!*" she toasted as she raised her glass to his. "To life!"

He lifted the glass to his lips and drained it.

She smiled and moved closer to him.

He slowly undid her blouse, fingers fumbling over all the little buttons, and slipped it off her shoulders. He looked at her breasts pressed against the black lace. He touched them hesitatingly at first, then harder. He reached around her and undid her bra. When he felt the tiny scars across her flesh, tears came to his eyes. Her nipples were already hard and he lowered his head and began kissing them, then sucking them gently and then not so gently.

Then he stopped and looked into her eyes.

"What is it, Grant?"

"I'm — I'm — I need you." His words came slowly; then his movements slowed just as his eyes glazed over. She could see him struggling to stay awake as he pulled her down to the bed with him and he continued to feel her body for another second. Then he passed out.

Rebecca waited for a moment, then got up and hurriedly put on her bra and blouse. She paused to look at him on the bed, then she drew the covers over him. "You'll never know what this took," she whispered, planting a kiss on his cheek.

She grabbed her coat and purse and headed for the door. Jimmy would be waiting downstairs.

*R*ebecca expected that Grant would be out cold for at least eight hours, probably longer. Earlier, Elizabeth had given her one of Santino's sedatives, promising that it would knock out a horse, especially when taken with alcohol. The worst memory that Grant would have of the experience would be a headache.

Jimmy was sitting in the limo outside the front door. "Rebecca," he asked very quietly once the car was moving, "what are you up to?"

"When did you start asking questions?" she answered, her mind already four hours ahead. "There's nothing for you to worry about. All you have to do is make sure Vinnie and Sal are out of the house and in a very public place, where people will remember you, after you drop off Santino's next visitor. Now, that's the end of the discussion."

"You know," he said, ignoring her instructions to drop the subject, "once before, many years ago, a younger version of Rebecca Sherman went off, half-cocked, trying to 'take care of something' herself. The fallout from that fiasco almost brought us all down."

"I know," she answered in a hostile tone. "And Jimmy Bono had to fix it. Well, you didn't, did you? The senator's still able to walk around — why couldn't you at least have shot him in the kneecaps instead of just breaking a couple of bats on them?"

Despite himself, Jimmy started to laugh. "That's what the IRA does," he said. "Don't mix up the Italians with the Irish."

She started to laugh, too, even though the memories were still painful to both of them.

"Jimmy," she said, more serious now, "Santino doesn't want anything to happen to you or the others. There's no old-time 'hit' going on here. Honest. Just a little friendly persuasion that only the two women he loves can handle. There's nothing to worry about."

*I*t was one o'clock in the morning when Rebecca Sherman and Elizabeth DeLuca sat down to share a pot of coffee. They began a long conversation about old hurts.

After a few minutes Rebecca confessed, "I was hurt before and after I got out of prison. I was devastated that Santino never called or sent any messages — not even when I was released. His Bermuda office still monitored my investments, but all our business dealings were done by accountants and the bank. He never made any effort to contact me directly."

Elizabeth nodded. "I should tell you what happened to Santino during that time. He broke down, literally, when you were sentenced to Midland. He locked himself in his study for three days and wouldn't talk to anyone. At first I was enraged — after all, I was his wife.

"But I knew why he was so crazed. It was because of you. And I hated you. I didn't know how to fight you. If you'd been younger, or prettier, then I'd have suspected midlife crisis, or just the usual macho male sex drive. But it was more than that. He was always fascinated with your brains, your spirit, and your intensity."

Rebecca felt her own face flush as she looked into Elizabeth's green eyes.

"After a while he stopped talking to me about you all the time, and only referred to you in passing as a part of his business, which he assumed didn't interest me. But I *was* interested. I was always very aware of his business dealings.

"You know, Rebecca, not all Italian women are dumb cows, good for nothing but cooking, cleaning, and making babies. I've always known the kind of business Santino was in, ever since that first night in Rome when he took me to his house after the explosion."

Rebecca nodded.

"And I chose to accept it. I loved him that much. Whatever my husband felt he needed to do, I was behind him. Many times I managed to make suggestions to him about people and issues without his even realizing that I knew exactly what was going on. He'd think I was just philosophizing — but it didn't stop him from following my advice occasionally, and I was pleased about that.

"So I'm not here tonight playing little Miss Muffet, pretending I didn't know the kinds of people Santino worked with and the serious decisions he had to make and then carry out. I knew it all. But I also knew the rules of the game, as you did. And despite my anger and my fear — and, yes, my jealousy — you were still a part of the business, and as such, deserved the respect you had earned. I loved him that much, too."

Rebecca drew in her breath.

"And I didn't want to lose him — not to you and not to the demons running around inside his brain. So I decided to take a chance. On the fourth day, when he still wouldn't come out of his study, I used the master key to open the door. I walked in and told him that I'd just spoken to you, which of course was a lie. His head shot up and his bloodshot eyes filled with tears, something I'd never seen happen before.

"'Is she okay?' he asked me, and his love and concern for you tore through my heart like a knife.

"'Yes, she's fine,' I answered him. 'If you want to send her any messages, or even if you want to see her, I'll help you to do it. I understand how much she has meant to you.'

"Then, he completely broke down," Elizabeth said. "A combination of fatigue and Scotch must have helped to weaken his defenses. When I went to him, he put his arms around me and cried bitterly, asking for my forgiveness. He told me he loved us both, would always love us both, but I was his wife and I was the one with whom he wanted to spend the rest of his life."

"Oh, Elizabeth," said Rebecca.

"So, after Santino and I spent most of that night talking," Elizabeth continued, "we decided to leave Canada and any memories of the past behind. We bought this townhouse and moved here. I decided to concentrate on my sculptures and my rare book collection. Santino began to spend more time with the boys, taking an active role in their everyday lives. And we started to rebuild our life together."

Rebecca bit her lip, not wanting to show how much Elizabeth's words hurt.

"After six months Santino returned to me in his heart as well. Once the kids were settled here, we returned to Mackinac Island, where we'd spent our honeymoon, and stayed for a month. We stayed in the same cottage, we rode our bicycles every day, and we took long walks around the island.

"I was determined not to lose my husband again, so I overcame my inhibitions. At first he was shocked by my sexual aggressiveness, but I know he enjoyed it, too. The last ten years have been wonderful. God has been good to me.

"The past is over now, Rebecca. There's no need to dwell on what happened back then. We have to move on with the task at hand."

Rebecca looked down, unable to meet Elizabeth's eyes. She felt enormous regret for the pain she'd caused this woman.

"I've noticed how Inspector Teasdale looks at you, Rebecca," Elizabeth said. "I know he has a wife and a disabled son. Think twice before you screw up his life.

"One more thing. No matter what happens from here on in, I want to thank you, Rebecca. Not only for being here now, but for letting go ten years ago — for loving Santino enough to let him return to us, where he needed to be. I admired you then and I admire you even more now."

Rebecca's eyes were full and she couldn't speak.

"It's almost time," Elizabeth said, looking at her watch.

*A*n hour later, right on schedule, the doorbell rang. Elizabeth crossed herself as she and Rebecca got up from their chairs, took deep breaths, and hugged each other. Then Elizabeth slipped out of the room as Rebecca went into the foyer.

"Hello, Bingo," Rebecca said as she opened the front door, a warm smile on her face. "Welcome to Boston."

She could hear Jimmy and the boys driving the limo away. In minutes they would be in a busy all-night restaurant, talking it up and making sure that the customers got a good look at them as they sat down and ordered coffee and burgers.

"Hey, where are the guards?" DeSalle asked.

"Oh, they're here. Don't you worry," she answered, the smile still on her face. "Come on, I'll take you up to the fifth floor. That's where Santino's bedroom is. Keep your coat on, but give me the gun. I'll put it in my pocket till you're cleared."

As they walked into the elevator, Bob DeSalle handed Rebecca his .38 snub-nosed revolver.

She put the gun in her pocket. Oh my God, she wondered, what if it's got an empty chamber and he jumps me? But no, they had a back-up plan. That's where Elizabeth would come in.

As the elevator doors closed, she leaned against the back wall, feeling calm, almost detached from reality, and pushed the number five button. Images of her gentle father Sam swirled around her, trying to distract her from what she had to do. She could almost hear him calling out to her. Becky, Becky, my *sheine maidele*, turn back! It's not too late. Turn back!

It is too late, Daddy, she thought. It was too late when I crossed that bridge a long time ago. And she thought of the blanket over her head and the hot knife on her breasts. She thought of all the people killed in the bomb blast and she thought of Santino's sons.

Rebecca was still smiling as the elevator passed the second floor. Then she took out the gun and pointed it.

It took DeSalle a moment to realize that the smile was gone from her face. In its place was a look of contempt and hatred. And his gun was pointed at his own heart.

"What the — ?" he started to yell as his eyes widened in terrified comprehension.

"Roberto Vincenzo! *Morte! Carogna!*" she whispered. Then she pulled the trigger.

As she looked down at DeSalle–Vincenzo's crumpled body, she remembered her dear, sweet Steven, and her friend, Dottie Smith.

"Now the two of you can rest in peace," she murmured.

*W*hen the doors slid open at the fifth floor Elizabeth was waiting. She was wearing jeans and one of her son's lumber jackets. There was an extra set of heavy clothing, which Rebecca put on as Elizabeth pushed the button that would hold the elevator doors open.

When she reached out to take Rebecca's arm, she noticed how white-faced and shaken she was. At first neither one of the women looked down at the body, but then Elizabeth mumbled, "God damned dirty bastard."

Her words broke the terrible tension. "Elizabeth," Rebecca said, "I hope it's not my presence that's affecting your language. Not very ladylike."

"Right now I don't feel like a lady," Elizabeth answered grimly.

"Are you going to be okay?" Rebecca asked.

"All I need to do is remember back to that scene in the park, where all those people were blown to bits by Vincenzo, and I'll be okay."

The two women then rolled DeSalle's body up in the blankets Elizabeth had put on the floor outside the elevator before he'd arrived. Then Rebecca picked up the towels Elizabeth had also provided, and mopped up the blood and flesh that had spattered on the floor and walls of the elevator. Surprisingly, she had stopped shaking, and felt much calmer now. Meanwhile, Elizabeth took the rope she had in her pocket and tied the blankets around the body. Together, the two women dragged him along the hall, stopping every few feet to catch their breath.

"This is going to be impossible," Rebecca said as she looked down at the body. "I should have thought about how heavy he'd be."

"You couldn't think of everything," Elizabeth answered. "Besides, it isn't impossible. We'll manage — we have no choice. Here, let's roll him along until we get to the door that leads to the rooftop. That'll save our strength. I'm sure we'll be able to push him through the doorway."

After a twenty-minute struggle they managed to get the body out the glass door and onto the roof.

"The townhouse next door is ours, too," Elizabeth told Rebecca while they stopped to catch their breath again. "It's used for Santino's European operations. There's an inside door between the two houses off the second-floor laundry room.

"People entering that house can get into ours without being seen and vice-versa. Anyone watching the place won't be the wiser. And we often use its back door to come and go."

"Okay, Elizabeth, then we've got to get him into the house next door, move him down to the back door and out onto the street, and away from here without anyone seeing us. God, why didn't I work this out beforehand? Well, I'll figure something out. I hope your car is here, as we discussed earlier."

It certainly had not been her first choice, forensics being so sophisticated. But there had been no other way to dispose of the body.

"Yes," Elizabeth answered, "and in fact, I left it parked on the street, right near the back door."

"Good," Rebecca said with relief. "That may make it easier to get him into the trunk. But then we'll have to dump him in the river. We have to!"

"Let's not panic," Elizabeth answered calmly. "I can always ask Jimmy to help."

"No!" snapped Rebecca. "We can't involve him! We'll just have to do this ourselves."

Just then the rooftop door of the house next door opened. Rebecca pulled out the gun. Jimmy, Vinnie, and Sal, the three old *compadres*, stepped out onto the roof.

"Okay, ladies, get lost!" Jimmy said, his eyes fastened onto Rebecca as he and the other two men walked toward her. "We'll handle things from here."

Vinnie was carrying a large tarpaulin, and he started to wrap DeSalle's body in it after handing the bloody blankets back to Elizabeth.

"Better put this through the laundry several times before you get rid of it," he cautioned. "Just in case DeSalle told someone where he was going and there's any questions."

"I told you to stay where you could establish alibis," Rebecca said plaintively. "Now it won't be over."

"It'll be over," Jimmy said. "First, we have an alibi because the time of death will be real easy to pinpoint. He ate on the plane and it's the food in the stomach and the stage of digestion that will nail the time of death pretty good. Second, and more important, Brattini issued a contract on DeSalle before he himself was killed. We just heard that tonight."

"Does that mean I get a reward?"

Jimmy laughed. "Maybe we could split it. Oh yeah, Mrs. Sherman, would you please stop pointing that gun? It's liable to go off again. Give it to me."

Rebecca stared at him, still holding the gun with her finger on the trigger, ignoring his request.

"Jimmy," she asked, "how did you know?"

"Sometimes you're like an open book," he told her. "I could see your mind was working when I tried to talk to you on the way back from the hotel. I figured you were up to something again.

"You forgot that I've been with DeLuca for almost fifty years, so when I saw it was Bob DeSalle at the airport, I knew right away he was no 'business partner.' I knew something wasn't right. You ladies better check the house for any traces of . . . well, you know what I mean."

As the three men lifted DeSalle's body and disappeared with it next door, the two women looked at each other, relief on both their faces. Then they walked back into the house and did as Jimmy had advised.

With their clothes changed and the washing machine hard at work, Elizabeth opened a bottle of grappa and joined Rebecca on the window seat in Santino's den.

"I'm sorry about what I said to you earlier about Teasdale," she said. "It was thoughtless and insensitive — and none of my business, really. You've put your life on the line for us, and whatever you decide to do is okay with me. I wish Santino could be told about all this, but of course he can't. I'm sure he expected Teasdale to carry out this job, and I can just imagine the size of the remuneration he must have offered him. But I'll make sure that whatever it was will be paid to him anyhow."

"You're right, Elizabeth," Rebecca said. "Santino must never know how the job was done, and neither must Teasdale."

I'm sure Santino does know, Elizabeth thought. I wouldn't be surprised if he knew what Rebecca would do even before she did.

"After all," Rebecca continued, "underneath it all, Grant is still a cop. The poor man must have been torn, needing the money to take care of his son and yet being asked to do something that went against everything he had stood for his entire professional life. Well, at least he's been spared that difficult choice." And others, she thought.

"You see, Rebecca, you do know what unselfish love is all about," Elizabeth said. "Thanks to you, Grant will have peace of mind — for himself, his wife, and his son. He'll have no choice but to take the money; otherwise the door will be left open for too many questions. And even though he might suspect that you were involved, he won't pursue it out of fear that you might be in even greater danger from the 'real killer.' I think he really cares for you, Rebecca, and, ironically, that caring will probably mean the end of any future for the two of you."

They sipped their drinks in silence.

Then Rebecca got up and walked over to the fireplace. "You know, when I was a kid in high school we studied *A Tale of Two Cities* in my English class. At the end of the story the hero makes a speech as he approaches the guillotine. It goes something like . . . 'Tis a far, far better thing that I do than I've ever done before . . . and so on. It had a tremendous impact on me. Now I understand what the author meant.

"I've come full circle, Elizabeth. I did what I had to do. I've paid my debts to my former enemies as well as to my dear friends. To Grant, whose protection probably saved my life inside prison; to you, who suffered because of my selfishness; and to Santino, who was once the love of my life. But now it's over. The world I've known for twenty-five years must be put to rest. It's time for me to move on with my life."

# 24

*November 23
1994*

*T*he pounding on the door wasn't as loud as the pounding inside his head.

"Grant!" his father called. "Grant, are you in there? Are you all right? Son, it's almost noon."

Grant staggered out of bed and opened the door.

"My God," his father said, "what happened to you? We tried phoning, but the desk clerk said you'd left instructions not to be disturbed. Surely you didn't forget that Mom and I were coming to meet you this morning?"

Oh God, Grant thought. I've been drugged! Why? She must know about DeSalle. What has she done?.

"Mom, Dad, have a seat," Grant said. "I've got to take a cold shower and make a phone call."

Just then the phone rang.

"Hello, Inspector." It was Elizabeth DeLuca. "I have some information for you. The documentation has now been processed and will be delivered to you within the hour. Everything's in order. My husband thanks you for your visit and your assistance. Mrs. Sherman has already left for the airport to return to Toronto. If there's anything we can do to make the rest of your stay in Boston pleasant, please don't hesitate to let us know. Otherwise I'll say good-bye, and thank you, from all of us.

Have a safe trip back to Florida."

The line went dead before he could say a word.

If the documents had been arranged, then someone had taken out Roberto Vincenzo, otherwise known as Bob "Bingo" DeSalle. And if he himself didn't do it, then who did?

Then he remembered last night's incredible passion with Rebecca. Did I only dream it happened? No, she probably hired someone to do the job and didn't want me to know. Perhaps DeLuca told her about Kevin and his offer to me.

He needed more time to sort it all out. But with his parents sitting across from him, it was impossible. But why had Rebecca left Boston without even saying good-bye? Well, Toronto wasn't that far away. Once he'd settled whatever problem his parents were having, he'd fly up to see her. But first he'd have to come to grips with his responsibilities and his guilt about Doris.

"Okay, folks," Grant said, turning to his parents. "Shoot. I hope whatever it is is important enough to wake me from the wonderful dream I was having."

*E*lizabeth and Rebecca had been sitting in the airport cocktail lounge for over an hour when the boarding call finally came. Bad weather had delayed the plane's departure.

"There's an old Jewish saying when good-byes are being spoken," Rebecca said, raising her glass to Elizabeth. "May you and your family live 120 years in good health and happiness."

"And may yours as well," Elizabeth said, kissing Rebecca's cheek. "We'll always be friends. We still love the same man."

# *Epilogue*

*A*s he looked around his parents' rustic cabin on the bank of the Quechee River, in Vermont, Grant Teasdale knew he had found a measure of peace. Doris and Kevin were at the piano trying to plunk out the tune "Deck the Halls with Boughs of Holly" while his parents were putting the finishing touches on the Christmas turkey.

Four weeks ago in that Boston hotel room, they'd told him about some old letters recently discovered in a metal box in a burned-out church in Pembroke. They were from the O'Connor and O'Grady families in Ireland asking the Canadian authorities about Sean and Mary O'Connor and their sons Grant and Kevin. The letters, which were dated 1956, had been hidden there by Father Thomas Wood almost forty years earlier. If not for the fire, they'd never have been found.

Grant had left for Ireland two days later. It had been an emotional reunion on that cold November morning when he stepped off the plane at

Shannon Airport and met his aunts, cousins, and, best of all, his ninety-four-year-old maternal grandmother Siobhan O'Grady. Tears flowed freely on all sides, and after their two-week visit, Grant felt like a man reborn.

Now, as he looked around the comfortable room, he felt surrounded by the love of his family, here and in Ireland.

My family, and keeping us together, is all that matters. Rebecca Sherman is out of my life forever.

*R*ebecca and Brad were sitting in front of the fire in their den discussing how well Lisa's wedding had gone. Rebecca rested her head on his comfortable shoulder and felt a contentment she had not known for a long time. Jean had joined them for cocktails before dinner and now the three of them were all laughing as they remembered some of the antics that had gone on at the reception.

Rebecca was determined to push the events of the last weeks out of her mind. Grant wasn't really the wandering kind, and an affair would have made them both miserable. More important, it would have made Brad and Doris miserable, too.

Bob DeSalle's badly decomposed body had recently been found floating in the Charles River. But before then documents relating to his "affairs" had mysteriously reached the press. So the police wrote the killing off as a "gangland murder," just as they had written off Brattini's death.

It's all in the past, Rebecca thought. Let it go. Concentrate on Brad now. Make it work.

At eight-thirty, the phone rang.

"Merry Christmas and Happy Chanukah," came the familiar voice.

"The same to you," she answered, her heart pounding. "How is your family?"

"Wonderful," he said. "Doris and I will be dropping Kevin off in Hallandale next week on our way home. I still have a fishing trip with some of my buddies waiting for me. I'm really looking forward to it."

After a few moments of awkward silence, Grant continued. "I have a story to tell you, and I can only tell it to you in person. Will you meet me the day after tomorrow? I'll fly up just for the day and take you out for lunch."

"Yes," she answered after a slight hesitation. "That's a very nice idea."

"I'll call you when the plane lands. Take care."

"You, too," she answered.

*E*lizabeth looked up at the clouds moving across the sky. It was a typical gray December day in Boston, and the streets were full of Christmas shoppers.

She pulled her fur around her as the first snowflakes began to fall gently to the ground. She turned away from the crowds headed for Filene's and hurried toward the Olde Corner Bookshop. They too had a sale.

Almost a year had passed since Santino's death. Soon she'd be having a memorial service and reception to mark the anniversary. She thought back to their last Christmas together. The two of them had been sitting on the couch in the living room watching their sons opening their presents. Santino's condition was deteriorating quickly. The doctors had warned her to expect him to slip into a coma at any time.

When she noticed the faraway look in his eyes, she'd asked him if there was anyone he wanted her to call.

"No, my dear," he'd answered, turning his head and looking tenderly at her. "Everything I want and need is right here in this room with you."

She went into the shop. The manager, who knew her, smiled. "Good morning, Mrs. DeLuca," he said cheerfully.

"Good morning to you," she answered as she headed for the art section.

After perusing the books on the table, she turned to some on a nearby shelf.

"Excuse me . . . "

Elizabeth turned and looked into soft brown eyes, distantly familiar eyes. Then she remembered. "Larry?"

He grinned at her and she smiled back. It had been fifteen years and his blond hair was now turning gray. But his dimples were still evident when he smiled. He was still a handsome man.

"Elizabeth, I can't believe it. You look the same."

"I can't possibly," she said, not taking her eyes off of his.

"You know, I've dreamed about this moment, but I never really expected it to happen. Whenever I come to Boston, I always come to this store, hoping — well, hoping to see you again."

Elizabeth shook her head and wondered how many times in the last ten years their paths had nearly crossed. They chatted a few minutes, then she asked, "Did you ever marry that girl?"

"Yes, in 1982. I've lived in Toronto ever since. Our daughter Megan was born in 1984. As a matter of fact, this trip is a belated birthday present for Meggie. Like me, she's an avid hockey fan."

"Oh, where is she?" Elizabeth asked, turning her head to look around the store. "I'd love to meet her . . . and her mother."

"I just dropped her off at the movies. Her mother and I were divorced two years ago. It was a mutual decision — as amicable as these things can ever be. Besides, I always had trouble shaking a previous vision. This woman I met in Boston."

She blushed but didn't say anything.

"I'm sorry about the loss of your husband, Elizabeth."

She really wasn't surprised that Larry knew who she was. Ten years ago, despite all the efforts to keep her and the twins out of it, the massive-media coverage on both sides of the border concerning Santino's activitiesincluded pictures of and references to his family. And at Santino's funeral, TV cameras and photographers had been everywhere.

"Elizabeth, can we go next door and have a coffee?"

She didn't answer right away.

"Come on, Elizabeth," he said with a big grin, "I won't bite you, I promise."

He opened the door to the coffee shop. It was steamy inside and it smelled of freshly ground coffee. He sat her down at a table and went to get two cups of cappuccino.

Elizabeth watched him carefully. Could it be? After all, as even Jimmy Bono had reminded her, she was still a young woman. Maybe all things do come around to those who wait, she thought. Life is really wonderful. You never know what tomorrow will bring. And I want to live.

# Acknowledgments

Much of the preliminary research for this book was done in Florida, where my good friend Linda Richman provided the hospitality and ambience that was so helpful during the early stages of the manuscript. I'm grateful to her, and to Bernie Gluckstein, who good-naturedly accompanied me around some of Palm Beach's seedier establishments in my quest for accuracy.

My gratitude also to: my colleagues in the Crime Writers of Canada, whose encouragement, advice, and moral support were invaluable, especially Rosemary Aubert, who did the first edit of the manuscript; James Dubro, who took the time to read and comment on it; and John North, whose suggestions were so helpful. My Italian connection, whose friendship and loyalty are as strong as their heritage: Dino Chiesa, Betty Disero, Pal Di Iulio, Pietro Gianmario, and Toni Varone. They provided diverse perspectives, Old Country anecdotes, and literal translations, which greatly enhanced the story I wanted to tell. Louis Chelin, whose Sunday morning walks with my husband produced the title. Dusty Cohl, who offered excellent and sobering reflections. Two very special lawyers: Peter Jacobsen and John Pollock. Some of the finest law-enforcement officers in the country who shared their expertise with me as I ran plot lines by them over and over again: Cpl. Fred Bowen and Cpl. Gary Uhlman of the RCMP, Det. Sgt. Larry Green of the OPP, and Inspector Roy Teeft of the Metro Toronto Criminal Intelligence branch. Rob Poulin and Dino, of the Business Depot, and Ralph Wilner, who came to the rescue whenever my computer broke down, usually the day before a deadline.

And finally . . . the last shall be the first: the Stoddart Publishing team. Nelson Doucet and Leona Trainer, who encouraged me to try my hand at fiction; Angel Guerra, whose marketing skills continue to amaze me; the editorial department, headed so capably by Don Bastian; three outstanding editors who worked on the manuscript during its development: Greg Ioannou, Janet Rosenstock, and Betty Jane Corson; and of course, Jack Stoddart, the boss himself, who had the vision, and the courage, to give this author another chance at life.